FiRETRAP

PHANTOM ISLAND

5

FIRETRAP

KRISSI DALLAS

THUNDERFLY

—— PRODUCTIONS ——

Published by Thunderfly Productions
Texas | www.ThunderflyProductions.com
Cover and Interior Design by Kristen McGregor
Edited by Katrina Elsea
Dorian Island Map Design by Athena Panthera (in 8th grade)

Published in the United States of America
ISBN: 978-1-73554-088-7 (paperback)
ISBN: 978-1-73554-089-4 (ebook)
1. Young Adult Fiction: Fantasy/Contemporary
2. Young Adult Fiction: Romance/Clean & Wholesome
www.KrissiDallas.com

FOR JASPER
MY VOLCANO-LOVING,
TORNADO-OBSESSED
FIRECRACKER OF A FIRSTBORN.

You were worth the wait.

SEPARATION

TRADITIONS

Perspiration beaded my forehead as I bent over the ground. Studying. Scrutinizing my work. There wasn't much time left, and it had to be perfect. My heart palpitated with adrenaline as I looked again over my shoulder to make sure I wasn't about to get caught.

Not that it mattered. This was tradition. But still… I was not good at being bad even when it was socially acceptable.

Fumbling with a different color of chalk, I made a few sweeping curlicues around the words. There. That was it.

"Perfect." Morgan nodded with approval, her two-toned hair bobbing on top of her head where she had piled it. She pulled out her phone and snapped some pictures. I gave a cheesy thumbs-up with my chalky hands. "Now let's find the others and get out of here before the cops show up."

"Cops are already here, Morgie," I reminded her, nodding at Hal, the school security guard, who watched us from the parking lot.

"I know." She grinned. "But it's fun to pretend."

We started to back away, skipping around the splashes of sidewalk art that ran up and down the front of the school. There was nothing but chalk stubs left in our guilty hands.

"Laura did a good job." Morgan pointed at the bubbly cheerleader handwriting shoe-polished across the front office windows.

"All those years making pep rally banners had to be good for something," I agreed, admiring her artistic flair. "Where did everyone go?"

The grounds seemed too deserted, when I knew there were about twenty seniors sneaking around our high school in the dark, including the valedictorian, salutatorian, a Rhodes Scholar, student council president (me), head cheerleader (Laura), captain of the state championship-winning basketball team (Caleb), modern medical miracle (Morgan), and a bunch of others who had worked hard to keep sparkly clean reps in our four years there.

It was the great unspoken rule that students in the graduating class pranked the school the night before graduation and got away with it—thus the reason Hal the security guard just sat back in his truck and watched, his presence there more to protect us than stop us.

Morgan and I tiptoed down the main breezeway of the school, now covered in blue and gold streamers with "SENIORS RULE" propaganda covering the walls. It felt good to leave our last marks on these hallways.

Because after tomorrow, everything would change. We would be graduates, and the halls that had borne witness to our lives for the last four years would only echo with our memories. Once the streamers and signs were cleaned up and the chalk easily washed away, there would be nothing left of us there. Our lockers had already been cleaned out, our academic and sports awards distributed, our yearbooks signed.

This was the last thing.

Bittersweet nostalgia filtered in as I followed Morgan through the darkened breezeway. I paused for a brief moment, turning a slow circle and taking in one sweeping glance. I wanted to remember this moment because my world would never be the same again.

"Whit," Morgan called from around the corner. "They're in the courtyard."

A few whispers and giggles wafted my way, so I ditched my deep thoughts in the dark breezeway and joined my friends. Caleb and Dillon were on the roof, hanging the last banner down into the courtyard while a couple of others gave them directions to make sure it wasn't crooked. The rest were sticking plastic forks in the ground.

"Forking the courtyard. Nice touch." I smiled before setting to work chalking the concrete picnic tables with the stubs I had left. In loopy handwriting, I spelled out "SENIOR SKIP DAY." Too bad we wouldn't be there to see the faces of our teachers and fellow students when they discovered our handiwork. Everybody knew the seniors skipped school the day of the graduation ceremony, just like they knew to expect some kind of pranking gesture from us tomorrow.

Once the banner was secured, Dillon and Caleb started dancing victoriously on the roof. A few of the girls whistled and cat-called at their antics.

"Guys, that's scary," I called out, pausing to watch them.

"We're not gonna fall," Dillon replied as he moonwalked past Caleb.

"That's not what I meant."

"Yeah," Morgan added, launching a fork at them. "We're still recovering from your scary dance moves at prom!"

That got a laugh from everyone. My eyes met Caleb's and my mind flashed back to how stunning he had looked in a tux as my date. Like a teenage James Bond who had oozed charm and more than a little mischief.

But then I gave him a real warning look. Seriously, the last thing we needed was for someone to get hurt. He blew a kiss at me in response, and my heart thumped a little harder. I reached in my back pocket to check the time on my phone and realized my phone wasn't there. I had left it in the car.

"Morgie, what time is it?"

She checked. "Almost midnight. Oops, we need to get out of here soon."

I had a midnight curfew, and Dad was not going to be happy when I missed it. He had been on edge all day and almost didn't let me go out for the Senior Skip Day pranks. Thankfully, Mom had stepped in on my behalf—but only if I was home by midnight.

"Pictures first!" Laura cheered. I tossed the chalk pieces in the trash and brushed my hands together, all the while carefully monitoring Caleb as he lowered himself from the roof. I breathed a small sigh of relief when he was safely back on the ground. He jogged over to me, his eyes dancing with exhilaration.

With a shake of my head, I said, "I thought you hated heights."

"It wasn't that high."

"You sure you're not just trying to impress a certain cheerleader?" I quipped, because joking about his mythical feelings for Laura helped me keep the boundaries in place between us.

"Nah. I don't have to work that hard with her," he threw back lightly. "She likes me the way I am."

I just rolled my eyes to mask what I really felt, which was... what? Guilt? Jealousy? Frustration? I wasn't sure anymore. All I knew was that I wished I didn't have to joke about Laura anymore. I wished Caleb held the title of Boyfriend and not just Best-Friend-Crush-Who-Won't-Commit.

Our exchange was interrupted when our friends grabbed us and squeezed us into a group photo. Laura had set up her camera with a timer. We smiled in the first one, then posed silly-faced in the second one because some traditions didn't die in elementary school. In the third one, I felt Caleb's arm slide across my waist and pull me closer. I wrapped my arms around his neck so that we posed cheek to cheek. I could smell his gum and the summery saltiness of his skin pressed against mine. For the last picture, we all did the best pop group album pose we could come up with. It involved a lot of smirk and sass.

We admired our hard work one last time, high-fived and hugged each other, and then exited the courtyard. Once in the breezeway, Caleb tugged lightly at my hand, beckoning me to stay behind.

"What's up?" I asked when it was just the two of us. His face was barely illuminated as he stared intensely at his cell phone in one hand.

"Hold on," he replied, and I glanced impatiently back at our friends waving bye to Hal in the parking lot and promising to find each other before the ceremony. Morgan pretended not to notice we were hanging back. She always did that... always tried to look the other way when we wanted moments of privacy. "And there it is. Midnight!" Caleb said triumphantly. "Happy eighteenth birthday, Whitnee."

"Oh." I smiled, just as a warm current of air blew through the breezeway, taking us both by surprise. My hair whipped around, and I held my breath for a moment, almost expecting… I don't know what. Random gusts of wind once meant something. But when it died down and nothing else happened, we both kind of laughed nervously. It was a breezeway by definition. No cause to freak out.

"That was weird," I chuckled, brushing my hair out of my face. Caleb must have been holding his breath too, because he released it with a low whistle. I turned a soft smile back on him. "Thanks for remembering at midnight."

His hands tentatively found my waist again. "Just wanted to be the first to say it." I went willingly into his arms and snuggled against his chest. Forget the fact that I was now officially breaking my curfew. All I wanted was to prolong that moment in Caleb's arms—even if it was in the middle of the high school hallway. I didn't know how many of these moments I had left. College was coming in a few months and I still hadn't made my final decision about where to go. The unknown future loomed over me like a shadow, a threat to everything I had built up in my life since last summer.

I pulled back a little and tilted my face up toward his. He had The Look again.

The one where his lips parted ever so slightly and the green of his eyes deepened with desire and his scarred eyebrow lifted in contemplation. I knew what that look meant.

I had seen it so many times over the last year, when too many perfect moments for a first kiss had passed us by. And why? What was our problem? I was getting tired of putting it off.

But he just stared at me, his conflict revealed in that eyebrow that couldn't settle on a position. Like he was waiting for something. Was he waiting for me to do it first? Was I just waiting for him? *Ugh.*

"Whitnee—" He took a breath, dropped his forehead to mine, and closed his eyes in frustration.

"You know you can just do it, Caleb. You've had my permission for a while now."

"Yeah," he sighed. "I know."

There was no sense in pretending anymore that I didn't want this. I wanted to be Caleb's girlfriend *officially*, and one itty bitty kiss seemed like a good first step.

Or one swoony, kiss-me-until-I-can't-breathe moment would work too. I wasn't picky.

"What exactly are you waiting for?"

That was when he pulled back and removed his arms from around me. I thought I saw his eyes flick to my necklace once as he said, "I don't know."

He did know. He just didn't want to admit it. At that moment, his phone started ringing.

"Ignore it," I told him. "Tell me what's wrong."

But he took a step away from me anyway and checked it.

"It's your dad." Caleb held the ringing phone out to me as "NATHAN TERRADORA" flashed insistently across the screen. "Did you not tell him you were running late?"

Oh, I was in trouble.

Sleep would not find me on this Island. The flames of doubt kept creeping to the surface every time I closed my eyes. I finally threw the blankets off and donned suitable clothing for a nighttime walk. Perhaps I could put my mind to rest if I went over the speech one more time. If I could only make myself feel as confident as I appeared…

Lightning lit the darkened corridors as I made my way up the narrow stairs. I hoped the storm relented by morning. We needed perfect weather for the coming events. It was extremely irritating to know I had control over every detail of the festivities except for the bloody weather.

When I pulled open the door, I could immediately feel the Dome's effects. My rampant emotions subdued slightly as I moved to stare out into the night sky. The rain pelted against the window, and angry tufts of cloud were visible when the lightning flashed behind them.

There was something about this kind of weather that vexed me. Or, if I was being honest, brought back memories better left in the past. Either way, I was not going to sleep any time soon. With a frustrated sigh, I turned toward the long meeting table in the room, prepared to review my speech.

But someone sat there at the table, watching me silently.

Instead of revealing how startled I was, I lowered myself into a chair across from her. "Why are you still awake?"

"Probably for the same reasons you are, Gabriel." She sighed and dropped her writing instrument on the table. Then she cupped her chin in her hands and rested her elbows on the table. When the lightning flashed, I did not miss how exhausted her green eyes were. "I keep worrying we are missing something or forgetting someone or failing at something—"

"Eden." I stopped her. "You have done a fine job. There are no holes in your careful planning."

She cocked one eyebrow wearily. "Yet you are also up here instead of sleeping peacefully."

"Ah, but that has nothing to do with *you* or your flawless job as my Advisor," I corrected her. "I just need more personal preparation."

"You say that, but you are quite good in front of a crowd. A trait that must come from your mother."

"That would mean it is possible to inherit something good from her. And we both know that cannot be true." I waved my hand dismissively. "Where is my speech?"

She shuffled some papers and then slid a few across the table. After she switched on a small light, we spent a few minutes in silence while I looked over the words I would speak at the opening ceremony tomorrow night. The storm pounded the Dome windows as I thought about the overall purpose of this speech and everything I had stood for in this last year. Justice. Unity. Change.

We had made many changes in a year. And even the opening ceremony itself would be unlike any before it; we had made certain of that. What we had planned was either madness or brilliance. I had not decided yet.

Finally I spoke. "There is something in this part of the speech that still does not feel right—" I stopped talking when I glanced up at Eden. She was waiting for me to finish my thoughts, but now that there was light cast on her face, I could see that her eyes were red-rimmed and puffy. "You have been crying," I blurted.

"Gabriel, please." She looked away, always loathing the moments when I could see her emotions so clearly. Sometimes I think she preferred me to believe she had no feelings at all. But I knew that was not true. Over the last year, I had seen a different side of her, a part that was softer and deeper than she ever let on when we were children. It was bound to happen when we worked so closely together.

"What has upset you?" I asked, knowing what it was but wanting to give her the opportunity to admit it.

"Nothing. I just came up here to work. There are thousands of people to coordinate on this Island over the next several days, which is not exactly an easy job. I do not wish to be distracted with anything else."

I studied her for a moment. She started writing again, purposefully keeping her face turned away from me. Perhaps I was asking too much of her. Perhaps it was unhealthy for her to live at the Palladium with me—away from her family.

"Have you talked to her this week?" I tried to make my voice as gentle as possible.

"Did you not hear everything I just said—"

"All I heard was your excuse for not visiting your sister. And it is not a good one."

I watched the pen fall from her hand, saw the tiny splash of one teardrop on the papers, and the urge to touch her—to give her some kind of Pyradorian comfort—was very strong. I knew her stubborn Geodorian self would not appreciate it coming from me, so I resisted. She covered her eyes with her hands, and her shoulders jerked.

"Eden." This was not right. She should be with her dying sister, not with me. "I think you should go."

"Go?" she repeated, pulling her hands from her face and staring at me incredulously.

"Yes. I think you should go and be with your family in Geodora immediately. I can do without you—"

"No, you cannot!"

I did not appreciate her tone. I most certainly could handle things without her.

If I had to.

"You are about to officially become our Guardian, and I am the one who has planned all of the events. There is no way I can miss the opening ceremony at the Watch Tower. No, I will go and see Elon when all of these traditions and ceremonies are over. I am certain nothing will happen to her before then—" Her voice caught. Everyone knew little Elon was at the end. It was surprising she had made it to this point. But, no, there was no certainty that she would survive to next week, not even to tomorrow.

And I knew Eden would never forgive herself if she did not get to see her again.

"Very well. I will take you to Geodora myself. Gather all of the paperwork." I stood to my feet as those wide, tearstained green eyes peered up at me in confusion.

"You cannot be serious. It is storming and we have to be at the Watch Tower tomorrow—"

"We will start our journey early with a short stop to see your family," I said calmly but firmly. "You know neither of us is going to sleep tonight. We are already packed. Everyone knows what to do. I say we leave now. Just the two of us. No guards, no advisors—no complications."

"I am sure your betrothed would not appreciate us sneaking off in the night together," Eden reminded me.

"Jezebel will just have to meet us at the ceremony." It would be better that way. Jezebel and Eden did not get along. In fact, Jezebel had become bent on getting along with no one lately. I was certain it had to do with my hesitance to make our betrothal public. I had put it off as long as I possibly could, despite pressure from Jezebel and her father. I just could not manage a marriage yet, not with every other political issue we had going on. And that was all marriage to Jezebel was—one more political issue.

"You do not need to add this to your worries, Gabriel. I do not wish for you to complicate matters on my behalf."

"Perhaps you have not considered the fact that I would like to see Elon for myself. I am her favorite Pyra, after all."

"You are the only Pyra she knows," Eden pointed out, but her tears had slowed and her face had lightened considerably.

It was true that I cared for Eden's little sister. Perhaps a visit with her would help me put this speech into its proper perspective. After all, how could I inspire an entire people if I could not take the time to hear its smallest voice?

"Come, I will have the wagon prepared. We leave within the hour."

"But—"

I held up a hand. "Ah, you just said I am about to become your Guardian. I think it is written somewhere in our agreement that you are not allowed to argue with me ever again. If I say we are leaving, then we are leaving." I grinned at her to show I was teasing. We both knew she would never give me total compliance in all matters, and it would only bore me if she did. But when a boom of thunder hit the Dome so fiercely that the whole room rattled, I lost my smile. The light on the table flickered with the impact and went out.

Eden whispered, "Maybe we should not go out in that storm."

I glanced out again, feeling that familiar indignation. A particular pair of gray eyes flashed across my mind as the lightning and wind hammered the other side of the window. So unpredictable was the wind, so uncontrollable. So utterly frustrating.

"No," I told her with confidence. "The storm will not stop us."

2

BEYOND MIDNIGHT

"I can't believe you waited up for me," I grumbled when I got home and found Dad chowing down on a bowl of ice cream at the kitchen table. Since Mom wasn't in sight, I assumed she was in bed asleep—like a *normal* parent who trusts her daughter.

"Midnight means twelve o'clock on the dot, not twelve twenty-two."

I dropped my purse on the table and went to the sink to wash the remaining chalk off my hands. "I've missed curfew before and you've never cared." After he had flipped out on me via Caleb's phone, I wasn't in the best mood.

"But you always texted to let us know. Tonight I was worried sick."

"How did you have time to worry sick?" I replied. "You called Caleb at 12:02 a.m., Dad. And when I found my phone in the car, I had missed eight calls from you… eight! Don't you think that's a little obsessive? Not to mention *embarrassing* for me in front of my friends?"

"All I want is for you to respect my wishes when I make them that clear."

I could feel my annoyance festering, but tried a different tactic instead. "I'm sorry I was late, but we were perfectly safe. I was with friends you know, and Hal the security guard was right there watching. Nothing bad could have happened."

"That's not what had me worried. I just wanted you home by midnight, Whitnee! Midnight, okay?" Dad huffed, and his spoon hit the bowl with a clang.

I reached into the fridge for a bottle of water, hiding my face so he couldn't see me roll my eyes. Nothing turned up the Dad Irritation Dial more than when I rolled my eyes. "What did you think would happen at midnight? That I would turn into a pumpkin on my eighteenth birthday?" I couldn't keep the sarcasm out of my voice. He was being so ridiculous about this.

I broke open the lid and drank the water down. When he didn't respond immediately, I turned back around. He was staring at the wall in front of him, his ice cream forgotten. Slowly, I lowered the water bottle to the counter, realization dawning on me.

"Is that what this is about? Did you think something would happen when I turned eighteen? Something *magical*?" I peered suspiciously at him.

He snapped out of it and met my eyes.

"No, of course that's not the issue." He sighed, picked up his bowl, and walked to the sink. "I'm just being overprotective, I guess. At least that's what your mom tells me."

Despite my frustration, I felt a chord of compassion for my dad. It hadn't even been a complete year since he had been reunited with Mom and me. I knew his fears ran deep. I knew because the same fears still haunted me. That one day I'd wake up and he'd be gone. Or that someone would find a way to rip our family apart again.

"I really am sorry I scared you," I conceded. "And if you had a reason to believe something could happen, you should have just told me. We can't keep secrets like that, Dad."

He rinsed out the bowl and wouldn't meet my gaze. "I don't have a reason to believe anything like that. I was just overreacting." I watched him thoughtfully as he dried his hands. I didn't really believe him. Not that Dad was a liar. But he had a way of only telling me what he thought I should know. And my definition of what I thought I should know seemed to be different than his. I was starting to suspect his fears tonight had something to do with the Island. That was only confirmed when he finally faced me and said, "But you would tell me if you *felt* something, wouldn't you, Whit?"

My hand went instinctively to the thunderfly necklace he had given to me. When I was on the Island, it would light up with a violet glow every time I touched it. The life force was no longer there once I returned to the Mainland. Even so, I never took it off. I don't know if I secretly believed it would light up again or what.

"Of course I would tell you that, Dad. Would you tell *me* if you felt something different?"

"Sure," he responded. But then we were scrutinizing each other as if we weren't sure the other one was being truthful. Had Dad felt something tonight and that's why he overreacted? The idea terrified me. I didn't sense anything different within myself. There had been the wind thing right when Caleb wished me happy birthday, but that had just been coincidence.

Right?

"If they shut down the portals like they were supposed to…" I started saying to myself like I had so many times this year.

"Then we have nothing to worry about," Dad finished routinely for me.

"Right. There's no way to get back. And even if there was, we're not going near a portal." He nodded absently. That was the thing about Dad and me. We acted as if we would never go back to that Island when deep down we found ourselves suspecting, worrying. Something within us still felt unsettled even a year later.

"Soooo…" I gave Dad an inquiring look. "Why exactly were you worried sick tonight?"

Dad forced a smile and gave me a hug. "I didn't mean to upset you, especially on your birthday. You've always been a responsible girl, and I've always been bad at letting go."

I squeezed my eyes shut, still sometimes amazed that he was there after I'd believed him to be dead for six years. "Who says you have to let go? I'm still here," I mumbled against his shoulder.

He didn't respond. With a pat on my back, he released me and stared at my face for a second. "Tomorrow is a big day. You should go get some sleep."

"I'm not really tired." I shrugged, then narrowed my eyes playfully. "Maybe this new *eighteen*-year-old wants some birthday ice cream. And to beat her old man in some video games."

He narrowed his eyes back. "Your mother will kill us if we stay up too late. We've got parties and graduation and traveling—"

"What she doesn't know won't hurt her."

He pretended to think it over as he reached into the cabinet and pulled out two fresh bowls. "I think I might need more ice cream. Just to make sure I have enough energy to gloat when I beat you in golf."

"You'll need the comfort food when I beat you at *racing*. Don't forget the sprinkles," I commanded and rushed off to get the game ready.

It wasn't until I was lying in bed later that night that I realized Dad never clarified what he was having a hard time letting go of. And that kept me up thinking for way too long.

"The storm woke her up and she is strangely coherent right now. You could not have chosen a better time to make a surprise visit." Joseph's voice was hushed as he led Eden and me back to Elon's room. "She will be so happy to see you. *Both* of you."

The lights in the house were dim in the early morning hours, and Eden's four other siblings were asleep in their rooms. Eden's parents seemed to have aged unnaturally quickly in the last year as they watched their second-youngest child fight for her life. If there had been a known cause to her illness, a proper treatment might have been found. But when a child grew fatigued and unable to connect with a life force for no reason, there was nothing to do. Gifting her would not work; healing her would not work. She was a delicately fading flower in the Geodora village.

And she was not the only one. Six other children had already died the same way this year. *Six*. More were falling victim to the symptoms. It was happening in all tribes and creating a panic.

I needed answers. I needed Elon to be okay. She had held on the longest of all the children. If we had just one success story, it could provide hope for the families suffering through this.

"Eden," Elon breathed happily when she caught sight of her oldest sister. Hesitating in the doorway, I watched Eden rush to Elon's bedswing and cuddle up beside the frail little girl. Elon rested her head on Eden's shoulder. "I am so glad you came."

Joseph and Joanna excused themselves to give us some time. I gripped Joseph's arm encouragingly as he exited. He gave me a thankful nod that made me glad I had forced Eden to come.

"I am sorry for not coming earlier this week. Things have been very busy at the Palladium," Eden explained, carefully concealing the shock I know she felt at the sight of Elon. I, too, felt it. The girl had grown even more thin and translucent since I had last visited. "Gabriel and I wanted to see you before we went to the Watch Tower."

"I wish I could see the new Watch Tower for myself." Elon's dark green eyes found me in the doorway. She tried to lift a tiny hand out to me, but could hardly raise it. There was a smile in her eyes, so I moved quickly to kneel by her other side. I took her weak hand in mine, trying to warm her with small doses of Fire. She felt so cold. "Gabriel, are you the Guardian now?" she asked me in a small voice.

I smiled. "Not yet. After this week I will be."

"And once you are Guardian, will you make every seventh day of the week Flower Day?" Her mouth turned up on one side, and she tried to giggle. That was our joke. Elon wanted one day a week for the entire Island to observe "Flower Day"—her own idea for a holiday.

"I have not forgotten." I winked at Eden, who frowned back at me. "We will all wear flowers for clothes and we will eat sugar flowers and drink flower tea. We will even make it rain flowers."

"And you will wear them in your hair, Gabriel, since it is getting longer again. If the Guardian does it, every one else will follow."

"Yes, any flower you want, I shall wear it in my hair." I played along.

"I want you to wear the Whitnee flower." She gestured to the bouquet of whitened flowers with gold slivers in them resting beside her bed. I tried not to reveal that familiar flash of annoyance at the name.

"I would be honored to wear the flower you designed." I squeezed her hand proudly. Even at such a young age, she had accomplished the one thing she had determined to do: create a flower the color of Whitnee's blonde hair. And it was the last thing she had been able to do with her life force.

Eden rolled her eyes at me and said to Elon, "You know he is just teasing you, Elon. It would be inappropriate to wear flowers instead of clothes. I can only imagine if Gabriel…" And then she drifted off, the color of embarrassment upon her cheeks.

I raised my eyebrows at her in surprise. "Are you imagining such a thing, Eden?"

"I just do not want you to raise her hopes over such a silly holiday," Eden replied curtly. But I was quite certain she had just been imagining me clothed in flowers, and I was extremely amused by it. I resisted the urge to picture her clothed only in flowers as well.

"I know we are just pretending," Elon answered simply. "Hand me a Whitnee flower, Eden."

Eden obediently pulled the flower from its bouquet, and Elon let go of me to take it from her. "Bow your head, Gabriel." I did as I was told and felt her weakly push the flower into my hair. "There. It shall be worn just like that on Flower Day," Elon declared when I raised my head for her to admire.

A short laugh escaped from Eden. "It is quite stunning on you, Gabriel. I think you should wear it when you give your speech tonight."

For Elon's sake, I agreed. "Maybe I shall!" But then I sent Eden a playful look and she just smiled back at me. It was good that we came when we did. There was a level of familiarity and comfort I felt around Eden's family in ways I had never felt with my own.

"Does that mean you are leaving soon?" Elon spoke up.

"Yes, we will leave later this morning, hopefully once the storm passes," Eden said with a yawn. "But we will come back in a few days when Gabriel receives his blessing from our tribe. Promise me you will wait for us to return."

Elon's sigh was barely perceptible. "I am waiting for the Pilgrim to come. Then everything will be okay."

My eyes drifted to Eden's, as I sensed the ache in her heart at Elon's words. Subduing my own sadness, I asked, "Do you mean Whitnee? Nobody knows when the Pilgrim will come, Elon."

"It will be soon," Elon told us. "Is that not what you taught me?"

"It will be whenever the Island wants it to be," Eden reminded her. "We do not always understand the Island's ways. But, yes, hold on to your faith, dear one."

Elon looked at me again and insisted, "It *will* be soon. The Pilgrim has to come… to save me."

It felt like a dagger twisted in my stomach as I listened to her bold faith in a person I was no longer certain about. Eden seemed at a loss for words.

"Would you like a light show before I go, Elon?" I offered, changing the direction of the conversation.

"Oh, yes, please!" she smiled and snuggled in to Eden's side. "No drakons or thunderflies this time. Just flowers that float."

I extinguished the lights and then created images that danced around the room—patterns of light to tickle her imagination, sparkling explosions of flowers to delight her. Manipulating light was one thing I could do well, and it was the only thing I could give Elon to take her mind off her sickness. It was not long before she and Eden grew drowsy with sleep. I hung one illuminated flower that glittered above their heads like moonlight, and I left them cuddled together in the darkened room.

Joseph and Joanna had also fallen asleep in the main room—probably feeling some ease now that someone was watching over Elon for a few hours. Quietly I proceeded to the guest room I used when I stayed in Geodora.

I placed the Whitnee flower beside my bedswing and stared at it. The thick petals curved outward, allowing the tiny gold veins to glint warmly in the dim light. It really was a beautiful and unique masterpiece of Geodorian work.

But I resented its inspiration. It had become easier not to indulge in thoughts about Whitnee—even though she was always at the edge of everything we did and every decision we made on this Island. She had left behind more influence than she probably ever knew. If she did know, surely she would have returned by now. Elon and Eden both believed she and her father would come back, but I was not so certain anymore. How could the prophesied Pilgrim abandon us? Unless neither of them was really the Pilgrim... Either way, we were still an Island of people waiting for a promise. Waiting for help that I could not seem to provide. The hardest part of my speech was going to be inspiring the people to continue to wait, to continue to have hope and faith when my own hope was fading quickly. If only we all had the blind faith of a child like Elon.

I spent some time thinking again about my speech before finally drifting into sleep for a few hours. By the time the dawn came, the storm had left us.

And so had Elon. She had died at some point in her sleep, right there in her sister's arms.

Not even the Pilgrim could save her now.

3

THE FRIEND ZONE

I woke up from my second dream ever about Elon. I thought about her every once in a while, but I hadn't dreamed about her since that night at Camp Fusion last summer when she had warned me "they" were coming for me. It had been the same night I had woken up using an Earth shield on the Mainland. That had been totally scary, especially when I found out that Elon had grown ill the same weekend of my dream. I never got to see her again, but the dream had freaked me out.

This time was different. She was perfectly beautiful and playing in the flower field of Geodora, her dark hair braided loosely down her back. I tried to get her attention. She looked up once as if she sensed something, but her eyes seemed to look right through me. After a while, she returned to her playing with a docile smile. It was a peaceful dream, but it still upset me.

Every once in a while, I woke up missing the Island. I don't know if it was because of dreams that I couldn't remember, or just because dreams and reality often seemed to blur in my mind. After being in two different worlds, the morning still confused me at times. Like I wasn't sure where I really was, or more so, where I was *supposed* to be. And the memories of last summer on the Island would filter in as I lay in bed, trying to determine my reality. But you just couldn't trust memories. They are suspended in time for a reason. And even if I did go back to the Island, I knew it wouldn't be like my memories.

Given enough time, things always change.

I stretched lazily and tried to clear my head of Elon and her flowers. My clock told me it was nine in the morning. I couldn't believe Mom hadn't come in and woken me up yet. The petrified Saint flower Caleb had made for me on the Island last summer glittered with early morning sunlight in the shadow box frame on my wall. My favorite words penned with his meticulous handwriting made me sigh and smile just like every other morning:

I'll always care, always try to find you—whether you want me to or not.

Caleb's steady heart beat out with every syllable. If he said it, I knew he meant it.

When I opened my door, pink and green streamers with balloons danced in my face. This was always my favorite part of my birthday. Not the presents, not the party. No, I loved waking up in the morning to find Mom's door decorations. It was her favorite tradition—and this year she had included plenty of graduate décor too.

I climbed through the streamers and made my way to the living room where all three of our suitcases were open and almost completely packed for our trip. Tonight, after the graduation ceremony, we were boarding a plane and heading to Florida. This time tomorrow I would be on my first Caribbean cruise. Mom and Dad agreed to take Morgan and Caleb and me somewhere tropical for our senior trip. We had invited Uncle Ben to come along too, but with Camp Fusion activities kicking off in a couple of weeks, he was needed around there.

Part of me regretted not committing to work again at Camp Fusion this summer. But I couldn't risk being that close to the Island—I wasn't ready to know if the portal was still active or not. I had to move on with my life, and so the part of me that had no regrets was primed and ready for some suntanning on a Caribbean beach with a good book in hand. Morgan and I had successfully convinced Caleb to attempt parasailing with us. In return, we had to ride jet skis, which sounded like fun as long as I didn't end up falling in the water. They didn't even try to talk me into snorkeling with them. After years of having a friend with an irrational fish phobia, you just don't ask anymore.

I bent down and pulled out my new black two-piece swimsuit with the adorable strappy cover-up and floppy sun hat. I don't know why, but I felt like Audrey Hepburn in it, and I didn't just pick it out for myself. Caleb had made no secret last summer of his appreciation of me in a swimsuit. But that had been almost a year ago. Maybe he needed a reminder that he could be attracted to more than just Gal Pal Whitnee's personality.

I rolled the clothes back up and stuffed it all into the suitcase. My thoughts were interrupted as I heard raised voices coming from my parents' room. I froze for a second, listening. It didn't sound like yelling—but that was some intense, emotional dialogue going on.

My parents never argued. Never. At least not in front of me. If they did when I was younger, I don't remember it. They certainly hadn't since being reunited last year. And, trust me, there could have been plenty to fight about given the fact that Dad was living on an Island for six years and being manipulated by another woman who claimed to love him.

I wandered over to their closed bedroom door, trying to catch snatches of what was wrong. Mom sounded like she was crying. Dad was talking fast, and I kept hearing "shhh" and "it will be okay." Mom's voice was muffled. She might have been rattling off phrases in Spanish, too, which did not help me understand any better.

My stomach flipped as I stood there alone in the hallway, listening to their desperate voices. All I could think of was the one night Mom finally broke down about a week after Dad had gone missing. I had heard desperate sobs coming from her room then, too—not unlike the kind I was hearing now.

It made me sick. I probably should have just charged in there and demanded to know what was happening. Or perhaps I should have just walked away and pretended not to notice. But something kept me rooted to that spot, right there in my pajamas and morning breath, listening.

Suddenly the door opened, and Dad and I came face to face with equally startled looks.

"What's wrong?" I whispered, fear clutching at my gut.

He seemed flustered as he grabbed me by the elbow and pulled me away from the door.

"I'm going to run some errands. Picking up your dress from the cleaners, last minute toiletries at the grocery store... Do you need anything else?" He busied himself looking for his car keys in the kitchen.

"Dad—"

"Uncle Ben will be here in a few hours for your birthday party. Your mom wants suitcases finished packing by then—"

"Dad, I heard y'all fighting."

He paused. "Apparently you heard nothing, because we weren't fighting."

"Then why is Mom crying in there?"

"Look, Whit, this is an emotional time for your mother. Just be gentle with her today, okay?" For a moment, he looked deeply sad.

So I nodded as if I understood. Emotional because of what? Graduation? Turning eighteen? Was it too much change for Mom all at once? Maybe it was a bit much for both of them.

I don't know if it was the look on my face or what, but Dad gave me one of his it's-all-okay smiles and tweaked the messy ponytail on top of my head. "Happy birthday, Baby Doll," he said and then he was out the door before I could say anything else.

Why did I feel like he was still only telling me what he thought I should know?

"The thunderfly is here. We need to leave."

I looked up from my papers to find Eden standing there, her satchel thrown over one shoulder.

I studied her thoughtfully, the way one arm crossed over her chest squeezing the strap of her bag as if it—or maybe she—would drop to the floor without it.

She could not be serious.

"You are not going with me," I told her calmly as I shuffled the papers into an organized pile.

"I do not remember making the decision to stay."

"You did not make the decision to come here, either. I did. And

I decided you are staying to be with your family through this. They need you—"

"No, *you* need me. We have the opening ceremony and then *four* tribal festivals in *four* days. You cannot possibly expect to do all of this without me. I have worked all year for this and I cannot let anything—"

"Eden," I interrupted her gently, coming around the table to face her straight on. "I can do this without you."

"Really, Gabriel! Tell me the order of the ceremony tonight and who is sitting where and what time you are being picked up to travel to Aerodora and who is supposed to accompany you for security—"

"We have a detailed schedule written down. And I can contact you by zephyra if anything is not clear."

I could sense the vibrations of grief pulsing all around her. She would work herself to death before she would just allow herself to mourn.

"Yes, but I am your Advisor—"

"And you just lost your sister—"

"And my presence here cannot bring her back!" she snapped, her eyes brimming with tears. "You cannot do this to me, Gabriel. I will *not* be distracted by this… I will *not*. My family knows how important this week is. And Elon knows I love her!"

"Of course she knows that," I agreed softly. I could not help moving closer to her. The cloud of emotional intensity was about to overcome her. I could feel it. "She waited to see you."

That was it. Eden completely melted into sobs. Her satchel dropped to the floor as she hid her face and cried, "I was holding her… how could I just sleep right through it?"

I had never seen my Advisor, my trusted friend, so broken. My arms were around her before I could think about what I was doing. And then her face was pressed into my chest as if we had done this before, as if I knew what it felt like to hold Eden so close. But I had never dared touch her. She had always kept me at a distance. Now my heart rushed with compassion for her, with sadness for Elon, with regret that she could not be saved.

"You must have given her great comfort, Eden, if she felt she could let go while in your arms." As horrifying as it was for her to wake up to that, I could not imagine anything more fitting for Elon than to die in the arms of a beloved sister.

There was nothing but the sound of Eden's weeping. I tightened my arms around her and felt her hands grip the front of my tunic as she released a flood of repressed emotion. Her hair smelled like sweet blossoms and her skin was terrifyingly soft, like the petals of the flowers in the room.

"Why are the children dying, Gabriel?" she sobbed. "We have to make it stop. Whatever is killing off our children is killing the heart and soul of our Island."

I did not respond, but the grim reality of her words weighed heavily on me. I did not understand what was happening on the Island, but I feared something was dreadfully wrong. The strange and unpredictable weather patterns, the unexplainable diseases, the deaths… it felt like we were being punished for something we did not understand. And it had become personal now that it had taken Elon's life.

"Eden, I know you want to leave the village, but I want you to trust me. I believe it is best that you stay here. Use your skills to plan a proper funeral for your sister. I will see you in a matter of days for the Geodorian Blessing."

She started shaking her head, but we were interrupted.

"Eden?" a voice called from the main room.

As if we had been caught doing something wrong, we both instinctively pulled away from each other. She wiped her eyes self-consciously and I smoothed the front of my tunic, which was still wet with her teardrops.

Eden sighed heavily. "Oh, I do not feel up to seeing—"

Abner entered the room. "There you are! I just got word about Elon." He rushed to embrace her right in front of me. Something inside me clenched at his familiarity with her.

Eden accepted his embrace and then pulled away. "Thank you, Abner. It was nice of you to come. Gabriel and I were just leaving—"

"Actually," I interrupted. "Eden was just saying goodbye as I will be leaving for the Watch Tower unaccompanied." I ignored the ugly look Eden gave me from across the room. We had an agreement; she was allowed to disagree with me in private, but the etiquette of her position was to help present a unified front to everyone else. Just as she had gotten better at not openly defying me over the last year, so, too, had I gotten better at listening to her. However, I was not backing down on this decision.

Was I sacrificing a tremendous amount by not having her with me? Yes. Was it going to make my job more complicated? Yes. But sometimes my job was to protect people from themselves. And Eden needed time to mourn and rest.

Besides, now that Abner was there, I would be leaving her in capable hands. The bearded Geoguard might irritate me at times for reasons I could not explain, but he did seem to care quite openly about my Advisor.

I scooped up the Whitnee flower that remained on the desk, tucked it into my satchel and proceeded to leave. I bowed slightly to Abner, one of the few other people I knew who was roughly my size.

"Best wishes tonight, Gabriel," he greeted me. "I was planning to be there, but in light of recent events with Elon…"

"I understand. I appreciate you taking care of my Advisor," I told him sincerely.

"I will walk with you to the thunderfly, Gabriel," Eden offered. But I knew better. She would just plant herself in the carrier and then I would lose this battle with her.

"No need. I know where to go." At the crestfallen look on her face, I added, "Please keep your zephyra nearby. In the event that I need you."

"You *will* need me," she retorted. With a small smile, I made my exit. "Wait!" she called out suddenly and came after me. "Did you decide what was wrong with your speech?"

I paused before saying, "No. But I suppose it does not matter. They are only words." Then I turned away from her, needing to leave before she could sense the lie.

She grabbed my arm and when I looked back into her face, her eyes were the color of moss—warm and exhausted. "Do not give up on this Island, or Whitnee and Nathan. I know your faith is weak right now, Gabriel. But great things happen to those whose faith is great."

The words were out of my mouth before I could stop them. "Elon's faith was great. And it did not help her."

At her sharp intake of breath, I immediately regretted what I said. But other than that, she just stared at me as if she pitied me. "I wish that you… I am sorry that…" She sighed, clearly flustered with her words. "Just do what you always do and you will be fine tonight," she finished abruptly and then turned around and left without another word.

I wished I knew what it was I "always do," according to her.

"Um, no, you totally don't look fat in that." I shook my head vehemently as Morgan paraded self-consciously out of my bathroom in her new swimsuit.

"Don't protect my feelings, Whit," she warned. "I know I've put on a lot of weight since last summer."

"Morgie, you put on *healthy* weight," I insisted. "You look great now. Last summer was not normal."

No, last summer was certainly not normal. It was not normal to find out your best friend had stage four cancer and you were the only one with the power to cure her. After I performed Transfusion, an ancient White Island ritual where I basically sacrificed my Water life force and infused it into her, Morgan had been healed of her cancer—and even became a real Hydrodorian as a result.

I grinned at the Hydro tattoo that showed clearly on her right shoulder. Morgan had determined in her heart that the day she turned eighteen, she was getting a tattoo just like the Hydrodorian birthmark. For her, such a mark meant healing, a second chance at life. Morgan had become a different person our senior year of high school. No boyfriends, more confidence, less fear. Coming pretty close to death had changed her perspective on the life she had.

Unfortunately Morgan's parents remained baffled at the changes in her, which was why Morgan didn't tell them about her new tattoo until four months after she had gotten it done.

"Are you sure my hips don't look too big? Maybe I should have gotten a different style—"

"No, this one is perfect for you! And you better be kidding me about your hips or you're gonna give me a complex about my own." Seriously, she was worrying for nothing. Morgan had curves in all the right places. "Now go change, so we don't neglect the party guests for too long."

"It's just our families," Morgan mumbled. She gave herself one last glance in my full-length mirror before disappearing into the bathroom again. I took the opportunity to check my reflection in the mirror too. I absolutely loved my graduation dress. Mom and I had discovered this amazing old-fashioned white sundress that was flattering and feminine with soft lacy patterns in the skirt and a petticoat underneath. It could be dressed up with heels and jewelry or dressed down with flip-flops and a jacket. Right now it was dressed up. And, of course, my thunderfly necklace glittered perfectly as my only accessory.

Mom and Dad had dressed in coordinating white and khaki so we could take some memorable family pictures for the wall. Mom, with her darker Mexican complexion, didn't look like Dad and me with our blonde hair and gray eyes. When I was younger, we used to joke about the blatant coloring differences. While I still favored my mom's face shape and features, I had been the only pale kid in my family—much like Dad had been growing up on the Island. But since Dad had come back into our lives, we really tried not to call unnecessary attention to the differences between us and Mom. Or to the fact that she had never been to the Island.

"So are you nervous about speaking at graduation?" Morgan called from the bathroom. I plopped down on the bed and hugged my fuzzy purple pillow.

"No," I answered. "Should I be? I'm just reading from a piece of paper."

"I would totally flub it. But you're a natural at speaking in front of people. That's why you're our President."

"Yeah, too bad I'm not a natural at walking. I'm more worried I'm gonna trip on my way to the mic."

She came out of the bathroom. "Are you wearing those shoes?" I kicked my heels out and nodded. She made a face and popped her gum wickedly. "Ooh. Good luck."

"Thanks." I threw myself back on the bed. All I had to do was present the Teacher of the Year Award from our graduating class. I had written my speech based on the essays submitted about this particular teacher. There was no way I could screw it up.

Morgan applied fresh lip gloss in the mirror as she added flippantly, "If you trip, I'm sure Caleb will be ready to catch you from the front row."

"Has he been acting weird to you lately?"

"In what way?"

"I don't know. He's been so distant with me. And—" I paused. "He still won't kiss me, Morgie. What the heck?"

She groaned and popped her gum. "You two are so weird. You're like the opposite of friends with benefits. You're like boyfriend and girlfriend—but with no benefits."

"We're *technically* just friends."

"You're totally *not* just friends. No guy dared to ask you out this year because they all assumed you were with Caleb. And the girls left Caleb alone because of you, even Laura. Y'all exude exclusiveness in your relationship."

I frowned at the ceiling. "But it's never been official. And every time I bring it up, he dodges the subject like it's a flying coconut. Do you think he's—" I sat up and caught her big blue eyes in the mirror. "Do you think he's losing his feelings for me? Maybe he wants to keep his options open for college." It was the first time that possibility had even occurred to me and my stomach tightened in response.

Morgan snorted, and it kind of made me feel better to see her react so forcefully to the idea. "He is definitely not losing feelings for you. Maybe he's just waiting for the right moment. Like on a Caribbean beach..." She wiggled her eyebrows meaningfully.

"Did he tell you that?"

"I'm just guessing."

I sighed, thinking about all the late nights together at Starbucks, lingering conversations in parking lots, prom and the after-party when we were all dressed up and exhilarated from dancing... Our first kiss should be natural, right? Not some big production he has to plan out. "I don't know. We've had so many perfect moments and we've come so close every time. I feel like something is going on with him."

"Maybe he's just worried about—" Then she stopped talking, like she was about to say something forbidden.

My eyes widened. "Morgie, have y'all talked about this?"

"Uhh…" She darted back into the bathroom and started washing her hands, avoiding eye contact with me.

"Oh my gosh, you *know*." I followed her, tossing the pillow aside. "Tell me what he said!"

"No way." She shook her head. "I promised both of you I would not get involved in this part of your relationship."

"I am your best friend! You don't keep secrets—"

"I don't tell Caleb the things you say, either. Respect the trio."

I gaped at her. How unfair! If she knew Caleb's problem, why wouldn't she just tell me? My friendship with Morgan should always trump her friendship with Caleb—it was Sisterhood 101!

"Does it have to do with me not picking a college yet?" I tried again, my mind rolling through any and every issue Caleb and I had discussed this year. At her stubborn silence, I added, "At least tell me what to do."

She dried her hands on the towel and then grabbed my arms. "Here's what you do: *communicate*."

"Tell *him* that." I frowned, afraid to assume the next thing that came to my mind. "I swear, if it's about Gabriel and the Island…"

She chomped down harder on her gum, which told me we had arrived at the real issue. We didn't really talk about Gabriel anymore. I didn't intentionally avoid his name like I had last summer, but it just didn't seem necessary to bring him up. He was a part of my past—a very strange and unsettling part, yes, but still. He wasn't in my present. We had moved on in our lives. "Morgie, I came to terms with all of that. Surely Caleb isn't hung up on what happened on that Island, because we all know I'm never going back. My life is meant for the Mainland."

"If that's true, Whit," she said gently, her oceanic eyes the shade of honesty, "then why do you still wait for that necklace to light up?"

My lack of protest at her assumption seemed to undermine everything I had just said, which was everything I tried to make myself believe.

She pointed at my neck. "You never take it off. We all know it's there. Even I find myself checking it every so often, wondering if someday—"

"It's just a necklace my dad gave me." My hand fluttered defensively to my neck, my fingertips pressing on the little glass thunderfly protectively. "I keep it on because—"

But Morgan's eyes bulged just as I felt *something*.

"Holy *beep*, Whitnee!"

I glanced in the mirror at the same time the warmth of the Firelight registered on my fingertips. The thunderfly lit up and cast a purple glow on my neck.

4

IN WHICH THERE ARE
COMPLICATIONS

"Hey, Dad." I grabbed him by the elbow. "Can I talk to you really quick?"

He took a big bite of cake and pulled his attention away from Morgan's dad. "Mmm-hmm. What's up?" I glanced at Mr. Armstrong, who allowed the interruption and sipped his punch slowly. I tried to pull Dad away. "We'll be right back, Mr. A. Sorry."

Dad took his sweet time following me, which gave Papi an opportunity to call out, "Whitnee, don't forget I brought my guitar. Nathan requested a special song for you to sing."

"He did?" I glanced at Dad in confusion just as my little cousin, Eddie, darted between us on his way across the room to tattle on one of his brothers.

Dad shrugged and his grin featured a dab of icing at the corner of his mouth. "Edelweiss," came his vanilla cake-coated response. Aww, I loved that song.

But not right now.

I called back, "Tune the guitar, Papi. I'll be back in a few minutes."

I steered Dad toward the back door and glimpsed Morgan trying to excuse Caleb from his conversation with her older brother. "Whitnee, what—" Dad started, but I shushed him until we were safely out on the patio. He took another gaping bite and looked at me expectantly.

"Um, can you explain *this* to me?" I made the necklace light up again. Cake spewed from Dad's mouth. Then he started choking and I had to wait impatiently for him to get control of himself.

"When did that start happening?"

"Five minutes ago."

He set his plate down on the porch table. "Take it off. Let me see."

I obeyed, trying to hide the tremors in my hands. As long as my hand was on the thunderfly, it remained illuminated. But as soon as it transferred to Dad's hands, it stopped.

He turned the necklace over and examined it. "Have you used any other life forces?"

"I haven't even used one."

"Well, yes, you must be. The Firelight connects to the Fire inside you."

"Oh." My head snapped back. Without hesitation, I turned my right hand palm up. With a snap of my fingers, a flame came to life and flickered like a little bonfire sitting in my hand.

I was connected to the life forces!

That was when Caleb appeared at the back door. He took one look at Dad with my necklace and another at the Fire that rested in my upturned hand and almost spilled his drink.

"Are you kidding me!"

"Shut the door," I chastised him. Imagine if our party guests saw me playing with Fire. He and Morgan joined us with questioning, nervous looks. Dad threw his hand over mine and closed my palm.

"I don't think you should play around."

"Why will the necklace light up for me, but not you? Can you feel the life forces?"

He concentrated for a moment. "No. I can't."

"Then why can I? What's happening, Dad?"

He shook his head, his face appearing deeply disturbed.

I turned to Morgan and Caleb. "Do y'all feel anything different? Morgan?"

She closed her eyes and held her hands out. "No," she finally said. Caleb just shrugged, clearly mystified.

I turned to face the backyard. With quick instincts that were still buried deep inside me, I shot a bright red Firedart at the ground several yards away. Dirt and grass exploded in the air, and a small patch of yard caught on Fire. I heard Dad grumble, but was too overwhelmed with the sensation of life force coursing through me again to even care.

Dad and Caleb rushed to stomp out the flames as I flexed the muscles in my hands.

"What's going on here?" Ben's voice came from the door.

"Oh, you know, Whitnee's just showing off her powers," Caleb muttered sarcastically. But when we all turned to give Ben our attention, we realized Mom was right behind him. I couldn't hide my golden eyes from her as we all tensed up, waiting for her reaction.

Very calmly, she stepped outside and shut the door quietly behind her. Then with wide, fearful eyes, she gazed from me to Dad. "Why are my daughter's eyes glowing?"

"We don't know exactly," I answered immediately, but Dad just locked eyes with her for a moment. Something passed between the two of them that I didn't understand.

"The Island has reconnected with her," Ben mumbled. "What about you, Nathan? Do you feel anything?"

"No." Dad looked to the man who had raised him like a father. "Why wouldn't it happen to me too? And why is she able to do this now?"

"It's happened before, Dad, and then it went away. This might just be a random thing that means nothing."

"Whitnee is connected to that portal, Nathan." Ben spoke heavily.

Mom and Dad were silent, and I had the distinct feeling there was a theory among the three of them that they didn't want to say aloud.

"Maybe it's a special gift from the Island now that she's eighteen," Morgan guessed, half-joking.

"Or maybe *somebody* on that Island didn't shut down the portal like he was supposed to," Caleb added. I turned my attention to him, trying to decipher his expression. He raised his eyebrows at me as if to say, *Somebody had to say it.*

"Well, it doesn't matter if the portals work or not. Nobody in my family is going near one," Mom stated fiercely. "Right, Nathan?

I will not lose my family again." Her eyes started to glisten with potential tears.

Dad placed a comforting arm around her. "Everything is okay, Serena."

"You say that, but Whitnee just blew up part of my yard." She gestured at the hole my Firedart created. Maybe it was the Fire life force within me or maybe I was just feeling sensitive to my Mom, but I could feel her fear radiating in terrified waves. I took her by the hand.

"Come here, Mom."

As the others watched, I led her to the hole in the yard. She stood there curiously as I knelt carefully in my white dress and placed both hands on the ground. I whispered with the Earth life force, and the ground began to seal itself back up. I coaxed fresh grass to grow over the damaged area and then sprinkled it with pink and yellow flowers. Before I stood up, I picked one bloom from its stem and then rose to my feet.

A single tear rolled down Mom's cheek as I held the flower out to her. "It's not all scary and bad. Sometimes these powers are beautiful."

Fierce, maternal arms pulled me in. "*You* make them beautiful, *mija*. That was incredible."

I squeezed her back and whispered, "I won't ever leave you, Mom." The Island wasn't my only threat. I was starting to realize that I had some deeply-rooted separation issues that were a huge part of my hesitance over a college commitment. I had gained acceptance to a few universities with scholarships, but one of these days, I'd have to make a terrifying decision. Whatever I chose was guaranteed to put distance between me and someone I loved.

But not today. No decision had to be made today, even when that meant that Whitnee Skye Terradora's name was called in that graduation ceremony with "Undecided" where a college should be.

"Don't use the life forces anymore, Whitnee. We need to lay low. Stay off their radar," Dad warned. "I mean it, Baby Doll. No more playing around."

"I had a feeling you would say that, Dad."

"Whitnee, *es hora de cantar!*" came Papi's voice. We all turned to find my boisterous grandfather smiling expectantly at the door with the guitar in hand. "Your guests are waiting—oh, Serena, I love the new garden." He gestured at the flowers I grew just two minutes ago.

I watched my mother take a deep breath and paste a smile on as she led the way back to the party. I copied her, flashing a reassuring smile at my friends. Mom's arm didn't leave my shoulders, and I still felt her touch as she sat close during the songs. Maybe she figured as long as she held on, nothing would change.

Maybe I hoped for that too.

"What do you mean *Eden is not coming?*" Thomas repeated. I ignored the doubtful look he exchanged with Levi.

"Exactly that," I replied. "She needs to stay with her family. She will join us in a few days." I did not need my friends questioning my decision—especially when my own doubts were too near the surface.

"That is terribly sad about Elon," Thomas mumbled. "Lilley will be devastated to hear the news. She kept believing Elon would make it through this."

I turned away from my closest advisors to gaze at the documents Eden had left with me. I was working very hard at keeping thoughts of little Elon far from my mind.

"I suppose it was good for you and Eden to leave when you did. However," Levi spoke up, "as head of your security, I would appreciate a little more warning in the future when the two of you decide to change your plans like that."

"Noted," I answered distractedly as I inspected the list in front of me.

"*Gabriel.*" Levi's voice had taken on an admonishing tone. "We cannot afford anything happening to either of you—not in this political climate and with your Guardianship so near to being official. There are new threats against you—"

"There are new threats daily, Levi," I reminded him, trying to make light of his concern. His protective instincts and attention to detail were the very reason he was the best candidate for my new personal security guard. They were also the very traits that my Pyra nature yearned to buck against. I understood the risks and had become accustomed to the danger that these tempestuous times created.

"If you care not for your own life, then at least care for the rest of ours. If you are in danger, then so is Eden and—"

"I understand, friend." I reached out and gripped his shoulder in reassurance. His words had hit their target and I was ready to move past them. I signaled to a Palladium servant. When he approached, I thrust a paper at him. "See to it that my mother gets this revised order of ceremony. By now she should be resting in the north wing."

"Actually," Thomas interrupted, "there were complications in transporting her and your father here. They are behind schedule, but I have been assured they will be here within the hour."

Of course there were complications. There were always complications when it came to my parents' cooperation. They might have seemed graciously aloof to the general public over the last year, but in private they found all manner of ways to make my life more difficult. Apparently my betrayal of their evil plots came with a cost—one I had to pay for every day with my sanity and peace of mind.

I gave Thomas an indifferent nod. "And what about the rest of the Council? Have they arrived?"

"Yes. Ezekiel and Sarah have been directing the entire set-up since yesterday. They have so much more experience than the rest of us."

"I am uncertain what I would have done without them this past year," I agreed. Ezekiel's life experience in matters of government and communication was a priceless source of wisdom for me.

"Zebedee and Zipporah arrived an hour ago and took over management of the food preparations in light of Joseph's absence. I was just informed that Jesse arrived and will be heading to the tower shortly," Thomas said, and then added casually, "Jezebel came with him, so we can probably expect her to come looking for you any moment now."

I felt myself frown before I could hide the expression. "Very well. Anything else?"

"Have you seen the Southern Beach yet?" Thomas asked, trying unsuccessfully to hide a smile.

"No, I came in through the tunnels. Why?"

"I have never seen such a crowd in all my life."

"That is because we have not had such an event in our lifetime. There has not been a transfer of Guardianship for thirty-two years," I reminded him.

"There have been people—mostly *girls*—camped out on the beach for days in order to gain the perfect view of their new Guardian. If you were looking for any distractions this week, you could find one easily."

"I do not wish to be distracted, friend, but thank you for your recommendations." I grinned at my Tribal Ambassador. Thomas knew exactly how to lighten an atmosphere. It was a key reason why I chose him to handle difficult affairs among the tribes—that and the fact that his prior travel experience had already given him good contacts and rapport in every tribe. "Let us not forget that most of the Island also came here to see the opening of the new Watch Tower," I pointed out.

"Of course. The new *Watch Tower*." Levi smirked.

Thomas clapped me on the back. "Sorry, friend, but it is no portrait of a Watch Tower that they are selling on the beach."

With surprise, I repeated, "They are selling portraits of me?"

Thomas's smile turned smug. He was responsible for the publicity surrounding this event. "And custom zephyra images of you coming off the beach after a swim."

"And do not forget the new Geo scent that you wear. That is apparently selling in mass quantities," Levi added.

I blinked foolishly. "I do not wear a Geo scent."

Levi laughed. "*They* do not know that."

"But, yes, I am sure they are just here for the new Watch Tower opening." Thomas looked entirely too amused. "I just do not understand why the most important person on this Island chooses not to indulge in the benefits that such a crowd of admiring women might afford him."

"Oh, come now, Thomas," a female voice interrupted hotly. "We all know that our Gabriel cares more for work than he does for *benefits*. Otherwise, I would already be a married woman."

Thomas winced. "I loathe it when she sneaks up on me like that."

I moved across the room to greet Jezebel. She might carry herself confidently, but the scorn of insecurity burned in her golden eyes. Of course she was displaying an indecent amount of her bare skin in the amber-colored dress she wore, and I had to force my gaze away as all the other respectable men in her presence tried to do. More than anyone, I had a right to appreciate Jezebel's physical beauty and allure. But most of the time all I felt around her were pity and a niggling sense of guilt.

I leaned over and dutifully dropped a light kiss on her right cheek, resisting the urge to wrinkle my nose at her cloying perfume. "You look beautiful as always, Jez. I am glad you are here."

She smiled adoringly at me, but her voice dripped with venom as she whispered back, "I might actually believe you meant that—if only I had pale hair and gray eyes."

I felt that dagger of guilt in my stomach. But I chased it with a numbing shot of annoyance toward Jezebel and the person to whom she referred. Before I could respond, she executed one more dig. "Or if my eyes were green and I was your most trusted Advisor, perhaps I would be the one you would run away with in the night."

And she wondered why I preferred Eden's company to hers?

"We had business to attend to, Jezebel. I try to keep you out of that," I responded through gritted teeth.

"Oh, of course, *business*. It is always business with you and Eden, I am sure."

"Jealousy is not flattering on you." I matched her tone, trying to hold on to what patience I had left. Her eyes were too dark with layers of makeup that probably masked the signs of the ugly tantrum that ensued when she found out I had already left. "And now is not the time for petty concerns. Can you at least pretend to be happy tonight? For the sake of the people?"

She narrowed those eyes at me. "Oh, yes, I have become very good at pretending."

I narrowed mine back. "Good."

"Gentlemen," Jezebel pronounced with a disingenuous smile. "Best wishes with the ceremony. I am going to meet my father." She flashed her eyes at me one last time and that was when I felt her loneliness radiating around her like a protective shield. I knew her harsh act was just a way to hide her pain, but I felt powerless to fix the deeply-rooted instability within her.

"Jezebel," I called out. She turned back around and I was certain there were tears in her eyes. However, words failed me as I just stared at her. If only we knew how to give each other the reassurance we both needed... but that had never been what tied us together. The bonds of negativity and rejection were the only bonds we had. And it was not much to build a meaningful relationship on.

She softened for the briefest of moments, but the distance between us felt like more than just a few feet. "Best wishes, Gabriel. You know where to find me in the crowd." She turned and sauntered away.

I watched her go with regret. I could feel empathetic for Jezebel all I wanted, but that did not change the fact that I could never give her the love she craved.

Thomas came up beside me. "*Do* we know how to find her? Without Eden, I do not even know the seating arrangement..."

I barely held back a sigh.

5

THAT AWKWARD
MOMENT WHEN...

"One more, Whit. I think my eyes were closed!" Mom exclaimed as Ben snapped another picture of me in my blue satin graduation gown, flanked by my two proud parents. I smiled radiantly, hoping the glisten of sweat in this Texas heat wouldn't make me too shiny in pictures.

"Those were really good, Serena. Come look at them." Ben held the camera out for Mom's approval. The grounds outside our football field were crowded with families taking pictures with their graduates. I had about five minutes before I had to line up on the other side of the stadium.

Morgan was in my peripheral vision, still posing with her family. I scanned the crowd of blue gowns for Caleb's figure. There he was. Lingering in front of the fountain while his mom and three sisters hovered around the graduation program. I wandered over to him, leaving my family to argue over whether they wanted a different angle of themselves in the multitude of pictures we had already taken.

"Hey." I bumped his side playfully, careful not to mess up the cap that had been strategically placed over my loosely-curled hair. "You look a little lost standing here alone."

He gave me his attention. "I forget how loud my world gets when all of my sisters are in town. I was enjoying a reprieve while they decide what torturous picture pose they want to put me through next."

I smiled compassionately. "Well, you do look handsome with all your special tassels. They're just proud of you."

"Yeah, it's like having four moms. I swear, if Carly makes one more comment about why I don't call you my girlfriend..." He grimaced, and I resisted the urge to comment on the same topic. "How are you feeling? Are you still *connected*?"

"Yep." I couldn't explain it, but I could sense the life forces brewing inside me. "I keep using them accidentally or something. See that one unnatural tree branch over there that's longer and flatter than the others?" Caleb followed the direction of my eyes. "We were standing there and I just wished for some shade out in this heat and then..." I gestured at the weirdly-shaped tree.

"Seriously? The branch just did that for you?"

"Like an umbrella." I nodded. "My dad almost flipped out again. And every time I touch my necklace" —I demonstrated— "it lights up. Look, you can see it through the gown."

He pulled my hand away and glanced furtively around us. "Yeah, don't do that right here. And definitely don't do that during the ceremony when you get nervous." He wiped the sweat beading on his forehead. "You don't seem as worried about this as I am."

With a shrug, I dipped my hand into the cool, sparkling fountain water. "I'm more worried about these shoes."

"Whit, this is kind of a serious problem."

"Well, I'm trying to do what Dad said and lay low, but the life forces seem to happen without my permission. I can either worry about it or just deal with it. Besides, my dad is worried enough for all of us." At the anxious look on Caleb's face, I joked, "Morgan thinks I should become a vigilante or something. I'd have to come up with a superhero look. So far, we agree it should include silver spandex to go with the eyes."

That earned an amused grunt from him. "In that case, please make pink hair part of your superhero look."

"You still have a thing for that pink hair last summer, huh, Caleb Austin?"

"I still have a thing for *you*—in any hair color. But especially in spandex. Or a bikini."

Yes, he remembered! Operation Cute Swimsuit was a go as soon as we got on that ship.

Though my stomach fluttered at his teasing, I played it cool. "I just have no idea what my superhero angle would be. Like, what would I protect people from?"

"Um, natural disasters? Except when you're the one *creating* them. We've seen your handiwork, Tornado Terradora. Ah! That's your superhero name. You're welcome."

"Funny." I rolled my eyes, but then I grabbed his hand and entwined my fingers with his. With a flirtatious smile, I suggested, "I'll be Tornado Terradora if you'll be my Lois Lane."

"Wow." He raised the one eyebrow with the scar slashed across it. "Weirdest thing you've ever said to me."

But his other hand found mine anyway and we stood there facing each other with the fountain behind us. I took a deep breath, wanting to lay the hint on thick. "But really, most superheroes have a special love interest who motivates them to keep going, keep fighting. If you could handle it, I'd choose you."

"If I could *handle* it? Pretty sure I know how to handle you." Of course he did. And the thought tickled my tummy. "And you know I've already been yours for a long time now, Whit."

"Really?"

His voice dropped to a tender notch as he tilted his head to the side. "Hey, why are you suddenly unsure of that?"

When he stared at me like that, I couldn't remember.

So I just shrugged it off with a smile. Those lips that I so desperately wanted to kiss turned up into an echo of my smile, and that thrill of adoration I carried for him bubbled up inside me. "Tornado Terradora thanks you for being the high stakes character in her superhero adventures."

While he continued to smile, those eyebrows grew conflicted again. "It's just a little problematic that it never seems to work out for the superhero and his—or *her*—love interest. There's always something preventing them from being together, you know?"

The weight of his words pulled my happy bubbles back down to earth. How was I supposed to respond to that? Was he playing along still or was there something else he was trying to tell me?

"Oh, that's a perfect picture, you two!" Caleb's oldest sister,

Carly, declared. She held up her phone. "Stay just like that with the fountain behind you."

I almost forgot to smile at first, but then Caleb's arm came around me and pulled me close. I felt a reassuring squeeze and heard him whisper, "Smile, Superhero. I'm not going anywhere."

So I did. Because Caleb's loyalty had never failed me.

"That's weird," Carly jerked her head up from the phone in confusion and then looked back at her screen. "Never seen a fountain act like that. Pretty cool what they can do these days." She stole one more picture and then walked back to Suzanne's side, mumbling, "Such a cute couple."

Caleb and I turned around to find long tentacles of water curling up into the air around us, sparkling innocently in the late afternoon sunlight. I took a step back and they reached out for me, as if wanting to caress my face. That was definitely not natural fountain behavior.

Caleb pulled me several feet away and the water went crashing back down into the pool. "Did you do that?"

"No," I cried, looking around to see if anyone else had noticed. "I mean, yes, but I didn't mean to."

"Your eyes aren't even glowing. It's like life force is leaking out of you or something."

"I hope this doesn't get out of control."

"I think it already is," Caleb murmured, staring back at the fountain.

"Time to go, y'all," Morgan chirped as she joined us. The graduates were starting to line up. Mom and Dad were behind her.

"We'll meet you out here after the ceremony," Mom reminded me for the fourteenth time. "You'll do great on your speech. Just take your time walking to the podium and speak clearly. Remember not to listen to the delay of your voice in the football field speakers or it will throw you off."

"Got it." I gave her a nod, thankful for her encouragement.

Dad gave me a hug and warned quietly, "Remember, don't use your powers!"

"It's not like I'm trying to, Dad."

"Y'all are so not normal people," Morgan said as the three of us waved and hurried away.

Once "Pomp and Circumstance" started and we marched out

on the field, my mind drifted to what lay ahead of me. Caleb and I were part of the Honors graduates on the first row. Morgan was only a row behind us since her last name was at the beginning of the alphabet. When they called my name to come to the stage and present the Teacher of the Year Award, I looked back to catch her giving me a thumbs-up. I smiled and then focused on just putting one foot in front of the other as gracefully as possible. My heels kept trying to stick in the grass of the football field, so it felt like I was going in slow motion. I made it to the stage and smiled brightly at our principal who smiled back encouragingly.

Oh, man, it's hot. Please don't let me melt onstage in front of everyone!

I should never have thought it.

In response to my dramatic thoughts, an unnaturally cold wind swept violently across the field. Caps went flying off my classmates' heads. People's programs flew away. My own cap was sucked up into the air and my hair sprang loose. The important people onstage held down their skirts and tried to keep the notes on the podium from taking flight. There were growing exclamations as the chilly wind buffeted everybody on the field. I could only imagine what my parents were thinking at this moment.

I slammed my eyes shut. *Stop it! Just stop it!!*

The wind died instantly. I froze. Were my eyes glowing or what? I glanced cautiously out at my fellow graduates who were all trying to straighten gowns and return lost caps to their owners. I wanted to cry. This was my fault.

"Whitnee!" It was Caleb. He sprinted to the stage and stood there on the grass, holding my escaped cap up to me. "Are you okay?"

I shook my head and felt the trigger of potential tears. "Thank you," I choked as I bent over to retrieve my cap. In a whisper, I asked, "Are my eyes normal?" He took a moment to meet my gaze squarely, and maybe he saw the fear there.

His voice was calm. "Yes, you're fine."

"Caleb." I could feel my pulse racing. "I can't do this. I can't control it. I feel weird—"

"Well, folks, gotta love our Texas weather," our principal joked on the microphone as people started reclaiming their seats. His voice boomed out into the whole stadium. "You just never know what's going to happen next."

Yeah. Especially when Tornado Terradora was around.

The crowd gave a distracted laugh and the rows of blue-gowned teenagers wiggled around and readjusted their appearances. My hands shook as I gripped my cap and cast another panicked look down at Caleb.

"It's okay," he assured me. "Nobody knows."

"Let's hear it once more for our Student Council President, Whitnee Terradora!" my principal announced. The crowd cheered again.

"Put on your cap and smile, Superhero. This is where the alter-ego begins." Caleb gave me a reassuring nod and then jogged back to his seat on the first row. Morgan was still on her feet behind him. She made a sympathetic "I love you" sign with her hands before taking her seat again. I took a deep breath, placed the cap carefully back on my head, and finished my hike across the stage to the podium.

6

SKIP DAY GETS REAL

"You look elegant as always, Abrianna," I greeted my mother respectfully. Her dress was a slate gray and, with her hair hanging loosely, she looked much younger than her fifty years might indicate.

"I was thinking the same of you, Gabriel. I am glad you chose the white and gold." She surveyed me with an expression of approval. "It is set apart and yet authoritative. Very appropriately designed."

I bowed slightly, hiding my surprise at receiving such a compliment. The parlor room with its high ceiling and vast windows felt cold and empty with just the two of us in there. "Hannah, Eden, and Jezebel selected all of my clothing for the week." I attempted to smile. "And believe me, with those three, my opinion mattered not. I only acquiesced to their wishes."

She smiled slightly. "A wise choice."

I wandered over to the window and chanced a glance at the sea of people awaiting our entrance on the topmost balcony of the Tower. I could faintly hear the drums and ceremonial rituals that Ezekiel was leading. Abrianna would go out before me and make a speech, starting off the week with her blessing over the future Guardian. It was the first time in history that the Guardian was being succeeded by her own offspring. It was also the first time in many generations that the transfer of leadership did not begin at the Palladium.

Centuries ago, the new Guardian was blessed at the old Watch Tower before traveling to each village for unique tribal blessings.

Since the Guardian was originally a position designed to watch over the people until the prophesied Pilgrim arrived, it was once sacred to initiate their leadership at the Watch Tower. It kept the position of power within its proper perspective and reminded the people of the hope found in the Island's ancient promises. But the Watch Tower had been in ruins that were all too indicative of our people's ruined and long-lost faith.

Due to my parents' limited power and maximum security over the last year, the transfer of Guardianship felt more like a formality than anything. I had already been governing the Island unofficially. My first priority had been to renew faith in the Pilgrim and in our Island. We began construction on the Watch Tower and restored the old glory of the Southern Beach immediately after the fires that ravaged it last summer.

My Palladium staff wore a new unified symbol of the swirling four life forces combined—the one Whitnee and I had found on the cave wall last summer. In the center of the design was a 'P' to symbolize both the Palladium and the Pilgrim.

And now here we were, bringing back ancient traditions. Despite the tumultuous time we were living in, I wanted to be the one to affect change, to gain the approval of the Island and its people. The problem was that I was working hard to restore a faith to the people that I myself was only barely clinging to. My questions and doubts about this Island and my real purpose had haunted me all year. Perhaps Eden was right and that was the real problem with my speech. I was no longer sure I believed in what I espoused.

"What was it like for you?" I spoke softly as I gazed down at the affairs below. "What was it like when you became Guardian?"

Abrianna joined me by the window and her voice was thoughtful when she answered. "I was so young—only eighteen at the time. As you now know, Benjamin, the Guardian before me was no longer here. Everybody believed Nathan was the Pilgrim, so you can imagine how those circumstances made for quite an uproar politically." I watched her expression glaze over as she remembered something long left in her past. "I had much to prove when I stepped into this position. I did everything I could to show the people that not only was I ordained by the Island to govern, but I was also the best person for such a task. I entered into an inter-tribal marriage, all in an effort to unite the tribes around me. I tried to break down barriers of distrust for our government." Her tone grew defeated the longer she spoke and I hung on to her every word, sensing that this was the most vulnerable she had ever been with me—and probably ever would be. "But somewhere in the middle of all that, I lost myself. Perhaps that is the burden of every Guardian. We want to make a difference in the lives of people. We want to give them hope. And we give and we give… and we forget to hold back some hope for ourselves."

For the first time ever, I could understand exactly what my mother meant. And that both terrified and comforted me at the same time. I did not know what to say at first.

"If Benjamin was not here to give you the Guardian blessing, who did?" I wondered.

"Ezekiel."

That surprised me. "Why Ezekiel?"

She sighed. "He was Benjamin's brother, a Tetrarch Council member and, of course, he was Nathan's father and extremely well-respected. I know Ezekiel did not want to do it, but I assume Nathan was the one who convinced him otherwise. Nathan always tried to help, always tried to protect me. In those days, I hardly realized how much I depended on him. I do so miss—" She stopped talking as if she had said too much. And she probably had. We avoided the subject of Nathan and Whitnee as much as possible. It was probably another one of those subjects in which we understood each other too well; discussing it was uncomfortable.

"Mother," I addressed her more personally. I had to ask the question I had never asked her before. "Do you believe in the Pilgrim?"

The piercing gray of her eyes turned sharp as she gazed at me. "I do not know what I believe in anymore, Gabriel. I lost my faith somewhere along the way. Or maybe I never had it to begin with. Either way, I am not sure it matters."

I could not read her thoughts, but my Pyradorian nature understood emotions. There was a thick wall of sadness around her that was impenetrable. As much as I did not trust her and did not even *like* her, she was still my mother. And at the moment, she was all I had.

The door startled us when it opened and the sounds of a cheering crowd filled the empty space. It was Sarah. "Abrianna, we are ready for you."

Abrianna smoothed her dress and began to follow, but then she stopped. With some kind of buried maternal instinct, she came back to me and kissed my cheek. The faint scent of her perfume brought back long-forgotten memories of the childhood days I would sit beside her and lean in close as she read historical tales of valor and courage.

I got the feeling she wanted to say something more. I waited, almost pathetically hoping for words of approval over more than just my wardrobe. But she never said anything and then she passed through the door and the crowd cheered. That was the mother I knew—the one who put on a smile for a crowd and kept her secret thoughts locked up tightly.

"I will be back for you in a few minutes, Gabriel. Get ready," Sarah called over her shoulder. I nodded and then I was alone in the room.

I wandered to the table and picked up the Whitnee flower Elon had given me. If Whitnee were here, this whole experience might feel different. But she was not coming back. She would not be by my side and I was not even sure I would want her there after all this time.

With self-inflicted torture, I stretched my free hand out and created a life-sized image of Whitnee a few feet away from me. She looked exactly as I remembered her that last day on the beach. She stood in that purple Aerodorian dress as golden wisps of her hair blew softly in a breeze that was not really there. She gazed at me with a half-smile, her eyes a light shade of gray that sparkled with some kind of emotion that I could never quite recapture in my mind. I used to indulge myself with this image of her whenever I missed her.

But it had been a long time since I had tormented myself with such an indulgence. And now it just angered me.

"You are not real," I said to her, my voice distorted with frustration. "And I cannot believe in you anymore."

Of course she did not say anything back because fake images do not talk to you. She only smiled at me, and I desperately wished then that I could just erase her from my memory completely.

"Gabriel," Sarah's voice interrupted as the door swung open again. I extinguished the image, but it was not fast enough for Sarah's eyes. She gazed longingly at the place where Whitnee disappeared. Then she gave me a knowing look and said, "It is time."

I followed her out to meet the familiar faces of our government and a roaring crowd that stretched along the beach farther than I could see.

I still clutched the Whitnee flower in one hand.

"Please don't be mad at me. I couldn't help it." I preempted my dad's reaction the moment I met my family again in front of the stadium.

Dad just pressed his lips together as my grandparents and cousins rushed at me with hugs and flowers. I did what I could to act normally, but normal was not at all what I was feeling. A splitting headache had formed behind my eyes and, truthfully, I just wanted to hide in my room alone. But that wasn't going to happen. Caleb and Morgan were already saying their goodbyes with their families and we would be leaving with our pre-packed trunk full of luggage straight for my house to change clothes and then on to the airport.

I hugged Papi and Mimi, Aunt Letty and the rest of them, and thanked them all for coming. Then it was just Mom and Dad and Uncle Ben.

"What happened out there, Whit?" Mom finally asked, concern etched all over her face.

I pressed a hand to my forehead and rubbed in circles. "I don't know. I'm sorry."

"Maybe going on this trip is a bad idea," Mom fretted. "If you can't control what's happening, then we should stay home and figure out a plan—"

"No!" I cried. "Gosh, no, Mom. I need a vacation. I just want to—I don't know. Can we talk about this at home?"

Mom wrapped her arms around me. "I love you, *mija*. You did really well out there—especially when I'm sure the whole thing stressed you out. Right, Nathan?" She turned to my dad who was being strangely quiet.

"Of course she did," Dad replied and then he gave Mom a slight nod and glanced around carefully. As if that was a secret cue, Mom said: "Ben, will you walk with me for a minute?" He agreed and the two of them left Dad and me alone, but still within sight.

Dad looked almost as exhausted as I felt.

"What? Am I in for a lecture or something?" I looked up at my dad and pitiful tears filled my eyes. "Dad, I feel like I can't do anything right with you—"

"No, no, Baby Doll." He reached out and pulled me in for a hug. "I am *not* mad at you—not at all. I'm just overwhelmed right now."

"By what? The life forces?" I asked weakly, my voice muffled in his shirt.

He held me out at arm's length and looked into my eyes. I was surprised to see tears glistening there in the sunset light. "By you, Whitnee Skye. I am overwhelmed by you and all that makes up who you are. Not just the life forces, but your maturity and your grace. I saw what happened on that field and I know what it's like to be shocked by what you can do. I know the panic that comes when things seem out of control. I saw you pull yourself together and still make a stunning speech. It wasn't just my little girl out there on that field; it was a young woman—a *graduate*—ready to take on the world with confidence."

"Oh," was all I could say.

"I don't say it enough, because I'm so afraid that if I admit how grown up you are... that if I tell you how proud I am of your heart and the person you have become—" His voice broke with emotion.

"Dad, don't do this right now." I fought back my own tears.

"No, listen. I need to tell you. I want you to know." His hand shook as he pushed back my hair from my face. "A father could ask for no greater reward than to see his daughter so capable and responsible and good-hearted. And I—" He paused as tears ran down both of our faces. "I want to remember this moment always. Being your father is my greatest blessing."

I leaned into his arms again. "I love you, Daddy."

Living without his hugs for six years made me appreciate them on a whole new level. A protective warmth sheltered me right there outside of the football stadium, as if Dad was both the source of and the barrier to these crazy life forces.

"Listen, Whit." He wiped his eyes and sniffed. "I'm going to take your mother home. She and I have some things to discuss before it's time to leave." We glanced over at Mom, who had a Kleenex pressed to her eyes as she watched us from afar. "You have a little bit of time with your friends before Uncle Ben brings the three of you home. You okay? You can handle this until you get to the house?"

"I got it." I nodded and tried to fix any makeup smears on my face. "Here, will you take my cap and gown with you and have Mom hang them up?" I unzipped the gown and folded it over his arm. The cap was already off.

Dad accepted them and twisted the tassel in his fingers. "I will always be proud of you, okay?" He started to back away. I nodded, afraid I wouldn't be able to speak again without crying. I waved weakly and didn't take my eyes off him until he disappeared from sight with one comforting arm around my crying mother.

I was soon joined by several classmates who made their goodbyes and planned to meet up again for summer parties. It was harder than it should have been to smile in the last few pictures we snapped. In the middle of all the embraces, I started feeling lightheaded and dizzy. Uncle Ben kept a watchful eye on me, so he didn't seem surprised when I finally moved his direction. I don't think I was even walking straight by that point.

"Something's wrong, isn't it?" he said.

"Yeah, I feel sick. I'm gonna grab Morgan and Caleb and we should go. It's practically dark out here anyway."

"Why don't I go get the car and pick you up? I'm not sure you're gonna make it through that parking lot," Ben offered.

"Thanks." He rushed off with phone in hand—probably calling Dad to tell him something was up. I caught Caleb's eye and motioned to him that it was time to go. Then I collapsed weakly on the side of the fountain. Geez. Had I eaten enough at the party? I needed to get out of there.

Caleb found Morgan, and by the time the two of them approached me sitting on the fountain, I could barely see straight. The world was tilting and blurring.

"What's wrong with you?" Morgan's voice echoed through a twisty, psychedelic tunnel.

"I think I'm sick," I mumbled, trying to stand. I could barely see the headlights of Ben's car pulling up. Caleb's arm came around me for support. "I haven't felt this way since—"

Oh my gosh.

I knew then what was happening. "Don't let go of me!" I cried and tried to get a firm grip on both of them.

"I got you," Caleb soothed. "I won't let you fall."

"No, that's not what I mean! Get Ben. Tell Ben…"

"He's right there with the car, Whit. Try to walk," Morgan coached, anxiety ringing through her tone.

I saw Uncle Ben get out of the car. I felt the tangle of Morgan and Caleb's arms around me. But then the world tilted and the colors flashed too vividly in my eyes.

For a moment, everything disappeared. But then with a thunderous boom, the world came back into focus.

Only it wasn't my world… exactly.

I was on a beach in the midst of hundreds of crouched and frightened people. A beautiful tower stood before me.

COLLISION

7

THE WRONG DESTINATION

The earthshaker lasted at least two minutes. I was just easing into the heart of my speech when a rumble started from beyond the beach and the whole tower began swaying slowly. When it grew more violent, my first thought was that we had somehow constructed a faulty foundation and the tower would come crashing down in front of our entire Dorian nation. But then people began dropping to the ground in fear and I realized it was not just our foundation.

The entire beach was moving.

Several people darted past me to try and take the stairs down to the ground. Levi stumbled in my direction, his first priority always to protect me. "No," I shouted at him. "My mother!" Abrianna was thrown against the balcony, dangerously close to toppling over the side. I would not be close enough to save her. Levi obeyed and lunged toward her.

Thomas attempted to usher Ezekiel and Sarah toward the stairs, but the older couple was tossed about mercilessly until Ezekiel fell to the floor where Zebedee and Zipporah had ducked. Jesse, Jezebel's father, was directly to my left, trying to crawl over to his wife. It was an absolutely terrifying and confusing two minutes as some either held on to the walls or tried to escape the dreadful shaking.

I was catapulted forward in my attempt to reach Abrianna and forced to grasp the balcony edge to prevent myself from plunging to my death. That was when I could see the terror in the people below, hear the screams and feel the panic.

Then it stopped.

The deep rumbling of the earth faded and the air was filled with the cries of the people. I released my grip on the balcony and straightened up to survey the beach more clearly.

I think I was the first to see her. She would never blend in on this Island. But more predictably, she appeared in the exact place on the Southern Beach that she always did—a location I had made the central viewpoint of the Watch Tower with a stone walkway and a custom-designed Firelight sculpture. She was bathed in a white glow beside the sculpture which now burned more brilliantly than I had designed it.

But it could not really be her.

Was this a hoax? Who was casting that image of her? What were they trying to accomplish? A hush fell on the crowd as people began to notice her standing there, the curly tendrils of pale, exotic hair blowing away from her face as she looked around in confusion.

"Enough!" I shouted angrily, trying to intimidate the person who would dare taunt us that way. At the sound of my voice, she turned her attention up to the tower. I *felt* her the moment our eyes connected and I knew then she was not just an image. I lost my breath for a moment as the reality set in. Everything else faded from my vision and thoughts, except for her.

But then people started crying out, "It is the Pilgrim! The Pilgrim has come!"

It was a delayed moment before I realized that people were not talking about *her.* No, they were pointing at something else, something up here on the tower.

I tore my gaze away from the beach and witnessed the expression on my mother's face. White with shock, she stared up at the pinnacle of the tower and leaned against the balcony as if her legs might give out. The topmost level of the Watch Tower was the highest point on the Island besides the White Mountain. And someone else with pale hair and a white glow stood there, overlooking all of us.

"Nathan," Abrianna breathed.

All chaos broke loose.

"Dad!" I cried out when I saw him up there beyond Gabriel's startled figure. My dad looked so powerful, so strong, so *special* as he stood atop the tower. How did he get up there? And, um, how did I get *here*?

Caleb and Morgan were gone. Had they transported with me and landed in their own locations like before? Or were they still on the Mainland? I had not used a portal this time. Something else—something unexpected—had just happened.

A woman grabbed my arm roughly. "Are you Whitnee? Are you the one they call the Pilgrim?"

Another woman standing nearby interrupted, "They say she can use all four life forces!" She marched up to me with crazy eyes and barked, "Did you just make the whole ground shake like that?"

I felt another pair of hands grabbing at me and the crowd started pressing in, asking questions, wanting to touch my clothes, my hair, my hands.

"Please, wait a minute." I tried to be nice, but my personal space was under invasion. I started shoving forward in the direction of the tower. I had to get out of this crowd.

"Do not let her go!"

"Show us what you can do!"

"My son is ill, could you heal him? I have heard—"

"Heal *me*! My arm is crippled—"

I shook my head, trying to make sense of their requests. "Please let me go. I will try to get you the help you need. But right now—" Somebody stepped on my foot and I tripped in my high heels. I was shoved roughly as more and more people crowded me. I could not even see the tower. I heard my dad roar, "Get my daughter out of that mob!" But the people didn't seem to recognize or care that they had created a panic around me. Just when I thought I would suffocate or be ripped to shreds by all their yanking, a huge flash of Fire exploded over our heads with a sharp sound like a gunshot. I cringed and screamed as the sparks rained down. So did the others.

"Back away. Now!"

Oh, *crap*. The bass-toned voice completely freaked me out more than anything else that had happened in the last five minutes.

The crowd parted and Eli came marching through—balder, bigger, and sharper than ever. "Give her to me." He held out those hands that had once wrung my own blood out of my arm.

I stepped back, stumbling over the people. "No! Somebody help me," I screamed. What was *wrong* with this place? How was it possible that the first person to find me was the one who tried to kill all of us last summer? Don't they lock up criminals like that around here? I no longer cared if I was being rude—I shoved people out of my way and tried to run. Didn't these people know Eli was a killer?

I face-planted into somebody, nearly knocking her over. "Whitnee, you are okay!"

I looked up to find Hannah there, her silver eyes illuminated. I threw myself at her in fear. "Hannah! It's Eli—help me—"

"Shhh, just stay with me." She wrapped one confident arm around me and thrust the other out defensively at the wall of people around us. "Clear a path for Palladium security. Immediately!" Her arm was scarred with discolorations from the burns she had suffered a year ago. They climbed up her neck. A swirling symbol I recognized on her purple uniform had a capital "P" in the center, and people actually seemed to listen to her as if she had authority and wasn't once upon a time a servant in the guesthouse of Aerodora.

She guided me forward as the people started making a path for us. When Eli flanked my other side as if we were old friends, I jolted with the instinct to run again. "Eli is on his best behavior right now, Whitnee. Just stay calm," Hannah murmured.

He marched beside me like a bodyguard, as if my safety and well-being had always been his utmost concern.

As if he wasn't a power-hungry psycho who had orchestrated my kidnapping and was responsible for Hannah's scars and for shooting his own son in the leg. I recoiled in disgust every time he brushed up against me.

I heard Hannah mutter quietly enough for only the three of us to hear, "And where are *your* guards, Eli?"

"I suppose I lost them in the middle of the earthshaker," he replied, keeping his eyes straightforward.

"That is rather convenient," she flung back, motioning to others in the crowd.

"There is nothing *convenient* about this situation. But I do believe it was rather fortunate that I was near enough to Whitnee to help," Eli retorted. I remained quiet, not feeling fortunate at all. Several other guards from different tribes found us and began organizing the people and recovering some sense of order. I glanced down at my feet to see where I was stepping.

The ground was littered with papers and pictures. I couldn't hold back my curiosity. I paused to bend over and pick one up. It was titled "The 30th Guardianship Festival" and it had a brief biography about Gabriel, a few historical facts, and an event schedule. There was a picture behind it, of Gabriel looking solemn and handsome in a Palladium uniform. He had the beginnings of a dark beard in the picture—like a five o'clock shadow that only made him appear darker and older than I remembered. The caption read: GABRIEL, PYRADORIAN, 30th GUARDIAN OF THE DORIAN ISLAND.

Uh-oh.

"Um, Hannah? What exactly did we just interrupt?" I whispered, staring hard at the picture and then glancing up at the tower that used to be nothing more than ruins back behind the trees. Gabriel stood there, overseeing my progress from the balcony. As I grew closer, I could make out the shadow of his beard and see the broad, powerful set to his stance. Good lord, he looked like a *man*. I wasn't even sure what I felt in that moment.

I raised my hand as if I was going to wave at him, but something about the fierce way he stared at me told me he would not wave back. I dropped my hand and resumed our trek to the entrance of the tower.

"Gabriel is about to become our Guardian," Hannah explained. "You are just in time for the fun. And what a beautifully designed dress you are wearing! I love it. The white matches Gabriel's attire, as well."

Only Hannah would notice such a thing in the middle of these circumstances.

We finally made it to the arched entrance of the Watch Tower and, right before I ducked inside, I heard Gabriel's voice reverberate over the crowd. "The opening ceremony will resume momentarily. For now, if you are injured or need help, please find your way to one of our HydroHealer Tents or send for a Healer to come to you. There are Palladium guards in the crowd who will assist you. Please do not panic. Our Island is safe and the Watch Tower is secure. We will continue on with our festivities in just a short while..."

"Hannah!" a guard called from inside. "We are up here!" The heavy doors closed on the crowd behind us as we rushed up several flights of stairs.

I ran straight to my dad when I entered a large parlor with a small crowd of people I had not seen in nearly a year.

"Baby Doll, are you okay?"

"Yeah. Are you?"

Dad nodded, but his face was contorted with anxiety. He led me straight to my Dorian grandparents, Poppa Zeke and Grandmother Sarah, who rested on a long tan couch with fluffy cushions. And then he placed himself between Eli and me.

"Why is *he* here?" Dad growled, his face turning red with anger as he stared Eli down.

"Remarkable question, Nathan. We are all wondering the same thing about you," Eli responded.

"I don't want you anywhere near my daughter or me."

"Nathan, perhaps you should calm down," Abrianna suggested, her composure clearly rocked. Her voice had a catch to it and she glanced nervously at another man in the room who I did not know, but who had a familiar face. "We have all just experienced a shock and are trying to remedy the situation. Perhaps you should explain what has happened to bring you back."

"I am not explaining anything as long as Eli is in this room." Dad spun around and cast his words at Poppa Zeke. "Why is he still the Pyradorian Elder? Did nothing change on this Island while I was away?"

"He is not the Pyradorian Elder," the man I did not know cut in. I studied him more closely. He seemed to be in his mid-fifties, handsome in a sort of cosmetic and fake way, and definitely a Pyra by the hazel color of his eyes. With a smile that seemed rather gloating to me, he proclaimed, "I am the Councilman for the Pyradora tribe now."

Dad frowned. "Jesse?"

"Hello, Nathan."

My eyes widened at the man who I now realized was Jezebel's father, the wealthiest man on the Island—and Eli's supposed best friend.

"I resigned from my position last summer, Nathan." Eli's voice was dangerously low. "I suppose the job had just become a little too *demanding*. Jesse was chosen in my stead."

I thought my dad might come unglued at that point. Fortunately, another Pyra entered the room in authority, interrupting the conversation with a haughty tone. "True, Eli, and since you are not a member of government anymore, you are not to be in this room. Where is your security?"

Gabriel.

"On their way," Hannah answered. "They somehow 'lost' him."

"I suppose we will have to make sure that does not happen again," Gabriel said. "Hannah, place my father in armbands for the remainder of the night and escort him back down. I need you and Thomas on the ground coordinating the crowd control. Give me a report immediately if the earthshaker caused any damage or injuries."

Hannah nodded obediently. Thomas weaved his way past Gabriel to follow orders, pausing to clap one hand on my shoulder in a friendly manner. "I am happy to see you again."

I couldn't help myself. I leaned in and gave him a brief hug, whispering in his ear, "Will you please find out if Morgan or Caleb are out there somewhere? I don't know if they transported or not."

When Thomas pulled back, his face was solemn. With a nod, he took Eli by the arm and exited with Hannah on the other side. I felt an old, wrinkled hand slide into mine and I turned back around for a closer look at Poppa Zeke. A smile broke out on his face as he pulled me in for a grandfatherly kiss.

"Poppa Zeke! You're hurt!" I cried, when I saw the blood through his clothing. His leg was propped up.

"Oh, I am just an old, clumsy man." He waved off my concern.

"He needs a Healer." Sarah directed her comment to Gabriel. I wanted to take a moment to study Gabriel and the obvious changes in him, but a blue-eyed gentleman with thick, dark hair and a thick mustache to match stepped forward.

"I can take a look at his leg." The manner in which the man knelt respectfully before Ezekiel made me like him immediately. Judging by the company in the room and his pale blue eyes, I had to assume he was the Hydrodorian Elder, the one who must have replaced the assassinated Simeon after last summer. It was a heart-wrenching moment as the memory of Simeon came alive in my mind again.

"No, Zeb, do not bother with me. It is merely a scratch," Ezekiel protested. "Sarah, darling, please stop fretting."

"We can call Lilley," a plain-looking woman with the other set of blue eyes in the room spoke up. "She is on the grounds somewhere."

"Lilley?" I piped up, gazing at her in curiosity.

"My daughter," she said and smiled warmly at me. "I am Zipporah. We have heard a lot about you and all that happened last year. My Lilley is a fierce believer in your abilities."

"I am a fierce believer in Lilley's abilities," I responded, thinking of the young Healer apprentice who helped me perform Transfusion on Morgan last summer. But I remembered something else too… "If you're Lilley's mom, then that means you're the woman Simeon's wife…" I trailed off, remembering the mysterious miracle of the little girl Simeon's wife had healed overnight after a tragic accident.

"Yes," she answered simply, seeing the direction of my thoughts.

But before we could say more, Gabriel interrupted. "We will have a Healer up here immediately, Ezekiel. Just rest for a moment." He crossed the room to give more instructions to the guards posted by the door. His face was hidden from me again and I swallowed down the frustration of having not been greeted directly by him yet. After all, there were important things going on and whatever had just happened had thrown a kink into their plan. I chose to admire the clear authority that Gabriel exercised over the situation, instead of giving more attention to the bad feeling stirring in my stomach.

I turned my attention back on my grandparents. Something about my grandfather seemed older to me. It had only been a year since I had last seen him, but it bothered me. It wasn't a difference I could necessarily see in his physical appearance. His hair was still silver, his skin still wrinkled. Maybe it was in the hand gripping mine at that moment—weaker, frailer. I lowered myself beside him, cradling his hand in both of mine.

"I have missed both of you so much," I confessed, overwhelmed suddenly that I was back with my other family. Back in the place that I wasn't sure I'd ever see again.

Grandmother Sarah reached out and grazed my cheek with her fingertips. "You are lovely as ever, my granddaughter. We have missed you more than words can convey."

"I apologize for breaking up the reunion, but we have a ceremony to complete and a festival to put on," Gabriel pronounced, his attention back on us. His words lacked any kind of warmth, and I didn't really think he cared about interrupting my tender moment with my family. When would he greet me as more than just an inconvenience? "Jesse, I need you to go find Jezebel and make sure she is okay. While you are out there, will you please coordinate with the Pyras in charge of the light show? Make sure they are still ready to go."

Jesse looked startled at being given a command to leave. "Surely somebody else can do such a task. I feel as if I should stay and hear more about Nathan's arrival—"

Gabriel held his ground unflinchingly. "Actually, there is no one else to take care of your daughter nor make the proper decisions regarding the entertainment later. We must try to make up the schedule somehow. I trust you to handle it."

"Zipporah and I will go down there with you," Zeb offered. "I would like to check on my Healers and make sure the food and refreshment tents are still in working order." He turned expectantly to Gabriel. "Unless, of course, there is something else you require of me, Gabriel?"

"That is exactly what I was thinking, Zebedee, thank you. We will fill you both in later on our Travelers," Gabriel replied. That left no room for argument from Jesse, who exited in a huff with a woman in tow—probably Jezebel's mother. She had the same exotic eyes as Jezebel.

"Levi." Gabriel addressed the Aerodorian guard who I just realized stood protectively behind Ezekiel. "Please take Abrianna to the northern wing."

"I am not leaving," Abrianna protested. "I am still the Guardian. I belong in here with Nathan and Whitnee."

Heck, no. I didn't want her anywhere near me, either.

Gabriel's voice was harsher than I expected. "You are the Guardian by title only. You do *not* belong here—"

Dad spoke up. "She should stay."

"What! No." I couldn't help my own harsh tone at my father's defense. Even Gabriel seemed a little put off.

"Whitnee—"

"Dad, no. I don't trust her and I don't want her here. She is not my family—"

"But she is mine!" Dad raised his voice. I felt Ezekiel squeeze my hand, whether in warning or in reassurance, I wasn't sure. But it made me shut my mouth and turn an angry look on my father instead. I suppose I would rather be present for any conversation between Abrianna and Dad—instead of worrying about what was going on in private.

"Don't forget about Mom," I muttered and I did not miss Dad's look of exasperation. "I'm just saying."

"Whitnee, how did you get here?" Dad asked instead of responding to my suggestive comments.

"I don't know. I just materialized. Like something brought me here," I answered honestly. But then I turned my attention on Gabriel, who was still carefully avoiding eye contact with me. "Do you know how that would be possible? Did you *do* something?"

Gabriel shifted his weight and crossed his arms over his chest—a mannerism I had come to know well last summer. "I have not touched those portals. I have no idea why you are here." Something in his tone made his words sound almost accusatory.

"The portals?" I repeated, standing to my feet. "Does that mean they're still open? You were supposed to shut them down, Gabriel."

"*Somebody* forgot to leave instructions for how to accomplish that. There is not exactly a 'shutdown' switch."

Um, it's called a sledgehammer, people. Pick it up and go to work on those orbs.

He took a step closer to me and I recognized the intimidation tactics. I knew him too well for that crap to work on me. I walked right up to him and pointed my finger. "So this is *your* fault. You didn't do what you were supposed to do and now I'm here instead of flying to Florida for my senior trip."

"Oh, I apologize." His voice was now dripping with sarcasm. "Did we ruin *your* plans? Did we interrupt something important in *your* life, Whitnee? Because in case you were not aware, you just dropped out of the sky and caused an earthshaker in the middle of my Guardianship ceremonies."

"Calm down, you two." Dad stepped in.

I was taken aback at how mean Gabriel was being. This wasn't how it should be. I mean, weren't we supposed to run into each other's arms and hug as if we were old friends who hadn't seen each other in a year? Wasn't there something in him that was happy to see me? Where did he get off being so mad? After all, I was the one who had been brought back here against my will.

"Bri, *you* knew how to shut down the portals." Dad turned on her.

"Is that *true*?" Gabriel growled, casting dark eyes on his mother.

Abrianna appeared startled. "I... I was not certain. There were complications."

Dad sighed as if her words exhausted him.

"So this is really Abrianna's fault?" I clarified. I just wanted it on record who Dad should blame here.

"But if we had shut down the portals, you would have been unable to come back," Abrianna admitted and then raised her eyebrows at Gabriel, as if he should understand.

I gaped at her. "That was the point!"

Gabriel snorted at my words. I was too flustered to address his attitude at the moment. Abrianna did not take her eyes off Dad to give me any sort of reaction.

"Dad, listen." I walked over to him, keeping my voice low. "We have to get back. Morgan and Caleb saw me disappear. So did Ben. And what do you think happened to Mom?"

"If Ben saw you, he'll connect the dots." Dad looked uncomfortable. "And your mother is okay. I was with her right before it started. She knew..."

I narrowed my eyes at him. "What do you mean, *she knew*?" Dad shook his head as if he didn't have time to worry about my questions. "Nathan Terradora, *did you know this would happen?*"

Dad paused before carefully choosing his words. "Only a few moments before it did. I did not know that we would transport like that, no. And I certainly did not realize you would be here too."

"What*ever*!" Once again, he was not telling me the whole truth. "Did the life forces on the Mainland not tip you off? When I was freaking ruining my graduation ceremony with weird natural disasters, you didn't think that *maybe* something like this was going on?"

"Watch your tone, Whitnee," Dad warned.

It was Abrianna who caught on to what we were saying. "Whitnee used life forces on the Mainland?" Dad and I turned and looked at her. There was something in her eyes then. Something glinty and weird and dangerous. I didn't like it.

Whitnee, watch what you say. We'll talk more in private. Dad's voice came through loud and clear inside my thoughts. I gave him one defiant look before dropping the subject and turning back on Gabriel.

"If the portal to Camp Fusion is still open, then Dad and I need to get to the Palladium. Tonight. We need to transport home."

Gabriel stared at me with a frown for way too long. "I cannot let you leave."

Excuse me, *what*. "You did *not* just say that to me." Apparently his voice wasn't the only one that could drop to a dangerously deep level.

"I was in the middle of a speech about the Pilgrim and the earth shook and then both of you just *appeared*," Gabriel explained, his arms still crossed and his face hard. "I will not let you disappear on us again when those people believe something ancient and supernatural just occurred. No. You will stay here in support of this government and these ceremonies. After it is all over, we can discuss your return home."

"Absolutely not. My mom and my friends are probably freaking out."

"Your mother is okay, Whitnee," Dad cut in, not helping my argument. At all. "You've got to trust me on that. Ben will know exactly what happened and will explain it to Caleb and Morgan.

Everybody else thinks we're on a family vacation in the Caribbean, so—"

"So what are you saying, Dad? That you want to stay?"

"I'm saying that we were brought back here for a reason," Dad responded and I couldn't help rolling my eyes. I cast my frustrated thought into his head: *In that case, I'd love to hear it!*

Gabriel might be right about this. We might need to stay—at least through the night.

Aloud I said, "I'd rather be in the Caribbean." I shot a furious look at Gabriel. "Hard to believe after such a wonderful welcoming committee, I know." I wanted to be far away from the guy who once held my heart and had now stomped all over the good memories of it.

"My decision is not going to change," Gabriel insisted.

Everybody erupted into different arguments at the same time. Gabriel seemed to just tune it all out as he walked to a table where a single white flower rested. I marched over to him, ignoring the tender way he picked up the flower and cradled it in one hand.

"You have got to stop being a crazy control freak," I seethed openly. He wouldn't look at me, so I grabbed his arm and forced his attention. I always seemed to forget just how much bigger than me he was. And double dang, he was still a hottie in all the right ways. But now he was a hottie with facial hair and a bad attitude the size of Texas.

Before he could infuriate me again, the double doors to the parlor flew open and in blustered Hannah and Thomas and...

"We are getting *really* good at finding our way around this Island," Caleb remarked as he and Morgan appeared.

8

ALL MY EXES LIVE IN TEXAS

I could not ignore the way her face changed when she saw Caleb. Nor did anyone miss her leap across the room and into his arms. I had to shift my gaze away.

It was Nathan who asked it first as he went over to embrace Whitnee's friends as if they were family. "How did you two get here?"

"Whitnee wouldn't let go of us. It felt like we got sucked in or something. Transporting felt very different than before," Morgan answered as Whitnee transferred her affections to the taller girl. "But then we got separated like always. We followed the sounds of the crowd."

"How did we transport from the football field?" Caleb wondered, his gaze resting suspiciously on me. "Did you open a new portal or something?"

I shook my head, wondering why everyone assumed I had something to do with their arrival. I needed a moment alone to subdue the rage I felt. A good leader could not lose control. And I felt more and more out of control as I watched the protective way Caleb angled himself toward Whitnee. He had grown enough over the year that he was now about my height.

"It seems" —Nathan walked to the window and gazed solemnly outside at the crowd— "that the *Island* did this."

His words were met with confused silence. Why would the Island bring them back here? And why now? Why in the middle of my speech?

"Regardless of the reasons, I have a crowd of people who are expecting an explanation for what just happened. What do you suggest, Nathan?" I asked, part of me hoping he had the answers that I was somehow missing.

When he turned back around, his response surprised all of us. "May I have a few moments alone somewhere? I need to think."

"You can use the Aerodorian library," Ezekiel answered. "It is two floors down from here, overlooking the beach."

Nathan looked to me for affirmation. I wanted to protest that there was not time to indulge, but something in the man's expression halted my words. Perhaps he needed to commune with the Island—a practice I had given up. If the Island would actually listen and respond to Nathan, then perhaps I should not stand in the way.

I nodded, but felt compelled to add, "Time is not a luxury we have at the moment. Please keep that in mind."

Nathan started toward the door and Whitnee followed. "I'm coming with you," she announced.

"No, Baby Doll. I need to be alone for this."

"Dad—" she started to plead, but he exited quickly with a firm shake of his head.

Caleb rested a hand on Whitnee's shoulder, reminding me of how the two of them used to infuriate me with their comfortable levels of affection. "What exactly is going on?"

"I don't understand what happened," she responded, shooting another angry look at me. I felt the Fire spike inside me. "And now I feel like Dad is hiding stuff from me again."

"Come here, Whitnee." Ezekiel motioned to her from the sofa. "Your father will know the right thing to do. Give him some quiet time."

Whitnee sighed and made her way to her grandfather. As she passed me, her frustration was sharp in the space between us. I allowed myself a moment to observe her. She had not grown taller as I had first perceived; she was merely wearing shoes that raised her height several inches. They did not look practical whatsoever, and I wondered how she was able to walk in such monstrosities. My curiosity led me to stare too long at her smooth legs until I was contemplating more than I should about her pale skin and the way she looked in that white dress. I tore my gaze away to find Caleb assessing me with cool, green eyes.

He was clothed in a manner I had never seen. His white tunic had buttons, a collar, and a red patterned scarf that was tied tightly around his neck and hung down his chest. Surely that would make a man feel choked and uncomfortable. He had tucked his tunic into light brown pants of a style I found intriguing. His belt looked like leather, and he appeared older and more confident than I remembered. Perhaps the strange clothes were creating that effect.

"Good to see you again, Gabriel." Caleb held out a hand to me and I hesitated before remembering their Mainland custom. I gripped his hand firmly and decided if he was going to be friendly, I would return the gesture. Before I knew it, Morgan slid an arm around my waist and leaned in to my side in greeting. I awkwardly lifted my arm to embrace her.

"Sorry we crashed your party," she apologized. Over her head, I caught the frown on Thomas's face. I understood exactly how he felt. How were we supposed to act when these people walked back into our lives after we had moved on? Thomas could so easily greet Whitnee the way I longed to, and there I was, able to embrace Morgan while he stood there holding back whatever was in his instinct to do.

"You look well, Morgan," I responded honestly. She had a much healthier glow upon her face than the last time I had seen her.

"Thank you." When she pulled back to look at me, her eyes sparkled like the sun on the blue ocean. "Look at you, the new Guardian!"

"Almost," I corrected.

"Right." She smiled sympathetically. "From the look of things, I guess we're just in time for the festivities."

"Yes, Whitnee's timing is always perfect, is it not?" My words were supposed to be an attempt at humor, but they ended up revealing too much of the bitterness festering inside me. Whitnee did not appreciate it.

"This isn't my fault, Gabriel," she proclaimed. "You were the one who didn't shut down the portals. I swear, if something happens to prevent my dad from coming back home with me again, I will *never* forgive you—"

"I have more important matters to worry about right now than your personal happiness, Whitnee," I responded hotly.

"This is about my *life*, not my happiness." She took a step toward me. "You have to let us go home."

But I held my ground. "People believe in you—or once did. You have to think about more than yourself right now."

"Says the selfish Guardian who just wants to use us as political pawns to make himself look good. It's amazing how much you've become just like your parents, after all."

That was it.

In a hazy cloud of enraged emotions, I strode right past Caleb and Morgan and straight down the hall. She had challenged my self-control and won. And she had done it in front of my mother.

I heard Morgan say, "Whitnee, that was mean..."

Thomas called out to me, but I found an empty room and slammed the door behind me, hoping he would not follow. I took a few calming breaths and paced around the room, trying to invoke the tranquility force that balanced out the fiery nature of a Pyradorian. It just did not feel powerful enough, and I shook with the urge to flip over a table or kick a chair across the room.

She had no right to force herself back into my life and try to control my decisions. This was *my* Island and *I* was the one who had been here to restore the chaos that her visit had created. She would have to do things my way this time.

I *did* bloody sound like my mother.

I was still holding Elon's flower in my hand, wondering if Nathan or Whitnee could have saved her had they only arrived sooner. Instead of just giving in to the terrible sorrow that threatened my composure, I fed the anger with thoughts about all the ways Whitnee had disappointed me.

Slumping into a chair, I forced myself to breathe evenly again. My gaze rested on the zephyra at the desk in front of me. Impetuously, I lunged for it.

"Eden." I barked at the device. It took so long to connect that I almost slammed it shut. Her concerned face appeared at the last moment. Something in me calmed, even though something in her appeared overtly anxious.

"Gabriel! Did you feel anything? We just experienced another earthshaker in Geodora, only this time I thought the Island would split in two. It wasn't like the small rumble we felt last month. Father and I could not reach anybody on zephyra—"

"Yes, yes. It happened on the Southern Beach, as well. I have our people checking in with the other villages to make sure all is okay."

Her face blanched. "Oh, my. All those people down there. Is everyone panicking? Was there damage? Injuries? I should be there. This was not on the schedule. We need to move to a backup plan—"

"Eden."

Her mind was in logical, fix-it mode and she hardly listened to me when the drive to organize took over. She grappled for papers in her bag. "Wait. What are you doing? You should be out on the tower right now. Was it bad enough there to interrupt the ceremony? We have Healers on call for emergencies. And I can get—"

"Whitnee and Nathan are here."

She froze and gave her full attention to the zephyra. "What?"

"I believe they are the ones who caused the earthshaker. They just *appeared*. Whitnee was in the middle of the crowd right by the statue on the beach. Nathan was on top of the bloody tower like a hero from another world." I rubbed my fingers along my growing beard as I thought over what I had witnessed. "Eden, there is no hiding their presence here this time. What happened was supernatural."

"Incredible." Her voice was in awe. "The time of the Pilgrim *is* here. Do you not see? The Island brought them back to help us! This is a sign, Gabriel. The fact that we chose to reconstruct the Watch Tower and host the opening ceremonies there—the Island is listening!"

I did not want her to be happy about this. I wanted her to feel my frustration, so I blurted, "If the Island brought them back, why could it not happen in time to save Elon?"

Her face fell. "Perhaps Elon was not meant to be saved, Gabriel. I do not understand and I do not wish to discuss it right now." She reached for her papers again and I still felt unsatisfied by her response. "We need to get security detail assigned to Whitnee and

Nathan. I knew I should have come tonight. I will pack a bag and take a hipposole there immediately. Perhaps we should—"

"No, I do not need you here. We will continue as planned, just on a delayed schedule," I assured her, even though there was a moment in which the thought of having her here to oversee this unexpected turn of events cheered me considerably. But I set aside my own selfishness and remembered the grief her family was enduring. "I will not allow *anyone* to deter our purpose."

She dropped her eyes and perused her papers, as if preoccupied. "What was it like seeing Whitnee again?"

I was not surprised at her candid question. What did surprise me was the strange way she avoided eye contact with me as she asked it. I knew I could not lie to Eden unless I wanted to face a full interrogation into what I was hiding. So I answered honestly.

"It was irritating, actually. She is just as stubborn as always. And she made it perfectly clear that she did not *choose* to come back," I added, though I was unsure why that mattered so much to me. "And then Morgan and Caleb appeared—"

"Morgan and Caleb transported?" she exclaimed, dropping her papers. "This is so strange! I do not care what you say, I must come immediately—"

"No." My irritation threatened to bubble over. I was tired of everyone questioning my decisions. "I made it clear that you are not needed here. Why do you not respect my wishes?"

I was shocked when her eyes turned glassy with tears again. I had never seen Eden cry this much, which was just another confirmation that she was not ready to be here. I was simply trying to protect her, but it felt like everything I said today was coming out the wrong way.

"Very well." She fought for control of her voice. "I will try to reach Hannah by zephyra and review some pertinent details about your schedule. Perhaps she will find my efforts useful."

"Eden," I tried softening my demeanor. There was no easy way to express the multitude of emotions coursing through me at the moment. However, the last person I wanted to upset over my own volatile impulses was Eden. "I do not mean to imply—"

"I know," she interrupted and sniffed self-consciously. "Clearly, I am not much help right now. I am sorry for the timing of these events. Is there anything at all you need from me right now? You must have called for some other reason." Her face looked hopeful and I suddenly did not understand what my reason for calling had been. It must have just become my nature to have her close by. She had moved into a separate wing at the Palladium this year. I hardly made any decisions anymore without her insight and knowledge—even if it was only what to have for breakfast, which we usually ate together. It was completely understandable that my instinct would point me in her direction. But I decided there was something I needed from her, after all. Something I could ask no one else.

Before I thought too long, I blurted, "Tell me how to treat Whitnee."

She frowned and tilted her head to the side like she always did when puzzled. "What do you mean?"

"I mean that I need your advice as a *girl*. Not as my Advisor," I admitted. "Jezebel is in the crowd and I have not even seen her reaction to Whitnee's presence... and yet..."

I heard Eden sigh and I knew she and I were entering awkward territory. But she was quite literally the only person I trusted with this problem.

"Be sincere in everything you do," Eden responded slowly. "If you still have feelings for Whitnee, it is understandable. We all know she is special to you."

"I feel nothing for her but anger—"

"Which is originating from *somewhere*, Gabriel," she pointed out, and a sympathetic spark entered her eyes. "I hope that you are not being unkind to her. Do not forget that every time she has come to this Island, it has been under stressful and inconvenient circumstances for her. We interrupt her life too."

I took a deep breath and considered that. "I do not know how to treat her in front of people, especially now that the entire Island knows she has returned. There were rumors before. About her and me." Now I was the one gazing off and avoiding eye contact with Eden. She knew they were more than just rumors.

"Well." She shrugged lightly and her words were flippant, like she was merely thinking aloud. "A crowd loves nothing more than a good love story. That is how your mother won them over eventually.

She put on a farce of unrequited love with Eli, and united two tribes who had been in major upheaval with one another."

I narrowed my eyes at her, entertaining new thoughts. "Are you saying you think I should give them a love story? Something to distract them?"

She hesitated to answer at first and now she was surveying me with her Geo eyes, the look that tried to see into my mind and motivation. Usually, I put up with it, but right then it made me uncomfortable. I glanced away and pretended to be preoccupied with the Whitnee flower resting beside the zephyra.

Finally she warned, "I am saying you should be genuine in your actions, and people will respect that. They have had a disingenuous ruler for too long."

I knew what she meant, but my mind was already turning over the possibilities of what the crowd might need now… explanations, hope, *love*. Perhaps I could give that to them, after all. Perhaps Whitnee's reappearance actually could benefit me in ways I had not previously conceived.

But it would depend on her cooperation.

"Gabriel, I am not sure I care too much for that look in your eye—" Her suspicions were interrupted when there was a timely knock on the door.

"I must go." I grasped at the opportunity to close this conversation. "Please contact Hannah and Levi and do what you feel you must, but do not leave on account of the earthshaker. We will have things under control soon."

I closed the zephyra before she had an opportunity to protest. Rising to my full height, I straightened my appearance and moved to the door.

It was Nathan. There was something determined in his face. And his eyes—the ones that still surprised me by how closely they resembled Whitnee's—were intuitive and alight with some idea. I had seen a similar look in my own mother's eyes when she was struck with brilliance—or madness.

"Come in." I stepped aside and felt a powerful energy in the air that almost pulsed around him as he entered.

Whitnee's father was a mystery to me. I could not quite understand him or the reasons why he had tolerated imprisonment for all those years. But I respected him. Something about him seemed right and just. Even kind. And I knew *no one* else who so easily received respect and love from my mother.

Nathan took a seat across from me at the desk. "Can I trust you with a secret?" he asked.

I am certain I did not contain my surprise within my expression. But I answered unswervingly, "Yes. Of course."

"I am not permitted to leave the Island right now. I do not need to go near a portal to know that the barrier will be back up for me. That being said, it is my wish that Whitnee and her friends go back home as soon as we can easily excuse her from the public eye. You and I both know that it is too dangerous here for her and I do not want people speculating that she could be the Pilgrim. I will shoulder that responsibility for you this week."

"Does that mean you are the Pilgrim, Nathan?"

His eyes pierced mine in a way that made me feel as if he was seeing into my soul. It was even more uncomfortable than Eden's stare. "What do you believe, Gabriel?"

I had to look away. "I do not know. But I suppose it does not matter now." I had defaulted to Abrianna's response, but I could sense my answer had disappointed him. I changed the subject back to what he was proposing. "If the Island brought you here and will not let you leave, how do you know that Whitnee is allowed to leave?"

"I don't." He scratched his head and sighed. "But there's only one way to find out. I know you have a tight schedule, but I would like to request transport to the Palladium first thing tomorrow morning. And I do not want Whitnee to know that I am planning to stay. Can you hold that secret?"

I paused before nodding. "She will be devastated, you know."

"Yes. But staying here would devastate her more."

I had no inkling of what exactly he meant. Sometimes it seemed like he did not give his daughter enough credit. As much as she had vexed me, I could admit that Whitnee was incredibly powerful and desired to use that for the good of others. She had strength that Nathan seemed to want to overlook. But as he was her father, I knew it was not my place to question his wishes.

With renewed purpose in his voice, Nathan said, "Now that we understand each other, I'd like to take a look at your speech. Some important revisions might be in order."

You better be right about this. Otherwise, we're asking for a whole lot of trouble here. I couldn't help asserting my warning into Dad's thoughts. There were definitely some cool benefits to being back on the Island. Like the ability my dad and I had to communicate directly through our minds.

His gaze slid sideways, but his expression wasn't exactly comforting.

I can't hide anymore, Whit. The Island made sure I had no choice this time.

Well, that was for darn sure. We couldn't pretend that Dad didn't appear atop the famous Watch Tower with no explanation. The coincidence of it happening in the middle of Gabriel's speech about the coming Pilgrim raised the hairs on the back of my neck.

In the same magical way I had heard Simeon project his voice over a crowd at the Lost Ceremony last year, the sound of Gabriel's deep reassuring tone settled over the beach below us where the sun was starting a slow descent into the water. I let my gaze linger on the ripples of golden, sun-washed waves as they rolled peacefully onto shore. The soft lilacs and pinks of drifting clouds shimmered in the sky. For a moment, I forgot all the things I dreaded about this Island and remembered that there was no other place that so vividly captured color and beauty in one sweep of the eye.

But then my eyes swept across the daunting crowd, and I could sense their fear and confusion as if it were a palpable part of the atmosphere.

Why do you really think we're here again, Dad? I felt a little lightheaded with a fear that I couldn't explain.

Perhaps it is merely to give credibility to Gabriel's speech tonight. I don't know. But don't worry. We'll stay tonight and then you three will go back through that portal first thing in the morning.

I frowned. *You're freaking me out again. I'm not leaving without you.* I felt like a broken record from last summer. Why did nothing ever change? And despite what I said earlier about wanting to get home, I had some hesitation now about leaving. I couldn't win.

We'll talk more later. Watch your expressions. Thousands of people can see you. He subtly directed his attention back on Gabriel but I was left studying his face for a sign of *something.* Anything. But, really, Dad had come back from his time alone seeming much more confident and less worried. I wish I felt the same.

"…and as you stand here before our new Watch Tower, I know you must be questioning its timing and significance. Even more so, I know that what just happened here on this beach is weighing heavily on all of our thoughts. I, for one, am just as shocked as you are." Gabriel's words pulled my gaze in his direction like a magnet. He stood directly to my left behind a stone podium where he paused for effect. *Here we go,* I thought to myself. I watched him absently take hold of that white flower again and rub the petals thoughtfully between his fingers—a gesture the crowd could not see, but one I found curious.

"What you experienced was frightening and confusing, as have been the other smaller earthshakers that we have experienced lately," Gabriel continued. At that, Dad and I both glanced instinctively at each other. I could see that this was news to him too. They'd had more earthquakes? Was that even scientifically possible on an island? "However, I want to remind you that this Island contains many mysteries. Some mysteries we might not understand now, but we have to trust that they are for a greater purpose in all our lives. I believe that the Island has brought us a long-awaited gift and that the earthshaker was caused by the power contained within this gift."

Gabriel paused again and this time, he turned to angle himself at Dad who stood beside me. With one powerful arm extended in our direction, Gabriel said, "I would like to re-introduce Nathan, the son of Aerodorian Councilman Ezekiel and his wife, Sarah, a man born right here on our Island forty-eight years ago, the gift that the Island has returned to us."

Dad came alongside Gabriel and bowed to the crowd in the traditional sign of respect and greeting. There was a collective gasp on the beach, and a slight buzz of conversation and energy went up into the atmosphere. Gabriel continued with more conviction in his voice. "Many of you older Dorians may remember Nathan and can recall the debate surrounding his strange birth. As you can see, Nathan has naturally pale hair and a pale complexion. Likewise, he has no birthmark and has been able to use all four life forces since childhood."

This was met with even more reactions from the crowd and I could see them shifting around down there in excitement. That uneasy feeling in my stomach intensified.

"As you might be assuming, fellow Dorians, Nathan fits the description of the Pilgrim, the one our ancient texts prophesy will come to bring us peace. Perhaps Nathan is the one we have been speaking of this last year and perhaps he is part of the great mystery this Island has yet to unravel. All I know is that I do not believe Nathan's arrival on the Watch Tower this evening was a coincidence."

And there it was. Gabriel was setting Dad up as the Pilgrim and I wasn't sure what impact that was going to have on Dad. Or on me.

Or on the Island.

As I watched Gabriel's expressions and body language, I had to admit that he wore the look of authority well. But I suppose he always had. He was clearly born and bred to do this, and as angry as I was with him, I couldn't help but admire him. Either Dad had coached him really well on what to say, or Gabriel was just naturally good at this. I had a feeling it was a combination of both.

Gabriel's solemn face broke into a smile then. Though it might have appeared to be a gracious smile to the crowd, I found it to be somewhat forced. "Nathan is not the only one to return to us. His beautiful daughter, Whitnee, has also come with him, and I ask you to welcome her as part of our Dorian family. I think you will find her to be a lovely addition to our Island as she has many exquisite talents of her own."

Well, that was a load of crap I didn't see coming. Trust Gabriel to both flatter and piss me off at the same time. He extended a hand to me and I donned my own cautious smile, stepping forward exactly as my dad had instructed earlier. Dad moved back for me as I placed my hand in Gabriel's.

Dangit. That little spark between us was still there and I completely resented it. I turned to the crowd and mimicked Dad's bow of respect, but before I could pull my hand out of Gabriel's, he raised it to his lips and kissed it.

In front of everyone.

My heart pounded harder as the slight tickle of the stubble on his face brushed with his lips across my skin. I felt the heat rush to my face, and I was actually at a loss for how to react. When Gabriel glanced back at me and our eyes met, it was not romance blooming there, but something else. Something I really didn't understand, but it flustered me.

Instead of allowing the moment to linger, I politely pulled my hand away from him and stepped back to stand by my dad.

Did you tell him to do that? I asked Dad pointedly.

He promptly responded, *Nope. But I will happily have a chat with him later.*

DO NOT, I warned as loudly as possible in the space between our minds. *Please don't start interfering with that again. I'm eighteen years old and I will handle this.*

Dad appeared doubtful. *Fine. But you might want to see the look on Caleb's face right now.*

My eyes could not catch Caleb's before Gabriel introduced him and Morgan to the crowd as "Travelers from the Mainland" who accompanied us here. They both stood to wave and bow from their places onstage behind the rest of the government leaders. When Caleb sat back down, he seemed to take an obsessive interest in watching the crowd. I hoped my stare was burning into his peripheral vision. I did not need Gabriel ruining things with Caleb! There was no longer a love triangle here. Just Caleb and me—two 'angles' who, um, had yet to connect the lines… or something like that.

I took Caleb's lack of acknowledgment as an opportunity to study the individual leaders of the Island. Jesse and Zebedee both smiled, but Zeb's actually appeared genuine. I searched for Joseph and Joanna and quickly realized they had been missing this whole time. I knew something else had felt off. Where was Eden? What in the world had happened to the Geodorian representation for such an occasion? My eyes wandered over to Ezekiel, who seemed solemnly proud of Dad's presence there. But something was wrong with Grandmother Sarah as she sat next to Poppa Zeke. She stared unseeingly at a spot on the floor and I thought I detected silent tears trickling down her face. As if she could sense me staring at her, she looked up and for a moment, my usually formal grandmother allowed me to see sadness and vulnerability plainly in her expression. Why was she so unhappy? Wouldn't Dad's return bring her joy?

I opened my mouth as if to say something, but shut it immediately as I was not in a position to do anything for her. She gracefully dabbed at her eyes and then went back to her expressionless state as she listened to the rest of Gabriel's words.

"I am sure you have noticed by now that our Geodorian leaders were unable to join us tonight." Gabriel bowed his head and closed his eyes for a prolonged moment. His voice was softer now. "Early this morning, I was privileged to speak with an innocent child who believed in this moment. She told me the Pilgrim was coming soon, that there would be healing and peace and hope on the Island. I confess that I did not have nearly as much faith as she did." He went back to cradling that white flower in his hand. "But she was not wrong. I believe you know the child of whom I speak—"

I think I did. Even before he said it.

"—Geodorian Councilman Joseph's daughter, Elon. She has suffered with sickness for the last year and I regret to tell you that she passed on into the next life this morning, not long after she proclaimed her belief in the Pilgrim."

"What!" I could not help my own reaction even as there were whispers of grief echoing across the beach. My stomach dropped to the floor and I grabbed onto my dad's arm to steady myself. I heard his troubled sigh.

Elon was *dead*? Poor Eden. Poor Joseph and Joanna. My dream of the little girl with flowers in her hair was still so vivid from this morning. A piece of my heart shattered. How could she really be gone? What had happened to her? Tears stung my eyes and blurred my vision of the darkening beach in front of me.

Gabriel held up the white flower in his hand. "Elon created this flower last summer right before she grew ill. She called it the 'Whitnee flower' as it was inspired by Whitnee's golden white hair."

I swallowed back my tears as Gabriel reached for me to join his side again. I was so taken aback by this news that I moved to him almost immediately. "In two days, I will return to Geodora to receive the Geodorian Blessing. On that day, I ask for the entire Island to wear flowers on your garments or in your hair as an honor to Elon and the other children we have lost this year." I felt him slide one arm around me and use the other hand to tilt my face up toward him. With grave intention, he tucked the white flower into my curls. "A perfect match," he mumbled. My chin quivered slightly with the sadness that wanted to leak out of my eyes. But I held it in.

Gabriel kept one sultry arm locked around my waist as he turned back to the crowd who resonated with weeping, sighing, and whispering. As if in tacit response to Gabriel's sudden touchy-feely inclinations, Dad joined his other side.

"Dorians," Gabriel addressed the crowd. His body temperature was unnaturally high as always, and being cloaked in it felt suffocating for a moment. "I want you to have hope as we enter this new era on our Island. Nathan's presence is proof that the Island still listens and still cares about us in the midst of our suffering and confusion. Nathan has asked me to assure you that he comes in peace and in support of this government." Gabriel glanced at Dad who nodded in agreement. "Though we do not understand the Island's plan, I trust that we will strengthen each other and work together toward a better future. Our government is strong and united and we will bring this Island into the next era where prosperity and peace will reign."

The crowd roared with applause and victorious cries. I tried to conjure a smile in return, but I was reeling. Gabriel accepted the crowd's response and then ushered us back inside the tower where everyone else on the stage followed. I could hear Jesse's voice announcing that the "light show" would begin after dark.

As soon as we were safely out of sight and back inside the muted tower room, I pulled away from Gabriel and faced him straight on. But before I could ask for more information about Elon, Dad barreled across the room with controlled anger. "Tell me exactly what you were thinking using Whitnee like that, Gabriel. We discussed that you were to present her simply as my daughter. Not as the Pilgrim and certainly not as your girlfriend!"

It was Abrianna who responded first. "Actually, Nathan, I thought what he did was quite effective. He kept Whitnee separate from the Pilgrim issue by setting her up as a personal friend to him. People will focus more on Whitnee in that respect and more on you as the Pilgrim. He protected her."

I shot a curious glance at Abrianna, my mind turning over her reasoning. That actually made sense. And I was a little disgusted by the part of me that understood her manipulative thinking.

"I promise you, Nathan, any pretense of romance was exactly that—an act," Gabriel informed Dad, who then turned uncertain fatherly eyes on me. I resisted flinching at the coldness in Gabriel's voice. I heard his point loud and clear. And I couldn't decide if I was hurt by it or not.

Instead of chasing that rabbit down a dark hole, I hugged my arms to myself and looked up at Gabriel, trying to sense the warmth that I knew was within him somewhere. "Elon." My voice felt thick, threatened by a barrage of emotion. "What happened?"

"She died in her sleep. Early this morning," Gabriel said, a sharp edge to his tone that hadn't revealed itself on that stage. The tender, compassionate leader was officially gone and replaced by some caricature of a stubborn Pyra ex-boyfriend.

"Gabriel, I'm so sorry," I said sincerely. "I wish I could've seen her again—"

"Yes, well, you were a little late." Gabriel marched away from me and acted as if the papers on the table were hugely important. His next words definitely rang with accusation. "She believed you would return to heal her. Clearly, she was wrong about that. I just hope your return now will do *something* good for this Island."

His words had finally hurt me the way I sensed he had wanted.

"Gabriel—" Dad's voice was reproving.

I held up my hand. "It's fine, Dad." I reached up and removed the flower from my hair. With a calmness I didn't really feel, I approached Gabriel's table and laid the flower down in front of him. His grief over Elon—and perhaps over things I didn't understand— was more obvious than he knew. "I'm sorry," I whispered. I meant it on behalf of Elon… and for whatever I had done to make him this angry with me.

He kept his eyes glued to the flower and refused to look at me.

I motioned to Caleb and Morgan to follow me. "We're going to the beach."

Nobody argued with me.

9

THAT 'SHIP HAS SAILED

"What the *beep*, y'all. I never knew food could taste like this." Morgan's words were distorted by a mouthful of pastry. "Seriously. These sticky bun things are sinful."

"The way you're moaning over them is sinful," Caleb teased as we strolled barefoot through the sand. We remained a short distance away from the general public along the Southern Beach.

Morgan waved a gooey, cinnamon-scented dessert in his face. "Come to the dark side and try a bite."

"No, thanks. I've got my eye on that one hut with the roasting meat." He nodded up ahead at the throng of people standing in line for food among the different vendors. It felt like we were on the outskirts of a typical Texas fair back home. Except there were no private beaches with this kind of view where we came from.

"Okay, so Thomas" —Morgan paused to swallow down a mouthful of sticky sweetness— "is definitely weirded out by me being here. Like, I had to just tell him it was cool. I didn't expect us to see each other again either, and I'm totally down with just flirting and nothing more."

Caleb eyed her suspiciously. "And what did he say?"

"He seemed relieved—like, he didn't feel like he had to act all committed or anything."

I watched her take another bite and gaze out at the ocean before I asked, "Are you really okay with being here again?"

"Sure," she answered easily. "Last time I was dying. This time, I'm healthy. And if he and I just play around the whole time, I'm good with it. I don't want to get serious about anything before college."

Caleb clarified, "So you basically just gave a guy permission to flirt with you with no strings attached?"

"He's a really good kisser, Caleb."

"Didn't need to know that, Morgan," he groaned while she just laughed and licked icing from her finger. "And maybe you should rethink your definition of flirting. Geez."

"I'm not saying it'll go there," she assured us, a wicked smile spreading across her features. "But I make no promises."

I could never understand Morgan's ability to move through guys as casually as she did. She had been so much more intentional with her relationships this year, keeping any potential dating partners at arm's length. If she was finally going to lower the drawbridge to Thomas, I wondered if it was because he meant more to her than she wanted to admit. And if Thomas wasn't madly in love with her all over again after twenty-four hours, he was stupid.

At my prolonged silence, she held out a sticky piece of bread to me. "Whit? One naughty little bite?"

I shook my head and glanced back. Our three tracks of footprints weaved around watermelon-sized seashells that seemed to have been placed strategically along the beach. Seriously, where else in the world could you find shells that huge? I knew I'd never seen them here before. Keeping a safe distance away from us were a couple of Palladium guards who fixed their watchful eyes on us. Of course we couldn't have escaped the Watch Tower completely. When we were here, we were always under surveillance.

"You're too quiet, Whit," Caleb remarked. "You know how much your silence scares us."

I couldn't bring myself to smile at him, even though I was thankful he didn't seem mad. "I'm glad it's so easy for y'all to adapt to being here again. Why don't I feel the same way?"

"Because we're not the ones the whole Island is watching," Morgan said.

Caleb's answer rolled out in thoughtful phrases. "About the only thing I get to choose when we come here is my reaction. So I'm trying to be different, to be better." He bumped my shoulder with his, attempting again to draw a smile from me.

I tried and faltered, worried about what he was really thinking. "Caleb, I don't want Gabriel to come between us this time. I need to know you trust me on this. I don't know why he's acting like that—"

"Oh, well, that part is obvious," Caleb said. I stopped walking and blinked up at him in confusion. He had rolled up his sleeves to his elbows, loosened his tie, and his dark auburn hair blew slightly in the beach breeze. He looked so cute all dressed up from graduation and then casually mussed up by the Island. My heart gave a little appreciative leap.

"I promise he doesn't have any feelings left for me. Everything he did onstage was just a self-serving act, like he said," I replied, which elicited a choke-slash-cough from Morgan as she finished off her snack. I ignored her as Caleb's eyes slid her direction before settling back on me.

"Well, that's debatable, but I'll save it for later," Caleb responded. "However, I do think it's time you tell me what happened between the two of you last summer."

Morgan started backing away. "Maybe I should give y'all some alone time."

"Of course not, Morgie. Stay," I assured her and she paused with uncertainty. I turned back to Caleb. "You know what happened last summer."

"No, I mean *after* we left you here. I have no idea how things really ended between you and him. I never asked for details because I didn't *want* to know." Caleb squared his shoulders and gave me a firm look. "But now I need to know. A guy only treats a girl like that when she's broken his heart."

"I didn't break his heart." I frowned, remembering that last time I'd seen Gabriel as I exited through the portal to Hawaii. I wished I could forget that angry look in his eye. Man, he really hadn't let it go, had he?

"Tell me what happened."

I sighed and shuffled around in the sand before finally facing the water and saying, "He wanted me to stay on the Island. Permanently." I paused and then added, "With him."

"What does that mean, 'with him'?" Caleb prodded.

"Probably the way it sounds. Like, by his side, a real commitment-type thing, I think."

I stole a glance at Caleb's reaction only to find him using his little knowing nod. "And what did you say to that?"

"Well, what was I supposed to say, Caleb?" I gave my attention to the enormous conch shell to my right, resting one bare foot on it. I was surprised to find it was abnormally warm. "I had no choice. I was leaving that night and it wasn't like staying on the Island was even an option in my dad's mind—"

"So you didn't choose to go home? You were just forced to dump Gabriel and leave?" There was an insecure edge to his tone now.

"No! I mean, circumstances matter, right? Wait, why are we talking about this?" I couldn't think straight and I did not want to say the wrong thing and upset the delicate nature of my relationship with Caleb.

"I really don't mind going back inside. I'll just go hang out with your dad," Morgan tried again.

"Stay, Morgan," Caleb responded.

"Why does she need to stay? Are you about to get mad at me, Caleb? Because I really can't handle that right now," I told him honestly, feeling a slight panic that things were about to go south with us.

"I'm not mad, Whit. Really. But I also know that I'd be lying if I said that I haven't worried about this moment for the entire last year. For some reason, I just knew you weren't done here... and that if we came back..." His voice trailed off.

I narrowed my eyes. "Is that why you won't kiss me?"

"O-kay," Morgan squeaked. "Now I'm out. See you guys back inside."

Neither of us argued with her that time and she made her escape quickly.

Caleb sighed and took a few steps so that he could stand in front of me, the conch shell between us. He really had gotten taller since the last time we were here. He completely blocked my view of the darkening ocean now. I drank him in, his stature, his natural charm, his broad shoulders. Without thinking, I leaned in and hid my face on his chest, my arms circling around his lean, muscled waist.

"Caleb, I feel like I'm losing you. With college coming and now this whole weird transporting thing… Please tell me what you're thinking." I stopped talking because I felt his arms come around me and his chin dip down to rest on top of my head.

There. That was the sweet spot. I could totally stay in that spot for the rest of my life. When he still didn't say anything, I pulled back enough to look at his face. It took him a moment to wrestle with his thoughts before he finally said, "I just feel like I'm still waiting."

"Waiting for what?"

"I don't know," he answered and I had a hard time sensing if that was the complete truth or not. "Waiting for something to happen or change or for the right moment."

"We are running out of moments!" I felt desperate as I stood there in his arms, a million unknown miles away from our home.

He pressed his lips together and glanced up at the sky. "What if the choice really had been yours? What would you have done? Stay here or go home?" I closed my eyes and rested my cheek on his chest again. I knew what he was really asking.

"Last summer doesn't matter. What matters is that I'm choosing *now* to go home. Tomorrow morning."

"But what if you're really supposed to be *here* for the rest of your life?"

"Caleb—"

"Whitnee, it's a serious question. I've always assumed you were meant to be at home with *me*—and yes, I do mean a 'real commitment type thing.' I thought that no matter what happened here, it was just for a certain time in your life. But some supernatural force brought you back here, something neither of us can control. Which makes me wonder what other things are out of our control that we just don't see."

"The same force that brought me here brought *you* too. That has to count for something."

When he spoke again, there was a melancholic honesty in his tone. "I just keep wondering if I'm messing with Fate. I get a sick feeling sometimes that I'm dreaming up a future that isn't really there… with a girl who won't be there."

His words gave me goosebumps. "Geez, Caleb, that's depressing. Stop with those dark thoughts."

"I know you sense it, too. Be honest and admit that's the real reason why you won't commit to going anywhere in the fall. You don't know where you're supposed to be. And I'm not talking about a college campus."

My eyes slammed closed as I battled that thought—to hear him say it out loud brought relief I didn't know I needed. He knew me better than I knew myself sometimes. But I refused to give it too much space to breathe, because with that relief also came a dose of stubbornness. Whatever did happen, I would fight this time to make it my choice and no one else's.

I pulled back and reached up to rest my hand on his cheek. My fingers traveled to his eye, touching the scar across his eyebrow and then the one at his temple from his accident on the Island. "Maybe you're right or maybe you're over-thinking things. Forget the girl of the future and look at the one standing right here in the present." His gaze finally met mine again and this time I smiled in reassurance. "This girl really wants you to kiss her before her eighteenth birthday is over."

He relented with a small smile. "I'll make you a deal."

"Quit stalling, Austin."

He seemed bolstered by my open affection as I felt his arms tighten around me. "I promise when you leave this Island with me—and we're safely together on the other side—I will kiss you and I won't stop until you tell me to."

"In that case, let's hit that portal up *now*."

He leaned over and kissed my forehead, his lips lingering there for a beautiful moment. When he pulled away, his eyes were tender. "Consider that a safety deposit."

"Signed, sealed, but not delivered. Super great." My words were brimming with sarcasm. "You are the master of ruining perfect moments with your over-analysis of everything."

"Trust me, it's not the perfect moment," Caleb's eyes shifted to a point on the beach behind me. "Gabriel's coming this way."

"What?" I don't know why, but I straightened up self-consciously which earned a meaningful raise of Caleb's eyebrows.

"Don't worry," I told him, but he just shoved his hands in his pockets and gave me a weak smile.

Morgan trudged along in the sand with Gabriel and her eyes were wide as she gave me signals that practically said, *I tried to stop him.*

"Did you need something, Gabriel?" I asked when he reached us.

"I would like to take a walk with you alone, if possible," he said, giving a cautious glance first at the crowd nearby and then at Caleb.

"Nope," I said, to the surprise of all three of them. "If you want to talk, you can do it in front of Caleb and Morgan. I'm not sure I want to be anywhere alone with you."

Gabriel rubbed his chin thoughtfully as he eyed the crowd again. "Very well. Allow me to apologize for my behavior since you arrived."

If he expected me to immediately jump in with an it's-all-okay-I'm-sorry-too response, he was dreaming. I remained silent and waited for him to continue.

"I was shocked to see you again and I did not handle it well. I am glad you returned, regardless of the reasons for it. I hope you will forgive my words earlier and understand that they were only words—not how I really feel."

I nodded to show I understood, although I wondered which of his words were true or not. I wasn't buying all the crap about feelings. Pyradorians were noted for their emotional nature where feelings dictated actions. Gabriel could deny his Pyra side all he wanted, but there had been true anger in his eyes earlier.

"I know that I am in no position to ask more of you, Whitnee, but I do have a proposition to make." At this, Gabriel glanced hesitantly at Caleb. "I know that you two are in a relationship, so I ask this with respect to Caleb, as well. But I need you to consider acting as my *personal friend* for the remainder of the evening. Or until you leave."

I didn't even look at Caleb, though I noticed we both conveniently avoided correcting Gabriel's statement about our relationship status. "What do you mean, your 'personal friend'?" I asked, already guessing where this was going.

"I mean you would act as a sort of romantic interest for me. But only in front of the crowd," he asserted when I snorted derisively.

"They need hope and, honestly, they need a distraction. You could provide them with both."

"Sorry, but I'm not going to pretend to be your girlfriend. Not after the way—" I stopped myself. "Just, no. That's a bad idea."

"Yeah, on the list of The Worst Things That Have Ever Come Out of Your Mouth, that has to rank number one," Caleb said, pulling his hands from his pockets to cross his arms. "I don't understand why you feel that's necessary, Gabriel. You're a good leader without the manipulation tactics. These people will follow your vision without you lying to them."

I was moved by the sincerity in Caleb's words. He was being very generous where Gabriel was concerned.

"I appreciate that sentiment, Caleb, but unfortunately, there is always a degree of lying that must take place in politics. If I told the people everything that really happened last summer—how their Guardian had faked a group of rebels just to scare them, how their Pyradorian Councilman betrayed this government and gave himself over to violence for the sake of greed and that he was *forced* to resign his position... There would be significant fear and mistrust on this Island, not to mention a lack of faith in our system. We have done what was necessary to maintain our way of life—and sometimes that included lying about the details."

"More lying will not help your situation, then. You're only asking for more problems," Caleb insisted.

"More problems will find me no matter what I do. At this point, I believe it is best for my reputation and for Whitnee's protection to let the Island believe there is a romance here. Would that really be that difficult to sell? After all, it was once a reality, or so I thought." Gabriel looked pointedly at me then and I felt my face grow hot.

"Well, it's not our reality now, Gabriel. And besides, my dad would never go for it."

Of that I was sure.

"He and I have already discussed the matter."

"And what did he say?" I pictured the foam at my dad's mouth when he let Gabriel have it for bringing up such an idiotic idea.

"He sees my side of it," Gabriel stated and my mouth dropped open. *No way.* "But mostly because he does not want people whispering about your role here as the Pilgrim. He would prefer, for whatever reason, for that title to belong to him only. And as my mother did point out, a romance better explains *your* presence here and takes the Pilgrim pressure away from you."

"Wait. My dad is *okay* with this idea?" I exclaimed and even Caleb looked distraught.

"He said it would be your choice. I am not allowed to force you into it." I just stared at him, dumbfounded. "Oh, and according to him, there would be no 'kissing stuff' allowed, to which, of course, I agreed. This is just an act for the people. Then you will go home, the portals will hopefully be destroyed once and for all, and we can feed a story to the people about my unrequited love in your absence. That will also free me from having to enter into a marriage any time soon."

My eyes connected with Morgan's and I could see in her face that she was actually considering the idea. "It does seem like an interesting political move," she mumbled.

"Morgie!" I chastised.

"Well, it's only for one night! And maybe it really would help the people of the Island after all the bad things going on. Everybody loves celebrity love stories—it gives them something to root for. We need a celebrity couple name. Like, Whitniel or... Gabnee."

"*Gabnee?*" I repeated as if that was the dumbest thing I'd ever heard. Because it was.

"That officially goes at the top of *your* Worst Things To Ever Come Out of Your Mouth List, Morgan," Caleb grumbled. "Maybe *you* should do it since you're so excited about the idea."

"No way." Morgan rolled her eyes. "I mean, no offense, Gabriel, you're just not exactly my type." He pursed his lips in slight amusement. "I'm not the actress that Whitnee is, either," she reasoned. "Caleb, it's just pretend. Like what she does onstage. And besides, you guys haven't even made any real commitments so it's not like you're breaking anything but your weird unspoken code of feelings for each other."

I widened my eyes at her. What was her angle by encouraging all of this? When she gave me a secret "trust me" wink, I started to realize she was just baiting Caleb. Regardless, Gabriel didn't need to know there was nothing official between Caleb and me! One look at Gabriel's face and I could see the wheels turning over what he'd just heard.

Caleb and I exchanged one prolonged look. "It's your choice, not mine," he said and it kind of bothered me that he didn't feel like he had more of a say. We both knew how much this choice mattered and even more so, I knew in my heart I could not do this to him. Even if it was all a farce. Even if Morgan thought it would push Caleb to finally see his own hesitations clearly.

I faced Gabriel. "I'm not going to pretend to be your girlfriend. Caleb's right about the lying. There are better ways to give people hope. I'll stand by your side as your *friend*. If the people want to imagine a romance here, then fine, that's their business. But I'm not going to intentionally deceive them. Does that work for you?"

Gabriel seemed to accept my answer or at least realize there was no argument that would change my mind. "Very well. I appreciate you at least staying by my side." He held out his hand to Caleb. "I would very much like for us to be friends, Caleb. I do not wish to cause problems for you. I expect you to take part in everything we do. And you too, Morgan. There are no secrets among us—you will be my special guests as long as you can stay."

Caleb stared hard at Gabriel's hand for a hesitant moment. Then he clapped his hand around Gabriel's for a firm shake. "Okay, man. I'm in, as your friend. Only because I do believe you are a good leader for this Island and if we can help in any way, we should. Maybe that's why we're here." Gabriel nodded thankfully, and my affection for Caleb swelled to embarrassing extents. Seriously, he was a class act. When he glanced down at me with a little bit of insecurity, I beamed at him and he let out a barely perceptible sigh. But then a slow smile spread across his face. To Gabriel, he added, "And since we're all *friends* here now, I swear, if you try to kiss my hand the way you did with Whitnee on that stage, I will be off this Island faster than you can call me your 'friend' again."

Morgan and I hooted with laughter and once Gabriel got Caleb's meaning, he released the first real laugh I'd heard from him in over a year.

"No offense, Caleb, but you are not exactly my type," Gabriel mimicked Morgan and sent a wink in her direction.

And then the four of us were chuckling together like we never had before. A flicker of happiness bloomed in my chest. Maybe being back on the Island wouldn't be so bad this time.

By the time we returned to the tower, the entire beach was sparkling. Every one of those huge shells on the beach had become a Firelight that cast a rainbow glow as far as I could see. When the music started for the light show, they flashed brilliantly in time with the drums.

I leaned over and whispered to Gabriel, pointing at the colorful beach. "I want to be down there when it's all lit up like that." He sat tall beside me, almost kingly-looking, in an engraved wooden chair with a back that rose up above him.

He dipped his face down to my level and replied, "If you behave, maybe we can go back down there after the show."

With an excited smile, I responded, "I'm behaving perfectly now that I've had something to eat. Did you see how nice I was to your mother?"

"We will see how long that lasts." His tone had a teasing quality and I felt myself relax a little more. It was nice that we could be friendly again. I looked over at Caleb and Morgan sitting to my right. Morgan gave me two thumbs up and Caleb just raised one eyebrow. I shared a secret smile that was just for him. He turned back to the show, but not before I caught the satisfied expression on his face.

Good. I would do whatever I could to make sure Caleb felt secure in my feelings for *him*. Nothing was worth losing his trust.

Suddenly all the lights extinguished on the entire Southern Beach, even on the Tower. A single rocket shot up over the ocean and we all watched its ascent with breathless anticipation. When it exploded, the flames took the shape of pictures. The pictures zoomed us closer to an Island with a beautiful tower on a beach. But I soon realized this was not the new tower Gabriel had just built. This was the tale of the original Watch Tower and of the stories from the ancient texts that involved a prophecy and a promise. As the images formed through chromatic light and flame against the backdrop of the dark sky, a female voice narrated the events.

I gave my attention over completely to the retelling of the Island's history—of a promise for peace that had not come, of the sacred tradition of the Guardianship. Until the Pilgrim came, the Island would set a tribal symbol in the sky every thirty years on the night of the new Guardian's birth. The Guardian was to protect and govern the people until the Pilgrim arrived—or so this was how the people of the Island interpreted the various visions and prophecies contained in the ancient texts.

In this particular story, the events of Gabriel's own birth were replayed. Just over twenty years ago, Abrianna gave birth at the Palladium to a baby boy. Shortly thereafter, the stars above took the shape of Pyradora's tribal symbol—the mountain with four rays coming out of the top. The only baby born that day with a Pyra symbol was the Guardian's own son. The people of the Island were shocked. However, they believed this baby was born for a special time and purpose, as all Guardians are.

Trusting the will of the Island, the people watched this boy grow up and take on more responsibilities. There were flashes of what I could only guess were scenes from Gabriel's childhood. He was a terribly cute little boy, with springy curls. I was mesmerized as I watched six-year-old pudgy-faced Gabriel teach himself how to make little Firelight creatures and flowers that danced around his face. His eyes were magnified with joy as he entertained himself. Then the images flashed forward a few years to where he looked like a preteen. He marched around a field with a little girl in tow, colorful flowers woven into her hair. At first, I was stunned to see the likeness of Elon in this little girl. But as the narrator talked of Gabriel's training in each village and his one infamous explosion in Geodora, I quickly realized I was looking at a young Eden, with her hands on her hips, correcting Gabriel's behavior.

I snuck a glance at Gabriel and found him smiling to himself as he watched the scene. When he felt my eyes, he gave a slight shake of his head and whispered in my direction, "Eden must have made them include that part. She loves to remind me of the day I accidentally set the field on Fire. Even though it really was her fault."

I just smiled back with curiosity and asked quietly, "Did she help you plan a lot of these events?"

"Of course. She has been my Personal Advisor since you left," he informed me. Then I felt his mood suddenly shift when he added, "I believe you were the one who recommended her." He directed his gaze back to the show, but I continued to study him.

What did that mean? Had he made her his Personal Advisor simply because I had suggested it? Or was there more between Gabriel and Eden after all? When I suggested that before, I had secretly believed that Eden could be a good romantic match for Gabriel, and I thought my hint had been pretty obvious. But if that had actually transpired between them, then Gabriel would not be using *me* to give the crowd a love story. Good grief, what was his problem?

"Is something wrong?" Gabriel finally asked, glancing back at me. I guess I had been staring too long.

I resisted asking more questions about what exactly was going on in his mysterious love life and just shook my head innocently. We both turned back to the light show in the sky and watched images of Gabriel training in offensive life forces. His powerful presence when he wielded the effects of the Fire life force made for some breathtaking scenes. Muscles rippled as he moved within their strange fighting formations, explosions bathed him in a yellow glow… By the crowd response on the beach, Gabriel had some devoted fans out there. I rolled my eyes at Caleb and Morgan. Caleb leaned back in mild disgust while Morgan watched appreciatively.

And it was only because I was looking away from the show and over at my friends that I saw exactly what happened next. A rocket-looking flame had launched from the beach, but instead of exploding into more images in the sky, it was on a clear flight path to the top of the Tower where we sat. Was nobody else seeing this? Everyone seemed immersed in the sexy images of Gabriel in the sky.

"Gabriel—" I started, but a brilliant display of lights and colors exploded in the sky as the dramatic finale to the light show hit its stride. For a second, I was almost blinded along with everyone else on the Tower. But not enough to realize that that fiery ball of destruction was about to detonate on *us*, instead of as part of the show.

Something told me an Earth shield would not protect all of us and definitely wouldn't be big enough to save the tower from certain collapse. With quick instincts, I darted forward in front of the others and pulled every bit of energy from every life force that I could. I shot two white beams of energy at the rocket-thing and missed.

"Get down!" I screamed and my third attempt hit its mark. The collision caused an explosion of flames, combined with two white electrical rings that rippled outward from the epicenter of the impact. When the beams of energy flashed over us, everyone was thrown backwards from the force. Only Dad and I remained standing—except now I was glowing with the exertion of all four life forces.

In front of the entire Island.

10

THE BEGINNING
OF A BROMANCE

I was a little slow at first to understand what had happened. Whitnee held her hands out in front of her in a state of awe and fear. She was coated in white light, and I knew the amount of life force power she was channeling at the moment could spin out of her control very quickly.

"Defenses!" Levi shouted, as if we had not already jumped to the alert. Ezekiel, however, looked as if he might collapse for good beside Nathan and Sarah. My gaze found our new Pyradorian Elder, the one who had been in charge of the light show.

"Jesse, what just happened?" I called, trying in vain to keep the accusation from coloring my tone.

"Your guess is as good as mine, Gabriel. I am on this tower with you," Jesse replied, and his perplexed expression was genuine. I still could not bring myself to trust that man.

"Gabriel, the crowd." Abrianna gestured over the balcony. I paused long enough to look and listen. Were those applause and cheers I heard?

"They think it was part of the show," Nathan realized. "Whitnee, get inside." She immediately obeyed and Nathan assisted his parents back into the Tower. Ezekiel was supposed to make the closing comments, but he was clearly not able. I looked to Abrianna as I debated what to do. She gave me a subtle reassuring nod and turned to address the crowd, using her Aero abilities to magnify her voice.

"This concludes our opening ceremony. Thank you for joining us for such a historic occasion! Please consult the Festival schedule for the activities in each village this week. Tomorrow we start the Tribal Blessing Rituals in Aerodora, my home village. As for tonight, the celebration on the beach will end at midnight..."

Abrianna continued with the instructions, her voice never catching with the fear that I could sense coming out of her. As she carried on, I scanned the sky and the beach for any signs of attack, my hands fired up by my sides. Had that been a rogue Pyra-tech accident or was someone aiming at us? Either way, we were fortunate that the crowd believed it was part of the show for Whitnee to display her powers like that.

As Abrianna finished, I extended my arm to her, waiting to escort her inside. We paused as Levi coordinated the Palladium Geoguards to construct a wide-ranging shield over the Tower. I wondered if that would have been powerful enough to stop the explosion had it been there in the first place. I had my doubts.

Zebedee placed a zephyra in my hands the moment the door closed. "It is Thomas on the ground," he explained. "Says he has the Pyra technician responsible for the glitch."

Thomas appeared on the screen with a Pyradorian I recognized. His name was Shad and while he was certainly a mouthy member of my tribe, to my knowledge he had never done anything to hurt others. "Shad, what happened to your Pyra-tech?"

"Sir, I launched it during the finale and the next thing I knew, it was out of my control. As if someone else took command of it," Shad explained, wide-eyed.

"How is that possible?"

Shad shook his head vehemently. "I do not know. But it was not me. It happened so fast that I did not even realize where it was heading at first. You have to believe me."

"We will question all of the technicians," Thomas added. "Maybe Levi should deal with Shad. I cannot tell if he is lying—"

"I am not lying!" Shad insisted, but Thomas dismissed him to someone else's custody and stepped away to talk privately with me. I tried not to think again about how much I needed Eden. Nobody could detect a liar as well as she could.

Eden will spit Geostones when she hears about this. I was certain I would not be able to stop her a third time from leaving Geodora.

"Gabriel, Eli is missing again. Hannah has a team looking for him," Thomas said quietly and I could read in his expression where his thoughts were heading. Eli could easily have overpowered that Pyra-tech.

With a sigh, I said, "Keep me updated. I want him locked up in the Tank and questioned as soon as he is found. Escaping a second time means he cannot be trusted to behave at these events. We need to find out how his security detail keeps losing him. And relieve them of their duties."

"Agreed. I will meet you later."

I slammed the zephyra closed only to realize that my mother still had a grip on my arm. She had turned almost as pale as the silver streak that ran through her hair. "Eli is loose?" she whispered.

"We will find him."

"Surely he would not be the one…" But she stopped because we both knew that surely he would. It mattered not how well Eli had behaved the last year under house arrest. He was still the violent and controlling man he had always been.

"Don't touch me!" Whitnee shrieked, drawing our attention as she shuffled to the corner of the room, trapped in a silver net of light. Nathan restrained Caleb from approaching her. "Is Poppa Zeke okay? I'm so sorry!"

"Nathan, she is not okay," Caleb said. "She's *vibrating*."

He was not wrong. Her appearance seemed to be blurring. Why had she not stopped glowing yet?

"Whitnee, can you disconnect from the life forces?" Nathan asked, stepping closer to her. She slammed her white eyes closed as if she was in pain and wrapped her arms around her stomach. Her necklace glowed so brightly, I worried it would explode.

"I'm trying! Do you hear that? That voice?" She looked up at her father again. "Is that you in my head? I've heard it before."

Nathan shook his head. "No. What is it saying?"

She gasped again as if she had been hit with a Firedart.

"Baby Doll, try to subdue the life forces. I'm afraid if I touch you, our life forces will combine and overwhelm you. You have to get it under control," Nathan coached. We all watched with bated breath as she struggled through it. I had seen her use all four life forces at the same time before, but she had never exhibited signs of pain. Clearly her attempts to gain control were not working.

"She cannot stop them alone," I said and strode across the room, knowing we had to do something. She saw me coming.

"Don't, Gabriel. I could shock you!"

"Would not be the first time," I muttered and melded my hands to hers. The shock rippled with a burn through my whole body, and a gust of energy pulsed out around us. Despite the sharp stabbing in my chest as I felt the pressure of her life forces coming up against mine, I exerted my tranquility force through our connected hands. This had always helped her.

But when she stopped breathing for a prolonged moment, I feared I was wrong.

Then the life force pressure around us collapsed and so did she. Right into my arms. Like she always did at some point. It was the most natural moment I had experienced with her so far.

"I'm fine, I'm fine," Whitnee muttered as she tried to regain control of her own body. Maybe she was, but a small part of me was not ready to let go of her. Without her permission and with great care in front of everyone, I swept her up and carried her to the couch. The tickle of her hair on my neck and the scent of her otherworldly perfume light on her skin brought back feelings I thought I had subdued. I hated them and craved them at the same time.

I did not have to look at Caleb to know everything I had just done irked whatever friendly feelings he had toward me. There was palpable irritation in the atmosphere between us. Maybe I should not have found satisfaction in that, but I did. Caleb might know Whitnee better on the Mainland, but he was no match for her on the Island. You cannot shrink from people with power. And that is what he always did.

To my surprise, though, Whitnee was doing her own shrinking away. I could not remember a time when she had not subtly leaned into my arms or tightened her grip on me when I touched her. So when she held herself very rigidly against my body and kept her face turned away as much as possible, the message was clear. My touch was no longer welcomed.

Once I deposited her on the couch next to Ezekiel, someone handed her Water and a thousand questions were fired at her from every direction. I stood back and let her father and friends attend to her, waiting impatiently for her to speak again.

Finally she leaned forward and focused just on Nathan. "I don't have life forces right now, so I can't—" She gestured to her head, signifying that she and Nathan could not communicate privately through their minds at the moment. Good. This was no time for their secrets. Her gaze rested on me for a few seconds. "Thanks for your help, Gabriel."

I tried to let that assuage the rejection I felt moments ago.

"That's it. First thing in the morning, you three are going back through the portal," Nathan announced to Whitnee and her friends.

Whitnee eyed him suspiciously, but Caleb was the one who addressed Nathan with fierce determination. "Either we all go or no one goes. That includes you, Nathan."

His words made me wonder about the relationship the two of them had developed. There seemed to be a mutual respect there— enough to give Nathan pause.

"I'm not repeating last summer," Whitnee added.

Nathan caught my eye, as if sending me a reminder to remain quiet about our earlier conversation. "We will leave that part up to the Island, Baby Doll. I think you need to rest for now."

"Fine," was her only response. It was perhaps the most dangerous response Whitnee ever gave to anyone. And I do not believe I was the only one in the room who found her passive agreement disturbing. After a moment of confused silence, I took control again.

"I believe we need to arrange transportation for Ezekiel and Sarah to go home tonight. He will need rest before the Aerodorian Blessing tomorrow. And that leg needs some attention." However, it was not Ezekiel's leg that really concerned me. It was his overarching frailty that had become more and more pronounced over the last year—a deterioration that did not seem to be missed by his son's keen eyes.

"That might be a good idea," Nathan agreed slowly.

To our surprise, Ezekiel's eyes filled with tears. "Please do not separate me from my family before it is time, Gabriel."

I had seen the Elder demonstrate a theatrical personality most of my life. But never tears. And never with such vulnerability. Whitnee laced her hand with her grandfather's and rested her head on his shoulder. "We're right here, Poppa Zeke."

There was so much tenderness there—a kind of family love and loyalty I had never known. And probably never would. However, very few people had garnered my loyalty and respect the way Ezekiel had—I would not want to cause him pain of any kind.

"Very well," I said. "I have other matters to tend to. Excuse me."

And I withdrew to the office, uncomfortable with all of the emerging emotions in that room.

Four more days and the Guardianship ceremonies would be over. Four days of travel and festivities in each tribe with a closing feast at the Palladium. Four days in front of crowds, saying the right words, graciously accepting the tribal blessings, and acting exactly as everyone on this Island expects.

And if I did not start getting more sleep, it would become four days of endless torture.

I trudged to the common room in search of food and maybe some spirited drink to help me sleep. No sooner had I poured the sharp-smelling liquid into my glass than I realized that I was not alone. Immediately I called the lights to full brightness.

Caleb lounged on the couch, staring out the window. "Guess I'm not the only one who can't sleep tonight," he noted, barely glancing over at me.

I reached for another glass and poured him a drink. He looked like he could use it. "Are the girls asleep?"

"Yeah. Morgan just went to bed a little while ago. Whit was wiped out the moment her head hit the pillow. Those life forces mess her up, man." He shook his head and rubbed his eyes. "This day will never end."

Wordlessly, I held out the second glass to him and he seemed surprised by the offer. Once he took it, I lowered myself into the chair across from him, curious to know what kept Whitnee's Caleb up at night—and why I sensed so much fear clouding him on that couch. But I did not ask. In fact, I could not think of one thing to say to him. Caleb and I had not exactly been on the best terms in the time I had known him. Being in love with the same girl had that effect.

We sat in silence for too many agonizing moments. Finally, he took a drink and proceeded to spit it back into the cup. "Ugh. Does this have alcohol in it?"

I gave him a strange look. "Do you mean spirits? It will help you sleep. Unless you are easily intoxicated…"

"I don't drink *spirits*," he said and set the glass down on the table with finality. What kind of a man did not drink spirits? "Besides, sleep isn't really a priority right now."

I shrugged. "I suppose you will be leaving the Island in a matter of hours anyway."

He snorted derisively. "You don't really believe we're leaving through that portal today, do you?"

"Nathan said—"

"I know what he said, but I'm not stupid. When have we ever left this Island on terms we all agree with? Whitnee and Nathan are hiding something—maybe even from each other."

I was impressed. Apparently Mainlanders had their own brand of magic for detecting lies—or maybe Caleb was just naturally good at it.

"And I'm the one who isn't leaving this time unless they all go back with me."

I respected his loyalty, but I had serious doubts that he was the one in control of that decision. Nonetheless…

"I suppose we shall see."

Caleb stood to his feet and stretched. "Do you think I could get permission to go down to the beach? I just need to go for a run or something."

I thought for a moment. That actually sounded enticing. With casual cautiousness, I asked, "Would you mind some company? I could use some exercise myself."

He raised his one scarred eyebrow at me. "If you think you can keep up."

That sounded like a challenge I would have no trouble accepting. "Then let us go. I am sure I can find you some comfortable clothing. And we will have a Geoguard gift you with life force, just to keep things interesting."

Twenty minutes later, we exited the Watch Tower and stretched on the front terrace as the clean up crews worked through the night to tear down the tents from the opening ceremony. The general public had been given a forced curfew to abandon the premises and return to their villages in honor of the week's upcoming schedule. Of course, there would still be a crowd from every tribe who would travel to each village to witness the blessing ceremonies.

"How about we follow the shoreline to the cove where I first met you?" I suggested, trying to stretch the tightness in my legs that continued to plague me since the drakon venom last summer.

He rolled his neck around. "Sounds good." And as if we heard the same cue, we launched into a sprint down the newly paved path. Eventually the path would end and it would just be a sandy beach. I still towered over Caleb by a couple of inches and though he had filled out some since I had seen him, I was still bigger. I should have had no trouble surpassing him.

Except that he was *fast*.

I was positive the sand would slow him down, but it was as if he regularly ran on a beach. Did they have beaches in the Texas that he came from? I did not remember seeing sand during my brief hours there. The gap between us started widening and I pushed harder in the moonlight.

I knew that my Palladium guards followed us from a distance, but they had been instructed to give us as much privacy as possible. I did not like the idea of them seeing me unable to keep up with a Mainlander. But no matter how hard I tried, I remained consistently behind him.

I could trip him with a Firedart… But I dismissed the temptation.

Sure enough, Caleb made it to the rock piles a full ten seconds before me. Not that it was a race. We were just out for a run on the beach, yes? I fought to hide the stitch in my side, regretting the times I had skipped my exercise routine lately. Blast those drakons! And I blamed Eden, as well. *Gabriel, your schedule is too full today.*

Exercise tomorrow. I would be sure to overrule her in the future.

"That felt good," Caleb gloated, hardly winded.

"How about a swim?"

He gazed around at the moonlight bouncing off the ocean. "Sure."

I pulled my shirt and shoes off and marched over to the rocks. "We will jump off the rocks into the cove." I was fairly certain Caleb had an issue with heights.

"Really? From all the way up there?" His hands raked through his hair as he stared up at the top. Not even the darkness of night could hide his discomfort.

"If you are afraid, you can stay down here—"

"Dude, *please.*" He rolled his eyes and shed his shirt and shoes. I turned my face away before he could see my smirk. We climbed in silence, feeling in the moonlight for the best route upward. Once we reached the top, Caleb's breath seemed to be coming out in shorter pants. "Are you sure that's deep enough for us down there?"

"Pretty sure," I said. "This is where Whitnee fell in last summer."

"Yeah. Question about that, and don't lie to me—you saw her on the beach long before she ever saw you, didn't you? You had already planned to reel her in with your muscles and long hair and all that aloof crap. So you took off your shirt and pretended like you were just taking a sexy little swim until *she* found *you.* Am I right?"

Apparently there was no fooling Caleb on *anything.*

"*A sexy little swim?* I already said you were not my type, Caleb."

"Answer the question, man."

"I cannot confirm any of that," I replied, not wanting to give him the satisfaction of being right. "But neither will I deny it. In any case, is it my fault that she liked what she saw?"

Ah, there it was—that spark of outrage in his face that said he wanted to pound my face into the rocks. I gave him one big smile before diving over the edge of the little cliff. A certain exhilaration came over me as I fell through the air and plunged into the cool water. When I returned to the surface, it felt like maybe some of my cares had settled down to the bottom of the ocean. I was surprised to see that Caleb had actually jumped in right behind me. I immediately started powerful strokes toward the shore. He would not beat me again.

This time he was the one ten seconds behind. He plopped down on the sand facing the water, and I decided to join him and catch my breath, pretending that ridiculous pain in my side was not there again.

"Just to be clear," I said through deep breaths. "No matter what has happened between Whitnee and me, she always chooses you. And probably always will."

"I wish I believed that."

That caused me to study him a little more closely. Did he really not know that Whitnee was in love with him? No matter how many times I had kissed her, I knew Caleb was not far from her mind. It was her unfading loyalty to him that chained her with guilt every time she wanted to give in to *me*. I thought back to Morgan's comment about the lack of commitment between Caleb and Whitnee. I had never heard of two people who so clearly cared about each other but took so long to commit.

"You hesitate too much, Caleb. Sometimes you just have to abandon caution and take what your heart wants. Before it is too late."

His eyes illuminated with the green glow of life force as he manipulated the sand under his hand into rippling waves. "Nice. Now I'm getting advice from the guy who caused my problems in the first place."

"I had mere weeks with her. You have had years," I reminded him. "Maybe I am not your problem."

His only response was to mold the sand into a compacted stone and launch it into the cove. Maybe I could not understand Caleb's reasons for hesitating with Whitnee, but I did understand the life force language of frustration. I shot my own Firedart into the ocean, making sure it landed a little farther than his. He retaliated with another Geostone aimed into the cove. It outdistanced mine by a healthy margin.

If he was going to turn it into a competition, then I would actually *try* this time. I fired up my strength and shot the Firedart high up in the air, but Caleb was ready. He launched a Geostone that caught mine mid-air and exploded in a flash of fire.

"Yes!" Caleb shouted, his hands thrown in the air in victory.

"Shoot again," I commanded, not impressed. Catching on to the game, he stood up. So did I.

"Okay—" He rubbed his hands together and bounced on his feet. "See if you can stop this." I could tell by the angle of his wrist that he was attempting to give the Geostone a right curve. Too easy.

My Firedart traveled around the other direction and met his Stone as if they were heading toward each other. The cracking sound of the two forces as they met each other echoed around the cove and life force rained down over the water like Pyra-technics. I waved to the Palladium guards that all was safe.

"Awesome!" Caleb exclaimed and I felt the smile on my face before I could hide it. He was a worthy competitor. "Let's do it again."

We shot into the cove over and over again—trying each time to create a bigger explosion. I showed him a few offensive tactics to improve his strength, but he was naturally adept with his aim and stamina. That part did not surprise me too much—Caleb had always demonstrated athleticism on the Island. I could only imagine what that looked like on the Mainland. It made me ask him more about his sport activities. He shared with me stories of "basketball" and "football" and events called "track and field." Apparently he *was* a trained runner.

We tried to think of ways to uniquely adapt these activities to life on the Island. We decided Aeros would have too much advantage levitating the ball to its destination, which required us to change the rules and parameters of the game. I was fairly certain with Caleb's knowledge and attention to detail, we were on the verge of creating a new Island sport that I could introduce under my Guardianship.

Once we had exhausted the subject, we started back to the Watch Tower.

"Can I ask you something off subject?" Caleb asked as we splashed through the shallow waves. I looked at him expectantly. "Everybody seems to accept the idea that Nathan is the true Pilgrim of the prophecy. But I'm pretty sure I've never heard your opinion on it."

I paused there on the beach, glancing around to make sure my guards were not within listening range.

"That is because I do not have an opinion either way. It seems to me that it is one of those mysteries that we will not know until we *know*."

Caleb nodded as if he understood exactly what I meant. "But here's the thing I can't get past..." He looked as if he was thinking hard about whatever he would say next. "If the Guardian is ordained in the stars as a temporary position until the Pilgrim comes, then it *has* to be Whitnee. Because she was born after you." I felt the heat inside me begin to surge nervously at his words. "That would make you the last Guardian, right? I mean, if the true Pilgrim really was Nathan, then why would the Island still ordain another Guardian after he was born? That should've made Abrianna the last one."

I rested my hands low on my hips, feeling those old questions and doubts rise up in me. Could I entrust them to Caleb? Or would saying them aloud give them power? In some ways, I feared knowing the truth for myself.

As I hesitated, Caleb added, "Gabriel, I don't want Whitnee to be the Pilgrim."

But I did. Because if Whitnee was not the Pilgrim—as Caleb speculated—then what did that make me?

The only answer I could give was: "I believe we will know the truth sooner rather than later." That did not seem to make him feel better. So I added, "For all you know, you will be going through that portal this morning with Whitnee and Nathan and all of this will be over."

I did not understand why, but neither of us seemed excited about that idea.

"You know yesterday was Whitnee's eighteenth birthday, right?" he said. No, I had not known that. I am sure my face showed my surprise because he continued, "Yeah. We also graduated high school. And the life forces just started reacting to her on the Mainland, as if we were here on the Island, but differently. She wasn't even trying to use them. And then, BAM! Right after our graduation ceremony, we transported here. Tell me none of that is a coincidence."

He watched for my reaction. "Am I correct in thinking you have a theory about this turn of events?" I asked him.

"I have a lot of theories—none of which make total sense yet. Maybe we'll know once we're in that portal room again."

I nodded, curious to know more about his theories. Instead, I reminded him, "We should probably return. I am sure the others will wake soon and wonder where we are."

He seemed to agree until a slow smile spread across his face. "You know the girls are still asleep. If it really is our last day here, don't you think a little harmless prank would make things interesting when they wake up?"

I grinned back at him. "What do you have in mind?"

It felt as if Caleb and I had just drifted off to sleep on the couches in the common room when we heard the first scream.

"AHHH! What is—who put a statue in my room?" It was Morgan. "Whitnee! Did you do this?" Caleb's eyes met mine across the room and we started chuckling with pride. He had created the statue out of the sand using the Earth, and I had burned a terrifying face into it. Then we planted it right in front of her bed for her to see when she woke up. Caleb had guaranteed me that Morgan was easily scared. He was not wrong. "Ugh, Whit! I'm gonna kill you!"

We heard Whitnee yank open her door. She must have seen the present we left for her in the hallway because the bloodcurdling scream that took place next was nothing short of brilliant. "*Oh my*— Caleb!" Caleb's head lifted off the pillow and glanced over at me through his laughter. "There's a fish in my doorway! A *monster fish*! Morgan, get it!"

"I can't help you because I'm trapped in my bed by a gargoyle!" Morgan yelled back.

"Daddy!" Whitnee called, then next was, "…Gabriel?" The panic in her voice gave me some satisfaction after the times she had taken me off-guard and "knocked me flat on my butt"—her words, not mine. I bit my knuckles, and Caleb was forced to smother his face into a pillow to keep from exploding into hysterics. Nathan came sprinting through the common room in the direction of the girls' rooms, but he paused when he caught sight of us and the tears of mirth streaming down our faces.

"Somebody get it out of here—ahh, I think it just flopped!" Whitnee cried and her voice started to catch with real tears. That was when Caleb dropped the pillow and we both sat up, a brief shadow of fear crossing over the room. I might have been the one to catch the oversized fish, but it had been Caleb's idea in the first place.

"A fish? Really?" A smile played on Nathan's face, clearly torn between fatherly protection and the unspoken appreciation of male camaraderie. He pointed at Caleb. "Do you *want* her to hate you for the rest of her life?"

"Does anyone care that I'm under attack?" Whitnee wailed. Under *attack*? No one did dramatics like she did.

"Me too!" Morgan howled. I supposed she had her moments too.

That sobered Caleb. He wiped his face and threw the pillow at me. "Dude, if I go down, I'm taking you with me." Then he left to go dispose of the fish. I was still laughing when Nathan cleared his throat and pointed me toward Morgan's room. Dutifully, I left too.

But it was worth it.

11

AN UNHOLY CONNECTION

Entering the Palladium for the second time was like visiting a recurring nightmare—different circumstances, same story. The interior hadn't changed much, but I suppose it did seem less intimidating knowing that Gabriel was in charge now. The few Palladium attendants left there were welcoming and curious—not threatening like last time.

Poppa Zeke, Grandmother Sarah, and Thomas had insisted on accompanying us. Levi reluctantly left his dutiful position as Gabriel's bodyguard to head to Aerodora with Hannah and secure thunderflies to meet everyone at the Palladium. Though Abrianna had secretly turned over her control to Gabriel, she was the one most familiar with the portal workings. Unfortunately, that meant she was still hanging around. I just wasn't buying her lies about not knowing how to shut the stupid thing down.

As we traipsed single-file down the stairwell to the Aerodorian elevator that would take us into the depths of the underground portal room, Caleb poked me in the back. "So are we gonna do this again, Whit? The fun thing where you hide a major secret from all of us right up until transport time?"

We were definitely back in that nightmare again.

Instead of confirming his suspicions, I said, "Morgan, is Caleb trying to talk to me again?"

"I don't know," she replied curtly, not even turning around to look at us. "He's dead to me."

127

"Too far, Morgan Maye," Caleb responded with mock hurt. "Take it back."

"I'll take it back when you and Gabriel fess up to what you did this morning," she retorted. "I peed myself at your little prank. Like, actual *pee*, Caleb."

It was always bathroom issues with Morgan, I swear. Caleb groaned as Gabriel spoke up from the back of the line. "I fail to see any proof for your accusations. Caleb and I could be completely innocent."

That caused me to turn around and shoot them both dirty looks. "As if the blossoming bromance between the two of you doesn't speak loads."

Caleb sent back a copy of my mean mug, but Gabriel's eyebrows furrowed. "What is a *bromance*? Wait—no, I think I understand."

I had to face forward again to conceal my amusement. I was dying to know what Caleb and Gabriel had been up to all night. They had been inseparable all morning and shared entirely too many private jokes to come across as even remotely innocent. Only two idiots operating on a lack of sleep would think it was a good idea to drop an ugly dead fish outside of my room. Like, I would rather Abrianna lock me in that tiny room in the Palladium and shackle me with armbands than ever have to see or smell that fish again. It was maddening that neither of them would rat the other one out, either. The part of me that liked seeing Caleb and Gabriel as friends was a little overshadowed by the uncomfortable part of me that intimately knew my separate histories with both of them. I mean, had I come up in their conversation? If so, under what horrifying context? And if I hadn't, then where did the fish idea come from?

Turds.

We all piled into the elevator. Morgan and I intentionally moved to the opposite side from the boys. With so many people in there, it took both Abrianna and Dad's combined strength to levitate the elevator using the Wind.

You seem too calm about this, Dad spoke into my head.

And you seem too nervous. I raised my eyebrows at him. His silver eyes stared back at me as if he was trying to read my thoughts beyond that. I wished I could read his.

Dad acted as if this would be the last time he'd see me. Normally, I would be furious and fighting with him about going through that portal. But I wasn't worried. There had been a voice in my head last night. And if what I heard was true, then things were about to get interesting down here. I needed to know for myself. And maybe Dad needed a reality check too.

The elevator finally stopped after a long, cautious descent. Everybody but Dad and me stepped out. We studied each other as if in a game of poker.

"After you, Whit," Dad gestured expectantly. With cautious steps, I exited the elevator. One step out and nothing happened. Every step after that was slow and earned suspicious looks from Dad. Ahead of me was the portal, humming with energy. The four orbs that represented the life forces rotated slowly in mid-air above the corners of a perfectly square platform. I remembered what Dad had said last summer about Abrianna's experiments with the portal: *She dug too far and harnessed an ungodly amount of power within that portal room. Now the portal won't turn off. It can still be open and closed for transporting—like opening or closing a door. But unlike before, the door is always there now—the connection is permanent.* It was like the orbs were already set—all we needed was to open the door.

The low vibration coming up from the ground seemed to grow stronger with every step I took into the room. It felt like I was standing too close to a bass speaker; my chest rattled disconcertingly. The others marched ahead of me and circled around the platform that would open up to Camp Fusion once those orbs were activated. An odd mix of feelings surged through me as I re-lived what it had felt like when Gabriel passed me off to Caleb last summer. When I had been ripped apart from a world and a guy that had stolen my heart. Even after almost a year, it was funny how quickly memories could invade my feelings. My eyes found Gabriel's across the room and for a brief second, maybe we shared the same memory.

But before I could give those thoughts a deeper assessment, I ran into a wall.

An *invisible* wall.

When I grazed my fingers across it, I could barely see the translucent shimmer of a barrier. I traced it like a mime in an invisible box, but there was no way through. Everyone else had just walked right past it with no problem.

Except Dad.

"No!" He yelled, pounding his fist on the barrier and drawing confusion from our friends on the other side. "Not my daughter! Please!" While I wasn't surprised by the barrier, I was caught off-guard by his violent reaction. His angry hands beat at it, causing reactive shimmers in the air. The rest of us could only watch with open curiosity. There was no breaking through whatever force field had gone up around Dad and me. The Island was not going to let either of us get any closer to that portal—just as I had expected. And probably as Dad had feared.

"Dad, it's okay—"

"No, it's not, Whitnee! It is *not*," he roared, still looking for a weakness in the invisible wall.

Caleb approached the barrier and extended his hand right through it. Then he stepped over the invisible line to stand beside us, as if nothing was there. "I don't understand," he murmured.

"We can't use the portal," I explained, feeling oddly calm about this turn of events. I tapped the shimmering wall. "The Island won't let us go home."

"This was not part of the deal," Dad continued, raising his eyes to the ceiling. He threw his arms out wide. "You have me here! Whitnee has nothing to do with this. Let her go home!"

Caleb and I exchanged troubled glances. I had secretly always guessed that Dad had worked something out with the Island in order to go home with me last summer. Maybe now he would admit the truth so we could move on with a plan. Caleb grabbed Dad by the shoulder. "Nathan, what does that mean? What deal?"

Dad wouldn't answer, but his characteristic pacing kicked in. The changing expressions on his face combined with his random pauses gave the indication that he was involved in some conversation the rest of us couldn't hear.

"You said last summer that the Island wouldn't let you enter the portal room." Caleb tried again. "Why is it blocking Whitnee now, too?"

Dad shook his head in frustration. "I don't know. I'm the one— she's not supposed to—" He couldn't even complete his sentences.

Abrianna spoke up. "Did you make a bargain with the Island, Nathan? Before you left?"

I might hate Abrianna, but I did like when she asked the questions I wanted answers to. Dad paused and shot her a warning look. "It's not that simple, Bri. I don't *bargain* with the Island."

Poppa Zeke approached Dad with gentleness in his voice. "Nathan, the Island brought you *and* Whitnee back for a reason. She is part of this, whether you like it or not. But that is not necessarily a bad thing. It is time you release some of your control and trust the bigger plan happening here." Dad rubbed his face and took a deep breath. I wasn't sure if he wanted to yell again or cry. Poppa Zeke added softly, "Sometimes our children are destined for purposes greater than we can imagine or protect them from. You are not the first father to have to let go, my son."

Those words seemed to break my dad. He looked to Caleb. "I don't suppose you and Morgan are willing to go back and tell Ben and Serena what's going on? The plan was to go straight to Camp Fusion if anything like this happened again."

I bristled inside that there had been a plan. And I hadn't been a part of it.

"Maybe it's time to bring them here," Dad continued, but then glanced between me and Caleb once. "I don't know what to do."

The discomfort that marked Caleb's face mirrored my own sense of panic. While I loved the idea of my mom coming here, I hated the idea of my friends leaving. Apparently Caleb did too. "You know I don't wanna go through that portal without y'all—"

"I'll go," Morgan volunteered. "You can just leave the portal open for me, right? I'll find them and we'll transport back to the Southern Beach." She crossed over to my side of the portal room and tucked her arm in mine. "Your mom deserves to see this place."

Mom… just the thought of her joining us here ignited hope on a new level.

"What if something goes wrong?" Caleb worried. "You shouldn't go alone—"

"I will go with her," Thomas volunteered.

Morgan beamed at him. "Can Gabriel spare you, though?"

Gabriel didn't really seem too excited about the idea. "We have a tight schedule. I will have to send others to help you back through as I do not have time to travel back to the Palladium until the end of the—" He paused and appeared to listen for something.

A low rumble like thunder seemed to start in the distance somewhere but then grew under our feet. The vibration in my chest grew to uncomfortable levels as it intensified all around me.

"Earthshaker!" Gabriel shouted. What in the world did you do during an earthquake when you were already deep below the surface of the ground? Our only way out was the elevator and that didn't seem like a good idea.

Morgan and I clung to each other, and Caleb instinctively swept us against the wall, using his body as a shield over us. Dad did the same thing for his parents and everyone braced against the increasingly violent shaking. It was as if the Island was being tossed about like a toy in the sea. How was this phenomenon even possible? Would this entire room cave in on us? Furthermore, why did I feel echoes of it *inside my own body*?

"I take it all back, Caleb!" Morgan cried. "I forgive you!"

I dipped my face into Caleb's chest and clung to Morgan, praying it ended soon. I felt his hand cup my neck and pull me in tightly before his whole arm hovered protectively over my head. He smelled faintly of saltwater and sand—exactly as one who had gone fishing in the night would smell.

He was *so* guilty.

But the longer the shaking continued, the more apprehensive I became. Not because I thought we were about to die. No, I was afraid that what we were about to do was breaking a Rule. As in capital R. I didn't completely understand the ancient laws governing this Island, but there was some kind of reverent fear that had struck me with dread. And I just *knew*...

The earthquake ended abruptly and the first words out of my mouth were: "I don't think we should open the portal." My statement came out at the exact same time Dad said, "Do *not* use that portal."

Interesting. He sensed it too.

"Why?" Thomas questioned.

But before Dad could explain, Abrianna called shakily, "I cannot feel my life force." She had gone noticeably white for such a tan person. "Nathan, why can I not feel the Wind?"

"I cannot either," Ezekiel said softly, his hands trembling.

Instinctively I felt for mine and I was certain that all four were still there, not to mention the vibration still humming inside my chest. Everyone else checked for themselves and reported that all was fine. Except...

"Mother?" Dad asked Sarah, and she shook her head.

"I feel nothing," she mumbled, folding her hands in front of her before Ezekiel wrapped an aging arm around her.

"Okay." Dad took charge. "That's all of the Aeros here besides me and Whit. You can't activate the portal without all four life forces. Obviously this is a message."

"They are also the oldest ones here," Gabriel pointed out and earned several perplexed looks. He explained, "Occasionally our earthshakers interrupt the life force connection for children and elderly."

Abrianna pressed an indignant hand to her chest. "I am hardly elderly!"

Dad turned a grave face to Gabriel. "It's time to tell me more about these earthshakers you keep having. When did they start?"

"Right after you two left through the portal. The first one was small and we thought it was just an after-effect of the portal closing behind you," Gabriel told us. "When it happened again, we started examining the volcano to see if it had become active. But there have been no signs of eruption, no smoke, no rising levels of pressure. And Pyras live on the White Mountain for a reason—we would know if it was the volcano. No one has sensed a change."

"Do they always originate from the White Mountain?"

"It is hard to tell, but sometimes I wonder..." Gabriel turned his gaze on Abrianna.

She cleared her throat and said, "They come from that mountain."

"It's gotta be the dang portal," I muttered.

Dad seemed to feel the same frustration as I did because he pounded on the invisible barrier again and made everyone jump. "You should have destroyed the portals like I told you to, Bri!"

"We tried!" she replied sharply. "Show them, Gabriel." She pointed to an ax-like weapon leaning against the wall.

Gabriel took a deep breath, as if uncertain, but then lifted the ax in both hands. As he brought it back for a swing at the closest orb, the one with the Pyra symbol, I yelped in panic. He was going to whack that orb and if he disabled the portal, nobody was going anywhere *ever.*

I wasn't the only one who reacted with a shout, but Gabriel followed through anyway. There was a flash of red light and the weapon bounced off the orb as if repelled by a magnet.

"Dude—" Caleb gasped and I just stood there in confusion.

"It cannot be destroyed," Abrianna said, not taking her eyes off of Dad. "Unless you know something I do not."

"I don't understand," Dad mumbled. "I damaged it once. What did you do to it that you didn't tell me?"

Abrianna just shook her head and lifted her shoulders in a tired shrug. "Perhaps the protective shield was placed there by the Island—to ensure you could come back someday…"

"Or," I accused, "when you merged the timeline between both sides last summer, you made it indestructible. Dad said the portal was an *unholy* connection. And you made it permanent." Was I the only one who saw the connection between Abrianna and every single problem on this Island?

"This is not good," Dad whispered and ran his hands across his face. Nobody said anything for a moment until he spoke again. "The portal in the mountain… is it the same?"

"That we do not know," Gabriel said, dropping the ax. The metallic thud echoed with grim finality. "We have not touched either of them again for fear of causing more earthshakers."

"Have you tried using life force to destroy it?"

Abrianna and Gabriel both shook their heads, and Gabriel said, "We could not risk activating it. Do you mean that even you do not know how to shut them down, Nathan?"

Dad had a strange look on his face then, and I couldn't read it. "We need to return to the surface immediately. I need to think. Everybody, on the elevator."

I had a million things I wanted to say, wanted to ask. But instead I just stared despondently at the portal for a few seconds. Mom and Ben were just on the other side somewhere. What were they thinking? How was Mom dealing with our disappearance this time?

"Dad, can you try to send a message to Ben through your mind? Like you did to me last year?"

Dad seemed to consider it for a moment. Then he closed his eyes and intense concentration came over his face. Everyone grew quiet, especially Ezekiel and Abrianna, who I imagined had mixed feelings at the mention of Ben. He was Ezekiel's brother and the man Abrianna had looked to as a father growing up. He was also banished to the Mainland by her. Because she was an evil, manipulative witch.

"I don't know if he can hear me," Dad said, opening his eyes. "It's fuzzy. My connection to you was stronger, and even then I wasn't sure if I was reaching you. But I tried. Let's hope it translates."

"What did you tell him?"

"That we were all here and safe, but unable to transport back yet. To wait at Camp Fusion until we can contact them again."

A trickle of gloom wound its way through me as I realized Mom would not be coming here. At least not in the foreseeable future. And I had no inkling of when I would be able to cross that barrier either.

"Whitnee?" Dad called when I lingered for too long.

I want Mom, I told him through our thoughts.

Me too, Baby Doll, he answered back. *Let's not give up on the idea, okay?*

I nodded, and his words gave me some comfort. Even if deep down I suspected it would never be that easy.

According to our Dorian friends, "earthshakers" weren't the only strange problems that had broken out on the Island since our departure last summer. There had been unpredictable weather patterns, damaging storms, and, even more upsetting, a growing number of children and elderly members of society losing touch with their life force connection. The malady seemed to target those who were already vulnerable, and it always started off with extreme fatigue. If it happened to somebody more than once, it felt like the stamp of death. Not one person had recovered once it started repeating. Elon had held on the longest, bringing hope to the Island that the Geodorian Elder's daughter might prove that whatever sickness was causing these problems could be overcome.

Until she died a day ago.

According to Gabriel, the earthshakers aggravated the life forces and created another kind of disconnect for people—similar to what we saw with Ezekiel, Sarah, and Abrianna in the portal room. Maybe similar to how I always felt after combining all four life forces. It was almost the same way that storms messed with our electricity on the Mainland—a temporary issue with no lasting effects. Even though the physical damage from the earthshakers had been minimal, that didn't make them any less disturbing.

It was no wonder there was such a sense of hopelessness and fear on the Island. I could sense it in all of them. The Dorians' homeland, their livelihood—*the very foundation of all they knew of the world*—felt out of control. They were powerless to stop whatever was coming.

But then Dad and I arrived.

And this little flicker of hope came to life.

I only wished that the nagging whisper of guilt in my head would go away. The one that kept saying I was to blame for these problems on the Island. Of course I wasn't to blame. I hadn't even been here, and the fact that I could feel the earthshakers radiating out of me somehow didn't mean—

Hey, Pilgrim. The voice chafed across my thoughts and brought me back to the present. There was only one voice that sounded like that and called me *Pilgrim* so boldly.

Boomer! I called out in my head as the thunderflies landed in front of us. Through the wind gusts tossing my hair around, I found the gigantic thunderfly with the trademark circular tie-dye mark on his body. He was my favorite. And those big bug eyes were staring me down.

Hey! You can communicate in my head now, he praised. *About time you came back.* His wings slowed and I left the others behind to greet him with a pat between the eyes.

You look good, I told him with a smile. *Can I ride in your carrier today?*

Always a place for you, Pilgrim, Boomer fluttered a wing at me. *Aerodora, here we come.*

We waited as a Palladium attendant brought some "thunderfly juice" for the three giant bugs to refresh with before carrying us to Aerodora.

When Caleb joined me beside Boomer, I muttered, "Maybe you should shower as soon as we get to Aerodora. The scent of beach and dead fish don't really flatter you."

Completely nonplussed, he threw long arms around me and squeezed. "I bet you'd still cuddle up to me anyway."

I tried halfheartedly to dodge the loop of his mischievous embrace. "No, thanks. I'm still mad at you."

"Of course you are."

"Just tell me everything you and Gabriel talked about and you'll be forgiven." I successfully crept away and placed Boomer between us.

Caleb cocked one eyebrow from across the gigantic bug drinking down his juice. "You sure are worried for someone who claims to have been completely honest with me."

I was the picture of innocence as I replied, "I've been honest with you. You're the one lying about your stupid pranks."

"Yeah, well, I'm about to get payback. You know I don't like riding on the back of these thunderflies." He patted Boomer's head. "You'll go easy on me, right?"

If you want me to give him a ride he will not forget, just say the word, Pilgrim, Boomer said in my head. *I can go higher than I usually do.*

I adored his loyalty. Aloud, I responded, "That's not a bad idea, Boomer."

Caleb's smile dropped. "What? What did he just say to you?"

"If we are to be on time, we must go," Gabriel called out. I obediently found my way to the carrier while Caleb harassed me for more information. Dad gently pulled Caleb back. "Ride in Gabriel's carrier, please. Whitnee and I need to be alone for a bit."

"Oh. Yes, sir," Caleb said. "Probably safer, anyway." He gave me a wave and pulled Morgan away with him. Gabriel didn't look pleased with the new traveling arrangement.

"Perhaps you need protection—" Gabriel started, but then stopped himself at the look Dad and I gave him. We were more than capable of defending ourselves, especially together. "What am

PHANTOM ISLAND BOOK FIVE

I saying?" he muttered to himself and walked off. Caleb pounded Gabriel's back as he passed and followed him with a half smile.

"See you in Aerodora," I called out.

Once we were settled into Boomer's carrier and achieved liftoff, Dad started talking over the wind and battering of wings.

"Level with me, Whit," he said. "Did the Island speak to you last night? When you were connected with all four life forces?"

"I think so," I answered honestly, assuming that was the voice I'd heard. "It said I couldn't leave yet. What did the Island tell *you*?"

"That I couldn't leave, either. But I already knew that would be the rule if I ever came back."

There was a catch in my chest at the casual nature of his words. "So you did make a bargain with the Island last summer, like Abrianna said—"

"No. The Island chose to give me more time with you. The barrier was removed so that I could go home with you. It was a gift, not a bargain." I didn't like where this was going. His eyes were such a clear gray as he sat across from me. His hands didn't fidget. He hardly moved, as if he'd known this conversation was coming. "You needed a father. And *I* needed more time with you and your mother. The Island saw my heart and allowed me to leave. But the condition was set—that I could only stay for as long as you needed me there and the Island could do without me here."

"I will *always* need you, Dad." How could the Island decide when I no longer needed a father? He was supposed to be there in every part of my life.

"You turned eighteen yesterday. You graduated high school. You handled all of the crazy things happening with such grace and patience. You remained calm when I didn't. I could practically feel the end coming and warned your mother something might happen. That's why she was so upset, and why I was so paranoid. But we had a plan. And I know she'll stick to it and wait with Ben at Camp Fusion until we can get in touch with her."

"How could you not tell me about this?" I felt so betrayed as I stared across the carrier at him. "What if the Island hadn't brought me too? I was completely unprepared for you to leave me again, Dad!"

"How could I have let you live in fear of that the whole time I was back? Besides, I didn't know just how much time I had. Could've been days or years..." He sighed. "Less than a year feels like so much. More than I ever imagined I'd have again with you and your mom—but so short at the same time."

It had been entirely too short. "So you knew you'd come back somehow but you didn't know I'd be brought back too?"

"Exactly. And I still don't understand."

"Why did Morgan and Caleb transport? And not Mom?"

"I think you act as a portal sometimes, Whit. That's why you experience life forces on the Mainland—you're channeling it through the portal, a bridge between two worlds. As for Morgan and Caleb—well, who are the two people you're the most attached to? Your power extends to them when it's time. Were you holding onto them?"

I nodded, remembering the moment. I didn't want to let go. "So did I bring myself here or did the Island do it?"

"Oh, I think the Island did it. It's powerful enough to work around or in conjunction with the portals to bring about its will. You are clearly supposed to be here, as proven by the barrier in the portal room."

I sighed and gazed out at the beautiful land beneath us. The trees were taller than back home and Boomer's belly almost grazed their tops. I could see the weightless effort of the thunderfly carrying my friends in front of us and knew that the one carrying my grandparents followed behind Boomer. The peaceful view and the breeze in the carrier helped me remain calm about my next words. "Caleb worries it's the fate of the Island or something, that maybe I'm supposed to stay here."

Dad remained silent until I looked at him again. "How do you feel about that?" he asked.

"I couldn't stay here without you and Mom. Or Caleb and Morgan." It wasn't that I didn't feel a pull toward the Island and its people. I did. More powerfully than I realized. But the separation from Mom and Uncle Ben was ripping me up. If I could get everyone to one place, maybe I wouldn't feel so torn. And the what-ifs of my next thought settled uncomfortably in my stomach. "Dad, what if the portal never lets me through again?"

"I think there is still much to be revealed before you start worrying about that, Whit. The Island is in pain. These deaths and earthshakers are originating out of that. I just do not know yet how and when to fix it. But once we do, things might look different."

"How in the world are we going to shut them down?"

"If the connection can't be physically interrupted, then I don't know yet. When we get to Aerodora, I'm going to study the ancient texts to see if there's anything that might help me understand."

"Do the texts address portals?"

"No, because something like that was never meant to be created."

That's right... an *unholy* connection. Did that describe me then? I was afraid to ask it. Instead I said, "Dad, shutting them down might damage the Island just as much or more than keeping them open at this point." He gave me a perturbed look, so I added, "I don't know how to explain it other than I feel a physical reaction to that portal in the Palladium. I think I really am connected *physically* to it somehow. But then I feel guilty, like I'm somehow the one causing all the problems the Island is facing."

It felt good to talk about this, even though it was hard to understand and even harder to put into words. Did I have a part to play in this just like Dad did?

"I agree we need to exercise caution with the portals—we don't know if shutting the Palladium portal down could cause some kind of physical harm to you. Abrianna might have actually done the right thing by leaving them alone."

I didn't disagree with him or find myself surprised at his theories. A part of me wished the portal to Camp Fusion could just stay open forever. That way, I wouldn't have to decide where to live permanently. We could all bounce back and forth whenever we wanted. But that didn't seem to be an option in Dad's mind.

Just when the cold grip of despair started creeping toward me, Dad reached out and took my hand in his. There was a flash of white light in our eyes as our life forces connected.

"Perhaps we're only meant to be here to help fix things once and for all. Then the choice will truly be ours. I'm hopeful we'll be reunited with your mom and Ben soon. I can feel peace even in these circumstances. Don't you?"

Years of knowing this Island and trusting its good will had trained Dad to look past the situation and find a greater purpose. I couldn't sense it the same way he did, but I could feel peace seeping through the connection of power between our hands. It worked its way quickly to my heart.

There was something so familiar, so pure, about the presence of Dad's life forces when they combined with mine. "Dad, the voice of the Island—the one I've heard in my head several times now—why does it sound similar to yours?"

He opened his mouth to respond, but that was when the other thunderfly leading us—the one with my friends on it—wailed and bucked and then started to fall like dead weight from the sky.

12

MIRACLES AND MISFORTUNES

"**D**ad, they're falling!" I screamed in horror as Caleb was tossed over the side of the carrier. Dad shot a levitation Wind to try and stop him from falling, and Gabriel reached out and grabbed onto Caleb's arms just before he himself was airborne. The bug seemed to have just stopped flying completely, and in a matter of seconds it wouldn't matter how good of a grip Gabriel had on Caleb.

Something is wrong with my friend, Boomer called. He dipped and dived to get closer to them. Morgan's screams on the wind shattered my nerves, and I couldn't take my eyes off Caleb dangling over the side—

"Whitnee, you have to help me levitate that thunderfly—they're going to crash!"

I leaned out of our carrier and mustered all of my Wind energy to slow the thunderfly's progress. It was *heavy*. My arms actually felt the pressure of the weight as I exerted more power. I pleaded inwardly with Gabriel not to let go of Caleb.

"Dad!" I reached my hand out, thinking maybe if we combined our life force energy together, we'd have more control. He caught my hand, and the clap of life forces strengthened our connection to the thunderfly. With just a few yards left to the ground, we were able to cushion the blow enough for the thunderfly to bounce and skid to a stop. That was the point that Caleb disconnected from Gabriel and his body rolled on the ground. A Water tunnel went up around him and blocked my view. Boomer hadn't even touched down totally when Dad and I jumped out and ran.

"Caleb!" I hollered and adrenaline propelled me toward the dissipating Water tunnel and his still figure. Dad ran to the carrier to check on the others.

By the time I reached him, Caleb groaned and turned over on his stomach.

"Tell me you're okay!" I cried.

He held up a dripping index finger and then crawled to a bush where he puked up his breakfast. Okay, that wasn't necessarily a bad sign. But I had never seen Caleb shake the way he did when he yanked on a giant leaf and wiped his mouth and face.

When he sat on his knees, he cleared his throat and mumbled, "If that's what you and Boomer planned—"

"Stop it." It wasn't funny. "I could've lost you." A strange hiccup escaped me at the thought. I took one hand and indigitated my fingers with his. An orange glow flowed from me to him and his shakes started to subside. Morgan and Thomas crowded around us. "Quick thinking on the Water tunnel. Which one of you did that?"

"Thomas did, after he secured me into the carrier with Water ropes," Morgan said and gave him an appreciative smile as she threw protective arms around Caleb's other side. "That was so scary. What happened to the thunderfly?"

We surveyed the damage on the ground where the giant bug crashed, and then gathered where Dad and Gabriel and the others examined its still body.

"Dead," Dad confirmed, resting a hand on the thunderfly's head.

"How?" Gabriel questioned, holding his body as if he was in pain.

"Heart attack?" Morgan guessed.

"Life force disruption?" Abrianna suggested. Could that cause a thunderfly to die right in the middle of flight? Because if so, I might not be traveling by thunderfly ever again.

"Or poison?" Levi suggested, and all of us looked at him in surprise. "Gabriel, how many people knew which thunderfly you would be traveling in?"

"I just picked a carrier—or so I thought," Gabriel mumbled, considering the possibility.

"There was a guy feeding the thunderflies before we left," Caleb remembered. "Is someone out for you, dude? Or are we going to chalk this up to coincidence again, like the rocket aimed at you last night?"

Abrianna was the next to speak, but it seemed more like she was talking to herself. "Eli is still out there."

Pilgrim! Boomer's voice choked in my head about the same time that he started thrashing around. High-pitched, scratchy noises came from his throat.

"Something's wrong with Boomer!" I shouted, but couldn't get near the bug while he was in such a fit.

"Maybe all of them were poisoned," Thomas realized.

Boomer, what's happening? Can you calm down so I can get to you?

His response scared me. *It is burning.*

"Somebody help him!" I cried.

"If he has been poisoned too, it is fast-acting. A Healer could not save him, Whitnee. Stand back!" Poppa Zeke tried weakly to grab my arm and pull me toward him and Sarah.

Boomer dying? Unacceptable. "Dad, save him, please!" The tears started pooling in my eyes as I watched him struggle to breathe. I dodged one gigantic flailing wing and made a leap toward his face.

Dad was faster than me. He planted his hands on either side of the thunderfly's face, but it wasn't the blue light of healing that glowed in the spaces of his fingers. It was white and it pulsed and flashed like nothing I had ever seen. Boomer became more frantic.

I called out to the bug, "Boomer, Dad is trying to help you. Be still and trust."

Please let this work. Boomer had been such a loyal friend and believer—from that first moment when he chased me down on the Southern Beach to the first time he entered my mind and made me think I was hearing voices. He was too innocent to die by the hands of a murderer trying to get to us.

Within a few seconds, his body went slack and he fell to his side, losing connection with Dad. Tearfully, I turned to Dad. "Is he…"

There was a breathless pause among all of us as we watched. Dad knelt down beside Boomer and listened. Boomer's wing flickered a few times and Dad's face relaxed into a satisfied smile.

"He's okay." Dad wiped the sweat that had formed on his forehead and stood up, only to be tackled by my hug.

"That was impossible," Thomas remarked to the incredulous group. "There is not a Healer who could have done that."

"I didn't heal him," Dad said. "The Island allowed me to save him. Let's go look at this other one too. I'm sure he is about to have the same reaction." Dad moved to the third thunderfly who had been observing his friends fearfully.

I pressed my face to the rubbery space between Boomer's buggy eyes, the ones that had once scared me.

"I'm so sorry," I told him.

There was a wheezy sigh that escaped him as his voice translated statically in my head. *Your father pulled me out of the clutches of death. I guess I have two Pilgrims now.*

I glanced back at Dad doing the same thing he did to Boomer on the other flustered thunderfly. "He's the real Pilgrim, Boomer." Perhaps for the first time, I truly *knew* that. Boomer made a strange, scratchy sound like a moan, so I rubbed his skin and hummed softly under my breath as if comforting a scared child. We both needed it.

Maybe there was a reason for why the mysterious voice I kept hearing practically mimicked Dad's aura of communication in my head. Maybe it was enshrouded in white pulses of light like Dad's because they were the same. Dad didn't bargain with the Island. He didn't have to. Dad *was* the Island. He was a physical incarnation of the Island's soul, born here on its own land and gifted with life forces in perfect symmetry.

It was time to accept the fact that he was more than just my father.

"One more moment, Gabriel. I almost have it," Hannah promised as Jezebel looked on disinterestedly. A glass of spirits rested in Jezebel's artist hands, which were still slightly stained from her last sculpting project. She had not moved from the lounge chair in my guesthouse room since we had arrived, and I lacked the willpower to make her leave. Clothed only from the waist down, I stood obediently in front of a mirror while Hannah made the finishing touches on the purple tunic she had designed for the Aerodorian Blessing ritual. Apparently, she was not pleased with a section of the gold stitching and wanted to fix it—an hour before things would be starting. The longer this took, the more self-conscious I felt about the drakon scars that slashed across my back right in view of the four other people in the room.

Levi kept up his running lecture about "assassination attempts" and how "ignoring them would be a lesson in foolishness." Nobody could figure out how or when the thunderfly juice stored at the Palladium had been poisoned. Had it always been that way? Or did someone slip it in there just for today? It was unclear, and that distressed Levi greatly. I was concerned and, yes, I was somewhat listening as he and Thomas launched vehement diatribes in my direction.

Thomas chattered on. "It took some intense concentration to answer the questions for the Zephyra Broadcast, and I believe I deserve an award for the fact that no report went out to the entire Island this morning mentioning a possible assassination attempt during the opening ceremony. Even when the correspondents asked some ridiculously suspicious questions about that explosion Whitnee deflected."

"You want an award for doing your job?" Jezebel asked. "Were you not brought on to coordinate the broadcasts and make Gabriel look good at all costs?"

She was not wrong, but Thomas flung back, "I was joking, Jezebel. Although, yes, some praise around here would be nice. I miss Eden. She at least tries to make me feel good about myself." He threw a mock-hurt expression my way.

"I think you are doing a wonderful job with publicity, Thomas," Hannah mumbled with a thread hanging out the side of her mouth. "I noticed the thunderfly death was also explained as accidental. And it enabled most of the report to focus on our beautiful Watch Tower and the excitement of the Pilgrim arriving."

I had to work harder than usual to keep my frustration from boiling out of my mouth. This entire week of festivities was becoming more daunting. We all felt it. That nagging sense of doubt in the back of my mind—the part of me that wondered if I was really fulfilling a destiny or just masquerading as someone with a purpose—kept fighting to take over my focus. I could not give it too much thought if I was to survive the week. Besides, there was no going back twenty years to erase the night I was born with all of this responsibility heaped on me.

Levi picked back up where he had left off. "Our security has already been stretched far beyond our resources. And now we have the Travelers to worry about—"

"I am confident Whitnee and Nathan can take care of themselves," I reminded him. They had already saved our lives twice in the short time they had been here. And Nathan saving two thunderflies from what had been confirmed as a deadly concoction of poisonous chemicals in their bodies was nothing short of a miracle.

"Whitnee and Nathan's abilities do not change the fact that someone is out to kill you. Maybe to kill all of us. And what about the protection of Morgan and Caleb? What about the fact that our group jumped up four extra people at all of these events? We were not equipped for that, and without Eden—" Levi paused and took a deep breath. "Hannah, do we have any word yet about where Eli might be? Surely Abrianna and I are not the only ones who believe he is orchestrating all of this."

Hannah glanced up at me first and then at Thomas and Levi. The scar along her neck tightened along with her muscles. "Once he overpowered his security detail, nobody could track where he went. It is as if he disappeared from the Island."

Of course he disappeared again. It was a talent of his. No matter what, my father remained committed to the preservation of his own greed and agenda.

"Did anyone else notice that Eli's disappearance was also conveniently absent from the Zephyra Broadcast?" Thomas jumped in. "Just me, then? Very well. I will accept my award when Eden returns."

"I would be happy to award you a kick in the arse," Jezebel responded. "These shoes are especially pointy today."

I should have locked Eli up in the new Tank we had built on the northern side of the Island as soon as it had been ready. It had been my own weakness to think that house arrest would suit him the way it had Abrianna.

Levi continued, "The problem with Eli is that we have no idea what other secrets he knows about this Island from years of ungoverned power. He could have several hiding places that we have not discovered yet."

"I agree with Levi," Hannah added. "I would not put these attempts to hurt us past Eli's range of ability."

"He did escape as soon as he had the chance last night," I agreed. "But the assassination threats started long before that." I watched Hannah's disfigured fingers stumble in her work for a moment and hated Eli for marring her beautiful skin and talents. Hated how his black rage invoked such fear in my friends. How they remained loyal to me despite my parentage was a gift I still could not make myself understand.

"Even under house arrest, he could have had people working with him—loyalty can be bought these days, and I am confident he still has influence with certain people. Which means there could be someone close to us giving him access to your plans," Levi pointed out.

"Like whom?" I asked. It was the question we often asked that rarely returned an answer. There were not many people left that we truly trusted. However, I noticed through the mirror that everyone in the room glanced nervously at Jezebel in the corner.

Apparently she noticed too. With a bitter snicker and a prolonged swill of her drink, she finally said, "I know what you are all thinking, and I do not trust my parents, either. So there you are. Arrest them if you want. How my father became the Elder in Eli's place is not a mystery. He bought the whole village out."

Of course we all knew that Jesse was a slippery businessman, and none of us trusted him simply because he had been Eli's best friend for so long. But Jesse's charisma, wealth, and extravagant parties were such a contrast to Eli's mysterious authority that the rest of the Pyradorians refused to question anything about him beyond the surface. We only informed Jesse of what he needed to know, and I knew Jezebel did not share information with him. She hardly had a meaningful relationship with her parents at all.

But despite our mistrust of Jezebel's family, we believed Jesse had a lot to lose by assisting in the murder of the new Guardian. If he was still involved with Eli and was the one planning—or even funding—these attacks, I could not come up with a real motivation for it. Additionally, I had not forgotten that he and his wife were on the Watch Tower with us when that explosive would have killed us all.

At the watery look in Jezebel's eyes across the room, I turned away from the mirror to gaze straight at her. "Do *you* believe your father is trying to kill me, Jezebel?"

Her face drooped slightly as she tried to hold my eyes with hers. "I believe..." She tilted the cup to her lips again. "I believe that I have run out of drink. Who moved the bottle?"

Thomas loomed near her with the bottle of spirits hidden behind his back. He glanced around bewildered while giving me a side wink. Thomas and Jezebel appeared to be trying even harder than usual to spar with each other in Eden's absence—as if Jezebel missed arguing with Eden, and Thomas felt that he needed to step into that role for her.

"It is rather early to be consuming so much drink, Jez. Maybe you should wait until we eat something first."

"It is never too early or too late for anything, Gabriel. We do not know if we will have the next moment. I say, drink to it. Here is to Thomas for successfully hiding all the ugly parts of this Guardianship business from the entire Island." She raised her empty glass, and Hannah sighed in exhaustion beside me.

"We will not give evil plans the attention they want," I said sharply, coming to Thomas's defense.

This was a scene we had all grown tired of, but Jezebel had no one if I abandoned her. And I was no longer certain if I allowed her behaviors and presence out of guilt, compassion, or simple cowardice.

"Here, Gabriel, try this." Hannah held up the finished tunic for me to slip my arms into. When I pivoted back around to look in the mirror, I was surprised. I could not recall the last time I had worn purple. Pyras typically avoided it. Even though I had been raised by an Aerodorian mother, I had been all the more opposed to aligning myself with her in that way.

Hannah frowned at me through the mirror. "Do you not like it?"

"He looks like a bloody Aerodorian, Hannah, what do you think?" Jezebel's bluntness always became more pronounced when she over-drank.

"Well, is that not the goal for tonight? To appeal to each tribe uniquely? We are trying to promote unity and—"

I rested my hand on her scarred one before she could get worked up. "It looks just fine, Hannah. You have done a wonderful job with the stitching and captured what is special to the Aeros. Thank you."

"I think you look quite handsome in it. And if you would just allow me to shave your face—"

"Nobody touches my face." I held up a warning hand accompanied by a short laugh. Perhaps I was intentionally bucking against Aeros and their clean-shaven preferences.

"Ah, that dusting of a beard is young Gabriel's work of art," Thomas piped up and propped an arm on my shoulder. His face was impish again as he looked into the mirror. "Makes him look older *and* find favor with the females."

"Really, Thomas." Jezebel stared him down haughtily from behind us.

"You said it yourself: positive publicity is my job." But then he whispered through clenched teeth, "Why do I even open my mouth when she is around?"

"Give me another drink, you thief, and I shall let it go," Jezebel bargained, but we were all interrupted by a knock at the door. Levi was the one to answer with extreme caution in place.

It was Ezekiel and Sarah.

"We would like to have a word with Gabriel alone, please," came Ezekiel's voice. I felt a slight alarm at this request so close to the start of the ceremony. I had felt sure they would be busy right up until time to begin.

Everyone exited the room quickly except for Jezebel. Hannah gave me a tight-lipped frown when she came back to assist Jez's wobbly steps through the door.

Ezekiel and Sarah politely ignored Jezebel's state as they moved further into the room. I rushed to help Ezekiel lower himself into the chair, and he squeezed my hands appreciatively.

"What can I help you with?" I asked them, my concern growing at their grave faces.

Ezekiel did not waste words, which was a noticeable change from his usual verbose personality. "Gabriel, it is time to tell you that I am having increasing trouble connecting to my life force."

My stomach clenched.

With a slow exhale, I lowered myself into a chair close to him and felt my eyebrows knit together in compassion. "When did this start happening?"

"Off and on for the last few months." I could see a tremor in his hands as he spoke. "I wanted you to know because I cannot be the one to give you my life force blessing tonight." He held up feeble hands. "I had hoped it would return in time, but it has not."

I was almost at a loss for words. "I am saddened to hear this, Ezekiel." The three of us did not have to say out loud what this really meant. Rarely did anyone lose connection with a life force more than once and live much longer—especially at Ezekiel's age. My mind unwillingly turned to Elon and I could physically feel the grief threaten to override my carefully constructed composure. Instead, I turned to questions. "Sarah, what about you?"

"I am still connected," she nodded. "And if it is all right with you, I will give the life force blessing in such a way as to make it look like Ezekiel is doing it. We do not want our tribe to know yet. And we certainly do not want to take attention away from you at such a big event—"

"Attention matters not when something like this is happening."

"It is good for the Island to focus on you and the restoration you and Nathan bring together. There is *hope*," Ezekiel interrupted. "Nobody needs to worry about an old man when there are far greater things at work."

His humility would have surprised me a year ago, but not in the man I had come to know so well since then—a man who had discarded caution to support me in this transition despite the murky history between our families.

"Ezekiel." I made him look at me, trying to keep the intensity of grief I was feeling out of my expression. "I fear that this is not happening because of your age. Some kind of *disease* is attacking our Island."

"I fear the same thing," he told me earnestly.

"How do we stop it before it is too late?"

Sarah leaned in closer to her husband. "We do not know, but the earthshakers must have something to do with it. Zeke's first interruption happened in the aftermath of the first earthshaker. Then it came back for a while." This did not bring me comfort.

"And it did not return today after the earthshaker in the portal room?" I clarified.

Sarah replied, "Mine did once we left the portal room. Ezekiel has not felt the Wind for a week now. This is the longest it has remained absent."

"Perhaps Nathan can fix—"

"No," Ezekiel said sternly. "I do not want Nathan or Whitnee to know right now. There will be a time for that. But it is not now."

I shook my head, wanting to argue. But I could see the resolution in their faces. And I respected them enough to obey, even if it was against my better judgment.

"Very well," I relented, trying to turn my thoughts toward logistics to help block out the intensity of emotion boiling inside me. Whitnee and Nathan would be crushed. "So how are we going to do this today?"

13

STARRING GABNEE

It was time to gather our group and make our way down to the lowest level of the treehouse village. The Amethyst Bridge was the centerpiece of the village where they held major events or announcements. The stage located there was visible to the entire village, allowing the Aerodorians to congregate on the interwoven bridges. I had not been there in a few years since most of my business with Ezekiel happened on the third level, but I was confident the surrounding bridges would be filled to the brim with more than just Aeros bearing witness to this event.

As Levi and Hannah bustled around trying to find all of our guests, my eyes spotted pale hair spilling down the back of a dark purple dress on the far end of the guesthouse bridge. I was compelled to go to her, but found myself pausing first to see if Caleb was near. Last time, I did not let his presence influence my interactions with Whitnee.

But now...

He was not in view, so I followed my instincts.

The pink hue of sunset cast a glow on her face as I made my presence known beside her. She smiled—which I took as a good sign—but she did not remove her gaze from the view of the ocean.

"I still remember the first time I came to this village. I stood here overlooking a stormy ocean and there was all this fear and confusion inside me. Tied up with other thoughts and... *curiosities*." Her smile

155

turned secretive and I wondered if she would admit I had been a source of her curiosity.

I dragged my eyes away from her to study the sunset before us. "And what do you feel now?"

"The typical fear and confusion," she answered and I was surprised to glance over and see that serene smile still playing on her face. "But it feels like home too."

Another good sign.

"It could be your home. If you wanted that," I reminded her, trying to keep my voice light, but hearing my tone come out more bitter than I felt at this point.

Her smile dissipated as she remarked, "I'm starting to think what I want doesn't really matter."

"It does to me."

"I appreciate that," she said lightly and I had trouble distinguishing if she meant it. "But you were in that portal room this morning. I wanted to go home, and yet here I am."

"Here you are."

"You sound unhappy about that too."

"Do I?" I leaned on the railing and angled my body toward her. "I suppose I have a lot on my mind. And having you here for all of this was a complication I did not imagine."

She finally gave up her view of the ocean to face me, and the moment that had been missing since she arrived finally happened— just her and me, actually looking into each other's eyes and trying to see beneath the surface. I expected her to launch an argument at me again about how this was not her fault, along with sarcastic comments about how sorry she was to complicate *my* life. So her actual words surprised me.

"Are you okay, Gabriel?"

I swallowed hard and thought about that for a moment.

"Yes." Actually, no. I had to *be* okay whether I felt that way or not.

"When I put myself in your shoes, I think about—"

"When did you put my shoes on?" That was a strange thing to do. She had not been near any of my belongings, to my knowledge.

"What? No, it's an expression." Her laugh transported me back to last summer whenever our two worlds caused misunderstandings.

"It means, when I think about things from your perspective, like when I let myself try to see the world through your eyes... like walking around in your shoes... Get it?"

"Ah, yes. What an odd expression," I commented, tempted to feel dense, but not when her eyes were alight with that affectionate amusement. She had always found our differences fascinating.

"As I was saying..." Her voice grew serious again. "I think about all you've been through lately with your parents and losing Elon and then Dad and me showing up—not to mention people trying to kill you twice in less than a day—and earthquakes, sicknesses and... and somehow all of this responsibility falls on your shoulders." She gazed up at me in concern. "I would want to run away."

My mouth had gone dry as I felt the heat in my chest surge again. She had not even listed everything, and it still sounded overwhelming when spoken aloud. The thought of running away stirred my Pyra instincts in ways only Whitnee's presence brought out.

But I had nowhere to go, and it felt suffocating.

Despite her compassionate words and her attempt to get "in my shoes" somehow, I could not make myself open up to her again. Not yet.

"A lot has changed in a year, Whitnee. This is my life now, and we are better equipped to handle it all than the last time you were here."

"I can totally see that. Your hard work really shows, Gabriel. And if it's not too weird to say, I'm really proud of you. I guess I—" Her hand moved as if she was going to reach out and touch me, the first sign of tenderness I had seen from her. But then she changed directions, swished her hair back over her shoulder, and folded her hands together instead. "I just want to make sure you're okay. And if you need my help with anything or just need to talk—" She stopped herself, maybe sensing how much I was holding back. "I hope you know that I still care and always will. About the *Island*, I mean."

I politely ignored how flustered she seemed all of a sudden. Her concern should not have mattered to me, but it did.

"And I hope you know that the offer to stay on the Island still stands. And always will."

Her eyes roamed over my face then as if trying to sense what I meant behind the ridiculous words I should not have spoken.

But even I was not sure what I meant. I was too volatile, and it was making me reveal long-kept sentiments that had no place in my life any more. While I was not certain when my heart would fully release Whitnee, I did know that what stood between us was different this time. I had naïvely offered her a place by my side, as my future wife, last summer. She had made it clear that was impossible and then vanished. The shame of that memory still stabbed at me as sharply as the drakon venom. A different kind of poison, but a weakness all the same, and I hated it. Last summer, I honestly believed that I would never see her again. Every storm or lightning strike or passing breeze had only stoked the petulant fire inside me. If I hated her, then I would not miss her.

But I did not hate her. And maybe it was time to quit my companionship with shame and anger.

In light of her offer to help me, I decided to take a chance. "May I request something of you during this ceremony? You are free to refuse it."

She gazed up at me with open curiosity. "Of course. What do you need?"

"If I reach for your hand at any point, would you allow that? Or would you pull away again? I want to respect your feelings. And since I am no longer interested in upsetting Caleb—"

"Did you used to try to upset Caleb?"

Her innocence was endearing and I had to press my lips together to hide my smile. She really did not understand men very well. "Maybe I should say that I want you—and Caleb—to trust my intentions. But back to my question about taking your hand—"

"You mean, to bolster an appearance of romance with the crowd? I thought we agreed we wouldn't do that."

"No." I licked my lips because for some reason they had become dry again. "Sometimes it helps anchor me. If someone—if *you*..." Words failed me because this suddenly sounded absurd. I did not need this. I just wanted some semblance of—

"That's fine," she agreed with that pitying compassion still in her expression. How wonderful that she could see what a babbling fool I was. I opened my mouth to take back my request but then she added, "It anchors me too."

In that moment, I believe we understood an aspect of our relationship that we had never defined. Putting aside all the romance of the past, a piece of ourselves needed each other. I was her tether to this reality. She was my connection to a greater purpose. Maybe we were stronger together or maybe it was the only remnant we had of the intimate things we had shared.

Either way… "Thank you."

She took a deep breath and nodded. I gave her my most serious look and said, "I am glad you are all right after all that happened today, especially after being attacked by a dead fish. Who knew they could do that?"

There came her smile again as she pursed her lips and shook her head. The urge to reach out and let her hair slip through my fingers as I had once done was overwhelming. Instead, I held back and enjoyed her reaction.

"You and Caleb might have some sweet revenge coming your way. Morgan and I do not mess around when it comes to pranks."

"Oh, am I to be afraid of you, Little One?" The nickname slipped right out of my mouth so naturally, I did not realize I had said it until after her eyes softened and our chuckles came to an abrupt end. To mask the awkwardness, I added, "If I blamed it all on Caleb, would I escape your wrath?"

"Caleb would not do something so stupid on his own. It takes two geniuses to incur my wrath like that."

"At least you recognize genius."

When I saw Levi waving, I offered Whitnee the crook of my arm to escort her across the bridge. She rested a delicate hand there, picked up the long hem of her dress, and glided the rest of the way by my side.

As we approached Caleb coolly observing us, I removed Whitnee's hand from my arm and held it out to him. "I pass the lady on to you. But be warned, her heart is full of revenge."

Caleb raised his eyebrows as Whitnee linked her arm in his and leaned against him more closely than she had with me. Any discomfort he might have had obviously melted into relief as her body pressed in to his side.

"She's all talk, man," he assured me, and we exchanged looks of solidarity. We were nonplussed by her threats, but it would be entertaining to see what the girls would attempt in return.

I was immediately flanked by Levi, Thomas, and Hannah, who launched into their concerns about the ceremony as we marched toward the treehouse elevators. Levi did not like how open to the public I would be during this ceremony. He had Palladium guards posted on every level watching for suspicious activity. Hannah was concerned about the appearances I would need to make for the ensuing night festival. She was supposed to manage that in Eden's absence while at the same time coordinating the formal dinner right after the ceremony. The decorators had not received a seating assignment list and some other issue with the floral arrangements had irritated her. I feared I might combust if they did not give me space.

As we waited for the elevating platform to be summoned, Thomas started murmuring his fears over Jezebel making a scene during the ceremony.

"I obliged her request for special seating because I did not want her burning the entire village down with her tantrums. But, really, Gabriel, she is not *well* and, as much as I hate to suggest this, she might need—"

But I never heard what Thomas suggested, because at that moment, the platform rose to our level. There stood Eden in a formal gown with shades of fading gray, green, and turquoise —the colors of the ocean—curving invitingly around, well, around *her* curves. Incongruous with her attire was that satchel hanging to one side. Parchment papers, fountain pen, and zephyra were carefully balanced in her hands with that characteristic look of concentration on her face.

I am not sure who was more stunned at the sight of the other— her or us—but my friends recovered before I did and rushed to engulf her in one united hug. They were followed immediately by Whitnee, Morgan, and Caleb.

"Oh, Eden, you're here!"

"Thank heavens. We need you!"

"I am so sorry about Elon. How are you holding up?" The last was Whitnee as she untangled herself from Eden's bare arms and helped rebalance all of her items.

"It is a moment-by-moment grief," Eden told her, but smiled lightly. "I am doing okay right now and am thrilled to see all of you."

She finally turned her sharp green eyes to me, still standing outside on the bridge, unsure of which feeling I wanted to act on more. I felt a visceral reaction at seeing her and yet all I could do was just take a deep breath and slowly exhale. She stepped away from the small crowd and faced me.

"How did you get here?" I asked quietly. It was such an unimportant question, but it was the first that came to mind.

"Abner brought me," she answered just as softly. I felt a confusing twinge of feelings at the mention of the Geoguard's name, knowing he had probably been a great source of comfort to her the last couple of days.

"Oh. That was kind of him. Where is he now?"

"He had to return to Geodora." She studied my expression which reminded me to conceal any emotion. "Do not be mad at me, Gabriel. I needed to come. My family understands how important this is." Her face was both fierce and pleading at the same time. "Plus, doing work might keep me from losing my sanity."

"I have been losing my sanity without you." I confessed the truth, not actually caring if anyone overheard me. Her expression relaxed into a strange kind of relief.

"We might as well lose it together, then."

I felt myself lean in closer so that I could take in her smell, which was always of fresh flowers—like the iridescent bloom in her hair. For some strange reason, I wanted her to fall into my arms again the way she had in Geodora. I was certain it was only pent-up energy over Whitnee. Not because Eden's lips glistened invitingly as she smiled up at me. I probably should have told her how beautiful she looked—even the weary shadows under her eyes did not dull the radiance in her face. That dirty, worn satchel thrown over such a formal dress demonstrated the typical dichotomy of Eden's commitment to soft femininity and relentless work. The heightened and confusing sense of awareness I had for her then frightened me enough to keep me from saying anything.

Instead, I offered her my arm as I had to Whitnee earlier. "Shall we?"

She grinned apologetically at my gesture and then held up her occupied hands. "No time for formalities, Gabriel. Too much to do."

Of course. She was here for business. How ridiculous of me to lose my senses so easily. I stood up straight again and gestured to where everyone waited on the platform, watching. "After you then, Miss Advisor-to-the-Guardian."

She did pause as if she wanted to say more. I suppose she changed her mind, though, because she spun back around to step onto the treehouse platform. It made me think that I should offer my arm to her more often—when she was not busy being my Personal Advisor.

Levi, Hannah, and Thomas immediately started launching their last minute issues at Eden, who already had a plan in place and an answer to all of them. A sense of pride stole over me as I listened to her. That bossy little girl I had known as a child had somehow become my closest ally as an adult, and I could not have been more grateful.

I stepped inside the tree, catching Whitnee's eye on the way. Her curious look had me once again worrying that she had seen something I had not meant to reveal.

The Amethyst Bridge was another gorgeous site in Aerodora that I had never seen before now. The stage and railings were embedded with lilac and orchid-colored jewels that sparkled in the late sun—the rays of which somehow peeked through the throngs of people perched on bridges around us. There were children dangling their feet, kicking around lightheartedly. Older people brought chairs to rest in during the ceremony, but they still leaned forward in anticipation. Babies babbled and grabbed at wind chimes. But most people stood and watched with respectful curiosity.

I let my gaze wander as I took in all the people looking down on us from the web of bridges above. A few onlookers waved at me as my eyes drifted their way, and I smiled in return. My vision finally settled back on Poppa Zeke, who was wrapping up his speech while Gabriel stood before him. Dad stood between me and Eden, and his focus never left his father and mother in front of him as they gave the blessing. I figured it was because he was trying to be vigilant in watching for impending trouble.

What's on your mind? I asked, feeling my Aerodorian abilities to be so much stronger and more natural when in the village.

Just watching, Dad replied.

Well, I could see that. But it didn't explain the sudden concern in his face.

We were probably all a little jittery with these public ceremonies. I couldn't help sweeping my eyes everywhere to make sure another explosive wasn't rocketing our way.

Not that anyone would mess with us once Eden got here. She had positioned defensive guards in a ring around the bridges and insisted on a Geodorian shield around the platform. Somehow they were able to make the green hue of the shield so light and translucent that you almost couldn't tell it was there.

Caleb and Morgan remained dutifully on my other side. Morgan watched the ceremony with fascination, but I could tell in my peripheral vision that Caleb was still trying not to notice just how high up we were in the trees—even at the bottommost level of the village. It was easy to ignore when you were on other levels. But this location definitely made you realize you were in treetops and not on the ground.

I adored this village.

My attention was drawn back to Poppa Zeke as he and Grandmother Sarah raised their hands in the air on either side of Gabriel. A beautiful silvery Wind traced a coil around Gabriel, originating at his head and moving down to his feet. His hair blew around his face and he stood perfectly still as the blessing shimmered and rotated around him. Just as this happened, the entire village raised their handheld wind chimes and set them tinkling all around us. The different tones of clinking wood and metal made a magical melody rise up into the sky and travel over the trees, as if winding its way to heaven. The gentle movement of Wind picked up and seemed to blow all around the shield protecting our platform, causing my hair to tickle my face.

Before I knew it, Eden whispered, "Nathan, Whitnee."

That was our signal to step forward and congratulate Gabriel. Dad took him by the shoulders and they bowed to each other before Dad hugged him. Gabriel's smile seemed guarded as he held one hand out to me—an anchor of safety in this magical world. When my hand slipped into his, I could feel the heat of his nerves leaking out through his Pyra palm.

I directed my most radiant smile up at him in front of the crowd, not as an act, but as a reminder to him that I was proud of his leadership. There was no reason for his self-doubt to creep in and steal the joy of this moment.

He took my other hand and suddenly leaned his face down toward mine like he always did when he was about to kiss me. I panicked and did some kind of a stiff dodging move until I realized he was just dropping an air kiss on my right cheek. The stubble on his cheek grazed my jawline and made me shiver.

"Relax, just a Dorian formality," he whispered so closely to my ear that his breath tickled and made me shiver again.

Why didn't we discuss this formality ahead of time? And, gah, why did he still smell like I remembered? Sun and coconut with maybe something a little new and woodsy within that fresh facial hair.

"Sorry," I whispered back. "Been a long time since you leaned in like that."

When he pulled away, he was laughing, like a genuine laugh. He lightly squeezed my hands, reminding me to soften the death grip I had on his. Despite my panicky heartbeat, my awkward reaction suddenly struck me as funny too, and a nervous chortle escaped. We faced the crowd with hands still linked and waved along with the others onstage. Abrianna came up to flank Gabriel's other side and gave him an air kiss on his other cheek. Just as he had done with me—a formality. Then she joined in the light applause and beamed at her son proudly as if she had always dreamed of this moment when her authority would transfer to him. The crowd picked up volume in their cheers for their former Aerodorian Guardian.

I wished I could trip her in front of the entire village.

"Thank you, kind Aerodorians," Gabriel spoke to the crowd. "The beauty of your village and your hearts shine brightly. I look forward to meeting many of you in person this evening as our celebration continues."

Poppa Zeke closed with a reminder. "Please check your schedules to see which businesses will be hosting our special guests after dinner."

I held on to Gabriel's heated hand until Eden motioned all of us off the stage. The guards remained around us as we moved toward the elevator. Dad lingered to attend to his parents, and as I finally wriggled my hand from Gabriel's to double back toward my family, Caleb muttered behind me, "It's so fun to watch you and Gabriel kiss and hold hands again."

Here it comes. "He kissed the air as a ceremonial formality. And I warned you about the hands; it was just to show a united front. Friend hand-holding. You and I did it for years."

"And there's *never* been any romantic feelings between the two of *us.*"

I took assessment of his rolling eyes, but could tell that he wasn't as sour about it as his words were.

Morgan jumped in before I could reply. "That was the most awkward and robotic I've ever seen Gabriel and Whitnee act with each other. It was almost painful."

I winced. "Do you think people noticed?"

"Not likely. I only noticed because I know how y'all used to—" She stopped at the narrow-eyed look Caleb gave her. "It was fine. The crowd loves 'Gabnee.' *And* it made some of those annoying fangirls up on that one bridge shut up."

Turning my attention back to Caleb, I reminded him, "You know there's no such thing as *Gabnee*. We were just playing the part of close friends—which we're supposed to be. If you need a little reassurance..." I grabbed his hand and "indigitated" my fingers with his. "This is real. Right here."

"Yeah, well, maybe Eden and I should hold hands during the Geodorian ceremony. I'm sure the crowd would love a fake love story for her too. How would that make you feel?"

"I'm pretty sure I wouldn't be the only one jealous." I wiggled my eyebrows which clearly caused him and Morgan some confusion.

But that was all we could say because we caught back up to the others in the elevator. Caleb and I released our entwined fingers but I was glad he remained close. Once my family made it on, Eden took control.

"We are going back up to Level Three for dinner with the Elders of Aerodora and their families. After that, Gabriel, Abrianna, and I will tour the business level to meet with villagers. Perhaps it would be better for the rest of you to remain on the third level until later when we go to the Nightingale. Trying to maintain a secure environment for all of you as we move from place to place is just too much right now. But it will be easy to secure the Nightingale before we arrive."

I bounced on my toes as I thought about returning to the dance club that had captured so many of my favorite Aerodora memories. That was when I had accidentally used Fire for the first time—while dancing with Gabriel.

I avoided any eye contact with him as those moments came charging back to my mind in glaring detail. I avoided Caleb's eye contact too, for that matter.

Ugh. Navigating the present while the past was still so fresh was quite a challenge this time around.

14

PROPHECY PROBZ

Truthfully, the part of me that loved to get dressed up and feel fancy absolutely relished every moment of the formal five-course dinner. Not only were the table settings and decorations silver-brushed and suited for royalty, but the food was a mixture of flavors we didn't get back at home. I wasn't sure half the time what kind of meat I was eating but chose not to ask. (Ignorance is bliss when on a magical Island.) The vegetables, fruits, and desserts were infinitely more flavorful than on the Mainland and I made sure I enjoyed them all to the last morsel.

Conversation was delightful enough. Eden had carefully placed Dad and me close to Gabriel and the Aerodorian Elders; Morgan and Caleb were a little farther down the table with our other Island friends. Every once in a while, my eyes slid to Caleb's at the same time his found mine and we shared a smile or made faces at each other. But when Eden left her place near Gabriel to mingle with the others, Caleb was immediately immersed in conversation with her.

I watched their antics for a while, trying to catch Caleb's eye again. He never looked away from her. Caleb and Eden were two of a kind, and I longed to be down there engaged in whatever revelry they were stirring up instead of sitting at the serious side of the table. It wasn't long before the conversation on my end turned to the Pilgrim, though, and I tuned back in.

One older gentleman sitting next to Poppa Zeke spoke up. "Nathan, forgive me, but I must ask: if you are the Pilgrim of our ancient prophecies, what role do you see yourself playing during Gabriel's Guardianship?"

I sensed Gabriel tense up beside me as we both gave Dad our attention. I was very curious to see how he would respond.

"Well," Dad cleared his throat and lowered his fork. "I am a native Dorian and a servant of our great Island first. I am not a governor. That role belongs to Gabriel and I will lend my support to him in any way that he sees fit."

"And what of the mysterious second part of the prophecy? How do you feel about that?"

Second part of the prophecy? I felt my expression turn to confusion, but Poppa Zeke jumped in quickly.

"Now, Amos, you know in some circles it is not believed that the second line is actually part of the Pilgrim prophecy. It could very well be just a philosophical statement, not one of prediction."

But Amos pressed Dad anyway. "How would you feel about it if it was a statement of prediction?"

Now I saw the discomfort shifting among Gabriel, Ezekiel and Sarah. Dad seemed indifferent as he responded, "It changes nothing about how I feel. As I said, I take my responsibility to serve our Island seriously. I do not know what that will look like. But I trust those answers will be given to me when the time is right." He took a bite from his plate and continued, "Until then, I recommend less focus on prophecies and more on the policies Gabriel would like to implement going forward."

That put a stopper in further questions and instead placed the attention on Gabriel, who wiped his mouth nervously with his napkin before finding his place in the conversation again. While the discussion turned to Gabriel's politics as the Guardian, I tuned it out and talked to Dad in our minds.

There's a second part to the prophecy?

Dad's eyes shifted my direction and shook his head with an expression that was clearly blowing off the question. *Nothing to worry about, Baby Doll. There are disagreements about it.*

Who cares about disagreements? You know the truth.

And you heard what I just said. Again, he seemed too casual. *There's no reason to worry about things for which we have no answer right now.*

But by course five of the meal, I still couldn't shake the questions stirring in my mind. Dad was my protector by nature and, therefore, tended to shield me from things that could be potentially upsetting. The fact that I had never actually gotten to read the entire prophecy in context started to nag at me.

Perhaps I needed a bathroom break.

I leaned over and whispered. "Gabriel, I'm so sorry, but may I be excused to the bathing room?"

"Of course," he answered in surprise, as if suddenly trying to read my motives.

"You all right, Baby Doll?" Dad asked, surveying me the same way.

My smile was innocent. "Yep. I'll be right back." I gave both of them an awkward grimace like I had to *go*, lovingly irked that they both knew me well enough to question me.

On my way out the door, I met Morgan and Caleb's questioning looks and mouthed "*bathroom*." For a second, I thought Morgan would get up and join me, but she was distracted by a question from Thomas. And with a small wave, Caleb was back in conversation with the lovely Eden.

To be clear, I did use the bathing room *first*. But then I happened to find myself at the front of the building instead of returning to the dining area.

The guards outside questioned me when I exited, but the lie came easily. "Poppa Zeke asked me to retrieve something in the Conclave. It will take me two minutes." Though they seemed suspicious, they couldn't argue with Ezekiel's special granddaughter. They stood back and watched intently as I crossed the intersecting bridges to the intimidating entrance of the Conclave. Fortunately, it was unlocked.

Apart from some dim lighting inside the massive foyer, the interior felt dark enough to hide me from the outside windows. My heels clicked and echoed, making me feel dwarfed underneath the transparent dome. As the distant stars in the sky peeked down at me, I marched past the ornate chairs lining the walls where the Advisors had sat the last time I had been here. With relief, I realized the thick oversized book of Dorian writings was still there on the desk where Ezekiel typically sat.

I climbed up to the platform behind the desk and grazed a tentative hand over the open page.

Well, crap. I had no idea where to go to find the Pilgrim prophecy in this monstrous thing. *Really* should've thought this one through.

"Where is it, where is it?" I whispered to myself.

Hadn't it been underlined or notated when Abrianna first showed it to me? I started carefully flipping through the leathery, yellowed pages looking for notations in the text. It was organized into short books, and the paragraphs were numbered. I tried to recall how deep into the book we had been that day I found out about the prophecy.

"Turn to page two hundred and two," a sultry voice called across the vast space, and I shot up guiltily, scanning in the dark. I could barely make out Jezebel's form reclining across one of the chairs that I must've breezed right past. Her legs were crossed over one of the arm rests, allowing her skirt to ride up high on her thigh. "You are looking for the Pilgrim prophecy, yes? Page two hundred and two."

"How did you know I was—"

"Because I know what a nosy little troll you are."

My head snapped back in shock. "Rude!" was about all I could manage in response.

"Oh, you understood me. Do they have trolls on the Mainland then?"

"Only the kind who pose as beautiful girls while treating everyone else like trash." I glared at her and hoped she wasn't stupid enough to miss my dig.

"Glad we understand each other then."

Ugh. How did she just throw that insult back at me like that? I saw the silver glow start to emerge in the palm of my hand. Slapping her with a lightning dart was tempting. But I fought back the life force coming to my defense.

When she untangled herself from the chair, gripping a bottle of dark liquid tightly in her polished fingers, I knew then what was fueling her lovely disposition. She tried to wobble toward me and ended up kicking off her shoes in frustration.

As if that's what was making her off-balance.

Adjusting the strap that had fallen down her shoulder, she plunked her bottle down on the desk across from me, folded her arms and rested her chin there. Bloodshot eyes looked up at me through insanely long eyelashes. Was she expecting me to do something while she stood *right there*? Just staring?

"You know," I said, "it's not nosy when it's my life being affected."

"It is all of our lives being affected. Quit acting like you are special." It was impossible to escape the swirling fumes of alcohol on her breath. She directed her attention to the ancient book resting between us and scrunched her nose. "What happened to this? The words went all wonky."

"You're looking at it upside down, genius." Apparently alcohol lowered IQ significantly. She snorted unattractively but kept watching my hands as I carefully turned pages. In a calmer tone, I asked, "What're you doing in here?"

"Taking a break. Thinking. Or trying not to think." She shrugged her thin shoulders, causing her strap to fall again. What would spoiled Jezebel need a break from? I wasn't going to ask aloud.

"Page 202," I breathed when I found it.

"I suppose you want to understand what brought you back this time."

"Now who's being a nosy little troll?" I started running my finger down the page.

"It should be a third of the way down. No, wait. The other direction. I think." She cast shadows all over the book and her breath was making me sick.

"Could you give me some space or something?"

"Are you worried about it?" she pressed. "Do you really understand who the Pilgrim is and what that means?"

All of her questions caused me to pause and survey her more objectively. Her interest in my thoughts suddenly seemed genuine. Maybe she had an opinion. "What do *you* think it means to be the Pilgrim?"

"I already told you I am trying not to think. Would you leave me alone?"

She was the one asking all the questions! She straightened up, unsteady at first, and then took a savage swig from her bottle. I resisted a retort because she finally stepped away. With concentration, I found the underlined portion of the prophecy. First I backed up a few lines because I had never known the intro leading into the prophecy.

> *Darkness will encompass the White Island and a gift will be sent. Blessed are the tribes who welcome this gift with humility and respect.*

Hmmm. Context actually matters.

> *This is the gift you shall receive: A Pilgrim resembling a native, yet of a pale color and missing birthmark, will appear in the midst of dark times. From this all-gifted Pilgrim, the tribes will learn the way to true peace, and the White Island will prosper.*

Okay, that was exactly as I remembered. And it still seemed as if it could technically apply to either Dad or me. But I read further down, past the underline.

> *Only the one set apart and pure unto the Island will be worthy of the sacrifice of glory, and only the one willing to sacrifice for the unknown will be worthy of peace and restoration. Therefore, live in accordance with the Island so that you will remain vigilant when the day comes.*

I kept reading for a little bit, but it seemed to go on about other things unrelated to the Pilgrim.

A "sacrifice of glory" and a "sacrifice for the unknown"? That word never seemed to invoke comforting thoughts. Sacrifice meant giving up something you wanted, maybe even loved. And my comfort-loving, first-world-problems side didn't like the sound of it.

"Why am I just now seeing this?" I muttered, falling back into the deep cushion of Ezekiel's chair.

Though the secondary paragraph seemed attached to the Pilgrim Prophecy upon first inspection, I supposed it could be speaking generically of all Dorian people. Maybe as a call for how to live their individual lives, as "set apart and pure unto the Island"? I had a feeling I would need to read this entire ancient book in more detail if I was ever to try and understand the principles that governed this Island. My head started spinning with theories, possibilities—some of which nauseated me a little.

My thoughts were interrupted when I remembered the crazy person sharing the room with me. Jezebel was wandering around, snapping her fingers by her side and leaving a trail of sparks.

With an uneasy feeling, I suggested, "We should probably get back to the party before someone comes looking for us."

"Nobody comes looking for me." The bluntness of her reply slapped me with unexpected compassion. She took another drink and then faced me. "Gabriel and I are still betrothed."

Wow. I guess we were going there.

When I didn't immediately respond, she continued, "I thought it was your fault. He fell in love with this magical princess from another world—"

A surprised laugh escaped me. "I'm not a princ—"

"When you left and broke his heart, I thought with a little bit of time things would return to normal. They never did. I blamed his work schedule and how he was always with Eden, who hates me. When he is with her, he seems…" She drank again. "But maybe it is not you or Eden or the Island or whatever destiny Gabriel thinks he is following. Maybe it is just *me*."

It took me a prolonged moment before I found my voice. "Maybe you and Gabriel just aren't right for each other. Maybe there's some other man out there who—"

"Save it, Your Royal Paleness. I have been with a lot of men." She marched up to me and set the bottle down on the desk again. Then she attempted to fix the lock of her hair that had come loose from its pins. "I could have my pick of anyone I wanted. I thought Gabriel was the best choice. But do I really *want* him? I cannot decide anymore. He has changed. And he clearly does not want me."

She was not finding success with her hair and made an even bigger loop on the side of her head. It was so painful to watch, I reached out. "Here, let me help—"

"I have it." She let go and patted the mess as if it was fixed. It wasn't.

I attempted a response. "I don't know why we're even talking about this, but I promise I was not trying to take Gabriel away from anyone. Caleb is the one I want to be with. Gabriel will always be special to me, but there are no feelings like that between us anymore. We've moved on. Maybe you should too."

Her lips slowly spread into a sinister smile that reminded me of the Grinch. "You really believe that about Gabriel? Okay, we shall see how things play out then. Tread carefully. Even he does not understand himself."

I decided I was fully uncomfortable now discussing these things with her. I stepped back down around the desk. "Let's go." Generously, I collected her shoes for her and held them out, but she had frozen with her back to me. Her hands flew to her ears.

"Jezebel?"

"Do you hear that?" Her voice was distorted with fear now. I didn't hear anything other than her sudden ragged breathing in the vast, high-ceilinged room. I reached out to her when she started convulsing with screams. "Make it stop! Get out of my head!" She flailed her arms out as if trying to escape an invisible net. Flames popped and sizzled out of her hands.

"What's wrong with you?" I tried to capture her hands to exert some kind of tranquility force and calm her down. Before I could even touch her, she whacked me so hard in the face that I stepped away to recover my vision. Unfortunately, it wasn't in time to stop her from spilling her liquor all over the ancient book of the Dorian Island.

"No!" I leapt toward the table.

I was too late. Fire sparked uncontrollably from her hands and made contact with the flammable alcohol that had soaked into the pages. Then the world around us began to shake.

15

SEAL IT UP

Jezebel's screams blended with the deep rumble and chaos around us. My mind flitted from *save the book* to *save Jezebel* to *save ourselves*, because I was pretty sure we were having another earthquake and we were on the topmost level of a treehouse village. I had no idea where to go for safety. All I knew was that if that glass dome above us was about to collapse, I didn't want my last memory to be of its shards impaling me.

I grabbed the tormented girl and had to drag her out of the Conclave because her alcoholic butt couldn't do a thing for herself. We barely made it past the immense carved wooden doors before I felt the heat of the flames erupt behind me.

Dad! I called out in my mind, as the shaker tossed Jezebel away from me. A quick impact to the head against the railing of the bridge and her screaming abruptly stopped. She crumpled like a dropped necklace just as Dad and everyone else spotted me across the intersecting bridges.

You were supposed to be in the bathroom! Dad's voice entered my mind.

Jezebel is hurt! I pointed to my feet and tried to drag her back to the solid porch of the Conclave. I will never forget the image of Dad, Caleb, and Gabriel as they came charging across the trembling walkway, the trifecta of my heart when it came to masculine heroism. Nor will I ever forget the sickening sound of splintering wood as the bridge ripped in half. Dad and Caleb were thrown into

175

the air like beach balls on a rippling blanket of wood, while a lasso of Fire whipped out from Gabriel and latched onto a wooden post just as the bridge slapped the side of an enormous tree. With one powerfully bulging arm, he held on and attempted without success to grab Caleb's outstretched hand.

Fueled by terror, I tried to shoot a levitating Wind at Dad and Caleb to slow their fall. My life forces short-circuited coming out of me.

"Oh, not today!" I screamed and exerted all my life force energy, not caring where I pulled from. The white hot electricity sizzled through me, capturing first Caleb and then Dad in a luminescent force field and freezing them in midair.

That gave me a moment to breathe and rise to my knees so I could yank them over to my side. They landed with a hard thud and gasped for breath on the porch, flames licking the edges of the building behind them. I released the pressure around them and realized the earthshaker had stopped.

But the pressure inside me had increased. The white light burned on my skin. I barely caught a glimpse of Gabriel climbing up the collapsed bridge like a ladder. A crowd of people had gathered on the other side to help him up—including Morgan who called out to me, horror painted on her face.

"Whitnee," Dad choked. "You gotta let go of the life forces now."

I don't know how... I wanted to cry out, feeling the panic in my chest. Once Gabriel reached the top and was pulled to safety, our eyes met and I knew we both felt the same thing as we gazed across the destroyed space between us. I needed him. He could collapse this power inside me, like he always had, right? He was strong enough to take the pressure. But he couldn't get to me.

I stood up, somehow noting a tear in my dress at the knee. I took deep breaths, I swallowed, I stretched, but I could not get it to release. Somewhere in the back of my mind, a presence tried to break in. It was obscured by the panic that increased when I realized the trees on this side were about to be engulfed in flames from the Conclave... which could potentially destroy the whole village, not to mention the ones I loved. My gaze rested on Caleb, whose frightened expression was illuminated in gold flickers by the fire that crept toward him.

Something about seeing him scared and in danger brought the pressure down in my chest. This time when I took a deep breath I held my hands out in front of me, palms facing each other, and concentrated all of the electric energy there. There were pops of light reacting to each other between my hands... purple, green, red, gold, and every shade in between. I could discern the unique components of each life force, but in a psychedelic fusion of senses.

"Get down!" I called to Dad and Caleb, my voice coming out thick and distorted. The atmosphere around me took on a jelly-like texture and everything seemed to slow down. I had seen this before on the Island. It was almost like the slow-motion manipulation of the world around me helped me see and sense more clearly. Dad and Caleb obediently hunched down next to Jezebel and, instead of releasing the forces in my hands, I launched them with smoky tentacles still attached. Like a locomotive on a fast track, they rushed around every corner, into hidden spaces, and through the vastness of the Conclave. I wasn't in the Conclave, but I could somehow see the path the life forces took through it. My hands became a vacuum as the wind and flames catapulted back into them. And then there it all was, a flaming globe of energy between my palms that blazed and sizzled without burning me.

The amount of power I felt in that moment was heady. It caressed my skin in new ways and intoxicated me with wonder.

Seal it up.

It was that voice again. The one that had a similar presence in my head as Dad's voice. Where Dad's voice shimmered in white light, this one beamed with authoritarian incandescence. I found Dad's face through the swirling lights and he seemed afraid. There was nowhere to send the fire, no way to release the life forces.

Keep it and seal it up, I was instructed again.

Keep it? Not release it? Had that been my problem all along? Maybe I kept trying to disconnect from them when I was supposed to carry them.

I shoved that sizzling orb into my chest and felt myself career backwards a step or two, my hair blown back by the pressure. If I wasn't burning before, I felt like I would then. But it only lasted a moment.

As I closed my eyes and took deep breaths, each exhalation powered down a life force in return. They were still there, but not in control of me.

The glow sealed itself back up inside my skin. And though I wasn't sure what my eyes were doing, one look at Dad's cautious relief told me maybe I looked normal again. The fire in the Conclave was gone and all that remained was the scent of burning wood on the fading wind.

"You did it! How did you release them?" Dad asked.

"I didn't release. I contained."

"You what?" A perturbed slant to his eyes said he did not understand. "Sit down before you pass out."

But I didn't feel faint at all. Normally I was ready to collapse after exertion like that. But I actually felt powered up like I had just guzzled an energy drink the night before a test. "I think I'm okay. Really."

I gave a reassuring wave to Gabriel and Morgan and all the others who had witnessed the entire scene across the bridge before I threw myself at Caleb on the floor and wrapped my arms as far around him as they would go. He was still shaking as he swept me onto his lap.

"I admit it, I'm freakin' Lois Lane and my girlfriend is Superman," he mumbled breathlessly, his words vibrating into my neck. "And yes, I have a fear of heights, okay? This trip is doing nothing to help that. If you didn't have these powers, if you hadn't caught me fast enough—"

"Caleb." I pulled back, feeling a glittery rush from my chest to my face. "Did you just call me your girlfriend?"

"I think I did." He tucked my loose hair behind my ear and the hand that cupped my neck found its grip. He wasn't shaking anymore. "Whitnee Skye, I would kiss the heck out of you right now if your dad wasn't sitting right next to us."

"I heard that," Dad called as he attended to Jezebel.

"Yeah?" I tilted my lips toward his, hoping maybe he'd change his mind. "Well, maybe later when Dad isn't—"

"I will *always* be around," Dad stated flatly, not looking at us. Caleb and I just smiled at each other, our faces inches away. He had called me his girlfriend. I had never been anyone's girlfriend. It sounded so committed. So important. So *perfect*. This moment definitely needed to be sealed with a kiss. From my *boyfriend*. Even if it was straight adrenaline fueling our intensity at the moment.

But that annoying Pyra, Jezebel, destroyed the moment like she had almost wiped out the Conclave when she said, "It's evil, that voice."

Oh, yeah. She heard voices in her head too. But I had a feeling what she heard was not the same voice that I was starting to understand.

"Don't try to sit up, Jezebel. You had a bad bump to the head," Dad coached as Caleb and I untangled ourselves to kneel beside her.

"You mean the voice you heard before the earthshaker?" I asked and her eyes filled up with tears as she looked back and forth between Dad and me.

She found a death grip on Dad's arm and he covered her hand protectively with his. "How often do you hear a voice like that, Jezebel?"

"During my worst nightmares. I cannot even sleep anymore in my house." She started sobbing and it was not the manipulative way I had once seen her do with Gabriel. It was ugly. "This awful chant starts in my head right before the earthshakers start. You have to get it out. He is ripping me *apart*."

If I could read my Dad's expressions well enough, I would say that real dread was there now. I had seen Dad rest gentle hands on people, but there was a ferocity in the way he gripped Jezebel's head this time—both hands pressing down at her temples as if he were trying to fight a battle in her mind. Her fear leaked out in fat tears that escaped down her cheeks.

"Help me!" she repeated hysterically until a blue glow filled the spaces around Dad's fingers and she calmed back down and seemed to fall asleep.

Dad pulled away with a sigh and rubbed his hands over his eyes.

"What does she mean, Dad?"

"The portal," he answered heavily. "The one in the mountain. It's definitely causing these earthshakers. And somehow physically oppressing her."

"But what about the voice? Who is she hearing?" Caleb's question was the same as mine. And I didn't expect Dad's answer:

"Destruction."

Words did not often escape me, but as I stared at Jezebel's weak hand resting in mine, the guilt overshadowed any coherent thing I should have said to her. Neither of us could even look each other in the eyes as the silence draped heavily over us in her Aerodorian guest room.

Finally, I asked the question. "Why did you not tell me, Jez?"

She remained focused on the fan above the bed. "Why did I not tell you that I heard a voice in my head every time the earthshakers happened and many times in between? Perhaps I did not want my sanity questioned any more than it already was, Gabriel."

"I do not think you are insane."

That was a little bit of a lie. The thought had come to me before. But now that I knew the truth—well, I had misjudged her.

"Nathan believes that I am channeling a tormenting spirit from the portal in the mountain. That my house's close proximity to it made me more sensitive to its power." She sniffed lightly. "And that my increased intake of spirit drinks made me more vulnerable to its manipulation."

"I am so sorry. I had no idea that is why you always wanted to be at the Palladium and not at home."

She grimaced slightly and I wondered what wrong thing I had said now. "Of course. That is why I wanted to be at the Palladium," she agreed. "To get away from it."

"And is that also the reason for your increased drunkenness?" I tried to understand her motivations, but the painful expression on her face made me feel that once again, I was failing at this.

"Correct." Her voice was flat and emotionless. "I drink to try and drown the voice out. Which apparently made it worse."

"Jezebel."

She was telling me what she thought I wanted to hear—which was an odd contrast to her usual habit of telling me things I wanted to ignore. What was happening here?

"Look at me," I commanded and squeezed her hand. Her mouth set into a stubborn line as she finally laid glossy eyes on me. "I am sorry that I have not been available to you as I should have been. I want to help you, but I do not know how if you refuse to tell me the truth."

"The truth?"

"Yes. What is it you are really thinking?"

"The truth, Gabriel, is that I do not wish to be betrothed to you anymore. You are not the same since the Travelers arrived last summer. And I am not the same since they left. I think we should both be free of this burden of commitment we carry."

I was stunned. Now that she was offering me the freedom I had wanted, I felt chains of self-condemnation. Had I driven her to this? Or was this really what she wanted?

"Jez, I always promised that I would take care of you—"

"It is time for me to take care of myself. Please do not mock me by pretending that you actually did want to marry me."

"There was a time…" I drifted off. Because there had been a time when marriage to Jezebel was the only good thing on my horizon.

"But you fell in love."

I could not look at her again. I assumed she meant Whitnee, and I was unwilling to sort through those memories. Instead, I brought her hand to my lips and pressed it there for a prolonged moment. Her stained artist hands were familiar to me. Everything about Jezebel spoke of my past. But she was not my future, and perhaps I envied her courage in being the one to finally end it.

"I am sorry." I did not know what else to say.

"I do not wish for your apologies. I just wish to be free."

"Then your freedom you shall have. I still want your friendship. I do not know this Island without it."

"We shall see," she responded emptily and something about it chilled the Fire in my ashamed heart. "In the morning, I will travel back to Pyradora and await your blessing ritual there. If I am to follow Nathan's advice and stop turning to the drink, then being around for Elon's memorial in Geodora tomorrow will not help. I had already planned to drink myself into oblivion just to get through it. I may not particularly like Eden, but her sister did not deserve—" And her words choked off.

With a sigh, I responded, "I understand." I too dreaded making my final goodbyes to Eden's little sister tomorrow. My mind was doing a good job of remaining in the present, moment-by-moment, instead of worrying about what came next. One event, one speech, one smile at a time. I would save the stress for when Eden sat me down with her schedule for the next day.

But perhaps I had made a huge mistake by not worrying more about Jezebel. Something in her fragile demeanor concerned me tonight. This change of heart seemed sudden. And she was almost too calm about it.

"I am sorry, Jez, but I have to leave now—I am supposed to make appearances at the Night Tour on the lower levels. They did not wish to cancel since the third level was the only one with damage." It was a little unnerving how quickly we could recover from these earthshakers, as if they were becoming part of our normal lives.

She smirked. "So glad I could be the one to help with that."

"As far as anyone knows, the earthshaker caused the fire. And Whitnee was able to save the building. The interior—along with the Book—was all that was damaged." Fortunately, we had a copy of the ancient texts in every village and at the Palladium.

Jezebel snorted and shook her head. "Thank the Island and its stars for Whitnee. How did we survive without her?" I was unsure how to handle her sarcasm. Whitnee had only ever been respectful of Jezebel. Perhaps I needed to remind her of that. But then she sighed and said, "She showed kindness tonight when she did not have to. I suppose I should be grateful even though burning up with the Conclave would have been a better fate for me."

"Jezebel!"

"Oh, Gabriel, cool your flanks. I jest."

I did not appreciate the nature of her jesting.

"But I suppose if you were to thank her for me, I would not mind. I do not know if I could choke the words out to her face." Jezebel's candor somehow always struck the right balance between obnoxious and entertaining. This time I did cool my flanks and release an amused sigh.

"Yes, I have a hard time inventing that conversation in my head as well. Under different circumstances, perhaps you would have been her friend."

"Different circumstances would be just that—different. However, I am keenly aware that I do not really get to choose my circumstances. I am just stuck in them. Like I am stuck on this Island."

"You are only stuck if you choose to be." I tried to encourage her, and her sharp eyes landed on me as if hearing something more in my words. So I added, "You have more power of choice than you believe, Jezebel. There is hope when you decide not to be a victim of circumstances anymore. I had to make that choice last summer too. I pray that you find that hope—that *power*—within yourself sooner rather than later."

If there was something Whitnee had taught me a year ago, it was that. Though she felt stuck sometimes too, we all watched her march forward with intention and boldness, making good out of whatever came her way. *You don't need me to make the right choices, Gabriel.* I could still hear her voice and recall her desperate face as it burned with pent-up passion and frustration in that mountain tunnel last summer. I allowed myself just a moment to relive the kiss that had blazed between us right after that.

But she had been right—there was always a choice to be made and we alone held sway over our own hearts and minds.

It was a shame Jezebel remained so opposed to Whitnee. I was convinced they could have found more in common with each other—things that had nothing to do with me. Perhaps Whitnee would have done a better job of keeping Jezebel from her own self-destruction.

I released her hand and leaned over to kiss her feverish cheek. It was the last kiss I would ever bestow upon her, I knew. I felt her lean in ever so slightly to my lips as if she knew too.

"I have to go, Jez. Long night ahead and even longer day tomorrow."

"I understand, go. But, Gabriel, make no mistake—" Her eyes suddenly scorched me with intensity. "Elon did not die—she was *killed*." A spark of fear made me flinch at her words. "It is as I told Nathan... something dark and violent brews on this Island. And if someone does not destroy it, it will destroy *all* of us."

16

EXPLODING ROCKS AND DEEP TALKS

My toes dug little tunnels into the dry sand, as if trying to plant themselves there. The moonlight was obscured by cloud cover, which gave the atmosphere a hazy quality. An intermittent breeze carried the sounds of Aerodora down to where we had congregated on the western beach. I watched Morgan and Caleb stroll barefoot in the shallow surf ahead, talking in low voices. I had a feeling it was about me and the strange things that had happened tonight, which prompted me to stay back. I had learned to respect the fact that sometimes they had to process things differently than I did when it came to this Island. Maybe it should have made me nervous or at least want to cut in on the conversation, but it was easy to trust my friends when they always ended up on my side.

Dad threw his sandals off and joined me for some toe therapy, and I asked, "Who are we waiting on again?"

"His name is Ehud. He's bringing my parents down here and then keeping guard over us while we work through some issues."

"Issues? That sounds bad."

Dad just shrugged. "You got a better word for your ability to infuse all four life forces into one? Or for the fact that you're hearing voices? Or for your connection to the portal?"

Nope. Issues worked just fine. But I still didn't understand his methods. "Why not use our friends or Palladium guards as security?

And why are we so far away from the village?" We were hidden even from the highest vantage point of Aerodora.

"Everyone is busy with the Guardianship schedule and I wanted some privacy, just us. To be honest, Ehud is the only other person I trust in the village."

"Who is he exactly?" I gazed around, wondering when this mysterious person I'd never even heard of would appear.

"He was my closest childhood friend, aside from Abrianna. When I came to Aerodora to spend time with my parents, he and I would play. He never judged me for being so pale compared to everyone else, never expected more out of me than friendship. He's also a great listener and probably knows me better than anyone on this Island."

I was always slightly taken aback when Dad talked of his experiences growing up. It still felt like hearing stories of a person I never knew. Every little tidbit he shared expanded my view of him as a total person.

And meeting Ehud was even more revealing.

When he came out of the trees, his silver eyes were the first thing I saw. He trudged behind Poppa Zeke who was propped up in a chair. It appeared that Ehud and Sarah had levitated him down to the shore as if he were in a wheelchair—with no wheels involved. That had to have taken concentration. I winced just thinking about how many times I would've accidentally dumped my weak grandfather on the ground if I'd been the one doing the levitating.

Upon closer inspection, Ehud was a short, chubby man with a bulbous nose and thinning dark hair. His smile was shy when Dad introduced him to me and, without thinking, I held my hand out to shake his. He stared at it for a second and then took a step back and shook his head silently.

"Oh, I'm sorry," I said with slight embarrassment. "I forget you don't shake hands around here. It's a Mainland greeting." I dropped my hand and smiled kindly at him.

His eyes flicked toward Dad before he held up his right hand and sheepishly pointed at it with his left.

Dad jumped in to explain. "Ehud was born with a deformity on his right hand. He cannot use life force out of it, so his life force strength is sometimes weaker than others."

"Oh." It was all I could say as I caught a glimpse of the shriveled nub where five long fingers should have been. Dad could have at least warned me. "I'm so sorry."

"Nothing to apologize for. He has many wonderful qualities and skills that don't require use of that hand. And, for the record, I have offered to heal it for him, but he never lets me. Stubborn man." Dad rolled his eyes at Ehud who waved Dad off in humility and made gestures similar to sign language with his left hand. Dad seemed to understand what he meant because he replied, "Yes, please keep this area secure while we are out here. I trust you, friend."

Poppa Zeke reached up to squeeze the man's forearm as Sarah patted Ehud's shoulder. "Thank you for your help, Ehud."

With a huge smile at Dad and another shy glance in my direction, Ehud set off to scrutinize our surroundings just as Morgan and Caleb joined us. When I gave Dad a confused look, he said, "Ehud is also mute. Did I forget to say that? I told you he was a good listener."

So Dad's only other trusted friend in the world was a man who didn't speak. Somehow it made sense.

"Family meeting time," Dad announced, and I appreciated how he brought Caleb and Morgan into the circle. He understood my definition of family. "We're all back here together. I don't know why or how it happened exactly, but I trust that it's for a good reason. And that it's *temporary*." Dad directed that word at my two friends, and when their eyes met mine, I could sense the relief they felt at hearing it.

So why didn't I feel the same consolation anymore? The looks on my grandparents' faces didn't seem too relieved either.

"We're going to stay until the end of Gabriel's Guardianship Festival and then we will try the portal again. However, I need to understand some things before this week progresses any further. Whitnee," Dad continued, "when you said tonight that you contained the life forces instead of releasing them, what did you mean exactly?"

"I meant that I didn't have to release them; I just had to hold on to them." I held my hands out palms up and then acted like I was pulling them into my chest. "Like sealing them up in my body."

"All that fire and energy... you just pulled it back into yourself? How did you not explode?"

"Geez, I don't know." Could I have exploded? That hadn't even occurred to me. "I felt better afterward. Instead of feeling out of control, I felt energized. Complete."

As Dad puzzled over that, Poppa Zeke spoke up. "Nathan, I have said it before and I will say it again. Instead of trying to keep her from using these abilities, you need to help her understand them. There might come a time when we need them."

"I realize that, Father, but I don't even understand them for myself."

"Maybe it is time to try," Sarah agreed.

Dad sighed. "Let's list out all the things you've been able to do when you combine the life forces."

"Super strength," I said. "Levitation. Or maybe it's electrocution, I'm not sure. But I'm able to freeze a person or object and force it where I want it."

"Yep," Caleb nodded. "Felt that. Didn't like it."

"Amen," echoed Dad.

"Well, maybe next time I won't save your lives then," I retorted, remembering my desperate fear as I watched that bridge collapse.

Caleb tweaked a lock of my hair. "It was better than falling to my death."

Dad continued, "Obviously, you can shoot things down, or blow them up."

"When she combined Earth and Water, she healed my head injury but communicated with my life force while she did it," Caleb pointed out.

"And remember when she had that dream of you in the Tank, Mr. T?" Morgan responded. "She combined Wind with Fire to see what you were seeing through your mind."

"Hmmm." Dad started to pace. "Maybe we should start with that one. Caleb, stand here. Whit, go to the opposite side and turn your back so that you can't see us." As we obeyed, Dad said to Poppa Zeke, "Can she practice through your mind?"

Ezekiel cleared his throat. "Maybe Sarah should try. I am not sure how clear-minded I am tonight."

I caught the look of concern on Dad's face, before he addressed Grandmother Sarah. "Mother, is that okay with you?"

"Of course, but you know mind communication is not my strength. What do I do?"

"Let Whitnee connect to your Aerodorian life force and then she's going to add in the Fire life force and try to see what you see—without looking at it."

I had never spoken to my grandmother through our minds. This would be interesting. I did as Dad instructed, facing the water and closing my eyes. It took a while to find Sarah's frequency with Dad's description. It was thin and fell across my mind in lacy patterns of silver light.

Grandmother Sarah? Can you hear me?

There you are, precious one. Your voice is so vivid and colorful.

I smiled even though her voice came back in echoes. *Okay, give me a moment to see if I can apply the Fire life force.*

I found the Fire within easily enough, but when I tried to add it to our conversation, the connection shorted out and I heard Sarah gasp. I turned back around in fear to find her pressing an aging hand to her forehead.

"It burned and the connection went out," she explained.

"I'm sorry!" I told her. "Maybe it won't work on everyone. Maybe it only worked between you and me, Dad, because you have all four life forces too."

"Let's test that theory, then," Dad said. "Mother, maybe you should sit and rest on that rock. Back to your place, Whit. Try connecting with me."

That was easy. Once we established our voice connection, I tapped into the Fire and this time, a picture started to take shape.

I see Caleb in front of you. I said telepathically. *Dang, he's cute.* His hair was thick and crazy on top and his athletic build was accentuated beautifully in that fitted gray tunic Hannah had found—

Spare me, please. Dad's thought interrupted mine and I wondered how much of that had accidentally seeped into his mind.

Dad's voice came out verbally this time. "How many fingers is he holding up?"

As if I was dreaming while awake, I saw Caleb hold up two fingers to Dad.

"Two."

Then he switched to seven really fast. "Seven... now he's dancing. Is that a bad version of the Running Man?" I started laughing as Caleb's antics grew more animated. "That's the sprinkler... oh my gosh, grocery shopping, really? Now Morgan is jumping in and they're going fishing... *Y'all.*" I lost my composure.

"Okay, cut it off," Dad said, but I didn't immediately, and I saw myself in Dad's mind as he turned my direction. With my eyes closed, I stood there laughing on the beach. It was really weird to see an image of myself that wasn't in a mirror. "Whit!"

"Okay, I'm done."

When I opened my eyes, Morgan said: "There she goes again. Silver eyes with gold rings around them."

Without missing a beat, Dad said, "See that rock over there? Combine all four, use the energy to pick it up and throw it out to sea."

I hesitated. "I've never really concentrated on what I was doing like that. It always seems to be in these extreme moments where I have to act forcefully and quickly."

"Right. This time I want you to try and think through it. Try to control it instead of reacting with it."

Control was the last thing I felt when I combined all four. But if he said so... I took a few calming breaths before powering on each life force inside. When they merged into one, that feverish glow spread throughout my body, lighting up my skin right there on the beach. I took a few moments to really understand each step in the process and feel the paradoxical pulses of power within my body. They were familiar and alien at the same time. Unnatural and yet *so* natural.

It was Caleb's comment to Morgan, though, that almost broke my concentration. "Is it just me or is she super hot when she lights up like that?"

"Caleb, I swear," Dad muttered. "You're gonna get tossed out to sea next."

Caleb widened innocent eyes at Dad. "Of course I meant hot like the temperature, Nathan."

No, he didn't. And I was totally okay with it.

"Let me cool things off for you, son." Dad raised a casual hand and blasted Caleb with icy Wind that sent him stumbling backward.

When Dad wasn't looking, I sent Caleb an appreciative wink and got a wiggle of his eyebrows in return. Who needed a cute new swimsuit when you could become a human glow stick and get your boyfriend's attention that way? I aimed both of my hands at that huge rock in the distance. I had no idea how to control the amount of force I was exerting, but the rock was bathed in electrical white light that sparked. I was able to rip it out of its roots in the ground, but as I started to levitate it toward the ocean, it suddenly exploded. Tiny shards of rock blasted away from the epicenter and a few fell as far as our feet.

"Yikes. Hot *and* scary," Caleb mumbled.

I dropped my hands, but felt the constricting glow still covering me as I explained, "I can't control the amount of energy as it leaves me. It feels kind of all-or-nothing once I aim."

"Maybe you need a better reason to control it," Dad reasoned. "Caleb, run out there and do your best Earth shield. Let her aim at you."

"Say what now, old man?" Caleb rested his hands on his hips and gave Dad a skeptical look. "She'll toast me."

Dad pretended to weigh that option, which brought out the chuckles from Morgan. But then he pulled Morgan and Caleb with him down the shore, calling out, "We'll do a four-on-one battle here. Fire up your defenses, you two. I'll use a Fire Wall. Ehud! Can you come form a Wind Blocker?"

Ehud stepped hesitantly out from the tree line where he had been scouting. There were some nervous signs made between him and Dad before he joined their line.

I frowned as my skin shimmered with power. It glowed for a reason. I felt indestructible. "I don't want to hurt y'all."

"Then try harder to control it," Dad hollered back. He seemed pretty confident, which probably meant his abilities could stand up to mine.

"Oh, this should be good," I heard Poppa Zeke say from the sidelines.

"Here we go!" I warned and then raised my arms and concentrated on the pulses of life around me. There were tiny rhythms like heartbeats that coated the trees to my right and the ocean waves to my left. Each grain of sand vibrated beneath my feet and offered up energy. I wasn't sure if I was sensing the Island or becoming part of the Island. What I do know is that when I finally aimed some of that pent-up energy toward my loved ones down the beach, I tried as hard as I could to hold some of the power back.

I saw my white hot energy match up against their four defensive life forces. They seemed to be able to hold me back, but I was also gritting my teeth trying to refrain from total exertion.

"Give us more, Whit!" I heard Dad holler, so I tightened the muscles in my body and felt the waves of power increase in intensity. The air crackled with electricity and as I pushed harder, the life forces started ricocheting toward the ocean, creating electric forks across the surface of the water. Just as I could see inside the Conclave earlier when I was "sweeping up" the Fire from outside, I could also follow the course my life forces took across the beach. Like a zoom-in feature, I could visually chase over the sand, through the air, and collide with Dad's Firewall before shooting sideways to the ocean and diving underwater with a sizzle. It was the strangest sensation to both conduct the power and become part of it. I got so caught up in the feeling, I almost missed Dad yelling at me to stop.

I reined the power back into myself, feeling that burst of clarity and euphoria almost like a drug. Everyone on the opposite end of the beach slowly lowered their defenses and panted for breath. They were up to their calves in sand, as if something had hammered them into the ground. Morgan called out, "That almost buried us!"

"I did that?" I repeated, as Caleb stepped out of the hole. "I wasn't even trying that hard."

"Thank God for that," he said, turning back to where his feet had just been. "The harder I tried, the deeper I sank. There was no forcing you back."

"I could definitely tell a difference when you were trying to hold back, though." Dad called and helped Ehud out of his hole. "That's a good start. But the question is—"

"Nathan!" Something in Sarah's voice to my right caused all of us to sprint that way. She was trying to rouse my grandfather who was slumped over in his chair. "He just faded. Help me revive him!"

Dad knelt in front of his father and placed careful hands on Poppa Zeke—one on his chest and one on the side of his head. After only a moment of blue light leaking out around Dad's palms, Poppa came back into consciousness and gazed around, confused for a moment. I breathed a quick sigh when it became apparent he had just passed out.

"Father, is there something you're not telling me?" Dad asked and then cast his gaze toward Sarah expectantly.

She swallowed noticeably but looked right into Dad's eyes and said, "He just needs more rest than he has been getting. Perhaps we should go back up to the village. Do not let us interrupt your work here."

"No, that's probably enough for the night. The kids wanted to go to the Nightingale soon anyway. We'll come with you," Dad said and silenced the rest of his parents' protests. He took charge of levitating Poppa Zeke's chair, and Caleb and Morgan dutifully followed. But I remembered my sandals still lying there in the sand. When I turned back for them, I discovered Ehud kneeling beside them, over the spot where I had stood earlier projecting the combination of life forces.

"Is something wrong?" I asked, peering in confusion over his shoulder.

He gestured and pointed down at the ground. I had to kneel beside him in the dark to see what he was seeing.

There was a crack in the earth.

A small one with sand pouring over the edge into the darkness below. It began where my footsteps interrupted the sandy beach, inches away from where I had kicked off my sandals. Without sharing a word, we followed the line to the edge of the foliage where it stopped.

Exactly where the indentations from Poppa Zeke's chair remained.

When our gazes met, I was thankful Ehud didn't speak. I was afraid of what he might say.

Later when Poppa Zeke and Grandmother Sarah were settled in for the night and we were just hanging out until Gabriel and the others returned, Dad found me alone on my favorite bridge outside the Western Guesthouse. I was mesmerized by the violent turn of the ocean's waves from this vantage point. The chaotic rhythm of those white tips echoed my thoughts as I turned over the events of the evening. Somewhere hidden from view on that beach was damage to the land that I might have caused. Damage that might have somehow found its way to my grandfather.

That unexplainable guilt had reappeared and I didn't like it.

"What are you thinking about?" Dad asked as he leaned over the side of the balcony and followed the direction of my gaze. "Wait—if it's Caleb, I don't want to know. Lock those thoughts up, my dear."

I had to laugh. "I really like him, Dad."

"I think we all know that."

"And he finally called me his girlfriend!"

"Yeah, I knew that was coming. I mean, your mom has been preparing me all year for it. But when Caleb came and asked our permission to date you, I was told I had to play it cool—"

"*What.*" Hold up. Caleb had talked to my parents about all of this? "You mean, he was already planning to ask me to be his girlfriend? Like... like, there was a *plan?*"

Dad had been caught and his face totally showed it. "You mean he didn't tell you that part yet?" Clearly not. I didn't even know what to say. "Great. Well, now you have to act like you didn't know anything, okay? He had a whole evening planned on the cruise—"

"Are. You. Serious!"

Dad winced and rubbed his forehead at my reaction. "Um, I'm not very good at this stuff. I guess you didn't need to know about the cruise either."

This just kept getting worse. Or better? Ugh, I couldn't pick an emotion!

"Let me get this straight: Caleb asked for permission to date me—and I'm assuming you said yes or we'd be having a totally different conversation right now—and he planned a romantic evening on our senior trip to make it official? Dad, I'm *dying*!"

"Why are you dying? Isn't that good news? You're shaking your head, so… no, it's bad news. Wait—now I'm getting an eyeroll. You know I hate that." Dad looked at me as if I had suddenly grown two heads and begun speaking in an alien language. "I clearly do not understand. What would your mother do in this situation?"

"She'd know that I'm upset about missing out on a romantic cruise date with the boy I care about and then she'd say, 'but, *mija*, how romantic that you get to be on a magical Island with him!' And then she'd probably get all emotional and spout off something in Spanish about how her little girl has her first boyfriend and I'd better not spare any details about our first real date! And now I kind of want to cry. But I also feel like happy dancing because I was *obviously* worrying for nothing all this time." With a dramatic sigh, I cast devastated eyes up at Dad whose expression had never looked so uncomfortable.

"That's a lot of emotional processing."

There was a bit of whine to my voice now. "Why did the Island choose *now* to bring us back here?"

Dad took a deep breath and tried to pacify me. "If I know Caleb, I'm sure he'll think of some other way to make things special for you. The kid adores you, which is the only reason I put up with him."

"You have more reasons than that," I reminded him. Dad and Caleb hung out almost as much as Caleb and I did. I pressed my lips together, but then an excited squeal still escaped. "That must be why he said he won't kiss me until we get back to the Mainland—"

"Okay." Dad held up a hand. "Where's Morgan? You need to process the rest of this drama with her while I go throw Caleb in the Tank until he swears not to kiss you until you're thirty. Maybe we need to have another talk about boys and boundaries and—"

"Nope." I held up a hand too, realizing I had tripped the Dad Alarm. We definitely needed Mom here. "Mom and I talk about that stuff. No need for you to jump in on it, Dad. I'm good. Caleb's good. We're all good here and the boundaries are in place."

At Dad's traumatized expression, I went ahead and changed the subject. "To be honest, I wasn't thinking about Caleb at all when you came over. I was actually thinking about some things you said last summer."

"Like what?" He was all too interested in moving to a new topic.

"When we sat on the roof in Hydrodora and watched the Lost Ceremony, you told me that it was the Island who told you to destroy the portal and leave by boat with Will Kinder. But when I asked you why the Island instructed you to do that, knowing that you wouldn't be back for a long time, you said you weren't ready to explain that to anyone yet." I glanced over at his face to see his reaction. "How about now?"

With a lift of his eyebrows and a sigh, he said, "I've kind of already explained that, right? I mean, I was never meant to leave the Island forever. Had I remembered anything after I sailed away, I never would have allowed myself to pursue your mother and a normal life on the Mainland."

"If people lose their memory once they leave by boat, then surely the Island knew that was a risk."

"That's the thing I'm starting to understand, though," he said. "Maybe the Island *knew* I would forget everything and fall in love with Serena. Maybe it was ultimately for the purpose of creating you. Which means, like I said today, you have a purpose here too. Among our people."

Our people. When would I truly own that identity? I could so easily feel at home on the Island, especially here in Aerodora. But sometimes I still saw myself as a foreigner here.

"What if my purpose keeps me here? Like it did for you?" I had to ask it, because the possibility was becoming more pronounced after that portal refused to cooperate today. He took a moment to think, and I watched the lightning in the distance out over the water. My Aero instincts told me it was just a passing storm and would not find its way here.

"We talk a lot about purpose and finding the right path for our lives, but sometimes we let the unknown future dictate how we're going to enjoy the present. Maybe our primary purpose is to make the most of each moment we're in." He pulled me into his side and planted a kiss on the top of my head. "Like, right now, I am thankful to have this moment with you."

"Me too, Dad." I leaned in and tried to exhale every worry suddenly fighting for attention in my mind. "If I ask another question, will you actually answer it instead of that thing you just did where you get philosophical and somehow avoid giving a real answer?"

"I'll try."

"What do you really think will happen to me if we destroy the Palladium portal?"

I felt him tense up and I pulled away to examine his face. "Best case scenario... nothing happens. Or maybe you lose your special abilities and that's all."

I wasn't really okay with that. Especially after that addicting feeling of mastering all four life forces combined. But I had to ask. "What's the worst case scenario?"

There was a glint in his eye. "Worst case scenario... let's just say we need to make sure you're on the Mainland side of the portal when it's shut down."

Because he still worried it could hurt me. That losing that connection, those abilities, might damage me here on the Island. He didn't have to say it out loud. "Well, this has been a fun conversation." We shared a sigh and directed our attention back to the storm in the distance. I remarked, "It's so dark and vast out there. Where the heck are we in the world?"

"In an undiscoverable place," Dad said and pointed out to the ocean. "Fun fact: the deepest part of the ocean where no sunlight penetrates is called the aphotic zone. On my last trip to Hawaii, we did some geological studies of minerals found in aphotic zones; I got to work in conjunction with a team of oceanographers and marine biologists to determine more about the depths of largely unexplored ocean and what organisms live there."

"And what did you find out?"

"That there are some deep, lost places in the world where light never touches and strange things breed."

"I don't think I want to go there."

He chuckled. "No, I don't imagine you would. The cool part was the bioluminescence, though. Some of the creatures had a chemical reaction that caused them to emit light—simply because they were alive. Can you imagine?"

"I'm trying to decide which is less terrifying: a regular fish or a glow-in-the-dark fish," I pondered.

"Oh, Baby Doll, I should never have taken you fishing as a child." Dad rolled his eyes and I resisted reminding him that it was a habit he hated. "The aphotic zone was an interesting study, and oddly enough, the idea that life not only exists in the darkest of places—out there in the middle of that ocean—but that it can find a way to produce light of its own has brought me comfort many times. No matter how dark my circumstances or future has seemed, I remember that maybe I can still find the light. That maybe I can still *be* light."

I studied his face, the gently graying temples of his blond hair, the sun-kissed wrinkles around his eyes, and the smile that brought them out. For the first time, I realized why sometimes Dad's smiles seemed sad. He had endured so much heartache and betrayal and loss in his life. Maybe I wasn't the only one trying to hold it together as we remained separated from Mom and Ben and everyone else. Maybe Dad felt the same anxiety I did, harbored the same separation issues that had plagued me all year too.

"Dad, how do you remain so positive when it seems like the rug always gets pulled out from underneath you? You never seem afraid."

His eyebrows lifted in surprise. "Oh, did I not display my fear and anger in that portal room enough, Whit? Because I never knew fear until I became a father and had to watch half of my heart walk around outside of my body. If something happened to you, it would damage me forever. Trust me, I have fears." He thrummed his fingers on the railing. "But I have faith too. And I choose every day to follow my faith instead of my fear."

I suppose that was a good way to live.

I leaned my head against his shoulder. "If I lost you again, it would damage me forever too."

The only response I got was his chin coming to rest on top of my head. I would have preferred more words, though.

17

THE BEARDED BEAUTY VS.
THE GREEN-EYED MONSTER

I did not often catch myself staring, but Eden must have called me out on it at least four different times through the course of the Night Tour. By the fourth time, she was actually showing real concern for my health. *Gabriel, did you hit your head on that bridge? Are you in shock? You keep dazing out on me. Maybe we should have cancelled this after what happened.*

I could only claim utter exhaustion. Because I *was* tired—in so many ways. And because if I started questioning myself, I might start to believe that I was staring at Eden more than anything else.

Her strength and beauty as she mingled among the Aerodorians were an unexpected comfort to me, but inspiring at the same time. She was graceful in conversation, yet confident in her opinions. Everything she said and did made *me* look good. I had seen her in this role all year, but as I waited at the entrance for her to make what felt like her fifteenth goodbye at the Music Center, I knew I was staring again.

Was she aware that her dress accentuated her feminine features in such a way that I had almost reached out to feel that swirl of sparkling stones around her waist those four times she caught me watching her?

Perhaps I really had hit my head. Touching Eden without permission would be asking for a Geostone to the gut.

Yet she let me hold her in Geodora.

She had also been overcome with grief and probably did not even remember that moment, so… No hands, no Geostones, no, thank you.

I tried not to appear impatient as I tore my gaze away and shoved all of my unhinged thoughts back into the Exhaustion category of my mind. At last, she stuffed everything into her handbag and joined me at the door. We exited without a word, waved to those who still stood outside, and then before I knew what was happening, Eden grabbed my arm and pulled me into a quiet corner of the village. Illuminated only by moonlight peeking through the thick branches around us, she dropped her satchel and leaned against the rail.

All formality gone, she reached up and started pulling pins out of her imprisoned hair. "Oh, I am glad that part is over. You did it, Gabriel. Well done, friend."

"*We* did it," I corrected her, allowing the use of "friend" to take root again.

"So many questions about Nathan and Whitnee, though. Perhaps we should have had them join us."

"Nathan would not have agreed. He wanted to keep political distance, for which I do not blame him. It is probably best for both of us."

"He is so wise, is he not? I wish I could sit down with him and really listen and ask questions. He has to be the true Pilgrim. There is just something about him." She wandered off into her thoughts and I felt my stomach clench a little in anxiety. Yes, I had questions too. But I did not know if Nathan would give me the answers I wanted.

As Eden absently twisted her hair around her fingers, I took a moment to stretch my back and neck where they so easily stiffened these days. "I am certainly glad you were here to navigate the questions with me. Especially since Ezekiel was not well and Abrianna spent more time posing for zephyra images."

"As if you did not take many an image with your eager admirers," she teased, and I recalled the band of young girls who traveled wherever we went until their parents called them home.

"No one was as obnoxious as Mistress Miriam who pinched my rear end the entire time we were in the library," I said.

Eden's laughter erupted. "I did not see any such thing. You must be joking."

"Eden. I have never been so pulverized in my life and that includes you pelting me with stones when we were children. How could you miss that? I am certain I will have little bruises on my left flank." I turned and gestured to my rear end, which caused Eden's laughter to come out more like high-pitched twitters.

"I did see her cling to your arm as if she could not stand upright without you. And her little white-haired head laying itself against your tunic—"

"She smelled like dead leaves carried in the wind."

"Gabriel!" Eden chastised. "You were probably the best thing about her day. You, with your golden eyes and tassels and that *very* Aerodorian purple outfit, probably set her little ancient heart to pounding." She reached out and playfully tweaked one of my tassels conveniently close to the bruises in question. "You two were perfectly adorable together. Had Jezebel been there, I am certain she would have been her usual jealous self."

It was a lighthearted comment, and one I normally would have laughed off, but not this time. I sobered and leaned against the wooden rail across from Eden.

"What? Did I say something wrong?" She ran more fingers through her cascading layers of hair as she surveyed my change in demeanor.

"Jezebel broke off our betrothal tonight."

Eden's hands faltered for a moment. "Is that why she set the Conclave on Fire?"

"No, that really was an accident, according to Whitnee. This was part of our conversation after she woke up again. Something is wrong with her, Eden."

"A lot of things are wrong with her," she muttered. "Although it is surprising. I was certain I would be planning a wedding ceremony after the Guardianship festivities ended."

I was aghast. "You believed I would marry her?"

"Well, you refused to end it." Her words made me feel foolish.

"I tried. Once. You know that. And there has not been a good time to revisit the topic." Why did I feel like I needed to defend myself now? The fact that Eden had assumed all this time that I was still going to marry Jezebel—just because I had not officially ended it yet—was frustrating. "I thought you knew me better than this, Eden. I have never dreamed of a wedding to Jezebel."

"Then what have you dreamed about, Gabriel?" Eden demanded in her unabashed way. I stared back at her, dumbstruck. I was not sure if I had dreamed of anything after becoming the Guardian. There had not been time. And there had been no signs with the portals that—

"Whitnee? Have you only ever dreamed of her?"

Encompassed by the soft light of the moon, Eden's face looked more vulnerable than I had ever seen it.

"I do not know," I replied honestly, because there was never really a point in lying to Eden. "I do know it is not like that with Whitnee anymore. And she will probably be gone at the end of the week." I stood back to my full height and took two steps closer to Eden. I could not tear my gaze away from the tiny glisten at the corners of her round, innocent eyes and the way she held her position no matter how close I came. "I suppose that I am truly free now to dream. To consider possibilities I had not considered before."

"That sounds..." She seemed breathless as she stood frozen before me. "...interesting."

"Does it?"

"Gabriel." She reached up and flipped a tassel on my shoulder. "You are staring again."

"Maybe there is a reason for that."

"I would love to hear it."

One glance down at her plump lips and I decided that my Pyra nature was dangling me over dangerous territory. She was Earth and I was Fire. Business partners and friends. I knew I should not read too much into the cloud of emotions surrounding her. She was still shaken from losing her sister and traveling and, oh, there was annoying Abner still part of the picture even if Jezebel was not. So I took a proper step back.

"You know I have not slept much," I answered, trying to gather the heat in my body back into a safe place. "We still have to make an appearance at the Nightingale before this day ends."

She blew out a breath and swept her hair again through her fingers. "Right. Of course. Then I can get out of this fancy dress."

I winced. Those were the wrong words for my extremely sensitive imagination at the moment. She reached for her satchel on the ground, and I stayed her hand. She did not pull away, though she did pause at my touch.

"Allow me," I insisted and quickly threw the satchel over my shoulder. Then I offered her my arm once again. "You have no excuse this time. Reject me again and I *will* take it personally."

She hesitated. "Do you think people will find it inappropriate? I am your Personal Advisor."

"You linking your arm with mine is a respectful show of Palladium solidarity. Nothing inappropriate about it," I assured her and she relented.

"Well, when you say it like that…" I felt her confident grip settle into the crook of my arm. "I must be exhausted too. Forgive me if I am misunderstanding you tonight."

The corners of my mouth itched to smile. "Now when we dance together the entire time at the Nightingale, some might consider that inappropriate. But you and I will know that you are only protecting my tender tushy from Mistress Miriam should she show up with her greedy little hands."

Eden's laughter carried on the wind as we ventured back into the village, arm-in-arm.

The Mainlanders might have been surrounded by a gaggle of admirers at the Nightingale, but it never seemed to faze Whitnee and Morgan to be the center of attention. Caleb, on the other hand, slipped out of the crowd and came up beside me as I ordered a drink. His fingers tapped the counter, pulsing out a nervous energy.

"Could you make my friend a Pomigold, please?" I ordered, and then assured Caleb, "It has no spirits in it—just fruit juices and coconut milk. Although I daresay you look like you could use a stronger drink."

Caleb smirked. "I'm getting extremely tired of almost dying every day around here. Falling off the bridge was *it*." His hands blazed a trail through his hair as if they were too restless to be still. "I don't know how you do it all the time, dodging death like it's not even real."

"Death is real. Fear is real. I have time for neither." I passed his frothy golden drink to him. We clinked our glasses together before taking a sip. The liquid spirits snaked a burning trail down my throat and left behind a calming warmth. We turned around toward the main floor again to watch the others frolic in time to the music. "Maybe you and Whitnee need a dance," I suggested, my words laced with meaning. "I am certain she would be more than willing to take your mind off death. It seems like there is some *tension* between the two of you that needs to be handled soon."

In my peripheral view, I saw Caleb's face break into a knowing smile. "I'm exerting self-control while we're on the Island. But I promised her once we were back on the Mainland, we would focus on *us*."

I faced him directly in exasperation. "Why on earth would you promise such a thing?"

His eyes were a protective shade of green. "Incentive."

"You believe she needs incentive to go back home with you? You are a fool, Caleb of the Mainland. Go grab that girl and spin her on the dance floor until you are dizzy enough to just kiss her. Or find a deserted bridge. That is what I would do if I were you."

"We all know what you would do, you raging pile of Pyra hormones. Stop talking about my girlfriend like that."

I had no knowledge of what hormones were, but my exhausted state and perhaps the tingle of the spirits were loosening my tongue. "I did not mean to imply that I wanted to do that to Whitnee myself."

"Oh, as if there's some other girl here you fantasize about. You wouldn't need a *Gabnee* if there were. Besides..." He took another swig of his drink and stood up a little straighter. "I don't want to do it here. There's too many people—"

"There are plenty of private places all over this village." I had mixed feelings about encouraging Caleb's affection for Whitnee, some filtered by truth and some grounded in selfishness. But aside from all of that, the imbecile needed a kick in the pants. "Stop making excuses."

"Nathan would kill me—"

"No, he would kill *me*. He looks at you like a son, can you not tell?"

He perked up. "You think so?"

I shook my head. "Now I am done with this conversation. When you decide to become a man instead of a—"

My insult was interrupted when someone shoved me from behind, causing my cup to careen across the floor with a slick trail.

"You imposter!" A man with silver eyes illuminated with harmful intent loomed toward me. Caleb's drink sloshed on the counter as he abandoned it to ignite green defensive fists. "You are not supposed to be Guardian. Now that the Pilgrim is here, you have no right to any authority!"

"Take a step back, dude," Caleb warned him as I felt the Fire rise to my own hands. There were some onlookers who caught on to the altercation despite all the noise of the club. Levi was upon us within seconds.

"I will only ask you once—remove yourself from the premises," Levi told him sharply. "You do not assault the Guardian."

"He is no Guardian! He is a fake and we will make sure the truth comes out—" But Levi, with the help of Thomas and a few Aeroguards, forced him out of the building, his shouts drowned out by the music. As if they had an internal alarm when trouble was near, Eden, Whitnee, and Morgan rushed over.

"What happened?" Eden demanded as Caleb and I relaxed our rigid positions.

"Some jerk tried to pick a fight with Gabriel," Caleb said as I retrieved my glass a few feet away, trying to contain my embarrassment at having been assaulted and accused of such things in a public place.

Whitnee was aghast. "What? Why?"

Before I could respond, Caleb told her, "He was just crazy. Clearly not a fan of the Bearded Beauty that is our Gabe." He made light of it, but the way his eyes slid my direction indicated that he remembered our conversation on the beach and was choosing to protect me anyway. This was not the first time I had been confronted with such accusations, but with Nathan and Whitnee back, it was certainly giving this vocal part of the population more leverage. Caleb patted me on the shoulder. "Shake it off, man."

"Are you guys okay? Or should we leave?" Whitnee glanced back and forth between the two of us as if trying to detect something.

"It *is* getting late, and we have early travel plans," Eden said, giving me a way out.

"Everything is fine," I assured them. "Let us stay just a little longer. I think Caleb wanted to dance." I pushed him forward a few inches, earning a glaring look from the foreigner.

"They are about to do partner dances," Eden pointed out and then offered, "I will dance with you, Caleb."

That was not *at all* what I had intended. With a sideways glance at me, Caleb said, "I would love to dance with my favorite Geodorian."

Whitnee was not at all rattled by the suggestion. "Better put some protective shields on your feet, Eden."

"Quiet, you," Caleb responded. "Or you'll be next."

"I'll happily be next." She wrinkled her nose playfully at him and the cuteness was somewhat nauseating.

"Let's go, Eden." When Caleb took her by the hand and Eden flashed a radiant smile at him, I decided I did not like that he called her his favorite.

At that point, Thomas rejoined our group. Levi had subdued my heckler and Thomas made me assure him I was okay. I was. But there was a rowdy group of Aerodorians blocking my view of Caleb and Eden and *that* was not okay with me.

"Thomas, they're starting a new dance. You interested?" Morgan piped up. "For old times' sake?"

Thomas's grin turned devilish as he threw an arm around her and led her away. About that moment, I found Eden. Caleb's hands were on her waist—the exact spot mine had wanted to be most of the night. I eyed them curiously for a moment, noting that Morgan and Thomas had reserved more distance between their bodies than Caleb and Eden had.

"What was all of that about?" Whitnee startled me.

"All of what?"

"Everything that just happened." She narrowed her eyes first at me and then searched the dance floor where I had just been staring. "What are you hiding, Bearded Beauty?"

"Nothing. It is as Caleb said. The man took issue with my appointment as Guardian and felt he should knock my drink out of my hand to make his point."

"I thought people didn't question what the Island ordained."

"Unless they think the Island did not ordain it."

She became transfixed on my face and I could almost see her mind connecting the pieces of the accusations. Her bright eyes grew shadowed as she tore her gaze from me and started scanning the room in suspicion. Over her head, I also noticed that the group who had overheard my assailant's earlier charges were now frowning in my direction and talking in hushed voices. Were they giving thought to the accusations about me? Perhaps I needed to go over there and make conversation to assure them I was completely, legitimately a good Guardian.

Whitnee noticed them too. "They seem to be staring for no good reason."

"Perhaps they have a problem with the beard then too," I muttered, feeling the discomfort snake across my skin. Suspicion and gossip should not bother me. But they did.

I felt Whitnee's hand curl into mine and her confident fingers pull me toward her. "I think it's time for Gabnee to distract them, don't you think? Let's dance and give them something else to talk about."

She was rescuing me and I had not even asked her to do it. I followed her willingly out into the mix of swaying and spinning bodies.

Once I had her in my arms, it was hard to not remember the last time we were here together. It was, in fact, one of the few times I had ever danced at all. I could still recall the fresh scent of lavender in her hair and the way her body curved against mine that night. The heat stoked between us had ultimately led to a discovery of her Pyradorian abilities. That had been the moment I knew she felt an uncontrollable attraction to me the way I had to her.

So many of our experiences last summer could be described that way—completely and utterly out of our control.

But not tonight. Our bodies did not mesh together the same way, though there was a comfortable familiarity to being this close to her. "I have not had a chance to say it, but you did a phenomenal thing earlier tonight, putting out that Fire the way you did. I knew you would find a way to harness your abilities."

"Strange how it worked, right? I've always thought I had to cut off the connection. But all along, I just needed to accept it, I guess."

It was an interesting distinction and did not make much sense to me. Whitnee was often a conundrum. But Eden and Caleb had just swayed into my view and I was distracted again.

"Does your boyfriend always dance that close to other women?" I asked, nodding their direction.

Whitnee turned to look. "They're not that close. About the same distance you and I are, right?"

Perhaps. They were so lost in a private conversation with only the music swirling around them that I was certain they did not notice us.

"Why does Eden always laugh so much when she is with Caleb? It is all they ever do, laugh and tell private jokes."

"Caleb's a funny guy." Whitnee shrugged. "Or at least he thinks he is."

"Apparently Eden thinks so too," I muttered and she pulled away to look over at them again, her steps slowing. Their heads dipped closer as Caleb said something apparently hilarious. "That does not bother you?"

"No." Her gaze landed on me with targeted suspicion. "Does it bother *you*?"

There I was, thinking and feeling things I should have under control. Mild laughter escaped when I said, "Caleb is not *my* boyfriend."

"Oh, Gabriel, I knew it!" She shook her head and then sang, "Somebody is starting to have feelings for his Personal Advisor."

I stared down at her in consternation. "That is not at all the issue here, and it is highly inappropriate of you to even suggest it." This made her laugh harder for whatever reason. And I was not interested

in discussing any romantic inclinations I might be struggling with—
she was too wrapped up in them already.

In true Whitnee fashion, she ignored my wishes. "Does Eden
know how you feel?"

"I did not say I felt anything for her. Besides, she is likely going
to end up betrothed to Abner."

"Ah, and you are still engaged to Jezebel." She pressed her lips
together and gave me a reproving look, but I could actually counter
that now.

"Not anymore. Jezebel broke off our betrothal tonight. It is
finally over."

Instead of the dramatic approval I expected from her, her face
darkened. "Jezebel was the one who ended it? For real?"

"Yes," I sighed. "And you can keep your comments to yourself. I
already heard from Eden how cowardly I must appear. I would have
eventually done it myself—"

"To be honest, it worries me about Jezebel. Something is off
about her."

"I thought we all knew that."

"No, I mean, after what I saw tonight, that doesn't seem like a
good sign that she is separating herself from you all of a sudden."
Her brows creased in concern. "I worry about her mental health,
Gabriel. I think she's way more depressed than she lets on."

Mental health. That was a phrase I had not heard. But I could
discern what she meant.

"I will check in on her," I promised. "She did ask me—in a very
Jezebel way—to thank you for your kindness to her tonight."

"Well, that's nice," Whitnee said. "And also completely not like
her. Please keep an eye on her, Gabriel."

I gave a nod and added Jezebel to the mental list of things I
needed to follow up on.

We swayed together in time to the swells of musical notes until
Eden and Caleb crossed Whitnee's direct line of sight. She started
back in. "If you're single now and Eden isn't engaged yet, then you
need to jump on this. That girl is fiercely loyal to you, possibly knows
more about the Island than you, and let's be honest, she's totally,
one-hundred-percent hot. If you won't say it, I will."

I would forever regret bringing anything up about Eden and Caleb. I took her words and spun them back on her.

"I admit Eden does look quite breathtaking tonight. Who can blame Caleb for being distracted with her? It is refreshing to see how little it bothers you."

She did not say anything, but her keen gray eyes were now focused on the couple in question. Perhaps my insinuations would take the focus off her intuitions. It did not seem to work at first.

Until she mumbled, "They do laugh a lot. I mean, he's not *that* funny."

Oh, I was a cruel person.

But we found ourselves stepping rhythmically in their direction anyway. When Eden and Caleb finally looked away from each other to find us next to them, they laughed again as if we had been the subject of their joke.

"Caleb," I addressed him. "I think my dance partner would like her turn with you." Whitnee rolled her eyes at me, but did not object.

"Oh, sure, yeah," Caleb searched our faces for a moment, before releasing Eden and adding, "I'm gonna take you up on that before I leave, Eden. We can ditch these two."

Eden laughed *again*. "It will be our secret."

"Secrets? From your Guardian?" I tried to joke as well, but it came across a little stiff and only earned a light chuckle from Eden.

"I would never," she insisted innocently, but sent a wink at Caleb.

Whitnee and I glanced at each other once before I found myself saying rather gruffly, "Eden, would you care to dance with me?"

"Oh. Of course." She glanced around the room conspiratorially. "Did Mistress Miriam show up?"

It took me an embarrassing two seconds to realize she was making a joke. My delayed smile finally appeared. As she stepped closer toward me, I forgot for a moment where my hands were supposed to go, so they just stayed at my sides for another embarrassingly prolonged moment.

But then Eden's hand came to rest on my chest and her other hand took mine. When our palms met, hers was confident and cool, like the earth on a dry, autumn day. I'm sure my presence felt sweltering to her, especially as my other sultry hand found a comfortable dip on the curve of her waist. Her curls still cascaded loosely around her face and almost down to those rhinestones at my fingertips. We kept a breath of distance between us, as if too afraid to touch.

"Gabriel, you need sleep. Your eyes are glazing over again."

For as smart as she was, she really had no idea. "If you would stop stealing my attention tonight, maybe I would stop staring."

Genuine confusion lit up her face as she stared at me. She was taller than Whitnee so I did not have to look down as much to see her so clearly. "What does that even mean?"

"It means that perhaps we should just dance and not talk." My arms tightened so that the space between our bodies disappeared. This time, she was the one who took two seconds to compose herself. But then I felt her body relax and her head dip toward my shoulder, and the blooming scent of flowers perfumed the space around my neck.

We might come from two historically conflicting tribes, but right then Earth and Fire coexisted in sweet harmony. That is, until Caleb swayed Whitnee right past me with a slight bump. When his wide eyes met mine, he mouthed and gestured behind Whitnee's back: *You. Eden. Tension.*

I could have pretended he was wrong. But instead, we traded secret smiles and led the girls across the dance floor, completely focused on the moment and nothing else.

18

THE REAL BLESSING

"The first Blessing Ritual in Aerodora, native tribe of our beloved Abrianna, was a success. Gabriel accepted the blessing from Councilman Ezekiel and his wife, Sarah. Even Nathan and Whitnee joined in the ceremony, showing a united front between the Pilgrim and the position of Guardian. While the ceremony was beautiful, the earthshaker that occurred over the Island last night did more than just alarm our tribes. A ravaging fire broke out in the Conclave on the Third Level—"

"Cool, it's like the news. Only 3-D," Morgan exclaimed when she entered the foyer of the guesthouse. I quickly shushed her as I watched the images of yesterday play out on the device in the center of the room. Apparently, there was a weekly Zephyra Broadcast that updated the people across the Island much the way our news media did. During the Guardianship festivities, it was on every morning to report what had happened the day before and it was only fifteen minutes long.

It was nothing like the vulture-circling scenes we got back on the Mainland. Only fifteen minutes a day of news? Sign me up.

Gabriel and his Palladium staff apparently watched it every morning to get a feel for how events were translating to the rest of the Island. I held my breath as they described the Fire being put out as an "act of miraculous ingenuity on the part of the Pilgrim's daughter, Whitnee." Someone showed an image of me dousing the flames before sucking them back up inside my glowing body.

"Does my hair always look that scary when I do that?" I mumbled.

"Yes, very 80s chic. With a little Bride of Frankenstein," Morgan said.

Yikes.

"Our young Guardian-to-be impressed business owners and leaders of the village during his Night Tour alongside his mother, Abrianna. But the real magic seemed to happen later that night at the Nightingale, the wind village's popular dance club." Images of Gabriel and me dancing together in which I leaned, laughing, into his chest played repetitively in front of us. I realized then that I had never seen what Gabriel and I looked like together. We seemed more natural than I remembered feeling. We really were complete contrasts to each other—in coloring, in stature, in everything. I started to see why maybe people found that so fascinating, and why Gabriel wanted to capitalize on it.

"Oh, aren't y'all cute." Caleb's sarcasm came from the corner, but his tone was only mildly offended. "He's not that funny, Whit."

"Neither are you," Gabriel tossed back just as mildly and then they both *laughed*.

As if they were *friends*.

Morgan widened her eyes at me and I shrugged. I needed to just accept it. There was absolutely nothing normal about my life being spent in two different worlds, so why would the only two boys I ever cared about *not* become friends with each other?

But then there were other shots of us all on the dance floor and a final view of Gabriel and Eden swaying together. Did her head curve into his chest more intimately than I had ever seen? Did his face seem more serene as it dipped closer to the flower in her hair?

"That is just asking for a scandal." Thomas smirked as he pointed to the image of Gabriel and Eden. "You two had better be careful or I will have to start addressing rumors about you."

Gabriel shifted uncomfortably in his chair, but Eden was quick on the response. "A dance hardly warrants a rumor. But yes, shut that gossip down should it arise. I do not want people questioning my focus as Personal Advisor to the Guardian."

"No one would dare question your focus, Eden. I was only joking," Thomas said, but his gaze lingered with curiosity at her when she turned her attention sharply back to the zephyra.

No wonder Gabriel refused to admit his feelings. Eden didn't appear to be open to that possibility at all. Or maybe she was in denial? Having spent a good amount of time there over Caleb last summer, I knew all about denial.

"While our Guardian-to-be and his friends spent time cavorting with the next generation of Aerodorians, Nathan was spotted coming out of the infirmary on Level One earlier this morning. Witnesses claimed he spent the night checking in on the sick and elderly and visiting old acquaintances from his childhood. While he claims to be the Pilgrim, the questions still remain: What does that mean? And what will he do next?"

Speaking of, I hadn't even seen Dad yet this morning and he hadn't been at the guesthouse by the time we made it back last night. I had been too tired to discover more, assuming he was with my grandparents.

Eden must have realized it too, because she got to her feet as the broadcast came to an end and the zephyra whirred down. "I think that was a sufficient report for yesterday's events. Well done communicating with the correspondents and protecting Jezebel's involvement with the Fire, Thomas."

"See?" Thomas said to Gabriel. "She appreciates the job I do."

"...Although I would like the next report to show Gabriel doing more than just 'cavorting.' We will need sufficient time for him to chat among the Geodorians today. And where is Nathan? It is time to leave or we will get behind schedule."

The vacant expressions around the room said that I wasn't the only one who didn't know where he was.

"It smells exactly as I remember it," Caleb said, breathing in deeply as our wagon approached Geodora through a tunnel of trees. His arm rested along the back of my seat the entire trip, and occasionally his fingers would graze my bare skin and send butterflies on a one-way trip to my stomach. Even now, he was close enough for me to feel the rise and fall of his greenery-adorned chest as he appreciated the familiar spices on the Geodorian air.

"We are arriving late, so everyone will need to move straight to the banquet hall in preparation for the ceremony," Eden reminded us.

"Sorry we're late," Dad apologized again, which Eden waved off respectfully.

It wasn't Dad's fault; it was the crowds of people who followed us to our wagon, insisting on just a touch from him. Some cried, others praised him for great deeds of healing and comfort, and some begged him for help. I had been ushered onto the wagon immediately with Caleb, Morgan, and Gabriel. From there, we had watched incredulously as Dad hugged, smiled, and gave each person individual attention on his way to us.

I could not forget Morgan's comment as the scene carried on. "Your dad is not of this world. He's just not."

Morgan had seen it since the first moment she met Dad. He was special in ways the rest of us weren't, and it was magnetizing.

When Dad had finally boarded the wagon, I asked him what all the talk was about and, more to the point, where he had been all night. We had only just found him feeding the thunderflies at the warehouse on the beach.

His response was casual. "I spent time on the lower level. Just checking on people."

Gabriel had remained quiet and reserved, speaking only when spoken to most of the trip. A silent and brooding Gabriel wasn't anything new, but he seemed distracted or displeased by something. Maybe he didn't like that Dad's admirers had outnumbered his as he left Aerodora. Or maybe it was that Eden was all business-like as she sat across from him, going over details of the ceremony.

But as we drew closer to the heart of the village, we all hushed. The road became lined with colorful flower petals and curious Geodorians who were so clothed in blooms themselves, it seemed like flowers were growing from their bodies. Green eyes competed for a closer look while the shouts and cheers grew in volume. I made sure my "Whitnee flower" was still tucked securely into my half-pinned hair, remembering that this day was special for more than one reason. It was the first ever Flower Day, given to honor Elon's life and Gabriel's ascent to Guardian. We all wore Elon's star-shaped white flowers with threaded gold somewhere in our hair or clothing. We also adorned ourselves with fresh green vines. I had wrapped a leafy vine up one arm and instead of having to pin it to the neckline of my sleeveless shirt, I just told it to stay there. And it did. Because that's what using the Earth life force could do.

We charmed vines to weave themselves around Morgan's legs up to her mid-thighs, like over-the-knee boots. With her short yellow skirt and her hair swept into a side ponytail, she looked like a character in a graphic novel. Eden and Hannah braided flowers into their long hair and let it hang loose down their backs.

"We renovated our outdoor theater this year in preparation for the Guardianship ceremony," Eden explained. "We planned so many beautiful things and then..." She trailed off and her ivy-toned eyes fluttered toward Gabriel.

"We will get through this," he said quietly. "It is understandable that a celebration is hard right now. Perhaps we can cut things short—"

"Elon would have wanted the whole Island to celebrate you. We will do her memory no justice by cancelling any part of it." They shared an intimate gaze that told me more about their relationship than anything I had guessed. These two did *life* together now. They respected each other. *Knew* one another.

Weirdly, I felt a sense of peace pour over me as I watched Gabriel and Eden reassure each other. They were like Caleb and me, maybe a year behind. I didn't realize the pressure cooker of guilty and confused feelings I'd stored up the last year until I felt them release right there in the back of that wagon. When I left the Island once and for all, Gabriel was going to be completely taken care of. He already had been, even if he didn't know it yet.

As if Caleb sensed it too, he glanced down at me. His hand curled completely around my upper arm and gently squeezed. There seemed to be zero tension between him and Gabriel, and that freed something in my spirit too.

But my warm fuzzy feelings lasted only until we reached our final destination, where Eden's family stood ready to greet us with forced smiles. Eden used to have five siblings. Now there were four, and the sight of one missing child assaulted me in the chest. It shouldn't have happened this way.

We alighted from the wagon, and the moment Dad wrapped his arms around Joanna, Eden's mom, she completely fell apart and soaked his tunic with fresh tears. I saw Eden's eyes fill up as Joseph patted his wife's back.

"Jo-Jo, we cannot do this here. The whole village is watching."

"Perhaps she could have been saved. If they had been here," she sobbed.

Dad's face was distressed as he held the weeping woman. I moved closer and rested my vine-wrapped arm around her back, my palm lighting up with the tranquility vibes of the Fire life force.

"Elon is in a safe and wonderful place now," I assured her, my words sounding empty to a mourning mother. "I dreamed about her the morning she died. She was playing in the flowers, and she was so peaceful and happy. It felt so real, I know that's where she is."

Joanna lifted her face to see me, her tears slowing. But it was Dad whose expression dramatically changed.

"You saw her back on the Mainland? Why didn't you tell me?"

I was at a loss for how to respond to that. Was that really important at a time like this? I hadn't *seen* her. I just wanted to comfort this family. I wanted to comfort *myself.*

"It was only a dream. And I didn't know then that she had died," I explained, trying to read his thoughts. "I've dreamed of her before on the Mainland."

A spark ignited in Dad's eyes as he glanced around at all of us, at the crowds of people moving closer down the road. He seemed to be wrestling with something, and I found myself holding my breath to see what was going to happen next.

"Take me to her," he said to Joanna and Joseph.

"What do you mean?" Joseph asked, flustered.

"I need to see Elon. Where is she?"

Joseph was confounded by the request. "Nathan, she has been dead for three days—"

"This way!" Joanna started pulling Dad down the street. "She is being held in the Preservation Room until we could have a proper memorial service."

Gabriel gave me a questioning look that I only mirrored back. Eden scooped up her littlest sister, Esther, and started following them without hesitation.

"Dad. *What* are you doing?" He didn't even answer; he was on a mission.

Curiosity propelled us all forward, past the banquet hall I remembered from last summer. Joseph led us between two buildings and down a path where lilies of white and red and orange seemed to lean in toward Dad as he rushed past them.

"You see what I'm seeing, right?" Morgan whispered, gesturing at the subtle but strange behavior of the flowers.

"Yep." I had seen nature react to him before. I couldn't decide if it was supernaturally breathtaking or horror-movie disturbing. The Island felt alive wherever Dad went.

Finally we came to a flat one-story building, shaded by huge trees and encompassed in a translucent green dome. Joseph manipulated the Geodorian shield to open for us but paused before opening the door.

"There is a cold shield over the table. It preserves the... the body better." He swallowed thickly. "But that is all that is in there, Nathan." A heart-wrenching sob escaped from Joanna at his words, and he turned to her. "Jo-Jo, that is not our little girl. That body is just a casing, a husk. She is *gone*."

But it was Dad's reaction that caused my own throat to seize up. He wiped at his eyes and in a broken voice he said, "I am so sorry I wasn't here. There have been so many on the Island... I should have stayed and done more."

"Don't say that, Dad," I mumbled, my own voice splintering with sadness. This wasn't his fault, and I didn't like hearing any regret over his time spent back at home with Mom and me.

"Whitnee," Dad said and reached for my hand. "Come in with me. I want everyone else to stay outside."

"What are you going to do?" Gabriel asked, warily glancing back toward the villagers who had followed us.

"Not sure yet," Dad responded. Caleb and Morgan gave me confused glances as I dutifully followed my dad into the frigid building. The door closed behind us with a heavy click that almost made me jump.

There was a figure on top of a table in the corner of the large warehouse-like room. Another glowing green shield cocooned the small frame inside and my knees started quivering. It had been almost a year since I'd witnessed death on this Island and I never wanted to experience it again.

Dad's hand was firm in mine as he practically dragged me over there.

She was skinnier and paler than I remembered, and *so* creepily unmoving. I could see what Joseph meant. And I remembered when Simeon died still holding my hand and what Caleb had once told me about his dad when he watched him die right in front of him. Dead people just looked, well, *dead*. The spirit—the essence of who a person was—just wasn't there anymore.

But the essence of nausea was definitely present in my stomach as I gazed down at her through the greenish hue of Earth life force. I recalled those sweet hands of hers braiding my hair last summer and how her little body had pressed near to mine whenever I sat down, always wanting to be close.

Dad's voice was barely above a whisper, but I still jumped when he spoke. "We need to remove this shield."

"Come on, really?" He was crazy. "We can see her just fine."

He ignored me and used his Geodorian abilities to collapse the shield. The medicinal smell of whatever spices they used to preserve her hit me first. Then the colorless, gossamer appearance of her skin nearly did me in.

I bit my fist to keep from crying out, but couldn't stop the tears from leaking.

"Baby Doll, death is not something to be afraid of."

Of all the things he could say… Death meant separation, and I hated it. All I could utter was, "Could we have saved her?"

"No. It was supposed to happen this way."

"Children aren't supposed to die, Dad."

He nodded and we both took a moment to compose ourselves. Dad sniffed and then crossed around to the other side of the table opposite of me. I watched him bow his head and lean both fists on the table. When his eyes closed, he almost looked as if he was in prayer.

But when he looked up at me again, his eyes had changed. The irises had a white circle and they seared me with intensity when he said, "Whitnee, I'm going to do something. And it will change things from this point on. But I need you to trust that I know what I'm doing."

"Of course I trust you," I assured him. "You're the Pilgrim."

Without another word, he put his hands on Elon's head and that white circle glowed brighter and brighter until I couldn't tell anymore where the light was originating from. I had to shield my eyes as the heat intensified around us. Then the burning whiteness took on the shape of smoke and poured into Elon's nostrils, causing her chest to rise and her whole body to lift off the table and hover in the air. Then she exhaled and the sound filled the entire room. I could feel it ripple through the air like a humid breeze, and goosebumps broke out over my entire body. Dad let go and her body slammed back down onto the table.

When she started twitching, I almost ran away. Something so unnatural had just happened between my dad and Elon—something so beautifully terrifying—that I was sure my tears were grounded more in fear than in any other emotion.

"Dad!" I choked out, taking several steps back. I was going to throw up if I attempted another word.

"Shhhh," he whispered in soothing tones from across the table. "Don't be afraid."

But I was. Elon stopped twitching and I stopped breathing. Dad said, "Wake up, Elon."

And then her chest started rising and falling with consistent breath and when she sat up, color and warmth were back in her skin tone. Her once pale lips were pink again and they stretched into a wide smile as she looked first at Dad and then at me and said,

"I knew you would come."

19

FLOWER DAY

Whitnee came out of the Preservation Room first. Either she tripped or her legs gave out—I am still uncertain—but I was the closest to the door and caught her by the arms. The wild look in her eyes was alarming.

"What has happened? What is it, Whitnee?"

She could not speak and I turned my Pyra senses on to full detection. She was brimming with a piercing fear and yet almost spilling over with *joy*. I tried to direct her to sit as Caleb came up to my side to help.

But then I heard, "Hi, Mama. Hi, Papa." And I knew that beloved little voice before I even saw her engulfed by Joseph and Joanna and the entire family.

Elon was *alive*?

There were screams and shouts of joy and confusion, and without any ceremony, they all toppled to the ground holding one another and kissing cheeks and heads and crying. The gasps and whispers and chatter started rippling through the crowd of Geodorians who had gathered outside.

I looked back at Whitnee who seemed incapable of controlling her own tears. "Did you—"

"No," she quickly clarified, using a leaf on her arm to wipe her face. "It was Dad. He brought her back."

All eyes turned to Nathan who stood in the doorway, witnessing the celebration. Eden was the first to break off from her family and run to him.

223

"Thank you, thank you!" she cried and clung to him. The rest of the family followed.

I could only stand there as if struck mute. How had this miracle occurred? And what did that mean about Nathan?

What did it mean for *me*?

"Gabriel?" Elon's voice pierced through all the other noise. She gently pushed away the tangle of arms around her so she could approach me. I got down on my knees so we could be eye-level. She still smelled of preservation herbs and oils.

"Hello, dear one," I greeted her, trying to swallow back down my own emotions but finding myself utterly unsuccessful. "I have missed you the last few days."

"I told you the Pilgrim would save me. Did you doubt it?"

I felt shame that what she believed so fiercely I had dismissed out of selfish skepticism.

"I wish to have your faith," I confessed to her and glanced over at Eden who watched silently with hands clasped to her chest. Elon looked around as if noticing where she was for the first time. At the sight of the weeping crowds, she shuffled closer into my shadow.

Then came her whisper. "Are you the Guardian yet?"

"Almost," I whispered back. "You are just in time for my Geodorian blessing."

"Is that why everyone is wearing flowers?" She peered shyly again out at the crowd of people. A few of her little friends waved back at her voraciously, but parents held them back.

"We wear flowers for you, Elon." I removed one of the Whitnee flowers from my necklace and settled it into her hair. "It is Flower Day! Do you not remember? Come, we must make it rain flowers."

She giggled and her thin little arms wrapped around my neck with strength I had not felt from her in a long time. I picked her up and put her on my shoulders. We faced the crowd together. "It is a miracle from our Pilgrim—Elon is alive! Let all the people and flowers on the Island rejoice!" And I summoned an explosion of Firelight flowers and petals over our heads to sprinkle down around us. The village erupted with cheers and the trees and blossoms began to dance from their rooted places in the ground.

"Gabriel." Elon pulled on the neck of my tunic to get my attention. "Hand me another Whitnee flower." I immediately obeyed. She tucked it into my hair above my ear like she had done the night she died.

"There," she said. "That is how you are to wear it."

"Anything for you," I acquiesced, catching Eden's eye again. Her smile was so serene as she gazed back at me that a sensation of happiness ignited in my chest—a feeling I was not sure I had ever experienced. It leaked out in the form of robust laughter. Elon's giggles joined in, and when the Mainlanders, Eden's family, and my own friends surrounded Elon and me with embraces, everything in my small world felt complete and whole for the first time.

"Gabriel, your flower is falling," Eden said as I shoveled a large bite into my mouth. I was certain I had never been so hungry in all my life. Instead of waiting for me to fix it, Eden reached out and pushed the obnoxious bloom back into place, poking my scalp with the stem. When I jerked with the sharpness, she laughed, and her fingers slid into my hair and rubbed circles above my ear for a few glorious seconds. "I had no idea a flower stem to the head was your weakness."

The flower did not weaken me, but I could not say the same thing about the impromptu head massage.

What I did say aloud was, "I am only wearing this for Elon. I look utterly ridiculous."

"And yet, you have somehow started a trend. I have seen countless young men wearing gigantic flowers in their hair the same way today."

With an amused sigh, I shook my head. "My first contribution as Guardian. I hope Elon is happy."

"Oh, she is," Eden assured me and we both glanced down the table where the little girl—freshly bathed and dressed like royalty— sat among her family with Nathan close by. She also ate her lunch with the appetite of a grown man. I suppose being dead and raised to life again might cause that. "It was very sweet of you to let her be part of the Blessing Ritual."

"Is that why I saw you crying off to the side?" I teased.

"I did no such thing." Her protest was pointless and she knew it. But did she know that I found it adorable how often she wanted to pretend she had no feelings?

I felt Whitnee elbow me slightly as she sat to my left. She leaned in and muttered, "If your mother touches my dad one more time, I might have to take her out with a cyclone."

My gaze locked on the two of them as they sat across from Joseph and Joanna. I thought Abrianna had been on her best behavior since Eli had run off. Whitnee did not understand how much Nathan's presence influenced my mother's kindness. But yes, Abrianna was also an attention-seeker and would always gravitate to the most powerful person in the room, barring herself, of course. "If you are expecting me to hold you back, you might be disappointed. The list of reasons I have for trusting my mother is practically nonexistent."

"He is a married man. And he's the Pilgrim. And he's my *dad*."

"And she is like a sister to him," I reminded her. At the thin-eyed look she gave me, I added, "Your father has many people who want to be close to him. She is not the only one doing a lot of touching."

Nathan, in fact, was drawing quite a bit of attention. The Geoguards ended up having to do more to protect him during the Blessing Ritual than they did for me. I was not jealous of the attention he was garnering, but I still felt uneasy about it. If he chose to leave the Island again, it could potentially create widespread problems. And where did this rule of peace, of miracles and blessings, end with him?

I did not understand it all, and every time I wanted to seek him out to discuss further, there was some other event to be held or place to be.

"Who is that?" Whitnee suddenly asked, nodding toward the Geoguard who approached to consult privately with Joseph.

"That is Abner," I muttered. I was never thrilled to see the man, though I could not understand why I disliked him even more since I saw him a few days ago.

"Eden's Abner?" Whitnee asked, which soured the food I had just swallowed. "Ohhhh. I see now why you grew a beard. His is quite stunning."

"Whitnee, behave," Caleb warned with a smirk from across the table. I had not realized he had been listening in, and I could barely concoct an annoyed glance at Whitnee's insinuations. I was preoccupied with whatever Abner and Joseph were discussing and why their eyes kept flicking this way. Why did Joseph suddenly seem uncomfortable?

Eden piped up from beside me, excitement coloring her voice. "Caleb! They are going to set up a game of coconut launch right after the meal. You will play, right?"

"Heck yes. But only if I get to be on your team," Caleb responded enthusiastically.

"Of course! Whitnee, will you play again? Morgan?"

Morgan chimed in first. "Would I be allowed to use a Water deflector? Because you know I can't green up like you Geos do."

"I am certain we could bend the rules for you," Eden laughed.

Whitnee responded, "No, thank you. I do not enjoy getting hit with coconuts. I think I would probably have more fun watching this time."

If she actually *watched* the game this time. I would never forget her first game of coconut launch. After an injury took her out of the game, she proceeded to fight with me until I was forced to kiss her to get her to stop wielding life forces like a maniac. It had been a confusing moment of infuriating desire that pushed me over the edge that night. And I did not regret it. I had never felt such a sensual clash of life forces as I had with Whitnee.

I might find myself distracted by Eden these days, but that did not mean that memories with Whitnee did not still stir embers of desire I had to douse.

The sudden flush to her cheeks told me she remembered it too. I averted my eyes to the afternoon sky and pretended not to notice.

But Caleb in his constantly observant and intuitive state had to have picked up on it. "Gabriel, maybe you should join us on the field this time." Of course he would want to keep me in his sight. But I supposed I had my reasons for wanting to keep him in mine too. "I'm sure they wouldn't mind you incinerating a flying coconut if you couldn't dodge it."

"I think perhaps my time would be better spent socializing with villagers as they watch the game, as Eden suggested this morning. No cavorting today, right?"

Eden's face dropped. "Oh, of course. What am I thinking? It is as if I forgot for a moment that I was the Guardian's Advisor and not just here at home. I can forego the game."

"Nonsense," I assured her. "This is a big day for you, for your family. I want you to enjoy every moment. I am sure your brothers and sisters will want to play out there with you. Please do not give them another reason to accuse me of stealing you away from them."

"Someone needs to assist you. Levi has no personality and Thomas has too much. He makes inappropriate jokes at the wrong times."

"Since when did Geodorians care so much for propriety?" I pointed out, which earned a reproving look from her.

"I am only trying to protect your reputation."

"Dad and I can make the social rounds with him," Whitnee offered. "Caleb has been secretly hoping this whole time that y'all would get to play again."

Caleb took a big drink of water before leaning back in his chair and sighing. "The world deserves to see our mad partner skills on that field, Eden. Give yourself a break and ditch the Palladium responsibilities for just one game."

"Eden!" The booming voice I had dreaded resounded behind me. Eden immediately turned and rose to greet Abner. I took my time with a drink before standing to my feet and clapping him on the shoulder.

"Thank you for bringing her to assist me in Aerodora," I thanked him.

"Of course. It was what she wanted," he told me and looped one of his large arms around her waist. "I apologize I am just now getting to talk to you. I was on perimeter security all morning. I am in awe that Elon is alive. You must be overjoyed!"

"I am," Eden smiled, though something in her demeanor seemed stiff. "It is hardly believable. My parents seem to have gained back years of their lives in just one morning."

"Yes, they look well. It has been awful to see them suffer."

I interrupted their little niceties. "Abner, have you officially met our Mainland friends? That is Morgan and Caleb." I pointed and they waved. Then I reached for Whitnee to stand by my side. "And this is Whitnee, Nathan's daughter."

Whitnee held out a hand in their custom of hand shaking that I had learned. Abner, unsure of what to do with that, grabbed hers with his beefy grip and brought it to his lips for a greeting kiss. Though he did so quite naturally, that old protectiveness for Whitnee filtered through me, and I wondered how Caleb was always able to stay back and observe Whitnee around other men (myself included) so casually.

"Have we met before?" Whitnee asked him, not removing her eyes from his face. I could sense her mind was trying to recall something.

"Actually, yes," he answered. "I met you the first time you were in Geodora last summer before your friends went missing. I was certain you would not remember me. You were quite distracted with many things that night—one being our future Guardian." He smiled mischievously at me, and I silently cursed the candor of the Geodorians.

Whitnee still seemed to be considering him. "Maybe that was it."

"Abner has been a family friend for years and a Geoguard for my father ever since the unexpected events of last summer," Eden explained.

"Well, we are more than just family friends at this point, right, Edie?" Abner laughed and squeezed her closer to him.

Edie? I could not halt my eyebrows from rising in surprise at the nickname. Eden's laughter was nervous when she deflected his comment and refused to look at me. "Abner, we are about to go play coconut launch. Will you be joining the game?"

"I would love to. But I will need to check in with your father first. He does not want to spare any security today." Then he turned to me. "We have had some protesters. Joseph wanted them removed from the heart of the village. But they are gathering in number on the outskirts. Making the same claims, as usual."

"The fact that they would question Gabriel's authenticity at birth is disrespectful," Eden huffed.

I had not shared my deepest fears with her, because what if they were right? I could not bear the thought of my friends discovering that I was a falsehood. Would they remain my friends if they did? Sometimes I wondered if Eden's heart was merely to serve the office of Guardian. If I were not in a position of leadership, would she still remain close to me?

There were really only two people I could consult about that bloody sign in the sky the night I was born, and I trusted neither of them to actually tell the truth. I figured I only had to keep these doubters under control a few days longer. Once Abrianna had officially passed off her Guardianship in the final ceremony and I was fully the Guardian, no amount of protesting would change it. The questions would die down. Things might return to normal. Or to something even better.

Unless Abner and Eden ended up betrothed... I could not bring myself to imagine how that would impact my relationship with my Personal Advisor.

"I think the supposed coming of the Pilgrim has caused a lot of questions," Abner said, once again voicing his opinions quite openly. "I was unsure if he was who the rumors claim until I saw Elon. Surely that is a sign that he is who they think he is."

"It certainly seems that way," Whitnee agreed. "However, that doesn't mean that *Gabriel* isn't who people think he is. My father does not have any desire to govern the Island. He feels that Gabriel is the man to maintain proper leadership over the Island, as he has already been doing. Dad trusts what the Island has ordained. Maybe everyone else should too."

There was a pause as Abner's mouth peeled back into a smile, first at Whitnee and then at me. "You have quite an advocate in her, Gabriel. Let Whitnee keep talking like that and I daresay those protesters might listen."

"Put me in, Coach," Whitnee said, as if in agreement. Eden and I exchanged confused looks.

"Do you mean, put you on a team for coconut launch?" Eden clarified.

"No!" The Mainlanders laughed, as they always did when their language confused us. "I meant, let me make the social rounds with Gabriel. Let me talk to people. Maybe I can help."

"She can be pretty persuasive," Caleb agreed. "But more importantly than that, Eden, we need to go strategize a plan for our team. I am not going to be the Mainlander who loses!"

"Oh, Caleb, you are also quite persuasive. Very well," Eden consented. I knew Caleb's words appealed to her competitive side and she used them to excuse herself. "I will find you later, Abner. Perhaps you will be off-duty for the dinner feast?"

"I will speak with your father," he said. With an affectionate tweak of the end of her braided hair and a nod to us, he left.

As the Geodorians finished their meals and we all started to walk to the playing field, Thomas and Levi flanked me on either side.

Levi started in first. "There are protesters—"

"I heard," I interrupted him. "I am certain you have it under control."

Levi just grunted. Thomas took his turn. "I have been instructed to stay close by, but to quiet my sense of humor. Since when am I considered inappropriate?"

"I think Eden has not forgiven you for that one dinner with the Councilmen."

Thomas rolled his eyes. "What is the point of working for the Guardian if you cannot wield that power to make a good joke?"

"That is *exactly* the kind of inappropriateness I am talking about, Thomas!" Eden's voice cut in as she marched past us with the Mainlanders in tow. "We do not use our positions to wield power."

"You are ruining my life, Eden!" he called after her, then leaned toward me and mumbled, "Does she understand what being the Guardian even means? It is power."

"I heard that too," Eden called back and Morgan stifled a laugh.

"Thanks, Morgan. At least someone around here finds me funny."

"Oh, I was laughing at Eden," she clarified, but then blew a kiss in his direction anyway.

That was the moment that Abner jogged past us and placed himself between Eden and Caleb. "Joseph gave me the rest of the day off to enjoy by your side. I can play in the game, after all. Tell me your strategies."

Caleb's pace slowed while Eden glanced back at me again. Why was she nervous around him? Or was I making her nervous?

"Great," she said and then started sharing her thoughts about the game. Everyone else kept walking until Caleb and I were the only ones hanging back.

Caleb said it first. "I don't like him."

Nor did I. But I did not have the freedom to be so vocal about it. "He is a good man. And he would be the best match for her within her tribe."

"Nah, forget the tribe loyalty. He's not the *best* match." We watched from a distance as Abner's arm went back around Eden's waist. It was amazing to me that she allowed someone outside of her family to touch her the way he did. She really must care for him.

"I can totally take him out of the game," Caleb offered. "Just say the word. I'll make it look like an accident."

My only response was to offer my fist the way he had taught me, the way he and his friends greeted each other or agreed about something on the Mainland. He pounded his knuckles against mine and when we pulled our hands back, our life forces met each other with a pop, sizzle, and bang.

I never would have guessed that Caleb would be the one to understand my deepest secrets without me having to speak them.

20

COCONUT LAUNCH,
TAKE TWO

The trees cocooned like a lush hut of greenery over my dad as he sat on the ground surrounded by thirty or so children. Elon sat in his lap while he told stories of the Island's history and hilarious accounts of life force accidents. At one point, Joseph had tried to make the children scatter so that Dad could go watch the game, but he was instantly rebuked.

I had never seen Dad so completely in his element as he was right there in a corner of that village sharing stories with the littlest Islanders and making them feel so important. For a few confusing moments, I found myself jealous of Elon getting to sit in my dad's lap, soaking up his presence and his words. The two of them were connected now in a way I could not quite pinpoint. And Dad was so immersed in his role as Pilgrim that he had hardly checked in on me today.

As if he could sense me watching him, his eyes found mine across the field and his voice entered my mind.

I love you, Baby Doll.

I smiled and waved. *I love you too. Even if you are ignoring me to hang out with a bunch of kids.*

Oh, did you want me in your business more? he teased.

Maybe a little, I admitted.

You and Gabriel seem to be doing fine without me. I'm really proud of you wanting to give truth and support to the people of the Island.

I'm really proud of you, Dad. Is that weird to say? I still trembled every time I remembered him calling Elon back to life, so it was possible I was a little scared of him too.

Not weird at all. Thank you.

I ignored the sting in my eyes that tried to trigger tears. I had felt increasingly emotional as the day went on. The love I held for my dad had somehow exploded even more as I witnessed his compassion and connection with others. I wished for the infinite time that Mom could see him like this. A part of me felt jealously protective of him. He might be the Pilgrim, but he was still my dad. We were still a family, and the little doubts about how we were going to make that work crept in every so often.

Doubts about returning to the Mainland at all lurked not too far behind the others, but if I gave them too much space in my mind, I might start to think living on the Island forever wouldn't be the worst thing—as long as Caleb and Morgan stayed too, and as long as Mom was here... and then the whole vicious cycle of worry started all over again.

Best to keep my mind clear and just focus on the present and trust that the future would work itself out soon. Faith over fear, like Dad had said.

While Dad had been busy doing Pilgrim-things, I floated around by Gabriel's side, speaking with villagers, listening politely as he answered questions and chiming in only when issues of the Pilgrim were brought up. I actually enjoyed meeting new people and seeing how drawn they were to Gabriel's strength and presence. We also did a lot of game-watching and cheering, especially as it got more intense out on the field. Caleb and Eden were spattered with coconut juice as they ran all over the field deflecting and launching coconuts the way we did at home in dodgeball.

I couldn't get enough of the view of Caleb's muscles tightening every time he threw a coconut across the line and the way his hair stuck up in crazy directions from the stickiness and sweat of the game. It was similar to how he had looked the night of the basketball championship. He had emptied all of himself out there on that court and then still made time among team celebrations to find me in the stands for one of those swing-you-around hugs. That had been the first time I thought he would kiss me, and I know I would have been okay with the sweaty and salty flavor that I was sure it would be. But then our parents had interrupted the moment with their congratulations. Dad had practically knocked him over in pride, dressed in his Lucky #13 t-shirt that Morgan and I had made for all of us to cheer Caleb on.

If Caleb were to finally steal a kiss after a victory today, I would make sure no one interrupted it. I had a feeling he was weakening in his resolve to wait until we returned home.

That thought had me intensely focused in those final moments of the game. Morgan got out and joined Gabriel and me on the sidelines as we cheered on Eden, Caleb, and Abner. The crowd grew more intense, and even Dad and the children joined the sidelines to watch. On the other side of the field, one of Eden's brothers (I never could tell the twins apart) launched a coconut right at Caleb. While his shield went up to deflect that one, another coconut flew from the other direction and smacked him in the left shoulder.

He was out, and from the look on his face, there went my chance for a victory kiss.

He jogged up to us on the sidelines, throwing out arguments and rotating his shoulder around.

"You okay?" I asked, immediately concerned. Last time he had taken a coconut to the head. I did not want to relive an injured Caleb.

"I'm fine. Just pissed." He still let me examine his arm anyway, and I caught him and Gabriel frowning at each other. "Abner is good out there, dude. I hate to admit it."

"Yes, I know," Gabriel grunted and then they both started shouting at a play on the field. Abner and Eden played well together—possibly an even better partnership than her and Caleb. Something I would never say to Caleb.

Or Gabriel.

It finally came down to Eden and Abner against one of the twins on the other team. With some teamwork, they launched coconuts until he tripped and couldn't get his shield up in time. The whole village turned upside down in cheers and chants. Then we all witnessed Abner hoist Eden into his arms and kiss her full on the mouth as the teams rushed forward to surround them.

However, Caleb, Morgan, and I might have been the only ones to witness Gabriel's crestfallen expression in the middle of the clapping and cheering. I was at a loss on what to say or do, and I suppose Gabriel felt the same way, because he turned around to leave.

Caleb grabbed him by the arm. "Hey, man. You okay?"

"Of course," Gabriel responded. "I am going to my room for a while." And he gave Levi and Thomas a severe look that said he didn't want any arguments.

"Gabriel—" I started, but Caleb gestured at me to let him go. Since Gabriel didn't even turn around at my voice, I let him.

"Whitnee, can we take a walk?" Elon asked, leaving Dad's side to approach me. The way that Dad scratched his neck as he watched us made me wonder if this was her idea or his.

"Of course. We don't have anywhere to be."

"I was hoping it could be just the two of us," she added and glanced shyly at Morgan and Caleb.

"It's because I stink, isn't it?" Caleb teased her, eliciting a giggle and shake of her head. "I need to head to the cabin to shower anyway."

"And I'm gonna make him stretch that shoulder out. Maybe he'll let me practice some Healing with Water on him," Morgan said, which brought forth protests from Caleb. Morgan just rolled her eyes at me and ushered him away. "We'll find you later."

Elon took my hand and led me down a private path in the direction of the flower fields. The scent of deep earth that had just finished drinking a fresh summer rain filled the air as we strolled hand in hand.

While she was very much alive, she also seemed somehow removed. As if she was made of something more now—maybe less of this world and more of the next. "How are you feeling?"

"Better with you and Nathan here." She allowed her free hand to graze the bushes beside us and little blooms appeared on every stem she touched. I tried not to be distracted by the lovely strangeness of it.

"I'm so glad to be here—with you," I said. "I never got a chance to tell you that I dreamed about you a couple of times on the Mainland."

"I know. I was there."

The hairs along the back of my neck stood up. "What do you mean?"

"I was there. In the dreams."

"Wait." I paused and knelt down so I could be on eye-level with her. "Elon, how is that possible?"

"The portal you used to come here made me sick last year. It is like Poison to the Island. Once it finds you, it takes away your life force. It found me and killed me."

Her dead face flashed in my mind again and I swallowed down the bile that threatened to rise in my throat.

"I'm sorry," I breathed. Her bluntly simple words propagated a fear that had taken root in my heart last summer, that I was somehow to blame for the problems on the Island. I already knew I was connected to the Palladium portal... connected to the *poison* she spoke of. Poison had been their word last summer for Morgan's cancer—something they knew as untreatable, unstoppable.

Cancerous. Did she mean it the same way?

"But what does the portal have to do with my dreams?"

"The Poison found me and tried to get to you on the Mainland, but the Island set me aside to help you. Do you remember when I tried to tell you that they were coming for you?" I did remember. I could never forget that night at Camp Fusion when I woke up with a green shield over my bunk bed with Elon's warnings echoing in my head.

"I do remember... you meant the ones who kidnapped me?"

She didn't answer directly. "When I died, I was taken to the flower fields to play until you and Nathan came. I could feel you there too."

"I dreamed that." In my bedroom at home... on my birthday.

"No, you were *there*. I felt you, but I could not see you."

It still made absolutely no sense to me, but at this point it didn't have to for me to believe.

"Why are you and I connected this way?" I took her other hand in mine as we faced each other. There was a subtle vibration between our palms, as alive as the earth beneath us. The plants around us started to sway and move, but there was no breeze.

"I do not know," she whispered, gazing around at the moving foliage. It was as if she were listening to something before her soft green eyes landed on me. "But I know that I was brought back to give you a message from the Island."

Now it was the hair on my arms standing up, trying to alert me to something. How could such a cute and innocent little girl creep me out so much? To be fair, I sensed my discomfort was less her and more the presence of something bigger and more powerful than us orchestrating things.

"What does the Island say?"

"You are the only one who can shut down the portal in the Palladium," she told me. "Not Nathan. It will be you. And when you do, there will be a difficult choice to make."

"What kind of choice?"

Her eyes welled up with tears as she shook her head. "I do not know, but I am so sorry."

"Oh, honey, why are you sorry? It's okay." I pulled her in for a hug and everything around us stilled again. I pressed my lips to her soft hair, still faintly smelling the preservation herbs of death that had embalmed her earlier that day.

"I am sorry because I think it will be hard," she cried into my neck and her words reverberated in my chest like a rapid heartbeat.

"Tell me how, Elon. Whatever you know, I need to know."

"I cannot see it. I only feel it. The Poison has to be stopped."

"Does my dad know all of this?"

At that, she pulled back from me to wipe her eyes. Her hands rested on my shoulders as she said solemnly, "Some things he will not know until it is time. Nathan *is* the Island. He is also your father. The part of him that belongs to you threatens his purpose. You must act carefully, Whitnee. All of our lives depend on it."

21

CLOSE ENCOUNTERS OF THE GEODORIAN KIND

The silence swirled around me like the steam in the bathing room. I wrapped a towel around my waist and shook the remaining droplets out of my hair before lowering myself to the bench. How could I be twenty years old and feel like I had already lived a lifetime of problems?

My head tilted back to rest against the wall and, as my eyes closed, I envisioned physically shutting out the world around me for just a few moments. As usual, I stoked the Fire life force within and allowed it to seep out through my damp skin. I could feel the tense muscles beneath my scars try to release the pressure that always found its way to my back. It had only been a year, but it seemed as if I would be forever bound to the effects of the drakon venom. Michael, my Hydrodorian attendant while growing up at the Palladium, had assured me that with time the pain would get better.

But time only seemed to complicate matters, never improve them.

And in the realm of complicated matters, since when had Eden's relationship with Abner turned physical? That kiss on the field did not look like a first. I wanted to erase it from my memory, but it puzzled me to no end. Had her frequent visits to Geodora over the last year been about more than seeing Elon and the family? Abner had been there for her through all of it. He had taken care of her family in her absence. I had always been aware of his fondness for her, but Eden always seemed more occupied with her work, with her plans, with *me*.

Her nervousness around the two of us began to make sense. If Eden and Abner were heading toward marriage, things would change. I was certain she would no longer want to live at the Palladium and act as my Personal Advisor once she was a married woman. Had I really expected her to stay by my side for the next thirty years of my Guardianship?

Gabriel, you are a fool.

Pathetic loneliness spiraled out around me as I realized I had an extremely limited vision of my future and even less for the future of the Island. I had lived moment-to-moment up to these ceremonies, trying to fix the damage caused by others, following Eden's ideas for restoration and change...

And now I might lose her.

A thud from the bedroom told me that someone had entered. I rolled my neck, guessing it was a member of my staff ready to go over the remaining schedule of the day. For the briefest of moments, I was tempted to remain perfectly still and silent in the hopes that they would go away and leave me to steam a little longer without interruption.

But, alas, there were responsibilities and festivities and other kinds of -ies that I was certain to be needed for.

I stood up and tightened the towel on my hips, then rubbed my eyes and looked in the mirror. My hair was almost dry and the stubble of a beard on my face freshly trimmed. As I turned to the door, it flung open and jammed into my foot.

I made a grunt of surprise, but it was nothing compared to the scream that escaped from Eden who was clad only in her undergarments.

Only in her undergarments. All that soft skin glistening with coconut juice took up every angle of my vision.

"Gabriel! What are you doing in this bathing room?" She yanked the door and slammed it closed between us.

"This is my room!" I could not move as I stared at the door, still only seeing her curvy figure in my mind's eye. "I always stay here..."

Did I not? Was I confused or was she? Every time I came to Geodora, I took the guest room at her family's main house while she stayed in her old room.

"No, you imbecile! Father put you in the bigger guesthouse with everyone else this time!"

"Is it not your job to inform me of that?"

"I cannot believe—" Her words grew muffled as I assumed with impure disappointment that she was putting clothes on. "Do not come out of there until we are both fully dressed!"

"Impossible, because my clothes are in there with you. Did you not see my satchel when you came marching into *my* private space?"

"What— where? *Ugh.*" I heard her banging around until she shoved the door open again without warning and hit me in the face this time.

"Could you please stop abusing me?" I grumbled as she thrust my bag through the cracked door. I yanked it away from her and then threw the door wide open before it could attack me again.

"I said to dress yourself!" she shrieked and her hands went to adjust the tunic she had thrown on haphazardly over herself. I had to force myself to avert my eyes again. Why did I find her so alluring? It was madness.

"My clothes are hanging in the dresser, not in this bag." I stormed over and wrenched the dresser door open, completely lost about which uniform Hannah had picked out for me to wear to the feast.

As I shuffled through the different decorated outfits, Eden burst out, "The green and gold one, Gabriel, you know that!" I finally found the one and then spun back around to discover she had donned shorts.

"This is your fault, not mine."

She gathered her wild hair in her hands, thick and wavy from her braids and tousled from the game. As she tied a loose knot on top of her head, she took a few breaths and had a hard time making eye contact with me.

"I apologize, I thought we discussed these arrangements this morning. I needed to bathe and all the other bathing rooms are being used after that game. I was so distracted that I did not even notice your—" She gestured at my belongings in the corner of the room.

"It is fine. You have seen me shirtless plenty of times."

"Being shirtless with pants on, and wearing nothing but a towel are two completely different things. You understand that, right?" She put her hands on her hips and stared up at the ceiling as if still trying to collect herself. "And I am certain you have never seen me in my undergarments, so there is nothing *fine* about this situation."

"Yes, I am going to have to work hard to get that image out of my head."

"You had better, or I will open a hole in the earth beneath your feet and seal it back up while you are still alive."

I winced. "That is harsh punishment for an innocent man."

"Gabriel." There was a bit of pleading to her tone now and it alerted me to the fact that she really was more embarrassed than I had realized. I could not recall ever seeing her cheeks that color of crimson as she stood across from me in that room. "If you do not stop looking at me like that, I might have to consider resigning my job and hiding in my parents' house for the rest of my life." The most enchanting look of shyness and awkward amusement came over her expression then, and it made me laugh.

"I do not know how I am looking at you, but please do not hide for the rest of your life. Let me get dressed and then you can use this bathing room." Once I was back on the other side of the door, I called out, "As for the matter of your resignation, I am sure it is just a matter of time anyway. Perhaps I need to start thinking of your replacement."

It was meant to sound like teasing, but once the words came out of my mouth, I regretted them. Especially when her voice came back startled. "What do you mean?"

Ah, she was going to make me say it. Very well. "Your relationship with Abner seems to have progressed."

"Oh. I suppose you saw him kiss me."

"Everyone on the Island saw it."

"So?"

So...? What game was she playing?

When I entered the bedroom again, she had her arms crossed over her chest, frowning.

"So, I assume he will be proposing marriage soon." I tried to connect the fastenings and hooks on the front of my vest, my fingers stumbling too many times. "And when he does, I doubt either of you will want to live at the Palladium. You will get married, live here in Geodora, have a dozen children, and you will forget that you ever worked yourself to death for a Pyradorian Guardian who once drove you mad."

There, that hook finally found its way through the hole. I looked up to find Eden's face still red, but with a completely different emotion.

"I never said I wanted to marry Abner."

"Does he know that? His intentions seem clear to everyone else."

"Maybe so, but I have not decided for myself—"

"What is holding you back?"

The question hung between us for too long as I watched her fidget with her hair again and then turn back to her bag on the bed. I waited for an answer that might give me some kind of indication that she had other reasons for not wanting to marry him.

"I do not know," she finally said, pulling thumb-sized bottles of oil scents from her belongings. Then her hands dropped to her sides as she met my eyes with a glimmer in that green. "Am I correct in assuming you have objections about a union between Abner and me?"

"Objections? You mean, other than the fact that it could significantly impact your job?" I wondered what exactly she was asking me to admit; Eden did not usually veil her thoughts. But my response was clearly the wrong one because a sizzle of anger passed across the room, originating from her.

"Has it ever occurred to you that maybe I do not wish to be married, perhaps never? Not every girl desires only to be a wife and mother to a horde of children."

That absolutely had never occurred to me. "But you come from an enormous family. I assumed you would—"

"Want to be just like my parents? After watching parts of them slowly die with Elon this year? Children have the power to cripple even the strongest person. It costs to love people so dearly and maybe I am better off not bringing more of that weakness on myself. Maybe I just want to be good at my job and make a lasting impact on the Island. Maybe having a husband and children is not for me. Would you support that if it was what I wanted?"

"Of course," I answered automatically. "I want you to be who you are, Eden. I am just surprised to hear this is what you have wanted all along."

"You never asked me what I wanted," she retorted. "So you can put your worry to rest over finding my replacement so soon. I will still work for you and do all I can to ensure your success as Guardian because it is what our Island ordained, and I believe in that. Now, if you will kindly leave, I need to get ready."

If I was supposed to be relieved by what she said, it was not getting through to my heart.

I was just her job.

I was distracted the rest of the day as Guardianship plans blurred and Eden took center focus in my head. Everything else became noise around me, and at some point I found another rare minute alone to take a stroll before the feast started. When I found myself wandering past the banquet hall and through the garden, I stumbled upon Nathan and Caleb who were reclining on chairs under a tree.

They both looked up, making me worry that I had intruded on a private conversation. I sent a nod at them and was going to continue past, when Nathan called out to me.

"Gabriel, come sit with us." He gestured at the empty chair on his other side. "We were about to go looking for you."

"Yeah, man. Take a break."

I hesitated a short moment before lowering myself to the chair, careful to not show the pain that shot straight up my back. "Where is everyone?" I wondered.

"The girls took off together earlier to the scent fields," Caleb answered. "I think Eden wanted to let them create their own perfume or makeup or something. I was like, 'no thanks' and found Nathan instead. They were giggling too much to even notice I didn't go."

"What a shame," I said. "You could use some eye shading to go with those ruddy cheeks of yours."

"Oh, yeah?" Caleb shot back. "All you need is some red lipstick with those long eyelashes and I could start calling you Gabriella."

"I shall take that as a compliment since I think it means you find me pretty."

Nathan let out a low whistle. "And to think you two fought over the same girl."

"A girl I won," Caleb reminded us. I was on the brink of responding tartly that he had only won because I had given up, but Nathan stopped us.

"Hey." He thumped Caleb in the arm. "My daughter is not a game. Watch yourself, son."

"I was kidding! You know she's more to me than that," Caleb said, but at Nathan's stern look, he backed down with a submissive "yes, sir" and then addressed me. "Speaking of games, *Gabriella*, did Abner find you? He had ants in his pants over something and needed to talk to you about it."

"Ants in his pants? He could not handle that issue for himself?" I was not going to help another man get ants out of his pants.

Nathan and Caleb roared with laughter. "I meant, he seemed anxious about something," Caleb finally clarified.

"Perhaps about the protestors again?"

"I have a feeling it was more personal than that," Nathan remarked, prompting questioning looks from us. "I overheard him talking to Joseph at lunch and I am guessing it's the reason he urgently wants to find you before the feast."

I gazed around in confusion, not finding the Geoguard anywhere near the area. "Tell me what you heard."

When Nathan hesitated, Caleb jumped in, "Does it have to do with Eden?"

Nathan's grimace affirmed it, and hope ignited in my chest. Perhaps Eden had ended whatever relationship they had and Abner was upset about it. Perhaps he expected me to talk some sense into her.

"Do you think something is wrong?" I asked, hoping very much that it *was*.

Nathan surveyed me with wise gray eyes. "I suppose it depends on your perspective. You care about Eden, yes?"

"She is my closest friend," I answered honestly to Caleb's sarcastic *psh* sound.

"In that case, maybe I *should* warn you ahead of time. Abner wants to propose marriage to Eden at some point during the feast tonight. He asked for Joseph's permission."

"And what did Joseph say?"

"He said it was your Guardianship festival and that you should decide if that was appropriate or not."

Why would Joseph put that decision back on me? I tried to reason my way through a barrage of feelings that ranged in varying levels of selfishness.

"Nope," Caleb immediately came to my defense. "Not appropriate at all. That dude needs to back off."

"I cannot say no to a request like that. It is not within my right."

"Sure it is. It's your festival! Tell him to wait," Caleb argued. "I can't even tell how much she really likes him, anyway. From the conversations we've had, she's been in survival mode this year, like you. I think she knows more about what the Island wants than she knows what she herself wants."

She had seemed pretty certain about it earlier. No marriage, no children. That seemed to shut down Abner's chances... along with any other person who might want to get close to her. If I told him yes, I could be setting him up for public humiliation. If I told him no, I appeared to be the self-absorbed Guardian who wanted every moment to be about me. Furthermore, Eden did not seem like the type of woman who had ever cared about big, public romantic gestures, and if she ever found out that I knew about such a proposal and did not tell her...

There was no right way to handle this.

"Eden is an extraordinary young woman," Nathan remarked. "She shows leadership and faith that I haven't seen on this Island in a long time."

"Her heart beats for our Island and our people," I agreed. "Why that sign did not appear in the sky the night she was born, I will never understand. She would have been an amazing Guardian."

"She is obviously destined for something different," he said cryptically. "And maybe it's okay for you to avoid Abner the rest of the evening. If he can't ask, he can't act. There's no need to rush these things. And I sense he is rushing for his own agenda."

I let that percolate between us as the zephyra sitting between Caleb and Nathan started flashing. Nathan answered it.

"Hi, Dad! Where are you?"

"Hey, Whit. I'm sitting in the garden outside the Banquet Hall. Where are you?"

"At the Scent Warehouse. Look what we made!" She held up a glass jar of brown oil, and Morgan's face popped in next to hers.

"It's the most disgusting scent you can imagine! Like a skunk had diarrhea." Morgan scrunched her face up. "We're gonna put some in Gabriel and Caleb's bedswings while they sleep tonight. Everyone will think they had an oopsie. Teach them not to mess with us."

"Really? That's your revenge?" Caleb scoffed and leaned in close to Nathan until he was in view of the girls in the zephyra. Their faces turned to shock.

"Dad! You could've warned us he was sitting right there," Whitnee huffed.

"Did you forget I'm a guy?" Caleb mocked. "I already know how to put the stank in things without your help."

Whitnee's expression soured. "Keep talking like that, Caleb. It's a real turn-on."

"If this was all you could come up with, you disappoint me, girls."

Morgan glared at him. "Don't tell Gabriel, okay? We could at least still—"

"Too late." It was my turn to lean in.

The girls looked positively furious. "Why did I even call? Morgan, put a stopper in this. It's making me sick." Whitnee handed the bottle to Morgan who disappeared from view.

"Bring that near me and I will make sure that it gets all over your fine evening dress," Caleb said. "You've been warned."

"No, *you've* been warned," she said looking at both of us in the zephyra. "We are not gonna forget—" She paused and looked away at something we couldn't see. All that could be heard was a loud pop and then yelling. I thought I heard a male voice in there.

"Whitnee, get down!" Eden shouted and I heard the sound of crashing bottles and life forces firing. Whitnee dropped to the floor.

"Dad—" Whitnee started, but then with a thump, her voice halted and the zephyra went careening away from her. The view of the warehouse ceiling went black, silencing Morgan's horrified scream.

22

THE WAREHOUSE

"They aren't answering. No one is answering. Why won't someone pick up the zephyra?" Caleb cried out with every pounding step we took. He led the way just a couple of feet in front of me with Nathan close behind.

"Whitnee isn't responding to my voice, either," Nathan fretted.

"We should have brought help." When Nathan had leapt up, Caleb and I had not even hesitated to launch into action too. Perhaps I should have collected some Geoguards first... "Contact Levi or Thomas, please," I instructed Caleb who had snatched Nathan's zephyra. I had not seen any of my Palladium staff in the last couple of hours. They had seemed to get my hint that I wanted some privacy.

"Wait! Stop and hide," Nathan hissed, leaving the path and darting out of sight. We each lined up behind a tree and stole quick careful glances around the trunks to view the warehouse in the center of the flower fields. There was not a single person in sight. Nathan warned, "We should not go tearing across that field out in the open. We don't know what we're dealing with."

Caleb's chest heaved with fearful breaths. "Someone attacked them. What if it was those protesters, or rebels? What if they took the girls?"

"Calm down, Caleb," Nathan whispered. "For all we know, it could've been a wild animal or something."

"I heard a man's voice!" Caleb insisted. He was not wrong—I heard it too. "And how is a wild animal attacking them any better?"

"Who was with the girls?" I asked, trying to get a grasp on the details. We might not know how many hostiles were in there, but I at least needed a count of everyone in danger.

"I think it was just Whitnee, Morgan, Eden, and Hannah. But there could've been other people already out here."

"Today is a holiday. Nobody would have been working," I told them. "Give me that zephyra." Caleb tossed it to me one-handed. I called for Levi first. No answer. Thomas was next and still there was no answer. "Blast!" I cursed under my breath, wondering if that device was even really working.

"We are wasting time!" Caleb grunted.

"Caleb's right," Nathan said. "I'll go around the tree line and try to enter from the other side of the warehouse. You two cover each other's backs and sneak through the flowers to that entrance. Shoot a flare up if you find something or need help."

Nathan hardly accepted our agreement before he crept away from us. Caleb dropped to the ground. "Let's army-crawl it." When I did not immediately join him, he looked up at me. "What are you waiting for?"

"Trying to distinguish what an army crawl is."

"Like this," Caleb wiggled on his stomach and elbows into the field. He looked like an oversized worm. And he moved about as fast as one.

"That is ridiculous. We will not get there until *tomorrow*!"

"Well, what do you suggest?"

"Normal crawling?" I dropped down on all fours and the flowers were high enough to cover me. I heard his annoyed grunt as he followed. Neither of us spoke again as we moved quickly and quietly, both trying to keep control of the cloud of fear hovering over us. The key was to keep my mind from envisioning the girls injured or lifeless on the floor in connecting lakes of blood…

I was not doing a good job with that.

I propelled myself faster, forgetting any pain that might be stinging my back and legs in this position. We reached the entrance of the warehouse easily with no sign of a problem. But there was also no sound coming from inside.

"We need backup. Maybe you should call Joseph," Caleb suggested. "Or your Palladium people."

"We cannot wait any longer! We need to see if they are still inside. I see no signs of a struggle out here, but the fact that I hear nothing makes me fear they were abducted." On that thought, Caleb leapt to his feet and ran to the door. "Wait! You cannot just barge in there—"

"Watch me." He yanked the door open as I came up behind him.

The sight before us was disturbing. All light had been extinguished and shards of glass crunched under our feet. That made us step more slowly and throw both hands out with only our defensive life forces lighting the way. We did not dare call out names in case someone else was lying in wait for us.

"Gabriel," Caleb breathed. "Is that blood?" I cast my light over to a trail of dark spots that looked as if they had been dripping from something—or someone. My heart plunged into my stomach. We followed the trail until it stopped in the middle of the warehouse between two tables.

This time his voice was high-pitched. "I'm scared to see what's under those tables." So I took a deep breath and swept my lit hands around.

Nothing. No bodies… or parts.

I took a moment to compose myself again. "It is clear. Keep moving."

"Look out!" Caleb shouted just as something came whipping past us in the air. In his startled state, Caleb conjured a half-shield, half-explosion of green light over us and the thing flew to a resting place up in the bars of the high ceiling.

"A bird," I gasped, its eyes lighting up in the rays of light. "Just a blasted bird!"

Caleb wiped the sweat from his forehead. "I'll kill that bird," he muttered as we started moving forward again into a more open space. Just as we cleared the tables, a glass jar exploded off the tabletop behind us, and we both hit the floor. About the same time, the ground started shaking and tossing us around like beads in a child's toy. A forceful wind cut fiercely across the warehouse, bringing pieces of debris that compelled us to shield our eyes as much as possible. But then from the corner of the warehouse, a murky, hazy light started flashing. With every flash, we could see

Whitnee's terrified face calling out to us, her eyes burning silver. She seemed chained in shadows, like she could not get to us. I had never seen such strange power. Where was the source?

"Whitnee!" Caleb tried crawling across the rippling ground to get to her, but with every flash of light, a dark shadow grew to my right. It took several flashes before I figured out what shape it was actually taking.

"Caleb, run!" I yelled and threw my body between him and the drakon that suddenly rose up on its hind legs. I cast a rope of fire to try and restrain it, but my aim was off. Within three flashes, I knew I would not be able to escape my doom this time. The drakon's venomous claws descended swiftly, tearing into my chest—and falling right through me.

What?

No pain came ripping across my body even as we tried to scramble away. Caleb screamed like a small child with one arm clutched around me from behind, shooting Geostone after Geostone at the drakon. All of which passed right through the creature and detonated on the warehouse wall.

At that moment all the lights came on and Nathan yelled across the space, "Okay, okay. I think that's enough!"

Whitnee untangled herself from black cloth in the corner, laughing uproariously. "Come on, Dad! We could've kept them going just a little bit longer."

Caleb still had not let go of his death grip on me. "What the—"

When Morgan, Eden, Hannah, Thomas, and Levi popped their heads up from around the warehouse, the laughter increased dramatically around us. It was hard to feel relief at their safety when we were the subject of their derision.

"We told you we would get you back," Whitnee announced and slapped her hand to Morgan's. "Thanks for the help, everyone."

Caleb and I were speechless. I tried to stand to my feet. "Let go of me!" I grumbled, throwing his arm off my chest. His mouth glubbed like a fish before he finally rose up again.

"Too! Far!" he screeched. "That was way worse than our prank!"

"You played with our fears, so we played with yours," Morgan said triumphantly.

23

POPPING THE QUESTION

Two more days.

That was all I had left here on the Island before I got to try that portal again. It seemed so short and so long and so… wrong. What was it about being here that turned my heart into a conflicted mush of feelings and fears? I missed my mom and kept imagining how the three of us could settle here together as a family. I imagined how much she would love it and how I was pretty sure her hot-headed Latina side would make her a Pyra. I could practically envision her eyes lighting up in gold and how she would use that warmth to spread love to others. I imagined her and Dad growing old here together with breakfast on the porch and walks on the beach.

But when I tried to smash Caleb and Morgan into the picture, the dream got more complicated. Not impossible, just complicated. And as the pressure of *two more days* settled in, so did a slight panic. Elon's words weighed heavily on my mind. I had chosen not to share them with anyone. It felt like a message the Island meant just for me and I wanted to respect that even if I didn't really understand it. The implications of me being the only one able to shut down the portal seemed to point to the fact that I might actually not get to go home. How did you shut something down and still be able to use it? And what could be a harder choice than separating myself from the Mainland?

The portal was a time bomb I would have to deal with, and the clock seemed to be counting down closer and closer. I couldn't shake the feeling that after two days, detonation might be coming.

That was the reason I arranged for Morgan and Caleb to join me on a canoe out in the middle of the river at Hydrodora a couple of hours before the Blessing Ceremony. Morgan steered us with her Water life force to a less crowded part of the village downriver, where most of the area was made up of houseboats. It was quiet; almost everyone had chosen their places on the shores of the main part of the village in anticipation of today's events.

There were Palladium security guards following us from a distance as protection, but other than that, we seemed to be mostly alone. When Morgan slowed the boat to a stop underneath an overhang of trees, they both gave me their full attention.

"So I wanted to propose something to you both," I started, folding my hands in my lap and taking a big breath. "What would you think about moving here permanently to the Island? With me. And my mom and dad."

They seemed stunned—as if that had been the last thing they expected me to bring up on this spontaneous escape. But it was Caleb's sigh that increased my nerves exponentially.

"Why are you asking us this? Do you *want* to stay here the rest of your life?"

"I don't know," I answered honestly. "Sometimes I think it wouldn't be the worst thing to happen. But not for the reasons you think, Caleb!" I was quick to reassure him. This had nothing to do with Gabriel. "Honestly, I'm a little worried the Island might never let me leave. I know we keep thinking that barrier is just there for a short time, but... what if it's not? I don't think I could stay here without you guys. I mean, Caleb, even you questioned if maybe it was my destiny—"

"No. The barrier will open back up. I don't believe the Island would force you to stay for long—"

"There is absolutely no way to know that. Dad was here for almost six years. But let's pretend for a moment that I *wanted* to stay here. Let's pretend that it's the only way I get to keep my family together. Would you even consider staying with me?"

Caleb's face dropped into his hands and I knew he was trying to weigh how to respond. Morgan chewed on her lower lip and gazed back at me in silence. I felt desperation start to leak into my words.

"Caleb, you and Gabriel and Thomas have so much fun together. You would already have guy friends you could trust. And Morgan, you're a full Hydrodorian here. Life force is in your blood now and everyone adores you. Who says we have to go to college somewhere and become big shots on the Mainland? I mean, what if a simple life here is where happiness really is?"

"There's nothing simple about your life here, Whitnee," Morgan pointed out and her voice had taken on that soft quality that it did when she was talking me down from something dramatic. Only I wasn't being dramatic. "What about our families? What about our friends at home? I can't speak for Caleb on this, but I feel like there's so much still on the Mainland that I haven't experienced. Not only that, but the love of *my* life is still out there."

"Or he could be here. I know you and Thomas have been sneaking kisses again, Morgie. You two could actually be in a real relationship if you stayed."

Morgan closed her eyes for a moment and took in a deep breath. "Whit, I'm not like you, okay? Thomas is my distraction. He's *my* survival tool when I'm here. He and I both know that, and we're cool with it. You and Caleb can judge that all you want. But if I stayed, Thomas wouldn't be my reason."

"Then what about me, Morgie?"

Her eyes became pools of conflict. "You're different, of course. You're my best friend. But I don't know how we could make it work—"

"We could just tell your families the truth," I jumped in. "You could say an actual goodbye and they would know you were safe living out your life on a magical Island somewhere." Okay, it sounded better in my head than when it came out of my mouth. I was basically asking them to leave their own loved ones behind—for *me*. The ridiculousness of it was starting to hit me, and my hands started sweating as I fidgeted with them in my lap. "Morgan, last summer you were the one who wanted to stay here."

"And you were the one who convinced me how unhealthy that was. I was staying to die, not because it was actually what was right for me. I know that I owe this place my life," Morgan said. "And it definitely wouldn't be the worst thing in the world to live here. I love being a Hydrodorian. But..."

"But?"

She took a deep breath, "Whit, please don't put me in a position of having to choose between you and my life on the Mainland."

I tried to hold onto my wavering strength as I said the thing I most feared. "Someday you might have to."

"That would be awful..." A tear wriggled down her cheek and it triggered my own eyes to water. I had meant for this to sound potentially like a good thing, but it was only coming out devastating.

"Caleb?"

He stared off into the water as if seeing something that wasn't there. "I have a full scholarship to A&M. I'm already setting up internships to go with my degree." His voice was so quiet, but I listened to every syllable with bated breath. "And even though I've tried to keep from saying it, I keep hoping—*praying*—that you'll finally commit to go there too. That maybe we can be a real couple and learn each other in all new ways. I can play intramural sports and you can organize parties and study sessions with our friends. We can do football games and road trips together to see our families. And we can be there for each other through the highs and lows of life. Then someday, when we're ready, we could get married and maybe run a campground together and raise children there. Morgan and her husband would be our best friends and we would just do *life* together." He finally met my gaze, and I felt myself choke into a half-sob, half-hiccup. "That's the future I dream about."

If I hadn't already wanted him forever, that would've done it. I had no idea he had thought so far or dreamed in such detail.

"That's beautiful, Caleb," I whispered.

"But that future is on the Mainland."

"Why couldn't we have a similar future together, just here on the Island? We could still—"

"It wouldn't work, Whitnee." Now he was the one who sounded desperate. "Morgan's right. There are too many things—too many people—vying for your focus here. At home, you're my best friend and the girl I've had a crush on since I was twelve. Here, you're the most powerful person around and everybody wants a piece of you. Look at how things have been the last few days. If you're not saving our lives, you're playing the part of Gabriel's political princess!

Where am I supposed to fit into that? This Island keeps trying to take you away from me and I won't let it. You were the girl of my dreams *before* we ever found this place. You still are. And you should get to choose your own future."

"I might still be able to make that choice, Caleb, I don't know. But if I chose the Island..." I paused and looked back and forth between both of them, trying not to stumble on my words. "Then I wouldn't be the only one who has to make a choice about the future."

They were mirror images of each other—twin faces of terror as my words invaded their comfort zones. Caleb's next words tumbled slowly out of his mouth like rocks slipping down a slope that didn't know how or where they would land. "I don't have a future on the Island. Morgan and I are Mainlanders."

Which meant I was not a good enough reason for them to leave it all behind.

"Caleb." I leaned forward and practically launched myself into his lap while the boat rocked. "Please, don't say it like that. I'm a Mainlander too." I reached my arm desperately behind him to Morgan and felt her lean forward to grasp my fingers. A flood of panic threatened to release all over Caleb's shirt. "Wherever I go, I want y'all there. I don't care where that is. I just don't want to lose you. Please tell me I won't. Please."

Caleb was there, arms tangled around me. And Morgan's hands surrounded mine and rubbed my arm comfortingly.

"We'll figure it out, Whitnee," Caleb soothed. "It's not worth freaking out about right now. Your dad will help us. He'll know the right thing to do. He'll get us all home."

I wanted to believe that. But Elon said...

"Promise me you'll at least think about it?" I asked, even though I knew it was unfair. "Promise that you'll be open to the possibility?" I couldn't see their expressions, but I did feel Caleb's muscles tighten reflexively at the same time Morgan's hand paused in its stroke.

"We promise to think about it."

If they had just lied to me, I didn't want to know. I could pretend that the bond between the three of us was strong enough to bridge two worlds. It was the only way I would make it two more days.

"Lilley!" I encompassed the young Healer in a hug as we boarded the ship that would host the Hydrodorian Blessing ceremony. "I love your short hair."

The now sixteen-year-old prodigy who had helped me save Morgan's life through Transfusion looked older with her hair cropped above her shoulders. She wore a white dress with a few sparkling blue stones sprinkled across the bodice—not her usual plain Healer clothes. She had brightened her soft features with subtle makeup and she practically glowed.

"Oh, Whitnee, it is so good to see you." She squeezed me back with fervor. "And Morgan, you look so healthy and beautiful. I am sorry that I had to leave so quickly the night of the opening ceremony—I missed greeting you! They needed me back at the Healing Center, especially as these earthshakers have caused so many injuries and sicknesses."

"You are a saint, Silly Lilley." Thomas came up behind us to embrace her. Morgan cast her eyes in my direction meaningfully. Lilley had always crushed on Thomas, her big brother's friend. Though Thomas was fond of Lilley, it seemed like maybe their age difference kept casting her in a little sister light to him. Of course, with Morgan dropping in again, I was certain he was always too distracted with his flirty Mainlander to notice the amazing young woman Lilley was becoming. It made me wonder about Morgan's words earlier... that Thomas was not her forever guy. Maybe she was preventing him from moving on too. One of Thomas's hands lingered on the small of Lilley's back in a friendly way, but I saw a slight blush to her face as he asked conspiratorially, "Now where is your troublemaking brother?"

"Below deck. Father has already warned him to stay away from the drinks today. Do not encourage him."

"I will go scour the area and remove all temptation." Thomas said and rolled his eyes. Ah, yes. Lilley's brother, Mark, had a drinking problem last summer that apparently carried over to this summer.

Once Thomas waved and jogged away, I dropped my voice so that only Lilley and Morgan could hear.

"What kind of sickness are you seeing with these earthshakers, Lilley?"

"Oh, it is awful. Every time one occurs, we see an influx of people afterward—some with injuries caused by collapsing buildings or falls. But then there are people who cannot connect to their life force. For most, it resolves in a matter of hours or days. For others, never again. If this disconnect does not stop, it will become the primary cause of death on the Island this year."

Curious to know what she had to say, I asked, "Do you have any theories about the earthshakers?"

"Well, Sapphira believes it is the volcano gearing up for an eruption to end all days." She waved that off, though. "There have been no signs of eruption and these earthshakers are far enough apart, not in any kind of pattern. But I do agree with Sapphira that they feel like a warning of something to come. I just hope someone is listening and figures it out. Am I correct in thinking perhaps *you* have a theory, Whitnee?"

I nodded slowly, but before I could respond, Eden called all of us to take our positions. The ship was about to float downriver in view of the crowd gathered on the shores of Hydrodora. I dutifully took my place between Gabriel and Dad, catching Abrianna's eye on the other side of her son.

"I do not have good memories on board a ship here," I muttered loudly enough for her to hear.

"All is safe this time," Gabriel assured me in a quiet voice. I'm sure he would never forget the day Simeon died, either. It was the first time Gabriel had ever killed someone, and that steals a person's innocence in unimaginable ways. Just remembering Saul and what that horrible man had done to hurt all of us gave me shivers on such a warm day.

"None of us have the best memories of last summer," Abrianna added. "Simeon was a good man. Even if he did meddle in business he did not understand—"

"Quiet yourself!" Gabriel seethed before I could come unglued at her comment. Even Dad glared at her and squeezed my hand in comfort.

Hydrodora held some of my darkest moments inside its watery boundaries. I felt like I couldn't hide from my feelings when I was here. And my emotional state only grew more chaotic as I watched Zebedee, father to Mark and Lilley and the new Councilman for the Hydrodorian tribe, give Gabriel a sprinkle of Water blessing in the ancient ceremony. The crowd cheered, the fan girls screamed, Dad and I did our formal bows and public congratulations to Gabriel just like the three ceremonies before, and all went according to Eden's perfect plans. Zebedee exhibited a smile full of mustache and white teeth and stuttered only once during his speech.

I liked him. But he wasn't Simeon. I would have given anything for a hug and words of wisdom right then from the white-haired man who gave me my health back. I could see the traces of his legacy all over this village, in the hearts of the Hydrodorian people and their peaceable ways—it was the only village we had been to so far where no protesters showed up.

As I gazed out across the water to the crowds of people, I felt each of them as if they were part of me. The Island *was* my home too, and these were my ancestors. I turned inward to remember what Simeon had said aboard his ship another time when I felt confused about the dichotomy within me: *Is love not the most important force of life? Just like the power of a life force, people are likely to achieve great things in the name of love. How could you really be the Pilgrim if you did not first love those you came to rescue?*

I might not be the Pilgrim, but I did feel love for this place that matched my heart for the Mainland. I only hoped it achieved great things in the end… and didn't leave me shattered.

Once we had docked and left the ship, Eden began organizing everyone according to the schedule. Gabriel and I stood off to the side as the Council Members asked clarifying questions. Poppa Zeke did not look well enough to be here. He had taken a break from travel while we were in Geodora but had insisted on joining us again in Hydrodora. I made a note to mention to Dad later that perhaps Poppa Zeke needed to spend some time at the Healing Center to see if anything else was going on with him. I really hoped I wasn't the cause of his deterioration.

My eyes roamed around the area as Gabriel and I smiled kindly at villagers who had followed us upstream, waiting patiently from a distance for us to finish before they approached. That was how I spotted Abrianna chatting with another woman. Abrianna's smile seemed too fake, and they were clearly talking in hushed tones.

"Who is that talking to your mother?" I asked Gabriel.

"I was just wondering the same thing." He left to approach them, and I decided to follow.

We got close enough to hear Abrianna declare, "I have no more to say." The woman paused in frustration before scampering away.

"Who was that?" Gabriel wanted to know.

"A disgruntled villager. Nothing of great concern, but something you will get used to quickly," she said dismissively, glancing once at me beside Gabriel. "What should be your concern is that broadcast this morning."

"I thought it was fine," he said.

"The focus was entirely on Nathan and bringing that girl back to life."

"Well, that was kind of a big deal," I threw in, wondering why on earth that would bother her.

"It was," Abrianna agreed. "A true miracle. But if you expect Nathan to ever have a chance at a normal life with you, then he needs to tone it down. His deeds are praised now, but the tide of favor can turn the other direction without warning. People are fickle creatures."

I wanted to dismiss her warnings, but something told me her lifetime of governing people had probably taught her some things. Back at home, I had certainly seen how fast people could turn on each other.

Still. My dad had done nothing wrong, and the people loved him wholeheartedly. Abrianna was just a manipulative, bitter woman about to pass on the only thing in her life that actually mattered to her—her authority. So even if she spoke from experience, I would never trust her motivations.

Abrianna continued, "This week needs to be about endearing *you* to the hearts of the people, Gabriel. A few angles of you strolling through a crowd and talking policies with people is not enough. You need to find a way to steal the attention back—for your good and for Nathan's."

"Like what? I am doing all I can."

"No, you are not. Try harder, son."

She forced a smile and flounced away before I could rattle off an unrated version of exactly what I thought of her tactics.

24

GARDEN OF MEMORIES

"I think I'm going to take a walk."

Caleb's head shot up from the game he had been playing with Morgan and some of the Hydros our age. There was a lovely breeze on the air as we overlooked the water's edge from the shore. Everything felt peaceful in this village. Enough for me to feel like maybe I could actually find some time to be alone and not freak everyone out.

"Do you want me to go with you?" he asked, even though I could tell he was really immersed in winning the game. I'm sure it was a matter of time before the locals had to declare the foreigner a winner on his first attempt at playing.

Seriously, it was unfair how competitive and talented he was.

I stood over him and looped my arms around his neck. "I really think I just want to be alone. I'm feeling a little claustrophobic and have had no time to myself since we got here. Y'all stay and play and just let me refresh myself for a bit."

Morgan's face turned alarmed at that. "You can't go anywhere by yourself."

Caleb added, "Yeah, especially because you have a bad habit of wandering off and getting yourself into trouble."

"Have I been like that at all this summer?"

"Well, there was the fire in Aerodora—" But he stopped at the pinch I gave him on the shoulders. "Other than that, I guess you've been a good girl."

"Exactly."

"But last time—"

"This isn't like last time, Caleb," I reminded him gently. "I promise that I have no sneaky adventures in mind. I just want to visit Simeon's memorial garden behind the Healing Center. I need to pay my respects to him while I have the chance. And it's something I'd like to do alone."

Morgan's expression softened at that. "I can understand that, Whit."

"I will make sure to tell Dad and take a zephyra and anything else y'all want me to do. I'll be back within the hour. And if you get antsy before that, you know exactly where to find me. I won't detour anywhere else. Is that good enough?"

They exchanged doubtful looks, but before they could protest and find my dad or insist on joining me, I patted Caleb's chest as if the case was closed. "Things are perfectly safe here. I'll be back soon—thanks for understanding."

And I padded away quickly in my white leather sandals. I would be shocked if someone didn't end up coming after me within the next five minutes. I tried to communicate to Dad, but he didn't respond. I wasn't surprised. His mind was a busy place lately. It wouldn't matter because I wouldn't stay gone for long.

I practically floated with the summer breeze as I greeted people I didn't know and waved at villagers playing in the river. My pale blue outfit (designed by Hannah) was perhaps my favorite of the week. It was a romper dress where the skirt tapered out longer on the sides. The bodice was embellished with a belt that featured a round pearlescent glass orb imbued with Water life force. Every time my hands passed over my waist, the Water swirled and sparkled. Between that and the Firelight thunderfly necklace that I still hadn't removed, I felt glittery even in broad daylight.

I could feel the longer back of the skirt billow out behind me as I passed the Healing Center. I took the barely worn path that led to a private spring Simeon had once kept a secret unto himself, noting the huge rock that marked where to leave the main path. A pulsing heartbeat sped my steps as I rushed forward to what I hoped was still a private area.

The steam from the bubbling hot spring came into view, curly tendrils welcoming me back to this place of sanctuary. I bent down to rub the small thin petals of the white saint flowers between my fingers and smiled.

Saint Simeon.

When I straightened up, I realized there was someone else in the little clearing. His golden eyes were appraising me openly by the time I noticed him.

"Gabriel! What are you doing here?"

"Trying to find solitude." He held a small branch in his hand and waved it in a circle. "When Lilley told me she had made this place into a memorial for Simeon, I felt it was appropriate to come here and I somehow convinced the others to give me some privacy."

"Same here," I admitted.

"How did you know how to find it?"

"Simeon let me run away here last summer." At the questioning lift of his eyebrows, I explained, "Morgan was sick and you were in a coma and I wasn't sure if either of you would live. I stood there in that spring and…"

And cried the life forces out of me. I even made it rain.

His eyes remained glued to mine, waiting for me to continue. But I knew memories were both precious and dangerous. So all I said was, "It's beautiful here."

"That it is," Gabriel agreed. "Would you like me to leave?"

"No, of course not. You were here first. Maybe I should…?" I gestured back from where I came, but he was quick to reply.

"Please stay. Do not let me bother you."

I smiled at him and strolled to the left, noting how much younger he seemed across the spring, playing with a stick. His tunic was ivory, like the flowers that bloomed all around us, but with aqua blue embroidery along the neckline and sleeves. His neck and wrists were adorned with braided leather of deep brown that matched the leathery brown pants he wore, and the aqua stitching continued down the sides of his legs. The gold emblem of the Palladium swirl hung as a small medallion around his neck. I could see Hannah's handiwork in all of it and was amazed at how every day she had incorporated the colors of each tribe into his wardrobe while still honoring his Pyradorian heritage. There had been gold accessories, stitching, and embellishments on each outfit.

"I wanted to say I'm sorry again for the drakon yesterday," I told him, breaking the silence we had fallen into. "That was bad taste. Once Thomas suggested it, the idea took off. I should've stopped it."

He kept his eyes on the branch, smoothing the leaves through his fingers. "It certainly worked. I am no friend to drakons."

I winced with guilt. "I haven't noticed you using a walking stick this time. I assume the injury got better?"

"Better, yes. But always with me. My body and strength will likely never be the same."

"I'm so sorry. Going into that cave was my idea. What happened was all my fault."

"Right." His face was mischievous. "Because you, being the *little one* that you are, obviously forced me to go into that mountain with you. I was completely innocent and powerless."

I pressed my lips together, trying not to remember that despairing moment when he had collapsed and I could barely get him up to the cabin. I picked up a white flower that had blown off its stem. With a gentle Wind, I levitated it to him. "Peace offering?"

He reached out and plucked it from the air. His lips curled into a smile as he tucked it into the branch. "I accept." Then he lowered himself with great care to the white stone bench that had been placed out there and it suddenly clicked why he always sat down slowly, as if his back might give out on him. I chose not to comment on it. He, however, had been entertaining a different trail of thoughts.

"Do you ever think about the last time you were here and the things we said to each other?"

Oh, lord. I didn't know if I was ready to have this conversation, even if it was long overdue.

"Sometimes." It was a careful answer and we both knew it.

"I realize I was a fool, you know. I was trying to rush something that had only begun to grow between us. I feel as if I should apologize for placing such an expectation on you."

I sighed and took a few steps closer. "You offered me a life here, one filled with your friendship and loyalty. That's not something to apologize for."

He seemed perplexed. "I meant it as more than friendship. You knew that, right?"

"Of course I knew that," I told him with a laugh. "And I believe time and distance have shown us both that there are other options out there, other people we could love and create a future with."

He leaned forward, resting his elbows on his knees, and doodled in the dirt with a sharp edge of the branch. "Perhaps that is true for you and Caleb. But it is much more complicated for me than you will ever know."

"How do you mean?"

"I mean that l do not see a future with love and commitment and hope in it the way that you do. My options are so limited that all I see is the prison of the job."

With a frustrated sigh, I sat down next to him on the bench. "Gabriel, if you are going to continue to deny having feelings for Eden, I might have to electrocute you—"

"Feelings do not matter if the other person does not feel the same way. Did we not establish that last summer?"

"How do you know Eden doesn't care about you like that? Because of Abner? Because from where I'm standing—"

"Because she told me."

"You talked about it?"

"Well, not exactly." He paused before sitting upright again and facing the spring. "But she disclosed to me that she did not ever want to get married. I think that says it, does it not? Her commitment, her *love*, is only for the Island and the government of its people."

"Did you tell her how you feel?"

"I do not even know if how I feel is real, Whitnee. Or if I am just trying to distract myself from—" He stopped and rubbed one hand across his stubble, as if trying to relax his jaw.

"Distract yourself from what?"

"From *you*."

Now I was the one staring hard at the spring, trying to ignore the rush of confusion his confession brought to the surface.

At my stony silence, he dropped his voice to that deep tone that almost vibrated across the bare skin of my neck. "Please know that I am not trying to win your heart. I am merely trying to be honest with you. I waited a year for you to return, to change your mind about us, to take charge of your choices—hoping I would be the one you chose. But I know now that what we had was not enough. And I do not know what I want to hear from you at this point… maybe just the truth. No matter how painful. Maybe I just want your complete transparency for a few minutes. Do not make me play Truth or Dare again."

I felt my eyes fill up with tears and I blinked rapidly to keep them from dropping. The worst part of all of this was that I finally had an inkling of what my rejection must've felt like. Looking up at the patch of sky in an effort to dry out my eyes, I confessed, "I'm sorry I made you feel that way and maybe now I understand it for myself. Caleb and I—" I paused, trying to gain control of my voice. "Caleb has always made it clear that his life is meant for the Mainland. He knows he's supposed to be there. And, ultimately, I have always felt the same. A future with him is what I want. And I'm sorry for how that must sound—"

"No apologies. The truth is what I want." He seemed to take that in stride. So I went on with my thoughts.

"The truth is that I question if I will ever return to the Mainland. I question if it's even where I want to be anymore. I don't see how the Island will let Dad come home again. There's no guarantee the Island is going to let *me* leave again either. And if I could bring Mom here before the portal is shut down… well, maybe things could actually work. I wouldn't be forced to go to college away from my family. If Caleb and Morgan stayed, we'd never have to be separated. It would be perfect, right? But when I asked Caleb to think about staying here with me, he—" My voice broke again and I had to swallow a couple of times before I could speak. "I don't think I'm enough for him to stay, Gabriel."

He didn't have to say a word, because we understood each other's hurts and insecurities in a new way now. He dropped the branch to the ground and one arm came gently around my shoulders. I leaned my head against the pocket between his shoulder and chest and accepted the comfort. We sat there in silence while I got my emotions back under control.

At one point, I thought I heard something in the trees and I sat upright immediately. Gabriel dropped his arm just as fast and peered out cautiously.

"Is someone coming?" I whispered, wiping my eyes and straightening my appearance, even though nothing was out of place. We waited for a minute, but no other sound could be heard.

"No one is there," Gabriel finally said. "It was likely a small animal."

"I should probably go anyway," I said, suddenly nervous for reasons I couldn't explain. "Is my makeup all smeared?" I gazed up into his eyes so he could check me, but the warmth I saw there radiated with more than just concern.

"You are perfect," he replied. And I almost left right then. I should have listened to my instincts, but my big mouth decided to say one more thing. Because I just couldn't leave things with the same kind of hurt he had shouldered all year. Not when I now knew the potential for that kind of pain.

"Gabriel, I never stopped caring about you." I kept my voice soft and slow because I think it was the first time I was admitting it to myself. "I think there's a part of my heart that will always belong to you. If I'm being honest, that's probably one of the reasons I've hesitated to make decisions this year. There's always been unfinished business on this Island—even between you and me. But maybe it's time to go ahead and finish it."

He seemed to be having an internal debate over something, and I tried to wait patiently for his response. "I understand. We both need that freedom to move forward. But I want you to know" —and those golden eyes were earnest and vulnerable and confident all at once— "if you end up staying here and Caleb does the wrong thing by choosing the Mainland over you—which I am certain will not happen—but if he does, I would still care for you. Even if it meant always taking second place in your heart."

"Oh, Gabriel, you deserve better than that. Someday, Eden is going to wake up and realize she has fallen in love with—"

"Perhaps love is more of a choice than just something to fall into. I would not have a difficult time choosing to love you, should we ever find ourselves in that situation again." He leaned on his hand, the one between us on the bench that barely brushed against my outer thigh and sent goosebumps along my neck.

With sincerity, I reached up to graze the stubble on his face—I had been curious to do so ever since I first saw him on that Watch Tower. It was softer than I imagined. "Thank you for listening and caring. That means more than you know."

And just before I got up to leave, his free hand cupped my cheek and directed my lips to his and there were prickles from his beard as he pressed in with that fervent heat. My mouth instinctively responded to the rhythm of his, because they were the only lips I knew. But then reality kicked in and my sanity returned and I flew away from him.

How in the h-e-quadruple-hockey-sticks did that just happen?

I covered my mouth in horror as we stared at each other from a few feet away. I didn't know what to say. And apparently neither did he. Paranoia filtered in as I surveyed the garden again, half-expecting Caleb to have stumbled upon that shameful moment.

Nobody was there.

When my wide-eyed gaze landed back on Gabriel, the guilt was taking shape on his face.

"That was wrong," he mumbled.

"*So* freaking wrong!" I cried out, the weight of my shame starting to overcome me as every curse word in the book ran through my mind. "Never again, Gabriel. I *choose* Caleb."

He could only nod, and then I ran away as fast as I could. Away from Gabriel, away from those feelings.

Away from a moment I could never take back.

Caleb could never know about it. It would ruin everything.

Everything.

25

INTOXICATED WITH SECRETS

I intentionally avoided any interaction with Caleb upon my return to the festival. For the first time ever, I felt genuine remorse over what I had done. If the bloody Mainlander had not become my friend, this would not be such a devastating issue for my conscience. But it was. And I feared for Whitnee if Caleb found out the truth.

"There you are, Gabriel!" Eden exclaimed when she burst into my bedroom on board Zebedee's ship to find me hovering over a drink.

"This is now the second time you have barged into my room unannounced. If I did this to you, I would lose my life," I chastised, glancing at her only long enough to see her annoyance. "I could have been naked this time."

I believe her cheeks would have colored again had she paused long enough in her mission to even hear me.

"You and Whitnee and Nathan are supposed to be making visits to the Healing Center rooms right now. They went ahead and started without you. Why are you hiding in here?"

"I am not hiding. *You* have been hiding from *me*," I corrected her, my mouth having a hard time forming words. "Or hiding things *from* me. Maybe that is what I meant."

"I am not hiding things from you—"

"Not even drakons? Bloody corpses? A *bird*?"

"Oh, pull yourself together—"

"Secret betrothal to Abner?" That gave her pause and she dropped her satchel and papers on the bed to come closer. Those Geo green eyes tried to pierce mine, and I hid behind a long swig of burning liquid. "So that is it. You are betrothed to Abner."

I had successfully avoided any conversation with Abner last night—with help from Caleb who always found something pressing for me to do whenever Abner came around. But what if the Geoguard had plowed ahead and proposed to her privately?

"No, I am not betrothed to Abner. Why on earth would you think that after what I—" She snatched my drink away and sniffed it. "How much of this have you had?"

"Only enough to dull the pain in my back."

She reached behind me to a large bottle that I had tossed in the trash. "Gabriel, did you drink this whole bottle?"

"No, of course not," I said. "Mark took a sip before he stashed it in here to hide it from Zebedee."

The angry wail that came out of her was not attractive at all. "You cannot be intoxicated right now, you stubborn man-child! What are we going to do? You were supposed to visit the sickly, then make an appearance at the children's party, do some water slides, splash some kids, smile and then have dinner in the Waterpark! I will have to contact Thomas and cancel, and that will ruin any positive publicity we worked on today. Tomorrow's broadcast will be all about the mysterious absence of the Guardian-to-be at his own festivities!"

She huffed back to her satchel and yanked the zephyra out.

"Is that all you care about?"

The words tripped out of my mouth and maybe slurred a little. But they must have landed a crushing blow to her anger because she flipped the zephyra closed, took a deep breath, and then perched herself on the bed to give me her full attention.

"Is the pain from the venom getting worse, Gabriel? Be honest."

"I think it is just exacerbated by all the strain of these festivities," I answered somewhat honestly. "I hardly sleep, and I am keenly aware that I will have nothing to be proud of by the time all of this ends."

Her eyes widened in shock. "What do you mean? You will be the Guardian at the end of all this—by this time tomorrow, actually. The future has so much possibility."

"This time tomorrow I will be more alone than I have ever been."

Her head snapped back as if she could not believe what she was hearing. It made me think the spirits were talking more than I wanted them to. Did I just admit my loneliness? To *Eden*? I prepared myself for a lecture about what a spoiled and ungrateful man-child I was… poor little Guardian who had everything he could want and was never happy with any of it. I could bloody well give the lecture to myself at this point.

But instead, she fidgeted with the golden Palladium medallion that dangled from her wrist and seemed to be conflicted about her next question. "Is this about Whitnee?"

I felt heat rush to my face and neck, and when I tried to hide my discomfort behind my drink again, I realized it was empty. I slammed the useless cup down on the table and drew in a heavy breath.

"You still love her," she stated.

"No," I disagreed, rubbing my eyes as I tried to make them more alert. "Whitnee and I have made peace with our past. She wants Caleb. And I want them to be happy together."

"But now you believe that means you will be alone the rest of your life? Impossible, Gabriel." She rolled her eyes and sent an exasperated smile at me. "You are the bravest person I have ever known. You are smart, fiercely protective of the people you love, and when you believe in something, you pursue it with every bit of passion you possess—which is incredibly more than anyone I know. You are also quite pleasing to the eye, which I hate admitting because we both know you are aware of your charm. Any woman would be honored to love you and be loved by you in return."

"Except for Whitnee. And Jezebel. And *you*."

No… I did not really just say that. Curse my lack of self-discipline with that bottle!

She stopped fidgeting and sat up straight. "Did you just put me in the same category as Whitnee and Jezebel?"

"No." I shook my head and tried to pull myself up out of the chair, hoping to end this conversation immediately. "You are a category unto yourself, Eden. Just ignore me—I am clearly out of my mind."

As I tried to pass her on the way to the door, I felt her hand slide firmly into mine.

"Gabriel, sit down. Talk to me about what is really going on."

"I think I have said enough."

"You need to say more," she insisted and pulled lightly on my hand to try and get me to sit next to her. But with my clouded mind, I did not trust myself. I yanked my hand away and lurched my way to the door.

"Gabriel."

I paused with my hand at the door, and decided to ask the question I had wondered all year. "Did Michael ever tell you?"

"Michael, your Healer? Did he ever tell me what?"

"About the other effects of the drakon venom?"

"He does not discuss your personal health with me. What other effects?" Now I could sense the alarm coming from her. When I turned around, she stood up to face me, fear crossing her features. "Tell me, Gabriel."

I leaned against the door and stared up at the ceiling for a moment. "The drakon venom was in my system long enough to cause permanent damage."

"What kind of damage? To what?"

"Like, my ability to produce children someday."

That was the first time I had said it out loud.

She took a step closer to me. "I am confused. Are you not able to..." Her voice trailed off in embarrassment, but I was quick to assure her.

"Oh, I am able. I am still a man and I can still... well, *you know*... if that is what you are asking." Now I was the one embarrassed that she would ever assume me *incapable*. "But it is likely that my attempts to father any offspring would be unfruitful." An awkward silence stood between us as we looked everywhere but at each other. "To be clear, I have made peace with the idea. It is probably better that I do not pass on the bad qualities my own father might have passed on to me. Nobody but Michael knows. And now you. I trust you to hold that secret."

"Why did you tell me?"

"Because contrary to what you said, not *any* woman would want me. And because it is strange the things you never knew you wanted, until you can no longer have them. And because I am damaged, and some days are harder than others to come to terms with that." I had not meant to say so much, but now it was out there.

I began to open the door, but her hand came down on mine and pushed it closed again. I turned around to find a mere inch between our bodies. Her chest rose and fell more rapidly as if she were suddenly nervous.

"Gabriel," she whispered between breaths. "When I look at you, I do not see damage. I see strength, forged out of survival." She gazed up at me through thick eyelashes that framed the most vivid shade of green I had ever seen on the Island. "I am glad you told me—I do not think any less of you. If anything, it increases my admiration for you. You are serving consequences for doing the right thing."

"I am hardly admirable, Eden." Of that I could be sure. I had done the *wrong* thing more times than I could count, which was what had brought me to this room when I should have been out there proving to everyone why I would be a good leader.

But she kept her eyes locked securely on mine. "Surely you know that I would not have aligned my future so closely with yours if I did not hold a tremendous amount of respect for you. I would not have moved to the Palladium for anyone else. You know I struggle to express my deepest feelings, but with you, Gabriel, I..." She fixed her gaze then on the medallion hanging from my neck, and her fingers grazed the emblem we had designed together. I held my breath as those fingers then traced a tantalizing trail across my chest until her palm flattened over my heart. Her voice was almost a whisper. "I know what I said yesterday about my job and my future, but the truth is—"

A sharp rap on the door made us both jolt, and Eden quickly backed away to gather her belongings on the bed while I tried to recover my senses.

"Gabriel, are you in there?" It was Thomas, curse him. "Everyone has been looking for you. You were supposed to be at the Healing Center thirty minutes ago."

I caught Eden's gaze again across the room and we both released a sigh. "Perhaps we can finish this conversation later? I really want to know where that sentence was going."

She smoothed her hair and collected herself before giving me a short nod.

I opened the door to Thomas and leaned on it weakly. "Eden found me. We have been discussing a change in plans."

Thomas peered around me to Eden who slung that satchel over her chest again, as if using it as a shield. "What is the new plan?"

"First, we need to sober Gabriel. Then try to salvage what we can of the evening." She was back to her usual self and charged ahead between us with the typical expectation that we would follow. "We need to come up with a good reason why he is missing the Healing Center visits…"

She continued to work through the details of her job, but I detected the trace of a sparkle in her eyes when she looked at me.

I sobered enough to attend the children's party at the Waterpark, but not enough to go anywhere without one of my Palladium staff as an escort. Caleb finally came up to me, bright-eyed, with a towel hooked over his shoulder.

"Dude, you ready to hit those slides?"

"I believe so," I answered slowly, a little nervous about the number of children ready to push their new Guardian down the first one. I tried to smile at them as I removed my sandals. More importantly, I tried to act perfectly normal around Caleb. He seemed oblivious to anything wrong, and for that I was thankful.

"Just do a few, Gabriel," Eden instructed. "Then you can sit and watch them play. They will love that just as much. And leave your shirt on."

"What? The Bearded Beauty won't be showing off all his bronze muscles today? Why would you deprive the people that way?" Caleb teased.

"Because nobody needs to see drakon scarring on their new Guardian," I reminded him.

"Yeeesh. Forgot about that. Good call." But then he removed his own shirt and added, "I guess that means I'll have no competition impressing the ladies then." I was the one impressed by how much he had bulked up in strength and definition over the year.

Not that I would give him the satisfaction of knowing that.

"Too bad they will be blinded by all that white skin." Then I turned my attention on the children. "Who is ready to slide? The first one to push me down gets thrown in the river!"

The laughter, the splashing, and the fresh water did more to raise my energy than anything else this week. Children did not care about policies and plans. They merely wanted to play. And for quite a while, Caleb and Thomas and I splashed in the river and threw kids up in the air to land in the water. Those Hydro children could do tricks we could not, even hoisting us up on waves and swimming such fast circles around us that we found ourselves in the middle of a whirlpool. Finally Thomas excused us for a break, to the disappointed groans of our young fans. We swam to the opposite shore from the slides and reclined on the ground, catching our breath.

"This is the closest I have felt to Camp Fusion in a long time," Caleb said. "Too bad Whit and Morgan are missing it."

"Where are they?" I finally asked, trying to sound mildly curious.

"Morgan wanted to spend some time with Lilley, asking her questions about Healing and things that happened last summer, I think. Whitnee and Nathan wanted some family time with Ezekiel and Sarah at the Healing Center. They said they would be here for dinner." He sat up and shook his hair out. "Whitnee's distracted today."

"How so?" I asked, feeling my heartbeat pick up with nervous speed.

"Just being more private and emotional, I guess." He seemed to force himself to make his tone light. "She worries about that portal more than she lets on. She's begging me to consider staying here permanently with her, because she suddenly believes it could be her destiny. I mean, I shouldn't be surprised. It's not like I haven't worried about this all year."

Thomas jumped in. "Then do you believe she is supposed to stay here? I once did. And I still wonder."

"I believe her dad will ensure she goes home."

I could not tell if he really believed that or was trying to convince himself.

I listened as he continued, "She goes through a version of this every time we come here—this dramatic struggle about where she belongs. Only this time she's making me question where *I* belong."

"Which is where?" Thomas asked.

"On the Mainland."

"Not with her?" I pulled myself painfully upright so I could observe him better. "When she asked you to stay, did you actually tell her that your place was *on the Mainland*?"

"Well, sort of—"

He was an imbecile. "Forgive me, but why would you not tell her your place is wherever *she* is? That might have helped ease her fears."

"Well, it's not that I don't feel that way!" he defended himself. "I would do anything for Whitnee. But I have to believe she is supposed to go back to the Mainland once her purpose here is finished. If I don't stand on that conviction now, she will lose herself here. I know you don't understand—"

"What I understand is that she opened her heart and shared her fears fully with you and you failed to validate them." If he had handled that better, perhaps Whitnee would not have found me out at that spring. Perhaps we would not have been so vulnerable with each other and fallen into that trap of desire. If I blamed Caleb, then maybe I could release this guilt I carried. With a shake of my hair, I said pointedly. "Of course if you cannot even commit to kissing her, then I suppose she cannot expect you to sacrifice everything for her."

"Whoa. That is a low blow, Gabriel!" Caleb spat.

"Wait, you two have never kissed?" Thomas repeated incredulously.

"Don't you start on me too, Thomas," Caleb said. "I have my reasons and, no offense, but you are not exactly the two I want advice from. You" —he pointed at Thomas— "have been sneaking kisses with Morgan the entire time we've been here even though your relationship is going to Nowhereville. And you" —he pointed at me— "well, I don't even have to say what's wrong with your advice on this subject."

"I just think she could use some reassurance from you," I finished, knowing I was right. "You love her, yes?"

"I mean, I haven't said it in those exact words yet. I was waiting for—"

"Always waiting," I interrupted. "That seems to be your favorite thing to do."

He angled his head at me and I wondered if he was contemplating hitting me. "You wanna talk about waiting? Let's talk about you and Eden. You clearly have feelings for each other and yet you seem to be waiting to act on that. Because you know the timing isn't right. Sometimes waiting is the right thing to do, so don't act like I'm just a coward unless you're going to say the same of yourself."

Before I could respond, Thomas spoke up. "Whaaaat? You and *Eden*?"

That Mainlander needed to shut his mouth immediately. But he did not. "Come on, Thomas. Gabe here has the hots for his Personal Advisor. But he knows that it needs time to grow, so he's playing it cool around everyone. Including her."

Thomas looked past me as if he were thinking back over every interaction of the last year. "I did not notice anything until the other night at the Nightingale. But then I laughed at the idea of a Pyra and Geo actually falling in love instead of trying to kill each other. Especially two as strong-headed as you and Eden. I suppose if I imagine it…."

As Thomas burst out laughing, I was the one wondering if I should hit Caleb. "How fantastic of you to discuss my personal life in front of *my* friends."

"Someone has to be able to talk sense into you when I'm gone," Caleb retorted and then softened his tone. "Because, dude, Eden is not a girl to lose."

"Neither is Whitnee," I said, and those Geo-like eyes narrowed. "Whitnee has chosen you and it was the right choice. Please do not mess it up."

He looked at me as if genuinely trying to see my motivation. "You mean that?"

"I really do." I held my knuckles out to him, anything to distract those intuitive green eyes from seeing what I was hiding. "Bestie?"

He seemed to relax and then pounded his fist against mine. The life forces dissolved in the air along with any tension. "For the restie."

"At the festie," Thomas threw in, holding his fist out. That earned him amused looks from us. "What? Do I not understand this game?"

After we threw Thomas back into the river and endured a soaking Water twister in return, Caleb and I shared a laugh, and I tried to make myself believe that all was actually well. He did not know what happened in that spring, and I would certainly never tell him. And maybe I would listen to my own advice and make sure Eden finished her sentence. If it was going where I hoped, I would be ready next time.

It was not until much later that evening that I had my first private interaction with Whitnee since the garden. She was about to enter her bedroom down the hall from me when I came out to find a bottle of Water. She had sleepy eyes and wisps of hair hanging loose around her face.

I paused at my door and so did she, but then she called out quietly, "Goodnight."

"Whitnee, wait." I was at her door in a few strides before she could disappear. "Are you all right? It seems you have been avoiding both me and Caleb all evening."

"And you can't figure out why?" she whispered, anguish swirling around in those gray eyes as she glanced once at Caleb's closed door. "I can't decide if I should tell him or pretend like it never happened. I can't even look at him. I made a huge mistake, Gabriel."

"So did I," I agreed. "I will never tell Caleb what happened today. I could not hurt him like that."

She closed her eyes and exhaled in relief. "Thank you. I just want to forget it ever happened."

That stung a little for reasons that no longer mattered. But I said, "No one ever has to know." And it was the truth. I had come to like

Caleb—to the point that I might actually miss him when—or if— he left someday. I did not want to ruin that for either of us.

"Thanks for understanding," she said, yawning before letting her tired expression fall into a light smile. "Goodnight, Gabriel."

"See you in the morning."

"Yep. Last day," she reminded me, then closed her door with a small wave.

I stood there too long, staring at her door. She was a closed chapter of my life now and though it ached in an unexpected way, it felt right.

26

STEALING BACK THE ATTENTION

Morning came quickly and Zebedee's boat made the gentle trek upriver where we would dock in Pyradora for the final blessing ritual. We Dorians had gathered around the breakfast table first, awaiting the morning's Zephyra Broadcast. I was under strict orders to remain as still as possible while Hannah tweaked a few things on the crisp red and gold tunic I would be wearing. Eden sat beside me and pretended to feed me like a baby since I could not move.

Nathan was the first to join us and almost as soon as he did, Abrianna addressed the table. "As this is our last day and it happens to be in Pyradora, I think it would be prudent to increase your security around the village."

"What do you expect to happen?" Eden narrowed her eyes and lowered the morsel of pastry I had already opened my mouth to receive.

"We all know Pyras can be wild. What if the protestors are there? What if people get too touchy with Nathan?"

"None of those problems have even come up the last couple of days," Eden pointed out.

"Why are you suddenly concerned about security?" I asked her, trying to read her real motivation.

"Yeah, Bri, just tell us what's on your mind," Nathan said.

"Very well. Eli is on my mind," she confessed. "His whereabouts are still unknown. And we are going to his home village. I just do not want him to try and sabotage events at the last minute."

"That is a worthy concern," Nathan replied thoughtfully. "Do you have extra security you can call on?"

Levi was the one to answer. "We do. I have some at the Palladium who could be there shortly. And I believe Abner was going to attend with your family." This he directed at Eden.

"Right. I had forgotten," Eden mumbled. "He is supposed to meet us when we dock. He can certainly accompany us as extra protection."

I turned my head, curious to read her expression, but Hannah directed me forward again. "No moving."

"Good morning!" Whitnee chimed in as she alighted on the patio atop the ship. Caleb and Morgan took the seats across the table next to Nathan, and Whitnee slid into the chair to my right. I could not get a complete view of her, but my Pyradorian nature sensed less anxiety emanating out of her this morning,

"I'm starving," Caleb mumbled, reaching immediately to pile fruit and pastries on his plate. "How soon until we get there?"

"Probably another hour," Eden answered, setting up the large zephyra in the center of the table so we all could watch. "Hopefully we fare well on the broadcast. It will instruct us on where to place our focus for this last ceremony. Today has to be the biggest and the best since it is in Pyradora. Your home village. Your life force. We have a breathtaking finale planned."

I did not have an excess of affection for the village since I had grown up at the Palladium. But there was certainly something special about being surrounded by your own life force and people who appreciated it the way you did.

"It's starting!" Morgan pointed at the zephyra, her mouth full of food.

The broadcast started with its usual retelling of the Hydrodorian blessing ceremony, mentioning who was there and who did what. Scenes of Nathan and Whitnee's presence at my side seemed to get a little more viewing time. There were also images of Nathan and Whitnee as they visited the Healing Center and chatted with the people getting help there.

"I apologize again for missing that," I told them and Nathan gave me a gracious wave of the hand as if it was okay.

Some of the best images were of me playing with the children in the Waterpark.

"Oh, I didn't get to see that," Whitnee remarked. "The kids look so happy!"

"We had fun," I said, still forced to look straight ahead at the zephyra.

"Those moments right there look wonderful," Eden gushed and Thomas agreed. "You seem so lighthearted and approachable. Well done."

"I can be lighthearted and approachable," I reminded her and heard her laugh beside me.

"*...perhaps the most stunning part of the day, though, was witnessing the romance bloom between Gabriel and Whitnee the Traveler. The two were caught exchanging affectionate whispers in a private clearing away from the festival.*"

My breathing stopped as a captured enactment of Whitnee and me kissing in the garden replayed several times. Her hand went to my face first, then I cupped her neck, and our lips moved together faster than I remembered. It cut off before Whitnee jumped away, only to repeat the whole torturous scene.

Someone *had* been watching us.

"*...could it be that the Island's next big event will be a wedding? Find out more as the festivities go on today in Pyradora—*"

Nathan was the one who launched himself at the zephyra and slammed it shut.

The silence at that table was so traumatic that nobody knew who to look at or what to do. I felt Hannah's hands release me, but it was the only movement that seemed to be taking place.

Whitnee and I started talking at the same time, directing our explanations to Caleb.

"That was not what it looked like—"

"We were just talking and—"

"...terrible mistake and we felt awful afterward..."

"It was an accident, and I swear, I don't feel that way about—"

"*Stop.*" Caleb finally commanded, dropping his utensil to the table. He glared at Whitnee. "That's why you wanted to be alone yesterday? To go meet *him*?"

"Caleb, let's go to another room and I'll explain—" Whitnee tried again, but Caleb held up a trembling hand and jumped to his feet.

"Explain what? That you and Gabriel have been meeting secretly to make out?"

"No," we answered adamantly at the same time.

"It was one kiss," Whitnee stuttered as she tried to speak faster than her mouth could go. "You know I was feeling overwhelmed yesterday. I am trying to do the right thing, trying to figure out where I belong and I was only sharing with Gabriel how confused I felt and how I didn't want to be separated forever from—"

"And let me guess, he took advantage of your vulnerability," Caleb spat. "Because that's what Gabriel has *always* done. As soon as you lower your guard, he swoops in and plays the part of your knight in shining armor."

My turn to try. "I was doing no such thing. We talked as friends—"

"Shut up, Gabriel." Caleb finally turned to me. "You have never in any way been a friend to either of us."

That burned in ways I never imagined.

Whitnee's voice rose steadily in pitch. "It was just a big mistake we both regretted immediately—the broadcast didn't even show that part! And I was only emotional in the first place because I was scared to lose *you*—"

"Well, congratulations." His voice was shockingly calm and controlled. "You two can have each other, because I am done with you. *Both* of you." He turned around to leave.

Whitnee turned to me, panic-stricken. "Gabriel, tell him!"

We launched out of our chairs to chase after him. "You can blame me, Caleb, because Whitnee would never—"

But Caleb spun around, and a sharply pointed wooden vine hurled viciously out of his glowing hand and paused dead center between my eyes. His aim always had been right on target.

"Oh, I do blame you. You pretended to be my friend." His voice was quiet—alarmingly quiet. I held up my hands and took a step back, seeing Levi ready himself for defense somewhere off to my side. "You earned my trust while you fed me lies. If you come near me again or try to speak one more word out of that lying mouth of yours, I *will* hurt you."

"Calm down, son," Nathan warned. "Don't do anything you'll regret."

"I already have." Caleb's icy green eyes turned on Whitnee. He recoiled the branch and dropped his fists to his sides. "I regret ever trying." Then he stalked away.

Whitnee's breath caught in a sob and Morgan was quick to her side. My sight somehow landed on Eden who stared back at me with disappointment and mistrust.

"Well, at least you successfully pulled the Island's attention back on yourself," Abrianna said, wiping her mouth delicately with a napkin. "A love story always works. No matter how complicated."

"Abrianna!" Nathan said sharply. "Your lack of empathy disgusts me."

I barely witnessed the shame that crossed her face before Eden stood up and quickly exited the patio without a word. I thought about following her, but my feet would not move.

"I have to go talk to him," Whitnee cried. "He'll listen if I can just explain."

But I had my doubts. Caleb was not a fool. Whitnee could try to explain it away however she wanted, but we both compromised our hearts yesterday.

Nathan was hesitant to let her go. "Maybe you should let him calm down first—"

"He wouldn't hurt me, Dad. Not how I've hurt him." And with that she shoved away from Morgan and chased after Caleb.

I found myself rooted to the spot, unsure of what to say, where to go. Morgan's blue eyes shimmered with dread when she turned toward me. "Did you know they were there watching? The correspondents? Is that why you did it?"

I could only give her a pained expression in return. Did I know they were there? No. Did I throw out my caution and do it anyway, knowing they were likely close by? Maybe.

Out of the corner of my eye, I saw Thomas's head drop into his hands, and I knew I had lost favor with him as well. I guess the loneliness was going to begin before the Guardianship Festival even ended. My loyal band of friends were dropping one by one.

"When will you all stop playing these games?" Nathan seethed, catching every eye left in the room before settling on me. "The people of this Island deserve better from you. Do the right thing before it's too late."

I caught up to Caleb in the hallway before he could slam his bedroom door in my face. I threw my whole body in the way and blocked him.

"Can we please talk this out? I am so sorry." My entire body shook badly enough that I worried life forces might start leaking out. I had never felt so apprehensive, and that included being kidnapped, threatened, stuck in a flooding underwater chamber, and hunted by a water beast.

He abandoned the doorway and moved purposefully to pick up his bag, tossing stuff into it.

"What are you doing?"

"I'm leaving."

He couldn't actually leave. We were on a *boat*. I shut the door behind me, trying to exhale the panic out of my chest. "I know you're hurt and angry and you have every right to be. But I need you to understand that what happened was an accident. I truly look at Gabriel as just a friend—"

"Friends! Don't! Kiss!" He violently pulled his graduation clothes out and whipped them in the air as if trying to release the wrinkles. "Morgan and I don't kiss. Kissing happens when there's attraction or a history. A *recent* history resulting in secret meet-ups. Which explains so much better why you suddenly want to stay on the Island!"

Oh, so much to respond to... and no idea where to start.

"First of all, this is a separate issue from staying on the Island and you know that. Secondly, I have not been meeting up with Gabriel, I swear." I cast wide innocent eyes at him, praying he'd calm down enough to see the truth. "He and I haven't even been alone together until yesterday—"

"And the second you were, *that* happened?" His hands shot through his hair and he refused to meet my eyes. "I guess you could hardly keep your hands off each other during the ceremonies—why would you hold back in private?"

I fought to stay calm. "I see how it looks that way." Because it did look bad. Every bit of it. Bad. "But every moment—besides the one yesterday—has been in full view of everyone. I've told you everything about our conversations. I promise I haven't hidden anything else from you—"

"Well, thank you for being *so* innocent and forthcoming." Aggressive hands tried desperately to smooth the clothes out on the bed. "When your lips accidentally fell into Gabriel's, it was really stellar of you to come straight to tell me, so I wouldn't find out some other horrible way, like in front of the entire Island and your dad and—oh, wait. That's *not at all* what you did."

"I should've told you immediately. I really wrestled over it, Caleb." I took a step closer to him, the guilt collecting in a ball at my throat. "Obviously I didn't want to hurt you, especially when I knew in my heart that something like that would never happen again. In my mind, it was settled, and I just wanted to forget it happened."

"You and your delusions about forgetting Gabriel," he snorted, still keeping his attention glued to those dang wrinkles he was intent on eliminating. "Absolutely nothing about you has changed this year. Nothing."

Whoa, now.

"That's not fair! I'm the one who has been trying all year to draw a commitment out of *you*. You were the one who kept walking away."

"And now you know why!" He threw his hands up in the air and then dug around in the bag again. "I should never have tried to make things work with you, with him... I mean, I became that guy's friend because I thought that maybe it would help ease some of your *neverending* drama here. I didn't want to act like some kind of jealous boyfriend this time—"

"You have no idea how much I adore you for that, Caleb. This week has been so fun because of *you*." I pressed my trembling hands to my heart, hating that this had burned him both ways because of his acceptance of Gabriel too. "And I know Gabriel genuinely cares about you and is horrified that—"

"That friendship is over. And so are any fantasies you had of me staying here on this Island." He stormed across the room for more of his belongings and then buried them in the bag. "To think that I was actually considering leaving the Mainland behind to be with you... I am so glad your true feelings were revealed before I made the biggest mistake of my life!"

"*Caleb.*" That hurt so freaking much. I didn't want to be his mistake. "Stop throwing things around and listen to me!" His hands paused and pressed to his stomach, and it looked like he might throw up. I was feeling nauseous too, so I swallowed hard. "If you'll stop interrupting me, I want to explain what happened yesterday. I don't want to hide anything from you."

"Fine, explain!" He gripped his waist and finally turned to face me. Now that he was still and his attention focused completely on me, my nerves skyrocketed.

"The truth is I went down to the garden to be alone—just like I told you. He was already there. We started talking and it led to how we left things last summer. You were right. I had broken his heart. And as he shared his *past* feelings, I could relate. I felt the same desperation when I thought about losing you to another world, Caleb. I told him I wanted you. And it was good to finally put that to rest."

"Ohhh... I get it." The sarcasm dripped out of him like acid. "So it was just one last kiss for old times' sake, now that you were so nobly sacrificing your love for each other."

"*No.*"

I got a close up of his sneer when he marched up to me so quickly that I had to take a step back. I tilted my face up to look into eyes that had never been as repulsed by me as they were then.

"Then what were you whispering to each other before that kiss? And why were you the first one to reach out to him? Don't even think about lying to me."

I broke down and hid my tears behind my hands. The contents of that conversation with Gabriel would sound so bad. He wouldn't understand.

But Caleb wasn't softening. He grabbed me by the wrists and pulled my hands away. "You owe me the truth."

I stared up at my best friend, my rock, my steady heartbeat. His hands shook and held onto me tightly as if my wrists were the only things keeping him from falling off a deadly precipice. I saw the dam of despair trying not to break across his face and I loved him so much that I couldn't lie to him or myself anymore. This had to be washed out of our lives if we were to actually recover from it.

"I told him that I had never stopped caring about him," I cried, the truth searing a burn across my chest. "I realized that it was just another piece to why I struggled all year deciding on college. I said that—" I couldn't get through this. I couldn't even breathe. "I said a part of my heart would always belong to him, but that it was time to go ahead and end this once and for all. He said he would care for me if you chose to go back to the Mainland, though he believed you would never abandon me. I thanked him and started to leave, and..."

And that did it. The dam broke and Caleb's eyes flooded with tears. He let go of me and turned away.

"No, Caleb, please don't cry. Please!" I threw my arms around his waist and he tried to peel them away. I wouldn't let go—couldn't let go—as my tears soaked into the back of his shirt. "Please forgive me. We can work through this. I will earn your trust back and you'll see... you'll see how much I love you."

It was the first time I'd ever confessed those three words to him and it wasn't at all how I wanted it to happen.

I pleaded over and over again, clinging to him as hard as I could, feeling his abdomen constrict with silent sobs. We stood there like that in the center of the room for a few minutes with only the sound of my weeping and his sniffs. Finally, he rubbed his eyes, wiped his face, and carefully pulled my hands apart from his waist. With quiet dejection, he lowered himself on the edge of the bed and stared at the floor. I thought I would pass out waiting for him to say something.

It was a scratchy and broken voice that emerged. "I need some time and space to think."

"Okay," I agreed, willing to give him whatever he wanted. "I'm sure you can miss the activities this morning. Then we can go somewhere and talk again—"

"No, I need more time than that."

"Whatever you need. We'll arrange it."

"Whitnee." His eyes finally met mine, but only for a moment as if it pained him to even look at me. "As soon as we dock, I'm heading to the Palladium and going back through that portal."

My breath caught again, and I felt dizzy. "You can't leave."

"No, you're the one who can't leave," he said coldly. "My time here is done."

I crumpled to the floor in front of him, trying to clear the dizziness away. When I reached for his hand, it was the first time ever that his fingers refused to tighten around mine. "Don't do this. Please, just wait things out with me. The portal is unstable. It could separate us forever."

"Then so be it."

It felt as if I'd been slapped. "You don't mean that."

He pulled his hand away and organized his bag more calmly now. "The whole Island has seen a public display of your relationship with Gabriel now. I can't stay here."

"Caleb, I am begging you to stay."

"Why? You already have a backup plan with Gabriel." His eyes watered again, but he seemed to swallow it down before continuing, "As long as this place exists, your heart will always gravitate to him. It's practically a freaking law of nature at this point, and I refuse to commit to someone who I can't trust to commit wholeheartedly back. He promised to take care of you, so allow me to free you completely of this burden over where you belong. I leave. You stay."

"That's not what I want—"

"But it's what *I* want."

I felt a moan escape as I teetered on the edge of the black hole we were falling into. "What about the future? What about your dream, that beautiful dream of us going to college together and getting married and—and… Don't give up on that, please. Don't give up on *me*."

He stood up with his bag. "Right now I can't see it, Whitnee. Not here. Not on the Mainland. Not anywhere."

"But I love you!"

"Don't," he choked. "Don't say that to me."

He could not have dug a deeper knife than that one. As he stepped around me to exit the room, I had the wild thought of grabbing onto his legs and not letting him escape. Or binding him up with all four life forces. I had powers. I could force him to stay.

But I didn't.

I doubled over and hid my face, trying to pretend this wasn't really happening, that Caleb wasn't really intent on walking out of my life forever. He said he would always be there, always find me, *always...*

But the click of the door pushed me over the edge of a hole from which I wasn't sure I would ever resurface.

27

DEPARTURE

The rest of the morning was a blur. Dad and Morgan found me on the floor. There were hugs and reassurances brutally combined with admonishment and tough love. I deserved it. I was not a victim—I had brought this on myself. And I had irreparably hurt the boy I loved, someone Dad and Morgan cared about too. The thought of Caleb going through that portal under these conditions brought on a full panic attack that took a while to get under control.

Dad ended up taking matters into his own hands. If it was because of his traumatized daughter or because he too had concerns about Caleb leaving, I didn't know. But he took Caleb somewhere private and all I knew was that when they emerged, the agreement was for Caleb to travel to Geodora and wait there until we had a plan for our return.

It still wasn't what I wanted, but it was so much better than the alternative. I started to breathe again. When the ship docked and the time to part came, I was so emotionally poured out that I felt dead inside. I watched from a short distance while Morgan hugged Caleb and said whatever it was she thought he needed to hear. He glanced at me uncertainly over her head, and I took a few nervous steps in that direction.

He started toward me too, but then stopped with a few feet between us.

The morning sun glanced across the top of his head, bathing his hair in a rustic gold color. It was devastating for so many reasons to see he had changed back into his khaki pants and button-up graduation shirt from home. The sleeves were casually rolled up, but he was neatly tucked in with that leather belt. His bag was thrown over one shoulder and he held onto the strap with one white-knuckled hand.

I spoke first. "Will you call? I mean, so we know you got there safely."

"I'll try," he said.

And then I waited there pathetically hoping that he'd change his mind and either stay with me or beg me to run away with him. At the very least, I hoped for a sign—any sign—that it was okay to hug him goodbye. My arms ached to embrace him, to hold him until everything around us melted away. But he didn't move an inch and neither did I. His eyes darted uneasily to something behind me and when I looked back, Dad was staring him down.

"I think it's time for you to go be the Island's golden girl," he said.

Standing before a crowd was the last thing I wanted to do. My composure started to slip, so I choked out, "Bye, Caleb." And I turned to walk off as briskly as my feet could carry me.

"Whit."

He called my name. My *nickname*. I only hesitated one second before turning back around.

He was fighting for composure too. Those conflicted eyebrows shadowed his swollen eyes, but he looked right at me.

"We *will* talk later, okay?"

Those five words carried on the breeze between us, and as I breathed them in, I could feel the ball in my chest loosen a tiny bit.

"Okay."

When he left to board the wagon with Abner who had agreed to Eden's sudden request to transport him safely back to Geodora, Caleb never once looked back at us. Morgan tucked her arm in mine and sighed.

"Maybe I should have gone with him. I hate to think of him being alone."

"That's what he wanted."

"Is it, though? Does anyone ever actually want to be alone?"

I didn't have an answer. I don't think I could've handled parting from Morgan too, but the thought of her being there to talk Caleb off the precipice of hating me for the rest of his life made me wonder if she should have gone.

"I'm sorry you're stuck in the middle of this," I told her.

"I hate it." She sighed again. "I can't defend your actions, Whitnee. I *won't*. Caleb deserves better than that." Ugh. Harsh Morgan words were so rare. "But I will never minimize the incredible weight of responsibility and pressure I know you feel between both worlds. Gabriel has been an integral part of your love for this world. And while I know you always want to do the right thing, it's hard when your heart is tangled in so many what-ifs. That's worth granting you a certain measure of grace, if you ask me."

Grace. I wasn't certain I deserved it.

"The heart is so fickle, so deceitful," I murmured. "Why do people tell you to follow it? It's not guaranteed to lead you in the right direction."

She squeezed in closer to my side. My eyes fell on my dad who was still watching Caleb's wagon disappear in the distance. Morgan followed my line of vision. "Maybe we're supposed to follow something—or some*one*—bigger and better than ourselves. Someone whose unconditional love and perspective never wavers— no matter how much of a mess we make in our lives." I studied her face for a moment as she gazed at my dad in reverence and adoration before giving me a small smile. I leaned my head on her shoulder and pondered her words.

Maybe so.

It felt like the crowd in Pyradora was the biggest we had seen so far. As we paraded through the village in open wagons, eye colors of every hue told me that most of the Island had gathered on the mountain for the finale of the Guardianship Festival. The Pyradorians themselves could easily be identified by the metallic jewels and vivid flares of color characterizing their brand of Island fashion. I smoothed the bodice of my dress—red and studded with tiny pieces of sparkly mountain rock—and then adjusted the heavy pieces of stone jewelry adorning my wrists and ankles. Though the colors and excitement around me were vivid, everything dulled without Caleb there.

With a deep breath and a nervous pat at the glittery gem holding half of my hair back, I told myself this was it. One more day. I could get through it with the hope that Caleb and I would talk tonight by zephyra.

But I was so restless. There was a steady hum in my chest that wouldn't stop, and I wasn't sure if it was the cause or effect of my anxiety. I just wanted it to stop.

I sat between Poppa Zeke and Grandmother Sarah in the back of the wagon, trying to soak up as much comfort and emotional protection from them as I could. We gazed up at the formidable mountain that rose ahead of us. Dad spoke up from the other side of Sarah. "The portal might be rippling out tremors from here, but I feel something else emanating out of that mountain. Do you feel it?"

I don't think I had really tried to tap into anything deeper than my own feelings this week. But now that I was in this village, maybe something did feel off. Then again, I wasn't sure if my emotional acuity was hindered by Caleb's absence or the effusive ranks of people all around us.

"What exactly do you feel, Dad?" I finally asked.

He closed his eyes then, as if trying to focus on something. The mountain was a perfect frame behind him when he answered, "Dread."

Perfect. That's exactly what this day needed.

He continued quickly. "After all of this is over, I'm going in there to shut that portal down."

"Would it make the earthshakers stop, Nathan?" Grandmother Sarah asked.

"That's the idea," he mused. "Once the job is done, we will see if the Palladium portal opens back up for us and we can get home."

"Except someone has to destroy the Palladium portal too," I reminded him, feeling my own sense of dread.

"We will find a way and make sure it's done this time."

Elon said it would fall to me to do the job. Did he really not know that? Perhaps I should tell him. I hoped it was simple. I *needed* it to be simple. Hopefully, I would know more after Dad disabled the one in the mountain.

I looked to the top of that volcano again, feeling like there should be smoke coming out the top… but it was just another clear, sultry day around here. Not a cloud in the vivid blue sky. I became aware then that Grandmother Sarah's hand in mine had tightened almost uncomfortably.

"What are you thinking about, Grandmother?"

She sighed. "I think that everyone should be extremely cautious on that mountain."

"We will, Mother." Dad patted her wrinkled hand and leaned over to plant a reassuring kiss on her cheek.

Eden traded seats with Thomas in order to be closer to us. Her gold pantsuit clung to her feminine figure, and even though she had worn ruby red jewelry in the same custom as the Pyras, she still had a characteristic star-shaped flower tucked into her hair. That floral pop of bright red matched the lip gloss she had chosen. "When we arrive at the Landing of Pyradora closer to the top, the ceremony will take place first."

"Is there room for all of these people up there?" As our caravan passed, I noticed the people followed behind us on the slow trek up the mountain path.

"The construction of the Landing is ingenious as well as beautiful. There is a significant space for village-wide gatherings, and the Fireports launch from up there." At my confused face, Morgan mouthed, "hot air balloons" and I remembered she got to ride in one last summer. "But almost the whole Island has come for the final blessing, so the overflow will spread out down the mountain. We will use voice projection so that everyone will be able to hear the ceremony."

I found myself stealing a glance at the front of the wagon where Gabriel and Abrianna stood and waved to the people. Gabriel and I had said probably two words to each other since the blow-up at breakfast. As I tuned back in to Eden's instructions, I really wanted to know how she had felt about that broadcast. Though I had no tangible reason, I felt like I had wronged her, too, by kissing Gabriel. She seemed to be extremely focused on her job since breakfast, to the point of forgetting to smile—not at all like the fun-loving companion to Gabriel that I had seen in Geodora.

"...for the actual blessing, it will just be Gabriel and Abrianna and Nathan, with Levi as security, along with Jesse and his family. You will board our specially-designed Fireport and hover out in view of the people along the mountain. The rest of the Councilmen— my parents, Ezekiel and Sarah, Zebedee and Zipporah—will have special seating with their families on the Landing. Whitnee and Morgan will remain with me and Thomas and Hannah on the main platform during the ceremony. There will be Pyra-technics shooting out in all directions, and let us hope none of them go rogue this time." She scrunched her nose and then added, "We almost cancelled that part after what happened at the Watch Tower, but it is very important to the Pyras to show off what makes them unique."

"Excuse me, Eden, but why am I not going on the Fireport with Gabriel and Dad?" I asked. "I've been there for all of the ceremonies."

"Well, for one, the Fireport is not big enough to hold everyone. We are cutting it close trying to squeeze Nathan on. And..." Eden paused and looked to my dad, as if questioning whether she should continue.

Dad said, "Gabriel and I agreed that you need some distance from the publicity today, Whit. He'll be fine without you."

I wondered if that was more Dad's suggestion or Gabriel's. Either way, I couldn't decide if I really cared or not. As exciting as a hot air balloon ride should sound, I had a hard time stirring up enthusiasm for any of this.

But by the time we arrived at the Landing, a bit of awe did creep its way in. The Landing was the most mashed-up version of Island beauty combined with old-world style technology I'd ever seen. There were coppery gears and steam engine-type mechanics that seemed to make the Landing almost float on the edge of the mountainside. One end of the Landing featured a stage that was artistically designed with glittering white stone and gold metal that swirled together to create a rich, almost theatrical backdrop.

Emblems of flame and sunlight were etched into the interwoven gears, and the tropical vegetation that grew on the mountain peeked out and softened the texture of all that brushed metal.

I had just stepped into a steampunk novel.

The Landing was well-named too, because stretching out from the stage, suspended by simple steam mechanics, was a flat bronze runway flanked by torches of dancing Firelight. The entire strip jutted out from the mountain to overlook the village itself. Buildings and homes were clearly set into the mountain, but with colorful fronts that, at this height and view, gave the appearance of confetti sprinkled down this side of the mountain. The winding roads were so packed with festive people, they were like colorful streamers. We were at the apex of a mountain-sized piñata. I couldn't help but think Papi back at home would have loved every moment of this fiesta. Mom would too.

I suddenly felt as battered on the inside as a real piñata, only instead of candy, it was more tears that wanted to spill out of me. This was such a beautiful piece of the Island, but all I could think about were all of my loved ones who weren't here to experience it with me. I took a ragged breath and found the courage to wave back at the people who tried to grab my attention in the audience.

At the farthest edge of the Landing—ready for flight—was their version of a hot air balloon. The balloon part shimmered in pale gold palm fronds and featured the same swirling design Gabriel and his team wore on their medallions—with the letter 'P' in the center. Each swirl rippled with lights in the color of each tribe—exactly as it had done on the doorway into the mountain at Jezebel's property. Behind it, you could see the vast Blue River winding its way south across the Island and the ocean stretching out beyond.

On the stage stood Pyradorian Councilman Jesse and his family. As we drew closer to them, I thought how Caleb would've hated being this high up, and my heart caught in my throat again. Abrianna and Gabriel stepped down first and greeted them all with a kiss on the cheek. Jezebel's smile was thin as Gabriel approached her and exchanged whispers. She at least seemed sober and dressed more modestly than usual. That bronze dress caught some of the sun-kissed highlights in her hair.

When it was my turn to greet her, I guessed, "You designed that Fireport, didn't you?" When she merely nodded, I added, "It's amazing. You are so talented."

I was going to move on, but she said, "That broadcast this morning was quite interesting. Might I ask where Caleb is?" Was she trying to bait me into some kind of snarky exchange? I didn't have the energy for a snide back-and-forth with her this time. When I failed to come up with words, she seemed to take a deep appraisal of my face, probably sizing up the puffiness I could barely hide even with makeup and doses of Water life force. "You should leave this Island before it destroys you."

I could not read her expression then, so I turned and walked away. I didn't need a reminder of how destroyed my future could be if Caleb didn't forgive me.

As the greetings and fanfare went on, Gabriel found his way to my side. His tunic was vivid red with a metallic yellow stripe that ran diagonally across his chest. Every aspect of his look was embellished with metal fastenings and stone-like adornments that almost gave the impression of armor, like a warrior prince, a commander of Fire. The gold flecks in his eyes seemed more vivid in his own village. Keeping those eyes on the crowd, he asked, "How are you feeling?"

"Like I've ruined my life."

"I understand."

I looked up at him, startled. "You're about to become the Guardian. People believe in you. And now you're the hero of a love story they didn't even know they wanted."

He grimaced. "People love the idea of a Guardian. But they do not know me. Nor will they provide friendship and companionship when this fanfare is all over. Likewise, when the love story abruptly ends, so will their interest."

He could still give them a love story. A proper one. A *real* one. "What about Eden—"

"Let us not talk about our Geodorian counterparts, shall we? I think we have done enough damage to them already."

"I'm sorry." I had lost count of how many times I'd said those words the last twenty-four hours.

"So am I."

A crowd of young people nearby started calling out to us and chanting for us to kiss again. I wanted to die. I had never had something so intimate be on display in front of that many people. Gabriel gestured for them to quiet down and then raised his voice over them. "A private moment like that should never have been broadcast. Please do not embarrass my friend."

They called back. "How soon will you be married?" and "You are disappointing eligible girls in every village!"

"No marriage plans right now. Thank you." With a gentle hand to my lower back, Gabriel steered me away from the crowd as the chants for a public kiss grew more insistent. I could detect Eden's annoyance as we followed her instructions and took our places onstage. The Councilmen for the other tribes moved to sit with their families in what looked to be the VIP audience on the Landing, and I caught a wave from Elon. Though I waved back with enthusiasm, something about seeing her set me on edge all over again. She was a beautiful miracle. But she was also a piece in a complicated puzzle that had yet to come together.

I glanced over at Dad and projected my thoughts into his. *Where exactly is Jezebel's house from here? I don't remember a lot in this village.*

Dad waved at the crowd and then nodded to the left up the mountain a little ways from us. *That blocked-off road will take us up there. The wealthy live closer to the top.*

At least we wouldn't have to fight crowds to get there. From the Landing down, every trail and road seemed packed with people. It would take hours to empty the village. I supposed that was why I saw dining tables already set for the new Guardian and his entourage on the outer edge of the Landing. Lunch with a view.

The Aerodorian voice projectors got in position to help amplify Jesse's words all over the mountainside. But just before it was time to quiet the crowd and begin, Jezebel, who stood to his left, started thrashing around as if something else possessed her body. When she dropped to her knees, Dad immediately moved to soothe her with a calm voice as Jesse scolded, "Stop this, Jezebel. Do not embarrass yourself."

It was just like in Aerodora. She clutched her head the same way, which made me rush over, a concerned Gabriel on my heels.

We formed a circle around her, trying to hide the scene from the onlookers.

Dad placed his hand on her head, but she was moving and shouting so much, he couldn't get her under control.

"Jezebel, talk to us. Is it the voice again?" I called, wondering if an earthshaker was about to start. "Dad, help her!"

With no warning, she stopped moving and her eyes turned *red*.

Pretty sure that was not one of the standard eye colors on the Island. Fear rippled through my body and I instinctively took a step back. She looked past us as if we weren't even there. Her voice came out in a deep, distorted tone and her eyes roamed all over the crowd—anywhere but at our faces. "It is time. All must be burned up by fire."

Goosebumps snaked down my back at the chilling sound of a voice that wasn't hers. She repeated the same phrases on a loop until Dad finally cried out, "Enough! Be gone!" He forcefully grabbed her head, and the white light of his hands grew in strength as he practically put her in a headlock. Her voice went from a croaking groan to a high-pitched female voice, and then she went slack and seemed to breathe again.

"Jezebel?" Dad asked.

Her fingers dug into his shoulders and her hazel eyes filled with pleading tears. "He owns me. I cannot be rid of him. Not unless—" She stopped and broke down, right there on the ground in her beautiful dress. Gabriel knelt beside her, patting her back and trying to shield her from the crowd.

"Who owns you?" he asked with his deep, authoritative voice.

"I must stop it," she said and then wobbled to her feet. As soon as Dad released her, she pushed through our circle and lurched purposefully down the runway to the Fireport. Her parents called out to her to stop, but Gabriel was the one in the lead as we all ran after her. She slammed the little door closed before Gabriel could jump inside the carrier.

"Get back, Gabriel. Please!" she yelled. I didn't like the wild look on her face.

"What are you doing, Jez? Just come out of there and we can go somewhere to talk. You are making a scene—"

"I am so sorry for what I have done to you. To all of you." She frantically heated up the Fireport, sending a burst of flame and lights into the balloon. The whole thing started to float.

"You have done nothing to me that warrants an apology. Just please come down from there and let me help you with whatever is—"

"You cannot help me. And if you could, you would not want to," she called out, desperation marring her beauty. Tears poured out around those golden-lit irises. "I am the one who orchestrated the assassination attacks."

"Jezebel!" her mother called out. "What are you talking about?"

"You...?" Shock registered on Gabriel's face.

I was just as surprised. Did I think Jezebel had been the portrait of integrity? Of course not. But murder did not seem to be her brand of poison either. Judging by the reactions around me, I wasn't the only one appalled and confused.

"The Pyra-technic at the Watch Tower? The thunderflies?" Gabriel gripped the back of his neck and looked over at Dad. Jezebel's sobs picked up in volume and hysteria with every question.

"He has tried to control me since we were young, Gabriel. Now he comes to me—sometimes in person, sometimes as a voice—and he threatens me. I felt powerless until Nathan cleared my head out that night in Aerodora. I cannot do this anymore. I have to get away from him."

"Get away from *whom*?" Gabriel tried again.

She had floated high enough that I saw a strange flashing contraption tied to the bottom of the Fireport. Something caught my eye about the odd material that matched nothing on the flawless design of the Fireport.

"There's something on the bottom of the Fireport," I pointed out to no one in particular, but it drew attention. "Is that supposed to be there?"

When Gabriel caught sight of it, his face changed dramatically. "Jezebel, you need to—"

"It is Eli I speak of!" she confessed, and I heard Abrianna unsuccessfully stifle a moan. "And he has people working for him, people who might be just as threatened as I, I do not know."

Can't say I was shocked to hear Eli's name come out of her mouth, but the level of disgust I felt for the situation was about to boil over. Who knew what kinds of awful ways Eli had threatened her? And what did she mean it was his voice she was hearing in her head? Pyras couldn't do that like Aeros could, right?

"Jezebel, jump out of the Fireport now and send it up. I will catch you. There is an explosive attached to the undercarriage!"

She wiped her face, took a deep breath, and with forced calmness, she said, "I know."

We watched with trepidation as she flew the Fireport up and away more speedily—heading toward the ocean. We followed her to the edge of the Landing, trying to weigh what should be done. But just as Dad called her name, the entire Fireport exploded and promptly disintegrated with a flash of flame and light.

Nothing but tiny burning strips of the leafy balloon rained down the mountainside as screams of horror filled the air.

28

CONFESSIONS OF A SOCIOPATH

Jezebel was gone. It happened so fast, I could not save her. My stomach wanted to revolt as I cried out in despair at the ashes that floated down around me.

But then I sensed him. He was there in the crowd somewhere.

Eli. The man who had given me my heritage and cursed it with his black rage. His violent depravity soaked into the emotional atmosphere as it always did when he was around. I slowly turned to face the distraught crowd and the devastated faces of my friends. Even my mother's usual poise seemed on the verge of collapsing.

I turned to Jezebel's parents first, trying to subdue the firestorm raging inside me. "Did you know about any of this? Answer truthfully as this could be the last thing you ever say."

Jesse's eyes were wide as he held onto his wife, who cried for her daughter. "I did not, Gabriel. We had no idea Jezebel was working with Eli or that she was under threat—" His voice gave out for a moment as the guilt and regret took over. "We always allowed her to do as she wished. I have distanced myself from your father over the last year, but I never would have thought he and Jezebel would try to kill us. We were on the Watch Tower that night. And we were about to board that Fireport with you!"

My eyes tilted to Eden. She would know if he was lying. When she gave me a subtle nod of affirmation that it was the truth, I let the matter rest for the present time.

"He is here. Prepare to protect yourselves." Instinctively, I planted myself slightly in front of Whitnee and Eden, but Eden took a step forward so that she was directly next to me with her eyes already lit up bright green. Dressed in shimmering pale gold, she coordinated perfectly at my side—right down to the scarlet flower behind her ear.

She gave me a fierce look. "Surely you do not think I need a protector."

"Of course not." I pressed my lips together because I had never seen her look so beautiful, so feral, as she did in that moment. "But perhaps a partner?"

"Always."

We scanned the crowd for the danger that we all sensed was out there. I could start evacuating the Landing, but I was unsure of what we were really dealing with. Rash decisions could lead to ruination.

As Nathan stood protectively near Whitnee and Morgan, I heard him say, "Whit, don't power up right now. Just stay calm and wait. I don't trust this situation." Then he muttered, "Show yourself, Eli."

Eden reminded me, "On your command, our Palladium security can start getting people out of the village. They will have to start at the bottom of the mountain as the roads are overflowing."

"Even if you do, we are stuck up here and Eli knows it." It was my mother who said it. "Make no mistake, he will punish innocent people for anything you do."

Hannah, Thomas, Levi, Eden and I formed the front line in a semicircle, eyes roaming everywhere. Someone suddenly came shoving through the crowd, calling for us, but it was just Abner.

Abner?

"I am here to help!" he bellowed and ran right up to Eden, embracing her awkwardly. She did not return his hug nor take her eyes off her surroundings.

"What are you doing here?" she asked, sounding annoyed and suspicious.

"Where's Caleb?" Whitnee piped up, looking desperately behind him. "Is he here?"

"No," Abner told her. "I did not have a good feeling about all of this after you requested more aid for the day. I felt strongly that we should turn around. He refused and demanded to go on to Geodora without me. So I left him with the wagon and fought the crowd to get here."

At Whitnee's crushed expression, Eden pressed him further. "Is that true, Abner? That does not sound like Caleb."

I agreed. No matter how upset Caleb was, I could not shake the feeling that he would not abandon Whitnee and Morgan if he had any inkling of danger on the horizon.

Abner shrugged. "He is a broken man."

That did not sit well with any of us for various reasons, but the moment was interrupted when a disturbance started at the entrance to the Landing. Eli, surrounded by about eight other people with black cloth masks shrouding their heads, took over the stage and faced us where we stood in the middle of the runway.

Nine people. We could easily overcome that many, but not when there were this many people all around us. Shots could be deflected and hit someone for whom they were not intended.

So I tried the diplomatic way first. "Eli, you are a traitor to the White Island on counts of murder, extortion, and threats to overthrow this government. Submit to armbands and call off your people."

He took a moment to look around him before bursting into that deep laughter I had heard on so many occasions when a beating was coming my way. One of the men in his guard must have been an Aerodorian voice projector because when Eli made a gesture, his voice boomed across the Landing and down the mountain. Everyone could hear him now.

"You are calling me a traitor to this Island? Let us talk about who the real traitors are."

"Should we fire at him before he starts spitting lies to everyone?" Thomas asked.

"No." I answered. "We could hit innocent people. We need to find a way to get everyone away from here, if possible."

"Do not attempt an evacuation, Gabriel," Eli called back, guessing at our conversation. "All along this mountainside are people with explosives mixed into the crowd. You do not know who they are. But on my command, they will eradicate half the population of the Island in one flash."

"He cannot be serious," Eden breathed.

"Which is why it is important for everyone to stay calm and wise. You will want to hear what I have to say," Eli roared. "And if either of you two become a problem" —he pointed at Nathan and Whitnee— "we will start terminating people at random."

I could not risk the lives of my people. How had he gotten past all of our security, known about all of our plans? Just through Jezebel? She had said there were more. Who else had he manipulated? He must have been hiding out in Jezebel's house, the one place we never would have searched. It had become a safehouse for *our* side. I felt betrayed and without one idea how to get out of this situation.

When none of us moved, the whole Island was forced to listen to his story. "I was a respected Councilman for the Pyradora tribe for ten years, and as a young man, I married the only woman I ever wanted—Abrianna, your Guardian. Together we raised a son who is about to become your next Guardian. I stood faithfully by my wife's side and supported her role as Guardian for nearly thirty years. But what no one really knows is that my wife has only ever been in love with one man. And it is not me. For the majority of her life, your Guardian has carried on a secret romantic relationship with the man you call Pilgrim." He pointed at Nathan and yelled, "Nathan left this Island when he was eighteen, only to return secretly seven years ago as Abrianna's lover—"

"Eli, I am warning you—"

"Everything you have seen Nathan do under the title of Pilgrim has been to win over your hearts and loyalty so that he and Abrianna could rule the Island together. It was not I who was behind the assassination attempts, Gabriel, but them. They have tried to get rid of you for years. Nathan was always jealous that Abrianna had a son with me; your mother despised the fact that you were born a Pyra. They have been the ones to orchestrate rebel attacks, protestors, anything they could to keep you distracted while they formed their perfect plan. And they pinned it all on me."

Lies. It was all lies and we all knew it. But the faces of the people watching this terrible scene unfold were confused, doubting.

"Watch!" Eli conjured images in the sky of Nathan and Abrianna when they were younger. A stolen kiss as teenagers. Embraces as adults. He had his hands on her in what I recognized as a Healer's posture, likely after physical altercations with Eli. But to the crowd, it looked extremely intimate.

"Dad..." Whitnee whispered, staring up at the images with disgust all over her face.

"None of this is true, Whitnee," he assured her.

"But that kiss—"

"We were young, a long time ago. Your mother is the one I love—remember that, Whitnee Skye. She was my choice and always will be."

Abrianna's cheeks were wet with tears. "Stop this, Eli!" She shouted and stepped forward, putting herself in the line of his attack should he do it. "Stop lying to our people about Nathan. I admit that I have always loved him—he is good and pure in heart in ways that you never have been. But he has never loved me back the same way" —she paused and looked back at Nathan as if admitting the truth to herself for the first time— "and there has never been any infidelity on my part or his. I will not let you destroy who he is as the Pilgrim."

"So you confess him as your Pilgrim!" Eli shouted.

"We have always known he was."

"Yes, I suppose we have." He descended from the stage and worked his way closer to us, but Abrianna did not back up. "Tell everyone how you have always known. It is time for the truth to surface. Tell them about the shameful secret you forced on me and have made me keep all these years."

She gazed out at the myriad of people who had once adored her, and I sensed the dread emanating from her heart.

"Tell your son the truth!" Eli screamed.

With her head held up, she slowly turned to face me, and I knew then exactly what was coming. I believe even she probably suspected I had known, deep down, all along. But she was owning her actions now. And someone was ensuring that she did it in front of everyone because her words were amplified and echoed over the crowds.

"I timed my pregnancy so that you would be born in a prophecy year. We silenced the real prophet who had confided in me that no sign would come that year. I knew it was because of Nathan. He was the Pilgrim and the Island would never ordain another Guardian. Things would have to change—and that might have meant losing my own right to rule." She took a shaky breath, but continued as if she could not go back now. "Nathan was gone from the Island, and I could not let everything unravel with no answers. We had a plan that, whenever you were born, whatever tribe you were given, Eli would set the sign in the stars. So he did. There was never supposed to be another Guardian. You have never had a destiny other than the one we chose for you."

There was a volatile reaction from the people as they took in this confession.

But my parents watched me closely for my reaction—one watched with thirst, one with regret. The truth about my birth did not impact me the way I would have expected. In fact, an odd sense of relief tried to find its way through the haze of anger. But hearing that I never had a destiny, was never special, not to the Island or anyone… that hit harder than I expected.

"Exactly what destiny did you think you were choosing for me?" I growled. "One that was easily disposable when the time came for you to try to dominate with your own power? *You* tried to do it last year" —I pointed viciously at her and then shot my accusation at Eli— "And now here *you* are, trying the same thing. Your reasons may be different, but you still did what was evil and have hurt us all in your path. Let these people out of the village and we can deal with this properly between us."

I knew Eli was not going to negotiate, but I had to try everything before I resorted to force.

Eli's eyes ignited, but not in the traditional Pyra gold as they always had. They were red, just as Jezebel's had been earlier. And I was not the only one puzzled by this. Gasps and whispers spread across the multitude. The ground beneath us began to vibrate ominously and I knew what was coming next.

"Earthshaker!"

We prepared as best as we could, but there was no way to know how weak or powerful it would be. Red life force dripped out of Eli's hands like thick blood, and he seemed perfectly in control when the shaking started. In fact, why did it seem like he was the one *controlling* the earthshaker? While everyone cowered to the ground to protect themselves and their families, I took the opportunity to fire at Eli who had closed his eyes.

It did not matter. A wall of furious flames went up in front of him and swallowed my life force. From behind him, three Firestones came rocketing our way. They detonated into Eden's defensive shield. We traded more attacks back and forth, with Eden successfully knocking one of their guards down and someone else's life force (maybe Levi's?) removing another.

But then the ground shook so badly that the Landing groaned with the impact and took on a slight downward tilt.

"Eli!" Jesse finally called out. "Please do not destroy our village. Tell us what you want and we will comply."

I growled under my breath. No, we would not comply with just anything. But I kept my mouth shut to see what his response would be.

"I demand the sacrifice of the Pilgrim—like the prophecy says. I demand that Nathan give up his rights to the life forces. He must appease the Primeval Spirit in the mountain or this volcano will blow and kill us all. You have felt the earthshakers, fellow Dorians. They are warnings."

The Primeval Spirit? I had never even heard of that before. What kind of lies did Eli think we would fall victim to?

"You have no proof of such a thing," I called back. "Nobody is going down inside the volcano with you." I knew what lay below. There was a portal, yes, but also a device Eli and Abrianna had once built that would allow them to take someone else's connection to the life forces. I was certain that was really what he wanted.

"Gabriel, do you think I am merely playing games with you?" Eli bellowed. "Perhaps this will change your mind."

With glowing red eyes, he lifted his arms and an explosive somewhere in the crowd to my right detonated. The horrified screams of the people whose neighbors or loved ones had just dissolved into ashes would haunt me for as long as I lived—even if that was only for a few more minutes. He must have set off two more further down the mountain because we heard the blast, heard the hysteria that accompanied each one.

"Shall I continue?" Eli shouted at us and the people cried out in fear. The shaking finally stopped, but the shouts of the crowd did not.

"The Pilgrim should be sacrificed! Send Nathan to the mountain or we will die!"

They were calling for his death. The same people who had praised him all week.

"No!" It was Whitnee this time and I saw her skin begin to glow in that silvery white light. "I will finish him."

There was still too much risk. Before I could get to her, Nathan was the one who stopped her. "Not yet! It's too dangerous."

The crowd turned into a mob as they called out for Nathan to submit to Eli. Pure fear coursed through every heart in that village. It would grow out of control very soon.

I turned to Nathan. "What do we do?"

"You let me handle this."

"Dad. You cannot give in to terrorists." Whitnee was quick to take hold of him.

"You're right, Baby Doll. But that terrorist is actually telling the truth about one thing. There is an ancient spirit in the mountain—a long imprisoned evil that has apparently found its power again through that portal, through their dark experiments with the life forces—" His knowing eyes were on Abrianna then. "How long has it had possession of Eli?"

She pressed her fist to her mouth and shook her head. "Hard to say. He has been quiet, obsessive, and withdrawn since you left last summer. I have never seen the red eyes, though." I saw her chin tremble with the threat of more tears. "Do not go with him, Nathan."

"For once, I agree with Abrianna," Whitnee said. "In fact, let her deal with him. She was the one who created the portals—this is ultimately all her fault!"

Nathan and Whitnee continued their conversation between their minds—I could tell from their facial expressions and looks of concentration. Nathan was solemn; Whitnee was becoming more upset.

He pulled the girls in close and dropped a kiss on the top of Whitnee's head and then Morgan's. Without another word, he marched out from our group and met Eli halfway.

"Start evacuating the village and I will go with you, Eli."

Eli grinned triumphantly. "No, the people stay where they are until you do your job. More explosives, remember? And perhaps Abrianna, Whitnee, and Gabriel should come too... we will make it a family affair."

"Not happening," Eden growled and shot with perfect aim at Eli's face. But two things happened at once. Someone counteracted her Geostone, causing it to explode into dust. And then there was another boom closer to me, only it took a moment to realize what it was.

Eden slowly pivoted to face me, her expression a mask of shock as she fell forward against me, clutching her lower abdomen. A deep red stain started spreading into the yellow fabric around her stomach as we sank to the ground together.

29

THE FALL OF A WARRIOR

Abner stood there with wicked red eyes, one hand still extended in Eden's direction with a dimming glow of life force. He did it. He struck Eden with a Geostone from only a few steps away. This time Whitnee planted herself in front of us, her hands and eyes fired up in sizzling white again.

"How could you!" she screamed.

When Abner lifted one side of his vest to reveal an explosive strapped to his body, I had the presence of mind to yell, "No! He could kill us all."

Whitnee stood facing him as if still debating; and in the distraction, other hostiles emerged from the mob of people on the Landing and surrounded us. Their eyes were all aglow with that same haunting red hue. Across their chests were explosives, each one pulsing with an ominous scarlet glow.

Nathan tried to turn back, but he was blocked by Eli's guards. Jesse and his wife were taken hostage and even Levi, Hannah, and Thomas were forced to back down in light of the risk surrounding us. Morgan, however, dropped to the ground next to me and helped me roll Eden over so she could examine her wound.

Abner muttered, "She was not supposed to get hurt. But she never really listens, does she?" He bent over as if he was going to yank Morgan away. In that brief moment, I considered the ramifications of giving him a Firedart to the head, but Morgan took us by surprise.

She aimed one hand up at Abner, blue life force swirling viciously out of her palm. "I won't stop *you* if you don't stop *me*. I have to help her."

"Morgie!" Whitnee cried, but Abner actually considered Morgan's words and decided to leave her alone. However, he turned those red eyes back on Whitnee who still had not powered herself down.

"Time for you three to go with Eli—or more blood will be on your hands."

Whitnee glanced down at me, but I could not find any path to calm. I held my closest friend in my arms while her blood pooled in front of me. Eden was unable to even cry properly; she could not move. Tears rolled down her cheeks with guttural moans of pain. She stared up at me in shock, and I removed her hand to place mine over her torn stomach. He could have severed her in half with such a close shot. She could not survive this without immediate help from a Healer. Maybe not even then. Perhaps if I cauterized the wound with heat...

"You are bleeding too much. I need to see if I can seal this," I warned, firing up my trembling hand.

"Stop!" Eden gasped. "Too exposed. Too open."

Morgan took over. "Tear off strips of fabric and start packing the wound. We have to stop the blood flow first. Pack in as much as you can, as deep as it will go. Then apply pressure—"

"Do as she says," Whitnee told me. "She's a lifeguard." When Whitnee sealed up her power and rushed forward to help, I had faith she could heal Eden. Healing had always come naturally to her. But Abner grabbed her by the arms and hauled her back several feet.

"Not you."

When she jerked her arm away from him, she was white hot again. "Touch me again and you lose your life!"

I yanked my tunic off and started ripping it into strips as Morgan felt with confident fingers inside the wound. Eden convulsed with pain, and I paused only to rest my trembling hands on her head and try to pass on Tranquility force. The flower in her hair fell to the ground.

"I'm sorry, Eden. I just need to see how deep it went and if I need to get anything out," Morgan apologized. "Gabriel, start packing and I'll give her doses of Water life force. I don't have a lot of experience, but I've learned some things—"

"What a waste of time," Eli laughed from a distance. "You cannot save her. Gabriel, get your mother and your Mainland lover and join Nathan. Or someone else dies." To our horror, he whipped a cord of fire around Elon where she stood on the sidelines and ripped her away from a hysterical Joanna and Joseph. "If you do not come now, she is next. Do you think you can bring her back to life a second time, Nathan?"

Joseph and Joanna started to launch attacks, but Eli's guards deflected them and held them back from charging Eli. People dropped to the ground in terror as life forces ricocheted in all directions. Eden cried out in anguish for her sister and her fingernails dug into my arm.

"Eli, you only need me. Let her go!" Nathan tried.

But I was quick to give in now. "I am coming! We will go with you."

This had to stop. Before Joseph and Joanna were killed too. Or had to watch their daughters die. *Again.* Before anyone else was hurt or terrorized by this scene.

Sweet Elon held my gaze with the perfect roundness of her eyes that were so much like her oldest sister's, the same shape as the eyes that were now squeezed shut as Eden writhed in pain against me. The little girl was oddly calm, as if perhaps death did not scare her anymore the same way it did all of us.

But Eli's grin was sinister—and familiar. "Of course you will comply for her sake. Because we all know her death was just a fabrication designed by Nathan and Joseph. Bring a young girl back to life and everyone will do whatever you say."

"Eli, you liar!" Whitnee shouted, and then glancing down at me, she said, "Gabriel, we need to go."

"No," Eden whispered, trying to beg me now with those eyes. I leaned down and kissed her forehead which had beaded with a cold sweat.

"Promise you will stay alive until I return. Promise it."

She could only nod, but the tears leaking down her face did not give me much hope. I tried to compose myself as I gently laid her head on the ground and traced tender fingers along her jawline in farewell.

Morgan cried out to Abner. "Give me Thomas. Please!" Abner hesitated a few seconds before flicking his hand to allow Thomas to join us.

My blue-eyed friend knelt by my side first and gripped my shoulder with confidence. "I did not follow you because of a sign in the sky. I did it because you had every reason to become one of *them*" —he nodded in Eli's direction— "but instead you became *you*. My friend. My Guardian."

I grasped at every word he said and held on to it. I had never felt so vulnerable in front of the entire Island as I did then—there were more than just drakon scars now visible to everyone. I looked up into the faces of my friends who, even though they were under threat, still featured the same ferocity and loyalty on their faces that I saw in Thomas. With a deep breath, I told them, "Try to keep everyone calm out here. And should events take a bad turn inside the mountain, I trust you to do what you think is best for our Island. I am so sorry this happened, that I am not who you all believed I was. I will do my best to fix this."

"We know exactly who you are, Gabriel," Levi declared and there was a chorus of agreement. "Go be the leader we all volunteered to follow. We will take care of Eden." I was surrounded by pure hearts, ones that would go down fighting before it was all over. I could not let that happen.

When I regained my footing, I took a few steps toward Abner, but he backed up and I saw him weaponize himself with life force. "Eden was always going to follow you to her death," he spat. "This was your fault."

Rage swept over me, and though I ignited with flame and fury, I held myself back from flying at him. "If you see me emerge from that mountain... start running."

Abner had no response, but he held his ground. I reached out for Whitnee's hand and felt a current of power that emanated out of her when our hands connected.

She sent Abner a scathing look before stepping out with me. I heard the determination in her voice as we marched forward together. "Time to end this."

It was exactly what I was thinking.

30

IN ACCORDANCE
WITH THE ISLAND

Entering the mountain again through Jezebel's secret screen door was terrifying this time—not at all like the adventurous curiosity that had led Gabriel and me here once upon a time. We were surrounded by Eli's weaponized guards, and if the pressure of imminent death wasn't enough to make it hot, then the heat in the volcano would surely suffocate us.

We mostly stayed quiet as we followed them down, down, down. We had long since passed the place where Gabriel had once kissed me, where I had tried unsuccessfully to convince myself he wasn't going to be a distraction for me, where I had learned he was engaged to Jezebel.

Jezebel. Such a tragic end to her life. It was almost unbearable to try and sort it out. I should've been nicer, should've recognized she was in trouble, instead of only seeing her *as* trouble. If I felt guilt about it, I couldn't imagine how Gabriel and the others would feel when there was time to actually process it all.

And then there was the pressing thought that kept taking root in my head…

"I remember where I first saw Abner," I announced quietly, my voice echoing in the tunnel.

"Where?" came Gabriel's question from behind me. Dad glanced back in curiosity.

"He helped Saul kidnap me at Camp Fusion. I only saw his face once when my blindfold fell down. He didn't have a beard then, but I remember those Geo green eyes now. I couldn't place his face in my memory until..." I trailed off, feeling my stomach lurch as if I might throw up.

"Until when?" Dad asked.

"Until he made that comment about Eden... that she wasn't supposed to get hurt." I could see Abner in my mind's eye so clearly now. Why had I not been able to connect the dots before it was too late? "I remembered his voice in the Frio River, 'you are not supposed to hurt her.' It was him. I knew it immediately. I'm right, aren't I, Eli?"

"You must feel terrible that you only now realized it," Eli mocked. I looked back at Gabriel with regretful eyes, and though he seemed just as pained as I was, I didn't see any blame there. "I almost got rid of Abner myself when he could not get Joseph's daughter to commit to him in marriage. He could only flatter so much Palladium information out of her. Either she is well-trained not to trust easily, or her feelings are shockingly devoted to someone else in this tunnel."

Oh, how I loved Eden. More than anything else, I wanted her to be okay. For Gabriel's sake too. Eli was not wrong in his estimation—the demonstration of devotion between Gabriel and Eden was undeniable. They deserved to explore that to its proper destination.

And that led me back to thoughts of Caleb.

"Eli, what did Abner do with Caleb?"

"You mean your Mainlander boy?" Eli clarified. "I have no inkling. But if he did what I expected, do not presume to find him alive."

"No..." Dad murmured aloud, but then came his Aerodorian voice in comforting rays of light. *Don't believe it, Whitnee.*

A burning sensation spread throughout my chest, and I thought my heart might actually fail at Eli's words. Gabriel's hands came to rest on my shoulders and I recognized his Pyra tranquility force seeping into my skin and coursing through my blood. I drank it in like a drug, hoping it could numb the paralyzing thoughts. "Caleb is smart. I am certain he figured out what was happening and has already arrived close by with a plan."

I wasn't sure how true that was either, but at least it was a better thought to hold onto. My senses kept trying to pick up on something out in the distance, but the power of the mountain kept interrupting my focus.

My thoughts reached out to Dad. *Remind me again why we agreed to all come down here to be assassinated.*

Dad's response came back. *He won't kill us. He wants our life forces first. But he has to take us into that portal chamber to do it, which gives us access to destroy it—along with sending that Primeval Spirit back to where it came from.*

He made it sound too easy. *What if the barrier is still up? What if this portal is indestructible too? You are not exactly helping me understand the plan here, Dad.*

That's because I'm kind of winging it as we go. Nothing is more powerful than the Island. We'll figure it out.

Once we figure it out, don't you think they'll try to kill us then?

Not if we subdue Eli first. He's controlling people with the red eyes— not like robots—but like speaking control over the dark desires these people already have in them. His followers aren't innocent. But I am not sure they would follow through this far if he wasn't strengthening their resolve. If we break his connection to the evil spirit controlling him, we break it with everyone. I am guessing they might come to their senses.

About that time, the tunnel opened up into the round chamber deep down in the center of the volcano. It was so hot that the air almost seemed distorted. There were no drakons—which I saw Gabriel scanning for out of the corner of my eye—but that table with the straps was still at the bottom of the circular descending stairs. I knew if I even tapped a toe on that flat surface at the bottom, the four towers around the circle would activate and open up the portal to Hawaii.

I moved slowly, wary of running into that same invisible barrier that blocked me from the Palladium portal. My senses were so overloaded that I felt trigger-happy. We all knew I could take Eli out in an instant. So what was Dad waiting for?

I soon found out.

"Eli, how were you able to summon the Primeval Spirit in here?" Dad asked.

Eli gazed at him in amusement. "I did not summon it. It found me after you and Whitnee left through the portal last year. When she opened it up again, a great power was unleashed, and it chose me to fulfill its purpose on the Island. Now it wants a sacrifice or it will destroy all the people with a fire storm unlike any you have seen." Eli shoved Nathan down the first few stairs. No barrier stopped Dad this time and something about that worried me. "You are the one the prophecy speaks of. Time to make your sacrifice. Time to bring peace for your people or judgment will fall upon their shoulders."

"What kind of sacrifice are you expecting?" Dad asked, regaining his footing on the steps.

"Your four life forces on that table. I am not the one who wants them this time. *It* does."

"Eli, this is madness," Abrianna said and I saw real fear in her for the first time. "You are being controlled by a force you do not understand. You must stop this."

Eli grabbed her by the wrist and slammed her against himself. "Being controlled by you was far worse, my dear. But no longer. I will let you watch the man you love die first. Then you can join him."

At least his intentions were clear. Which made me wonder what he had planned for me and Gabriel. I wasn't freaking out yet, though. I was preparing mentally and emotionally to destroy Eli before he could kill one more person. I was also keeping my eye on Dad and waiting to see how he would handle things.

Though Dad backed down the stairs slowly, I noticed he also shuffled himself closer and closer to the tower marked with the Hydro symbol that controlled a quarter of the portal. In a blaze of silver light, he shot a lightning dart at the ceiling above Eli, loosening a few large boulders. We scattered away—Gabriel and I took the opportunity to shake our guards as we ran around the room toward the Wind tower. Dad used the Wind life force to transform the falling mountain rock into a missile and detonate it straight into the side of the Hydrodorian tower.

They bounced off the surface like rubber balls on a gym floor, emitting a flash of red light... just like the Palladium portal. As we all defended ourselves from the onslaught of exploding rock, I witnessed Dad then fire a Water spear at the tower. But instead of blowing it to pieces, the tower activated.

The sound of Eli's laughter across the chamber was louder and more distorted than normal.

"Oh, did I forget to tell you? The portal cannot be destroyed," Eli announced happily, as if this would shock us. "Believe me, I tried. No amount of physical force can affect it. You cannot even try to use a different life force to damage it. But go on and keep trying. Every time you feed the life forces into it, you give more freedom and power to the Primeval Spirit. And we feeeeel it." He breathed in deeply and I swore I could detect smoke on his breath. Abrianna wrenched herself free from his grasp but had nowhere to go with his guards hemming us all in.

Now what?

Dad, let me destroy it. If I combine all four life forces, you know it could be powerful enough to—

No, Whitnee! Dad's Aerodorian voice almost made my head hurt. *If you touch any of that portal with your abilities, you could set that ancient monster free completely.*

"Nathan, you are out of options," Eli said calmly. "You need to appease it. You need to surrender your life forces to the Primeval Spirit at that table before it rages out of control. Another earthshaker could bury the village—"

The talking was getting on my nerves. Careful to avoid the portal towers, I pulled my energy from every life force and the white electricity shot straight out of my hand and found its way to Eli. Last time he couldn't fight against it, and a dark part of me was pleased to see my power envelop him and begin to squeeze the breath out of him.

But then something odd happened... the red glow of his eyes spread to his face and his head and then down until it covered his entire body. With a burst of power that seemed to match my own, he cast off my electric prison and pushed back with his own sizzling force.

Red and white energy pushed against each other across the portal. I exerted all of my strength, but he was stronger and overcame me. The red hot force reached my fingertips, but I broke off the connection and leapt behind the tower just as his life force— was that even what it was?—shattered the wall behind me and sent more rock shards cascading everywhere. Another rumble started in that room and spread outward.

Dad, what do we do? I cried out. Gabriel tried to help me up, but was yanked away by the guards.

There's only one thing left, Whitnee. His voice came back. *I have to sacrifice my life forces.*

You can't give them to Eli—have you lost your mind? I shouted inside my mind. *It will kill you!*

I'm not giving them to Eli, was his resolved response.

Then aloud, I heard him shout. "Okay, Eli, I give in! You're right—it was always going to end like this. A sacrifice has been demanded. But you have to do something for me first."

"Oh, Nathan, as if you are in a place to negotiate with me." Eli's laugh was too amused for the situation. "But what do you want?"

"I want your guards to take Whitnee, Gabriel, and Abrianna back to the village safely. Once I know you have kept your word, I will finish this."

"What?" I cried, stepping out. "No, I'm not leaving you down here!"

"Whitnee, I don't want you to see this part, okay?" Nathan said. And then only to me, he said, *Once you're out of the tunnels, you three can easily get rid of every one of those guards. Eli will lose his power over you.*

But what about you?

If I can make it out alive, I will. Baby Doll, this is the only way.

There's gotta be a way to shut down this portal. That's where it's coming from, Dad. If we had a—

I know exactly how to destroy it. But I need you out of here.

"Very well, Nathan." Eli gave in and directed his followers, "Take Whitnee and Gabriel to the surface. Do not do anything with them until you hear from me again."

"And Abrianna," Dad demanded.

But Eli stood his ground. "No. She stays to watch. She would refuse to leave you anyway."

I couldn't see Abrianna's or Dad's reactions because the guards were upon me. Gabriel held threatening hands out to them. "Do not touch her. Nathan, is this really what is best?"

"Go with the guards," Dad confirmed and I tried to get a read on what his game plan really was. Dad pleaded with his eyes and, though everything in me wanted to argue further or think of a different plan, I knew I needed to trust him.

"Come on, Gabriel. Let's do what Dad says."

Gabriel and I remained protectively close to each other as we gave ourselves up. Eli's guards started to usher us back to the doorway we had come from. But my eyes never left Dad's.

You're coming out of here, right? Am I really not supposed to do anything?

Shake off those guards as soon as it's safe to do so and then get everyone off this mountain.

What does that mean—

Eli raged, "What are you and Whitnee communicating about, Nathan? Are you trying to trap me?" Before either of us could respond, he commanded, "Stop! Kill Gabriel and get armbands on the girl!"

I was not submitting to armbands and I would not let them kill Gabriel. In a flash, I put a green shield up around the two of us just as Gabriel's hands became blowtorches. We stood back to back and tried not to flinch at the barrage of attacks coming at us.

"When I drop the shield, I'm going to let loose a ring of electricity and zap them all at once, okay?" I heaved with energy.

"What if you activate the portal?"

"I'll have to risk it! Get down and put a Wall of Fire up around you so I don't accidentally hit you too."

"Ready," he said, but before we could enact our plan, the ground beneath us started shaking again. The violence of it catapulted us sideways. Even the guards were knocked over, and I lost connection with my Earth shield. In fact, it felt like I had been punched in the back.

The room became pressurized until a burst of heat in the center of the portal blasted upward. The shaking grew more tumultuous, and above all of it, Eli screamed, "What have you done? Stop that!"

I finally found out what caused the tremor. Both of Dad's hands were pressed to the Hydrodorian tower. The rock liquified into an electric blue substance and then melted down and disappeared. Dad crumpled to the ground as a crack spread from the bottom of the stairs across the room.

"Dad!" I screamed at the same time Abrianna called out to him. I crawled across the shaking ground, but one of the guards got a hold of my foot. As I tried desperately to kick away from him, I saw Dad gather his energy again and stumble around the circle until he reached the Geodorian tower.

"You angered it." Eli's eyes stopped glowing red and he looked afraid all of a sudden. "It will destroy everything now!"

"Not unless I destroy it first!" Dad bellowed. He tried to press both hands on the Geodorian tower, which was all the way across the chamber from me, but dramatic shaking rippled out from the center of the portal floor. The guard who had my foot lost his grip and rolled down the stairs like a pebble. The crack in the floor of the cave widened and I had to look away as blazing hot lava popped and sizzled and swallowed the shrieking guard.

Dear lord, it was happening.

The volcano was erupting.

31

STEAL, KILL, AND DESTROY

Eli didn't even say anything; he took off running toward the tunnel that once led to Dad's cabin on the other side of the mountain. His goons released us and made an escape back the way we had come—toward Jezebel's house. Gabriel started after Eli but had to take cover when he aimed attacks back at us.

I had to help Dad. How was he destroying it?

"Dad, tell me what to do," I cried out as I ran back to the tower on my right marked with the Aerodorian symbol. Just as I reached out to touch it, my hands hit an invisible barrier... again.

"No!" I screamed and pounded on it. I ran around looking for a weakness, a gap in that shimmering wall. "I can't get to you. Dad! It won't let me—"

"I need you to get out of here," Dad yelled back, as the table that had once been part of the cave floor down there started to crack and sink into the pit of lava. "The volcano could blow at any minute!"

"Then let's go. Surely the volcano will destroy the portal."

"It won't. It will destroy the Island. You have to get up to the surface and redirect the explosion—use your abilities to create a firetrap. You're the only one who can do it. As I shut down each piece of the portal, it will temporarily shut down that life force across the Island. But not for you... your power comes from the other portal."

"Well, then let us help you destroy this and get out of here together—"

"Whitnee."

I stopped at the authority that rang out around the cavern. Even the shaking ground lowered to a tremble at his voice.

"Do you not understand?" This time sorrow and desperation entered his tone. "I have to transfuse each of my life forces back into the portal. Giving them back to the Island is the only way. You can't help because you need all four to save our people. The Island is protecting you, so get out of here now!"

Realization started sinking in. He was the Pilgrim. The sacrifice. It would take four life forces, four *lives*, to destroy that portal.

Or one person who had been gifted with all four in a moment like this.

A chunk of the cavern loosened and fell down into the center of the pit, causing the lava to lap up the sides of the stairs.

"I can't leave you, Dad," I cried, tears mixing with sweat as I leaned against that dang invisible blockade. "We'll wait. We'll get you out of here once you're done."

"Gabriel, she still doesn't understand. Take her, please. For me!" I had never heard his voice sound so panicked. "Judgment is about to rain down and I won't be able to stop it if I wait much longer. Once I destroy the last tower, the volcano should seal back up too. But as your father, *I can't do that* until I know you are safe."

I shuddered as Elon's warning came back in full detail... *The part of him that belongs to you threatens his purpose. You must act carefully, Whitnee. All of our lives depend on it.*

An indefinable roaring sound rushed around the cavern just then and made the hair on my body stand up.

"What is that?" I looked around, feeling the presence of something inhuman.

"The Primeval Spirit is erupting with the volcano," Dad realized. "I have to destroy the connection, the portal, before it escapes completely. Whitnee, run, before it tries to get to you!"

Gabriel started pulling me toward the tunnel. But I shoved him away. "No, I can't leave—I can't do this—"

"I love you, Baby Doll. Save our people."

Our people.

With a shout, he released his Earth life force into that tower.

It cracked into a million pieces, dust vanishing into the sweltering heat. I didn't just see Dad stumble with the effort, I felt it inside my chest. A part of him was dying with each destroyed tower. I wanted to go to him, to take this burden from him. To figure out another way—

But Abrianna was the one who grabbed me by the arm and propelled me forward. How dare she try to separate me from my dad when this was all her fault! I was about to reach out and grab her by the hair when Gabriel picked me up, threw me over his bare shoulder and carried me out of the collapsing chamber. Chunks of mountain rock fell all around us, glancing off my back, whacking me in the head as I screamed for my dad. Lava shot up and steamed from the pit as the floor finally ripped in two. How would Dad ever make it? He was almost to the Pyradorian tower when we entered the tunnel and part of the ceiling crashed down and blocked my view of—and my way back into—the portal room.

Gabriel was forced to set me down. "Run, Whitnee!"

"He won't make it out of there if I don't stay... he'll die!"

"He is already dying." It was Abrianna who said it, and she turned back to stare at the collapsed entry into the chamber.

Gabriel took me by the arms and shook me. "If we wait for him to finish, there will not be anything left of him to rescue. Go!"

He acted like he was going to pick me up again, but somehow through my hysteria I started running on feet I couldn't even feel. We passed the little lights that dotted the corridors and flickered with every impact. I knew at any moment the whole mountain could explode and that was the only thing that kept me pressing upward and forward. But I couldn't let Dad stay in there alone. Not when I had the power to be there too.

I activated both the Wind and Fire life forces in my head—the combination that allowed me to see what he was seeing.

I'm here, Dad. I tried to force myself to sound calm for his sake. The connection between us felt fragile. But the view started to come and I could see his hands pelted with crashing rock as he pulled himself up to the Pyradorian tower. Why were his hands bloody? What was happening to him in there? *Just two more, Daddy. You can do this.*

Thank you, Baby Doll, I thought I heard him whisper.

With his hands pressed to the tower, he laid down his Fire life force and the tower went up in flames and then ashes. As he started to fall again, it felt a knife to my stomach. I faltered and slumped against the wall of the tunnel, trying to breathe. I lost visual of him. And the tunnel suddenly went pitch black.

Gabriel slowed and grabbed my hand. "What is it?" he gasped.

"He just destroyed the third tower. Fire," I wheezed. "I can feel him dying."

Abrianna panted behind us as Gabriel tried to conjure a flame in his hand. Nothing happened. "It is gone. My life force."

I squeezed my eyes shut, trying to contain the moan of grief that wanted to escape.

"We have to keep going. Do I need to carry you?"

"No." I caught my breath again and we kept climbing back through the rumbling walls that threatened to crumble around us. Blasts of heat rippled through the tunnel.

As we rushed through the dark, I tapped back into the only life force I knew he had left—Wind.

Daddy, are you still there?

He didn't answer.

Dad! Nathan! Answer me!

A flickering white light appeared in my mind.

Can you hear me? You only have one more.

Are you to the surface yet? His voice was faint.

Almost. I think. I wasn't sure.

It's exploding. Burning. I don't know how to reach the other tower.

I ran harder, starting to recognize the familiar parts of Jezebel's tunnel.

"Up ahead, Whitnee. We are almost there!"

Outside, the air was so thick with smoke and ash that it looked like nighttime. Lava crept down the lush green mountainside, burning everything it touched and spreading quickly. It was only feet away from us. It would not be much longer before it flowed all the way down to the Landing and the village below. And that was assuming more didn't explode out of the top. I tried to use the Wind to blow the smoke away and to give me a view. As far as I could see down the mountain, the people were in chaos. We ran as fast as our feet could take us on the twisty trail toward the Landing a little further down. I tried Dad again.

We made it out. Dad, you can finish this.

I'm so sorry, Whitnee. So sorry I couldn't be the father you wanted.

My heart split in two and I stumbled. *You're the father I needed. And you're the Pilgrim. I believe in you.*

I don't know if I can do this. I think my leg is broken and I can't stand up. The tower is floating further away from me. And there's a presence in here... so dark... it wants to swallow me. It bites and whispers lies. If I don't stop it, it'll come after you. After all of you.

I looked up at Gabriel and Abrianna who had stopped to help me.

"He can't do it. He can't reach the fourth tower..." I felt dazed. Fire dripped down the mountain above me, too close to Jezebel's house. "I need to go back. I need to help him. Maybe I could levitate him..."

Abrianna took a deep breath and her eyes lit up silver. She stood up straight and said, "I will help Nathan. You are the firetrap." Then she charged back up the trail.

"Going back in that tunnel is a death sentence!" Gabriel warned.

"As long as I have the Wind, I can push through cracks and get to him. Now stop talking and do what you must." I wasn't going to argue with her, though I had mixed feelings about her aiding my father in completing his death. This just couldn't be happening. Shock was starting to creep its way into my system. I knew because I was becoming calmer. Like I was removed from reality.

Dad, Abrianna is going to help levitate you to the tower. At least I thought that was her plan. I tried to swallow, but my mouth was so dry. When Dad didn't respond, I tried again, saying words I didn't want to say, trying to strengthen him. *I know you can do this. And I'll stay with you until you do. I'm not leaving. Let's finish it, Dad.*

Okay. He flickered. *Let's finish it.*

Gabriel pulled me to my feet and we descended again. The Landing was rocked by a dreadful explosion above us. People were trying to evacuate, but the crowd couldn't move fast enough down the streets. Boulders rolled down the mountainside, new cliffs formed in the broken earth, and the lava oozed closer. My friends and family remained there on the Landing, congregated around Eden. Somewhere not too far away, I heard Zebedee and Joseph shouting orders, trying to organize the evacuation. Lilley and Morgan knelt by Eden.

"How is she?" Gabriel asked immediately.

"She faded, we think," Thomas said. "My life force left me and so did Lilley's, but Morgan has still been working on her with Lilley's guidance. We think we bought her some time, but unless Lilley's healing abilities return... Nobody seems to have life force except the Aeros. And Morgan."

"Nathan said that might happen, but it should be temporary. Where are all of Eli's men?"

Hannah explained, "When the Pyra life force quit, so did the power in the explosives. We took out some of our captors, but Abner got away. Then we tried to evacuate the mountain in an orderly way, but everybody panicked and started running."

"Where is Nathan?" The quiet question came from Grandmother Sarah who, though she asked, did not seem surprised that her son was not there. "He is still in the mountain, yes?"

My eyes filled with tears. "Yes." I ran into her arms and felt Poppa Zeke's frail hands pat my back. "He wants you to get to safety, while he shuts down the portal. Abrianna went back to help him."

"Is Eli there too?" I heard Joseph ask.

"He took the tunnel to the other side of the mountain when the eruption started," Gabriel told them and he cursed under his breath. "Eli and Abner... both gone! If anyone sees Eli, you are to execute him immediately. No questions asked. Abner, though... I want him brought to me alive."

As if in response to his words, an ominous explosion from the top of the mountain shook us and the Landing lurched, slanting down more, causing all of us to fall over and start sliding. I saw Gabriel pull Eden into the shield of his body and try to secure Morgan. I did the only thing I could think of and called on the Earth. Roots shot out of the mountain like tentacles and secured the Landing enough for us to scramble onto solid ground. We all looked up fearfully as a deep rumble shook the air, not the ground. It was that otherworldly presence again, that demon of darkness building strength above us. The hairs all over my body stood up as if commanded by something evil.

"What is it?" Hannah whispered next to me.

That was when I took charge. As I spoke, I used the Earth life force to braid branches and twigs and roots together—anything I could find close by—to create a stretcher for them to transport Eden. "Gabriel, if you can find a path to get off the mountain, try to get everyone to Hydrodora. The river will naturally stop the lava, if it makes it that far. Morgan, stay with him and keep working on Eden. You're gifted through me now, so you can still use Water life force. Levi and Hannah, come with me."

Gabriel marched forward first and cupped my face in his hot hands, desperation leaking out around him. One thumb wiped away the track of my tears. "You will be okay?"

I placed my hands over his and gave them a squeeze of confidence. "I'll try to contain the eruption. Do what you can to get our people to safety."

Our people. Because that's who they were. Dad charged me to protect them, and I couldn't let him down.

With a firm nod, Gabriel bent down to shift the colorless Eden onto the mat, the spindly purple scars across his back flexing with the effort. Morgan grabbed my hand. "I believe in you, Whit. And I believe in your dad. It will be okay." She didn't understand what Dad was doing, and there was no time to explain. But I let her blind faith bolster my confidence anyway. Thomas picked up one end of the stretcher, and Morgan and Lilley flanked Eden's sides. Joseph and Joanna started herding everyone forward. Only Elon stayed in place, staring up at the dark clouds churning above us.

"It is the Poison." She lowered her eyes to my face, and that expression pierced me with dread. "It will take the Pilgrim and destroy the Island."

I couldn't focus on that. I needed to hold it together, and those big green eyes were making it impossible.

"Go with the others, Elon." She turned away sadly and obeyed.

When I turned to Levi and Hannah, they were resolute. "Tell us what to do."

I led the two of them back up near Jezebel's house, which had now been engulfed in flames. The sound of glass popping and the lava tracks coming toward us did not slow me. "My dad is destroying the portal. Once he does, the eruption should stop. But until he can shut down the last tower—the Aerodorian one—we have to create a firetrap. I need you to spread out and blow the smoke and ash away so I can see. Try to deflect any debris that might hit people. I'm going to try and create a barrier around the mountain and force the lava to flow into the ocean on the other side."

We set ourselves a short way above the crowds of desperate people. The lava streams spilled on top of one another and were practically upon us. It was excruciatingly hot and almost impossible to see.

Dad, I'm still here. I knew he hadn't successfully gotten to the Aero tower yet—I would've felt it.

He said something, but I couldn't make it out.

I accessed every life force—feeling the Wind, Water, Fire, and Earth swirl inside me until the power was uncontainable. With a wide sweep of my arms, a white-flamed barricade spread in front of me and licked outward until it circled most of the mountain. I couldn't physically see the other side of the volcano, but when the atmosphere took on that jelly-like, translucent quality again, I could visualize the entire scope of the Island. I could see myself spreading around the mountain. The river of lava lapped up against my wall of energy and rerouted itself. My perspective shifted higher until I could almost see the exploding tip-top of the mountain.

"Whitnee, you are levitating!" Hannah called out. Her voice was too far away and her words almost didn't register until I looked around through my own eyes. I hadn't even meant to do it, but I had risen up off the ground somehow. Seeing the earth so far below me was suddenly intimidating, and my concentration wavered.

That left me completely unprepared for the moment a giant face formed in the ash cloud at the top—not a human face, but the face of a monster. And it shrieked so loudly that I was sure the entire Island and maybe even the Mainland somewhere out there could hear it. I felt the hot steam of its breath as I blocked my face and ears with my arms. There was a smell like rotting eggs, like sulfur, that gagged me. My firetrap almost weakened, and I was about to fall to the ground like a pebble.

Except it was Dad's voice in my head. Or maybe it was the Island's. The two were meshing into one.

Be gone!

The mountain shook so hard that a split in the earth started from the top and raced downward, ripping through the Pyradorian village and all the way across the Island parallel to the Blue River. The sky thundered and became like night, and I started to fall with the final blow of death.

But it wasn't my death.

It was the death of the Pilgrim.

My dad.

The face in the clouds gave one last scream, coughed up balls of flame that rained down around us, and then disintegrated just like Jezebel's Fireport.

With one final shout of grief, I pushed my white flames as high and as far into the sky as they would go, and every bit of lava and debris was turned to ash and dust. Then I slammed back to earth and let the darkness sprinkle down on me until I was nothing more than an extension of the ground.

32

THE APHOTIC ZONE

We were still on the mountain when the white flames overtook the sky. We cowered when the darkness roared and the world around us broke into pieces. And we cried out when we saw Whitnee fall like a star unhinged from its home in the sky.

"Oh, no!" Morgan gasped into the deafening silence that followed.

As all became still around us, a heavy darkness pervaded the atmosphere. It was not just the lingering ash and smoke. It was something thicker. Impenetrable. We never knew the quality of light and sound that the life forces had brought to our existence.

Until they were gone.

It felt as if the Island itself had just died and I knew then that we were in trouble. It was the middle of the day, yet we had been cast into night with no warning.

"Nobody move," I commanded, having a very difficult time seeing anyone around me, least of all my own hands on Eden's makeshift mat.

"I cannot see a thing," Thomas said as we set Eden down. I wiped my eyes of the grit that collected on my skin. It wasn't until Morgan's hands lit up blue on Eden's stomach that I was able to make out the faint shape of my friends.

"This is the only light I have. But I need to keep working on her," Morgan told me.

"Thank you, Morgan, keep her alive," I said, the cries and

mourning of my people rising up all along the mountainside. This was chaos; we needed our life forces back. How long would this interruption last? "Stay here and stay aware. I need to go back for Whitnee and the others."

"Move carefully, Gabriel," Joseph said. "There are cracks in the earth."

I took his advice and stepped gingerly back up toward the area I had seen Whitnee fall. It had seemed close to Jezebel's house. As the scent of smoke grew more powerful, I called out to Whitnee, to Levi and Hannah, and I finally got a response. With quicker steps, I followed the sound of their voices until I found the spot where Whitnee lay.

"She is waking up," Hannah informed me, reaching for me in the dark until I came to kneel securely next to her.

"Dad..." Whitnee moaned and I felt in the dark until my hands found her body curled into a ball on the ground.

"He saved the Island from complete ruin. And so did you," I said in a feeble attempt at comfort. She had just lost her father. And I was concerned about what that meant for the rest of us, as well.

"I need to go back in and find him. What if he's still alive somehow—"

"You said you could feel him dying," I reminded her. "What do you feel now?"

A sob broke out. "Nothing."

"We need to get off this mountain."

"I can't do it, Gabriel," she cried. "My dad is gone! This wasn't supposed to happen. I need to at least recover his body—"

"You will not find a body." The voice belonged to Abrianna who coughed as she approached us in the dark. I could not see her, but she sounded like she was limping and wheezing. I was compelled to go to her. When she found my extended hand, I could feel her shaking. "The entire cavern went up in flames and caved in when he shut down the last tower. I cannot believe I made it out."

Another sob from Whitnee. Even with my Pyra life force absent, I felt her grief in my own chest. She was right—it should not have happened this way. I resolved then that I would go back into that mountain as soon as I could to see the truth for myself. But for now... "I am horrified over this loss, but we must go."

Whitnee continued to weep as Hannah comforted her. But Abrianna's bruised voice turned sharp. "Your father did not die in that mountain so that you could lie here and cry about it."

Before I could rebuke her, Whitnee started to glow with fury as we watched her rise up and clamber to her feet. I caught a glimpse of Abrianna's ash-covered expression as the two of them glared at each other.

"This all happened because of you. You killed him!" Whitnee accused, her skin getting brighter with every syllable.

"We can discuss blame another time," Abrianna replied. "Right now, our world has been plunged into darkness. More people are dying as we stand here. And *you* are the only one with life force."

That gave Whitnee pause as she blinked a few times and then looked out around her, as if noticing it all for the first time. "Why is it still so dark?" she mumbled.

"We do not know," I said with forced gentleness in my voice. "You are the only light we have right now."

She looked down at her hands and her glowing body and whispered, "We're in the aphotic zone."

"The what?"

She sniffled as she wiped her cheeks. "The deepest, darkest part... it's like he knew."

I was not following her thinking, but something had gotten her attention in a dramatic way. "Whitnee," I tried again with more insistence. "We need to lead people off the mountain to safety. Can you light up as brightly as possible and show us the way?"

"Yes." Her voice shook. But then she rested those shimmering white eyes on me and held out a trembling hand. "If you walk beside me. I could really use an anchor right now."

"Me too." I accepted the shock of her powers as our hands fused together. Then I found a broken branch on the ground. "Can you light this on Fire?"

She lifted her free hand and when she touched the wood, it sparked and sizzled with life force. It did catch, but the flame was white with a blue center that did not seem to burn the wood. Not the same Fire I knew. I handed it to Levi to help light the way.

Hand in hand Whitnee and I walked down the mountain. The crowds watched from afar and then parted and fell into line behind us when we passed. Whitnee blazed brightly by my side, as if the ash had been burned off her skin. The scarlet stones on her dress flickered almost like Firelight. As I came across broken branches, I held them out for her to ignite and we passed back the torches for people to use. But she never said a word. Something in her presence quieted the fear in the atmosphere and even in my own soul. I called out instructions and encouragement as needed and, even though my entire rise to Guardianship had been exposed as a lie, the people still listened and followed. My friends fell in step with us and I tried to keep my hope alive that Eden would be okay. Morgan had hardly taken a break, and for that I would be forever grateful.

At one point, we came upon a crying child of about five or six years old. I paused to kneel beside the boy. "Are you hurt?"

"No. My parents disappeared over the edge," he cried and pointed. Whitnee cast light in that direction and we saw an endlessly deep gap in the earth below. She and I exchanged despairing glances before I turned my gaze back to the child. His golden-brown eyes shone with tears.

"What is your name?"

"Jasper."

"Named after a stone, a strong rock. Which means you must be very brave." I spoke gently. "I am Gabriel. I will make sure you are safe until we find your family."

"I know who you are." He wiped his eyes and sniffled. For a moment, I saw a reflection of myself in this orphaned Pyradorian boy.

"Hold my hand and walk with me, Jasper."

He placed his little hand in mine and though I could not transfer Tranquility to him without my life force, his tears seemed to slow once he anchored himself beside me. Something about the simplicity of his trust gave me renewed purpose.

Whitnee's eyes brimmed with tears when I glanced at her, but she still said nothing, and we continued our slow journey.

Hydrodora never felt so far away as it did the day that turned into night. But we finally made it there. Whitnee extinguished her glow and the people used their torches to make Fire in the village. There was plenty of food left over from the Hydrodorian Blessing feast and it was quickly distributed to the masses. The sick and injured were given beds wherever they could be found, but still no life forces returned. Elon took over watch of little Jasper for me; her tender spirit had a calming effect, and he was soon asleep beside a Fire surrounded by Eden's siblings.

The Councilmen stepped up to their leadership roles and organized what they could with what they had. Meanwhile, I made my mother take a guarded room in the Healing Center away from the crowd—not just for her benefit but because I did not want any riots to break out after her lies had been exposed. At the moment, everyone seemed unified for survival's sake; but when the life forces and the light of day returned, I feared for the reaction of the masses. All of this damage would have to be explained and her actions called into account.

But I could not think too hard about such things when each moment already contained more than I could handle. When the village seemed to be under control, Whitnee and I found ourselves in Eden's room inside the Healing Center. The lower half of Eden's body was submerged in a murky pool of Water where Morgan worked under Lilley's instruction. Over in the corner, Joanna prepared an herbal mixture to help alleviate some of Eden's pain.

"I'm sorry, y'all, but I think I need a break for a second," Morgan finally said, doubling over in pain.

"The Shadow Effect can be very draining. Drink some water, Morgan. You have done amazing work so far," Lilley encouraged.

Morgan climbed out of the water and wrapped herself in a towel. Whitnee handed her a bottle of Water, which Morgan quickly drank down. Then she rested her illuminated eyes back on Whitnee. "You would probably do a better job than me. I have just been trying to repair the tissue and cells, working from the outer edges in."

Whitnee gazed down at Eden in the Water and I could see the distress in her face, the hesitance in the way she held her hands to her stomach. "I suppose I could try," she whispered.

"Please try," I begged her. The sound of my own voice seemed foreign. As if the weariness in every part of my body and the guilt in the dark corners of my mind had found their way to my throat. Surely Whitnee could fix this. We needed one of her miracles.

I lowered myself beside the pool where Eden floated, across from Whitnee. She knelt down and the strands of her hair that had come loose from the jeweled clip looked more silver than gold. Her hands dipped into the water and just as the blue light began, she started gagging.

"Whitnee?" Lilley called out in alarm.

Instead of answering, she crawled over to a bowl on the floor near Eden's mother and vomited. Joanna dropped down with a wet cloth and began wiping at her forehead. I had to work to keep the sound from affecting my own stomach.

"I can't do it," Whitnee cried. "I can't even look at her! That Spirit—I can still feel it. So much death and destruction. Jezebel disintegrated. Dad burned to death in the volcano. Eden is practically ripped in two. That poor little boy's parents... And Caleb—" She retched again into the bowl.

"Shhhh," Joanna soothed.

"I'm sorry, Joanna, I'm so sorry. I want to help her. I just..."

"You have saved enough lives for one day," Joanna assured her.

But that was not good enough for me. "We need you to save one more! We have all been through a nightmare, Whitnee, and I am sorry for that. But if you do not help Eden—"

"Hush, Gabriel." Joanna held up a hand to me, taking on that maternal dominance I had heard her use with her children many times. "We have seen nightmares, yes. But we have seen far more good than we deserve. Let us not be ruled by fear. That is the tool of our Enemy."

I took a deep breath and abandoned my protests, feeling empty inside. Whatever that thing was in the mountain, that Primeval Spirit... it had robbed us of our sacred connection to the Island. We were an incomplete people without our life forces.

And then there was Whitnee with her unbroken and seemingly infinite power—I did not understand where it came from. Her thunderfly necklace pulsed erratically with every ragged breath she took, making the room flicker.

"Try to calm down, Whit," Morgan coached, stumbling to her side.

"I can't. C-Caleb's in trouble too. I don't know what to do. I feel so—" Her words turned to more retching and sobbing, and I could not contain my sigh.

"I will go get more clean towels and something for all of you to eat. I believe Whitnee is not the only one exhausted." Joanna patted Whitnee's back. Before she padded away, she fixed me with a fierce gaze. "What happened to Eden was not your fault. You know that, yes?" I felt my own breath vanish for a moment as her words tried to cut through the guilt and disgrace that weighed me down. "My daughter has a strong heart. That is why she chose *you*. Be the man she believes you are and hold to your faith in our Island."

I swallowed with difficulty and matched her gaze. "I will."

With a confident smile that seemed beyond any normal person's capability under the circumstances, she left the room. Morgan and I exchanged weary looks.

"It's okay," Morgan told us. "I can keep working on Eden. I feel like I'm getting somewhere."

"Eden does seem more stable," Lilley added. "She is only alive at this point because of you, Morgan. You *can* do this. Your body— and the life force that flows through it—knows what it is like to be completely healed. Just continue to let the Water guide you where you are uncertain."

I let my fingers brush across Eden's forehead and run through her hair in the dim light of the dancing Firelight—actions I wish I had taken before now. To my surprise, she stirred, almost as if leaning toward my touch.

"Eden? Are you awake?"

Her eyes fluttered a bit, but did not open. Lilley massaged her arm lightly, washing off the blood stains with gentle strokes. "She might be able to hear you, Gabriel," she encouraged softly.

The sound of Whitnee's heaves faded as I thought back to this morning after the broadcast... when I had sought out Eden to apologize or at least to talk about what had happened. But I had found her locked in her room, pretending to be busy with all of the plans for the day—plans that we would never see come to fruition. She had refused to let me into the room and acted as if all was fine.

But it was not all fine.

"There are so many things I did not say," I whispered, and I saw

Lilley try to look away and pretend that she could not hear me. "Things I should have said a long time ago. When you are well, I promise I will say them. But right now, I hope you know how brave and beautiful I think you are. Your friendship has been my favorite part of the last year, and I want many more years of it." I grabbed her hand out of the water and pressed it to my cheek. "Stay here with me." They were the same words I had once said when I invited her to live at the Palladium. She stirred slightly again, but did not respond or open her eyes.

"Gabriel." Whitnee's hollow voice echoed across the room, and I looked up at her. The pain that passed between us was something neither of us had to say aloud. "I'm sorry, but I have to leave. I'm going after Caleb."

"No." Morgan tucked her arm in Whitnee's. "Send the others to look for him. I don't want something to happen to you too."

"What else could possibly happen to me? I promise you, I will never power down again under threat." There was a chord of anger—maybe even of violence—in Whitnee's tone, and I could not decide if it unsettled me or satisfied me. "I think Caleb sent me a warning or distress call with the Earth life force earlier. The portal jacked with my ability to decode it, but I know he reached out. And I can't—" Her voice broke again. "I can't lose him too. You stay here and keep working on Eden. I'll find a way to contact y'all later—"

"I will go with you," I stated.

"You're needed here too, Gabriel."

"Not as much as you need me. I am the reason Caleb left, so the responsibility to find him falls on me too. Besides, you do not know your way around the Island like I do. And you should not be alone in the event that you find..." I trailed off at the traumatized looks on Whitnee and Morgan's faces. "We should go before people start looking for us."

"I will let the others know when I see them," Lilley offered. "My father can oversee things in your absence."

He would have to—I was technically not the real leader of our Island. For a lot of reasons.

I pressed the palm of Eden's hand to my lips. There was nothing I could do for her. And I needed to feel in control of *something*. "I will come back for you," I promised. *You have a sentence to finish.*

Gently I released Eden's hand to rest on her chest, trying to walk away with a semblance of her unshakeable hope and belief in the Island's greater purpose. Maybe it was my turn to carry that faith for both of us.

When Eden did not move again, Lilley said, "Eden is a warrior. She will not give up. And neither will we."

"I hate this. Be careful. Both of you." Morgan hugged us with tears in her eyes.

I gripped Morgan's arm with gratitude. "Thank you for taking care of her. Regardless of what happens, you have done a remarkable job."

She patted my hand and then said to Whitnee, "Find our boy." Whitnee only nodded and then Morgan threw off her towel to enter the water again.

We grabbed a few supplies on our way out of the Healing Center, including some hooded robes that would help cloak us as we left Hydrodora behind. Once we made it to the abandoned outskirts of the village where it was too dark to see, Whitnee paused and placed her hands on the ground. Her eyes illuminated with the green hue of a Geodorian.

"I don't know if you can hear this or not," she whispered into the blackness of the jungle that stretched before us, "but we're coming for you, Caleb. I *will* find you."

"Any chance you can put out a similar message to Abner?" I asked with brewing rage. "Because I am coming for *him*." And for Eli. And for every person who played a part in our Island's destruction.

Whitnee glanced up at me for a moment, as if checking to see how serious I was. But then her face turned savage. This time, it was vengeance that rippled out through her hands as she sent out another message. I hoped it reached them.

When she rose to her feet, we were connected by a thread of dark determination. Whether it was right or wrong hardly mattered. "We'll find him," she vowed and it was unclear who exactly she meant. But it made no difference.

The one thing I did know for certain was… "We will find them *all*."

TO BE CONTINUED ONE LAST TIME...

Get early access to Earthbound, the final installment of the Phantom Island series, as it's being written on Kindle Vella's interactive, digital reading platform!

Paperback and ebook to release when the Kindle Vella experience is complete.

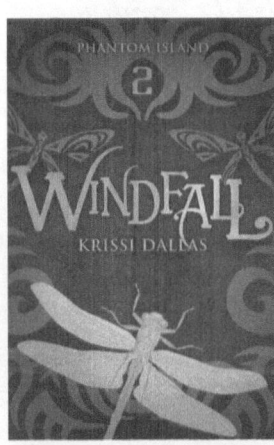

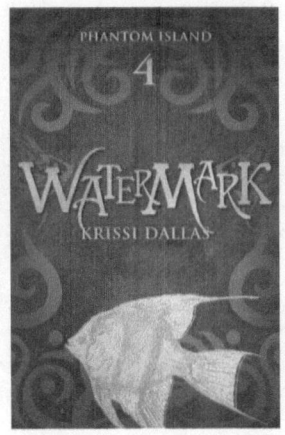

THEY THOUGHT IT WAS JUST ORIENTATION FOR PILOT TRAINING.

Until a bomb went off in the heart of D.C.

When perfectionistic seventeen-year-old Olivia McKenzie shows up for flight school orientation, she and three other famous teens are instead recruited as spies and tasked with infiltrating a network of teenage terrorists. Flight simulators, laser tag games, and dance club missions as training? Party on.

Until a bomb goes off and the killer refuses to speak to anyone but Olivia.

While the countdown is on to stop the next attack, a world of violent secrets starts to awaken skills and passions Olivia didn't know she had... particularly for a teammate who turns her own heart into dangerous territory.

Take a thrilling, interactive flight aboard the romantic spy thriller Icarus Flight School on Kindle Vella's episodic storytelling platform or in paperback and hardcover.

HE'S A YOUTUBE STAR.
SHE'S HIS NEIGHBOR AND ENEMY.

Until a challenge with half-a-million dollars shows up.

Daisy just wants to graduate high school and save her family's riverside campground. High-school-dropout-turned-YouTube-star Caz needs more subscribers before his sponsor dumps him. They're neighbors and sworn enemies until half-a-million dollars shows up from a mysterious donor who challenges the two to recreate a series of famous movie scenes on live broadcast within 48 hours. The only thing that could jeopardize their prize money is the one challenge they can't control—falling in love.

Check out the new romantic comedy by Krissi Dallas exclusively on Kindle Vella—available in the Kindle app for iOS/Android and the Kindle Fire. First three episodes are free!

ACKNOWLEDGEMENTS

I never intended nor dreamed that it would take seven years from the release of *Watermark* before the fifth book in this series could come out. Yet in that time and in His infinite wisdom, God has been so good to me and I believe His timing is always perfect. I am always first and foremost thankful to my Savior, Jesus Christ, who brings abundant grace and renewed purpose into my life no matter how many years pass.

And in His goodness, He has blessed me with people who not only unconditionally support me mentally, spiritually, emotionally… but who have also held a special love for this series for over a decade. So bear with me as I try to share my gratitude in a list that will never cover everybody who has made an impact in my Phantom Island universe.

Thunderfly Productions would certainly not exist—nor could it have produced five books in a calendar year (yes, I said FIVE, people)—without the steadfast commitment and skill of Kristen McGregor and Katrina Elsea. Kristen, thank you for being the one to say, "Hey, if you want to start all over and take back the work that was stolen from you, we can do this." I know you've probably regretted it ever since because it was endless hours of work that you don't get paid enough for, but still. You started this journey with me in 2011, and I'm thankful to have you continue it with me. Also— you're a freaking graphic design genius. Katrina, thank you for making my words concise, coherent, and *complete*. These books feel as much yours as they are mine. You have endless patience and skill and have given so much more time and energy to my stories than they deserve. Thanks for knowing all of my secrets and keeping me off the ledge so many times.

To my husband, Sam—you are the dream, babe. I wish all women had husbands who believe in their talent and back that belief up with real action the way you do. Forever my favorite.

To Jasper and Caspian—you are two amazing, energetic, and adorable reasons why there has been a seven-year gap in this series. Being your Mommi is the most rewarding job ever.

To my family—Bonnie, Randy, Mike, Sandra, Kevin, Michael, Susie, Vic, Tiffany, and Cameron—a girl could not be more loved by you. Thank you for always speaking life into me and my work. Especially you, Mom. None of this would have happened without you.

To my fellow writers/authors—Jill Cox, Sandra Fernandez Rhoads, Allison Duke, Stacy Wells, Heather Reid, and Jennifer Looft—I'm so thankful I can "talk shop" with you any time of the day or night. Thank you for the hours you have spent reading and writing with me and exhorting me forward when I wanted to give up. Thank you to my Art House Dallas Fort Worth Writers group—Sarah Ndjerareou, Shari Bower, Sara Hill, Shannon Holt, Stephanie Suire, Maggie Philpot (and Sandra, again)—you ladies came into my life at a pivotal point and the Lord has blessed me through you, your art, and your encouragement.

Y'all, I have the BEST beta readers ever—it's too bad the world will never see their texts as they read *Firetrap*. Super entertaining. Thank you to Hayley Chandler, Kaydi Shaw, Leigh Ann Eddlemon, Laura Longmire, and Shannan Horton (my cousin).

My life would not be complete without my teenage beta readers and budding novelists known as the Cuteness Factor Creative Club—Jaylin, Naomi, Josephine, Emma, and Sophia. I can't wait to read your published works someday, girls. You all have amazing talent! I must give a shout-out to Rahab and Symphony for being such ultimate fans that they got an early preview of this book, too, and kept all of its secrets! And a special thanks to Naomi and Jaylin for running the Zephyra fan account on Instagram. (Go follow @_.zephyra_)

A big, self-serving thanks to my hair stylist, Holly Ritchey, who is ultimately the reason I have been identified in public so many times over the years as "that author of those books." Seriously, you are an artist and an integral part of my author branding.

David Elsea won't ever see this because teen romance makes him puke, but I am indebted to him for making my awesome promo videos, audiobook intros, and for coining the title of "Fandom Island." Thank you for supporting even when it's not your bag of chips, dude.

To Gabi Graves—thank you for your uninhibited love for this series and partnering with me to spread the fun. Keep shining your light in Hollywood! I am forever your fan.

U.M.E. Preparatory Academy—thank you for helping me re-launch and reinvent myself after all these years and for letting me love on your kiddos. Teaching is the other half of my heart.

Reece Prairie Baptist Church—you are my *people*. Thank you for how you have impacted my life and our community. You are the salt of the earth.

And to my readers—thank you for waiting. Whether you've waited seven years, seven months, or seven minutes for this continuation, you are the reason this book exists. Thank you for not giving up. Thank you for lending out your old copies, for constantly buying new ones, for posting, talking, and asking about Book 5 even when my answer was "Um, I'm still working on it..." There's one more book left and I look forward to experiencing the end with you. Until then—when the world is on fire with ugliness, despair, and hate—be the light, be the *firetrap* with your kindness and goodness and grace.

KRISSI DALLAS

prefers her music loud and Junior Mints fresh
when she's writing late at night. She married her
best guy friend from college and together they
have two boys—a messy inventor and a blossoming
musician. Teaching junior high reading keeps her
young and teaching teen Bible study keeps her
wise. She has a hard time not hugging during a
pandemic, so you can send her virtual hugs on
Instagram, Facebook, and Twitter.